Hidden Lives

By Judith Lennox

Reynardine
Till the Day Goes Down
The Glittering Strand
The Italian Garden
The Secret Years
The Winter House
Some Old Lover's Ghost
Footprints on the Sand
The Shadow Child
The Dark-Eyed Girls
Written on Glass
Middlemere
All My Sisters
A Step in the Dark
Before the Storm
The Heart of the Night
Catching the Tide
The Turning Point
One Last Dance
The Jeweller's Wife
Hidden Lives

JUDITH LENNOX

Hidden Lives

REVIEW

First published in Great Britain in 2018 by
HEADLINE REVIEW
An imprint of HEADLINE PUBLISHING GROUP

1

Cataloguing in Publication Data is available from the British Library

ISBN 978 1 4722 2399 9 (Hardback)
ISBN 978 1 4722 2400 2 (Trade Paperback)

Typeset in Joanna MT STd by
Palimpsest Book Production Ltd, Falkirk, Stirlingshire

Printed and bound by CPI Group (UK) Ltd, Croydon CR0 4YY

MIX
Paper from
responsible sources
FSC® C104740

HEADLINE PUBLISHING GROUP
An Hachette UK Company
Carmelite House
50 Victoria Embankment
London EC4Y 0DZ

www.headline.co.uk
www.hachette.co.uk

To Oliver Winter Smith

Acknowledgements

Many people helped me in the course of writing this novel. First, I would like to thank my husband, Iain Smith, who drove me around Sussex, organised our travels in Spain, and was a knowledgeable and patient source of information on aviation.

Heartfelt thanks are also due to my sister, Danielle Stretch, for helping me understand printmaking and etching presses. I am deeply appreciative of Steve and Rosie Garwood's warm hospitality in Sussex. To my daughter-in-law, Victoria Bethencourt-Smith, thank you for our enjoyable conversations about Spain and the Spanish language.

Some novels have a more difficult birth than others, and this was sometimes a painful one. So I owe a great deal to my agent, Margaret Hanbury, whose steadfast support was invaluable. Many thanks also to my editor at Piper, Bettina Feldweg, for her incisive and helpful comments. Finally, the suggestions of Clare Foss, my editor at Headline, were both insightful and imaginative, and hugely influential in giving Hidden Lives its final shape.

Prologue

They climbed out of the Austin Twelve. The air was perfumed by the scents of woodland: earth and rotting leaves and something that was meaty and acrid. Edith pictured spores floating across the road from the fat, yellow fungi that gripped the tree trunks. It was colder than in London, colder even than Nutcombe, in the valley, where they had stopped to buy peppermints at the village shop. She drew her fur collar round her throat.

'Jumping Jehoshaphat,' said Cyril. He was looking at the house.

'Do you like it?'

'I'm not sure,' he said. 'It's frightfully bedazzling.' He took a few paces back, pushing his spectacles up to the bridge of his nose. 'Do you know, I think I do.' He kissed her. 'I think I shall love it.'

'I knew you would.' Edith felt giddy with freedom; a day away from her household duties, a day spent in the company of her two favourite men, in this beautiful, light-filled house.

She had known that Cyril would adore the Gull's Wing.

How could he not? The fairy-tale palace of glass and wood and stone perched beside the ridgeway that ran along the top of the hill. Her father's clever, controlling hand was evident in the apparent simplicity of the structure, which had the appearance of being so lightly sketched in it might be blown from the hilltop by a gust of wind. A row of columns, which must surely be too fragile to bear the weight of the slanting, overhanging roof, ran along the front of the house, their slender forms echoing the tall, spindly conifers of Paley High Wood, across the road. Pale grey weatherboarding glittered in the winter sunshine, bringing to mind the sails of a ship . . . or the wing feathers of a seabird.

Cyril had parked the motor car behind Edith's father's Bentley. She said, 'Daddy must be indoors.'

The front door was slightly ajar. Cyril pushed it open. 'Mr Lawless?' he called out. 'Edward? We're here!'

Hearing voices from the upper floor, Edith said, 'I didn't know Mama was coming, too.' As they climbed the stairs, she explained to Cyril, 'Daddy put the drawing room on the first floor to make the most of the view. The kitchen and scullery, that sort of thing, are on the ground floor.'

Entering the drawing room through the wide double doors, Edith first saw her father, smiling as he came towards her, his familiar, uneven gait a consequence of a cycling accident in Berlin in the years before the war.

And then she saw Sadie, standing by a window, and her happiness trickled away like water let out of a basin. She had not expected her sister to be here: Sadie, who would steal their father's attention and capture the limelight with her prettiness and vivacity; Sadie, who would spoil her day.

Cyril put his arm round her, showing her that he understood how she felt. He said to her father, 'Stunning place, Edward; you are to be congratulated.' But Edith was unable to disguise the expression of resentment and disappointment that sprang to her face.

Events of great significance occurred and you hardly noticed them. Her father had invited her to Sussex to see the finished house and she had gone to the Gull's Wing that day expecting to have him to herself, only to find out that Sadie was there as well. Part of her had known at the time that she was ruining her own day, that her father would turn away from her monosyllabic responses and talk to Sadie instead. He might have done so, anyway. They conversed so easily, he and Sadie, switching from light chatter to deep discussion with a naturalness that eluded Edith. She tried too hard and, in her conscientious search for the intelligent or witty phrase that would win his approval, must have come across as slow and stolid.

So she sulked through the remainder of the day and, when they parted at five to drive back to London, she gave her father an aloof farewell and a chilly kiss, not realising that it would be for the last time. Shortly afterwards, her parents travelled to France, so they did not see each other over Christmas. Three weeks later, the plane in which Edward and Victoire Lawless were flying from Le Touquet to an airfield in Sussex crashed in a snowstorm near the coast. There were obituaries in the newspapers and the phone rang constantly as friends and colleagues called to offer their condolences. They were there and then they were gone, erased by the whirling whiteness.

As she wept uncontrollably, Edith gasped to Cyril that her father would never be proud of her now. He shook his head. 'He was proud of you, my darling. I know he was. It was quite plain to me.' His words gave her some solace, but then, after the will was read, she discovered that, though Cyril was the wisest man she knew, and hardly ever wrong, in this instance he was mistaken. She, Edith, loved the two houses her father had built in Sussex, the Egg and the Gull's Wing, and yet he had left both to Sadie. If he had bequeathed the Gull's Wing to her and the smaller Egg to Sadie, that would have been fair, as Sadie was the younger sister, but even if he had only given her, Edith, the Egg, she would have known that he had thought of her – had loved her.

The shock of it made her feel sick at first – then angry. She howled to Cyril that she would contest the will. Gently, he explained to her that such a course would be futile. The will had been properly drawn up and witnessed. Edward Lawless had neither lacked capacity nor come under undue influence.

Edith blamed Sadie. It was only much, much later that she came to realise she should have blamed her father.

'Sadie's unmarried,' Cyril said, trying to reason with her. 'She's little prospect now of ever marrying. That's why your father left her the houses, to give her some security.'

Bitterly, Edith responded that it was Sadie's own fault that she was unmarried. What man would marry a woman who made herself disreputable by wearing peculiar clothes and insisting on earning her own living? A woman who swore and smoked in public?

'Edith, Edith,' Cyril pleaded. 'Please don't hate Sadie. It will only hurt you.'

And it had. She let her sister slip so easily out of her life. Sadie, who could brighten up a room, who was as flickering and changeable as a woodland stream, who could be lively and fun and dazzling, but could also fall silent and shut you out. Since the day Sadie was born, she had conjured in her elder sister such conflicting, complicated emotions that, in the end, angry and exhausted, Edith ran away from them.

Chapter One

Edith Fuller's friends and bridge partners were rising creakily from the table to stretch their legs and chat to each other as the funeral luncheon came to an end.

Robert Martineau put his arm round his wife's shoulders. 'How are you doing?'

'I'm fine,' said Rose. 'I'm going to miss Granny, though.' She smiled up at him. 'I'll miss our lunches: curry and pink blancmange.'

'I know, love.' Robert glanced at his watch. 'I have to go.'

'I thought you were taking the afternoon off?'

'Too much to do, I'm afraid. I'll see you later.' They kissed and Robert left the room.

'Rose.'

Hearing her father's voice, she turned. 'Didn't Katherine do well, Dad?' Her six-year-old daughter, Katherine, had read out Rudyard Kipling's 'If—' at the funeral service that morning.

'I had tears in my eyes, I must admit.' Giles Cabourne opened the door of the function room. 'There's something I need to talk to you about, Rose. Shall we go out here, where it's quieter?'

She checked that Katherine and her younger sister, four-year-old Eve, were still talking to an old friend of the family and followed her father into the corridor.

'Your grandmother appointed me as one of her executors,' Giles said. 'Apart from some minor bequests, she's left everything to you, Rose.'

'Oh, Dad.' She put her hand to her mouth.

'It's not a fortune, but there's a useful sum of money, and her flat, of course.'

'I didn't know. I wasn't expecting anything.' But then, who else should her grandmother leave her property to? A widow, Edith Fuller had had one daughter, Rose's mother, Louisa, who had died nine years ago. Rose herself was an only child.

Her father said, 'And there's a house in Sussex, too.'

A waitress in a black dress and white frilled apron rushed by with a tray of glasses; Rose and her father flattened themselves against the wall to allow her to pass.

Rose said, startled, 'A house? Dad? What house?'

Giles ran a hand over his fine, sparse, silvery hair. 'I vaguely remember hearing about it, years ago, but I'd completely forgotten, to be honest.'

'A house . . .'

'Apparently it's in the middle of nowhere. I've no idea what sort of condition it's in. According to Edith's solicitor, she'd owned it for a long time. She never lived in it; always let it out. You know your grandmother, Rose – she wasn't the confiding sort. Anyway, it's yours now, love.'

One of her grandmother's schoolfriends, a tiny woman a head shorter than Rose, wearing a black hat and a lavender crepe coat, emerged from the function room to take her leave. Hands were shaken, thanks and good wishes exchanged.

When they were alone again, Giles took an envelope out

of his jacket pocket and handed it to Rose. 'Edith left instructions in her will that you should be given this on her death. Perhaps it'll tell you something about the house.'

She felt dazed. 'Granny never said anything to me. Never.'

Glancing through the glass door, she saw that Eve was carefully pouring salt from the cellars on to the dining table to make a little white, powdery mountain.

'Dad, I have to go.' She hugged her father. 'A flat and a house . . . Goodness.' Then she went back into the function room and took her daughter's hand, steering her firmly away from the table.

You would have had to look at Katherine and Eve twice to see that they were sisters. Katherine was tall, slim and gangly, and had inherited her mother's grey eyes along with her Martineau grandmother's fine, straight, sandy hair. Eve was short and stocky, her eyes brown like Robert's, her hair a mass of dark curls. Katherine was loving and generous, a perfectionist who demanded high standards both from herself and other people, but was capable of being impatient and prickly. Eve was a small bundle of energy, a chatterbox, a slapdash, happy-go-lucky child who was sometimes overcome by sudden wild outpourings of grief. You saw they were sisters in their quickness and liveliness, and in the shape of an eye and a limb.

Eve was tucked up in bed in the Martineaus' house in Walton-on-Thames. Rose kissed her goodnight and went to Katherine's room. Her elder daughter was in her pyjamas, kneeling on her bedroom carpet, wrestling with her Spirograph set.

'Aah!' A shriek of frustration. 'The pen keeps coming out!'

'Put it away for now, darling. Away, love. You can play with it again tomorrow. Where's your book? You can read till eight.' Rose tapped the clock on the bedside table.

After she had settled Katherine, she went downstairs. Robert came home shortly afterwards. In the kitchen, Rose made two gin and tonics while the supper bubbled on the stove. She gave one of the drinks to Robert. Then she told him about her grandmother's will and the flat and the house in Sussex.

'Good God,' he said. 'My wife, the property magnate.'

'This house . . . I'd no idea it even *existed*. I expect it's a dilapidated old dump. I wonder why Granny never told me about it. It's a big thing not to talk about, don't you think, a house?'

'Pretty big.'

'It's called the Egg. Isn't that weird? Granny's father built it. You know, the architect.' She gave him a close look. 'Robert?'

'Hmm?'

He was giving the appearance of listening, but he wasn't, not really. His dark brown eyes were focused on some middle distance and Rose knew he was thinking about something else.

She said, 'Is anything wrong?'

'Wrong?' A quick smile. 'No, of course not. Are the girls asleep?'

'Eve, probably. Katherine, not a chance.'

'I'll go and see them.'

'George phoned,' she called after him as he went upstairs. George was Robert's elder brother, unmarried, a civil servant in the higher echelons of a government department. The two brothers didn't get on.

Looking back at her, Robert frowned. 'What did he want?'

'To talk about your parents' anniversary party.' Lionel and

10

Mary Martineau were shortly to celebrate their ruby wedding. 'Speeches and flowers.'

Later that night, she climbed into bed and curled up against him. He turned to her and his fingertips ran up the little bones of her spine and she shivered. Their lovemaking was quick and rushed and needy.

Afterwards, Robert fell asleep, but Rose lay awake, the events of the day tumbling through her head: her grand-mother's funeral, her unexpected inheritance – and the house in Sussex, the Egg.

In her letter, her grandmother had written,

In the 1920s, my father, the architect Edward Lawless, built two houses on the land he owned in Sussex. Both were of a modern design. My father used to say that they were his masterpieces, his legacy. He and my mother had intended to live in the Gull's Wing, the larger house, which he built on the ridgeway, but they died in January 1929, very shortly after it was completed. The house was then sold. I am bequeathing to you, Rose, the smaller of the two, which has always been known as the Egg. It has been let out, but my last tenant, Mr Manners, who lived there for more than a decade, died six months ago, so it is currently unoccupied.

And then a series of rather involved directions – a road beside the church in Nutcombe . . . park on a bend, halfway up the hill . . . a path through trees. And two keys, a Yale and a smaller key, enfolded in a square of paper.

She was thirsty; she went downstairs to the kitchen and ran herself a tumbler of water. She knew little about her great-grandparents, Edith's parents. Edward Lawless had been an architect, who had died in a plane crash along with his wife – that was about it. Now she had discovered that they

11

had built themselves a house, the Gull's Wing, but had never lived in it. Perhaps her grandmother had never spoken of the Sussex house because it had been too intimately bound up with the tragedy of her parents' death.

You put a lot of yourself into a house. She and Robert had bought their home, a four-bedroom Edwardian end-of-terrace, five years ago. They had fallen in love with the high-ceilinged rooms and the way the sunlight poured through the windows on to the wooden floors. There were dusty plaster mouldings and tiled fireplaces and a long, thin garden in which rose, honeysuckle and bramble made intricate knots. After they had moved in, they had replaced the pre-war decor and fittings, teaching themselves to plumb, rewire, paper and paint. They had celebrated the project's completion with a bottle of champagne on the terrace. The garden was still a tangle; neither of them was a gardener.

Though she didn't miss the mess or the exhaustion, Rose found herself recalling their shared absorption in the renovation, and their closeness. If they had moved into the house now, they would have had builders in. Robert's businesses – two garages, several small engineering concerns and his most recent acquisition, an air-freight company – had flourished in the last couple of years, and he would not, these days, have been able to spare the time.

She had been twenty-one years old, a couple of months out of university, when she and Robert had first met. She had been trying to decide whether to take a further degree, weighing up a yearning to be out in the world against the practical advantages of being Rose Cabourne, M.Sc. She had taken a summer job with an engineering firm to earn money and gain experience while she made up her mind.

When the director's secretary went on holiday, Rose was

asked to fill in for her. Robert was visiting, that day. She greeted him at reception. On the stairs to the upper floor, he found out her name; in the corridor between the stairs and the office, he asked her out to dinner. She must have seen something in him more durable than his obvious handsomeness, presence and charm, because she said yes.

Robert was the sort of man you couldn't help but notice: tall and broad shouldered, outgoing and confident, darkly good-looking. He had a look in his eyes which told her that her answer was important to him, and an air of drive and determination. Over dinner, she discovered that he was smart, funny and generous as well.

Six months later, they married. Katherine was born the following year. Her second name, Louisa, was for Rose's mother, who had died of breast cancer three years before that. Eve Mary Rose – the Mary after Robert's mother, who, hale and hearty, lived with her husband in the Martineau family home in Oxfordshire – was born two years later.

Rose put away some dishes that were draining beside the sink. The mild boredom she had felt since Eve had started school in mid-April, her flatness and lack of focus, and her dissatisfaction, which she tried to suppress, with the domestic tasks and social obligations that filled her days, settled round her like a scratchy wool garment. Once, she had had ambitions. Once, she had pictured her life as purposeful, even extraordinary, and yet somehow, without her ever quite choosing it, she had become a housewife like her mother, who had never worked outside the home. Rose had assumed she would be different, but here she was, holding dinner parties for Robert's business associates and picking up his socks. There had been a time, before Katherine was born, when she had let Robert's laundry accumulate on the

13

bedroom floor to make a point. Now, she couldn't be bothered and picked things up.

Sometimes she felt as if she were thinning, shrinking, becoming less than she had thought herself to be. The balance between her and Robert had shifted. His working hours were long and irregular, and he often took clients out to dinner in the evenings. Sometimes she accompanied him; at other times he brushed her offer away, telling her she would be bored.

Perhaps she should look for a part-time job – though, with a rusty physics degree, little used, and hours that must be fitted round her daughters' schooling, it was hard to feel optimistic about her chances. But it troubled her that the crossword was the greatest intellectual challenge of her day, and she knew that she sometimes blurred with a drink the long, quiet evenings after the girls had gone to bed.

Mentally, she scolded herself. It was becoming a habit, this chewing over of discontent, this searching for a way out of . . . what? A comfortable, affluent life. She had her own car, regular holidays and a cleaner. She had two beautiful, healthy daughters and a husband who loved her.

And yet she missed Eve, her baby, her chatter and her hot little hand in hers as they walked to the shops. She disliked the silence that settled in the empty rooms and the lack of shape to her days when the girls were at school, and found it hard to accept that the tumbling emotional intensity of early motherhood was over for ever. Perhaps they should try for another baby. She was only twenty-nine, plenty of time.

It occurred to her that her grandmother's unexpected bequest meant that suddenly she had plenty to do. A flat to sort out, a mysterious house in Sussex to visit. The prospect cheered her. She took the glass of water upstairs, slipped into bed beside Robert and fell asleep.

The Weybridge flat was crammed with dark, heavy furniture and souvenirs of Edith Fuller's years as a colonial wife – prints of Old Delhi, a black wooden figurine and, in front of the fireplace, the flat, faded skin of some unfortunate beast.

Rose tackled the wardrobe first. Clothes were so personal, so imbued with memories of the wearer. A wine-coloured coat with a fur collar conjured up an autumn outing to Bushy Park, her daughters running in and out of the trees and the distant deer little more than shadows in the mist, while her grandmother spoke of safaris in Kenya. A Liberty silk scarf impregnated with Arpège, her grandmother's scent, made tears spring to her eyes.

She had come to know her grandmother well only comparatively recently. During Rose's childhood, Edith and her husband Cyril had lived abroad – first in India and then, after independence, in Kenya. Airmail letters had arrived regularly, twice a month; when her grandparents visited, they stayed at the family home in Weybridge, where Rose's father still lived. And then, after a month, they flew home, back to Africa, and Rose would not see them again for another three years. When Cyril died, Edith had sold up her house in Nairobi and moved back to England. Rose's mother, Edith's daughter, Louisa, had been ill by then, and Rose and her grandmother had given each other what comfort they could. Though Edith had neither sought nor encouraged emotional closeness, they had loved and respected each other.

In a drawer, Rose found treasures: an evening gown of peppermint-green satin, cut on the cross, a pair of pale grey glacé kid gloves and a tiny, beaded handbag, which she put aside to take home with her. The Dennis Wheatley and Eric Ambler paperbacks, authors that her grandmother had favoured, she would take to a second-hand bookshop. She set aside half a dozen volumes of Indian military history that her father-in-law might enjoy.

But what should she do with the ivory bird cage and the spectacularly ugly elephant clock that her grandmother had treasured? Or the cream-coloured Wedgwood dinner service and Midwinter teapot, which, though beautiful and inti-mately connected with her grandmother, she would worry about every time Katherine or Eve came near them? Rose wondered whether the house in Sussex — the Egg — was as stuffed with furniture and knick-knacks as the flat. She hoped not. A rental property, it was more likely to contain tired rugs and sofas and ill-assorted plates and mugs, sourced from jumble sales. What should she do with it, this unexpected inheritance? Robert assumed she would sell both properties as soon as probate was granted. Rose hadn't made up her mind yet.

She decided to tackle the padouk cabinet next. This was a large and cumbersome piece of furniture, topped with scrollwork covered in gold leaf; there were cupboards and drawers above and below, its central section a writing desk.

Opening the desk, Rose peered inside and examined the contents of the pigeonholes: a green Osmiroid fountain pen, a bottle of Quink and half a dozen pencils; a pair of scissors and a roll of Sellotape; bills and receipts, bound together with elastic bands.

A tiny ivory handle that one might easily overlook revealed a shallow drawer beneath the pigeonholes. Inside it, she found a foolscap-sized folder, covered in orange paper printed

16

with yellow and gold birds. When she opened it, letters and a handful of photographs spilled out: a man wearing a sola topi, riding on the back of an elephant; a baby, its tiny crumpled face peeping out from a froth of lace.

On the front of a plain white postcard, someone had drawn a pen-and-ink cartoon of a woman wearing a drop-waisted, calf-length coat with a fur collar and a cloche hat. The hat was pulled down low over the wearer's eyes and she was teetering along the pavement on high heels. Rose turned the postcard over. On the back of it was written, *Don't I look just le dernier cri, darling? If only I could see where I was going!* It was signed with an initial, S.

Rose made herself a cup of Nescafé, her grandmother's preferred hot drink. Lunches in this flat had meant instant coffee from a Minton pot while they shared the box of Meltis Newberry Fruits, another of her grandmother's favourites, which Rose always brought as a gift. Edith would regale her granddaughter with stories of India and Africa while Rose tried to stop Eve picking up precious and fragile objects. Edith Fuller's voice had been clear and imperious. She had cultivated that tone, Rose assumed, when addressing dhobi wallahs, house boys and maids – the accoutrements of a different and vanished life.

She put the coffee cup on a spindly side-table and sat down on the sofa with the writing case. A photograph slipped to the floor and she picked it up. The black-and-white snap-shot was of two young women. Both were wearing shapeless, calf-length coats and complicated hats of some heavy fabric, perhaps velvet. Though the photo must have been taken fifty or sixty years ago, Rose recognised her grandmother instantly. At eighty years of age, Edith had been tall and raw boned, her beaky nose jutting from a long, narrow, high-cheekboned face. And so it was in the picture, though here the angles of nose and jaw were softened by youth, and Edith's hair was dark, not silvered.

The young girl standing beside her was shorter and slighter. Her features were symmetrical and attractive, her smile open and friendly. A large tassel hung jauntily from the brim of her hat and rested on one shoulder, and she had raised a hand to push a strand of fairish, windblown hair from her eyes.

Rose turned the print over and read the two names written in faded ink on the back. Edith confirmed what she had already worked out: that the taller of the two women was her grandmother. The other was called Sadie. It occurred to Rose that this Sadie might be the 'S' who had drawn the sketch on the postcard.

She took a few mouthfuls of coffee and examined the letters in the writing case. Unfolding one, she felt a mixture of curiosity and a reluctance to invade her grandmother's privacy. The letter was from someone called Margery Burton, and although purporting to be a friendly note, it was in fact begging for money. There was also a large bundle of letters from Cyril, her grandfather. Perhaps they were love letters. She put them aside. Another collection, tied up with a pink ribbon, were from Louisa, her mother. Rose had letters from her mother at home, which had been sent to her when she was at school and university. Since her mother had died, she had not been able to read them. She wondered whether she would ever be able to read them again.

She thought she had taken all the letters out of the case, but then a narrow compartment revealed a bundle tucked inside it. Opening an envelope of heavy cream paper, she glanced at the name at the foot of the page.

Sadie. So this letter had been written by the pretty, fair-haired Sadie of the photograph. The handwriting, though old-fashioned in style, had an elegant clarity.

Rose began to read: *I can't possibly see Philip Sprott every fortnight, Edith. It would be far too expensive, what with his fees and the train fare to London. And, anyway, I feel perfectly well now. You mustn't worry about me, honestly.* Exasperation seeped through the phrases.

In another letter, picked at random, Sadie wrote, *I shall be coming up to Town from the 5th to the 9th. Will it be convenient for me to call? It seems ages since I saw Louisa. Is she home from school yet?* And, further down the page, *The Egg is perfectly delightful at this time of year, the primroses are out and the birds singing merrily. I do hope you will come and stay with me soon.*

That was interesting. So Sadie had been living in the Egg. The letter heading confirmed this: *The Egg, Paley High Wood, Nutcombe, Sussex.* Perhaps Sadie had been a tenant of Edith's — but, no, the tenor of the letters indicated a closer relationship. Perhaps Edith had let her friend stay in her house for a while.

Rose checked her watch. It was almost quarter past three; she must shortly drive to Walton-on-Thames to collect Katherine and Eve from their school. She began to shuffle the correspondence back into an orderly pile.

A name inscribed on the back of a flimsy blue envelope caught her eye: *Sadie Lawless.*

Rose frowned. Her grandmother's maiden name had been Lawless. Had Sadie Lawless been a cousin of Edith's, perhaps? She skimmed through the short letter. And then had to read it a second time to make sure she had understood it properly.

Sadie's letter told her two things. The first was that the Egg hadn't always belonged to Edith. In the early 1930s, it had

19

been owned by Sadie. And yet – she glanced at the date – in October 1934, Sadie had given the house to Edith.

The Egg is now yours, Edith, Sadie had written. *I have posted the papers to Mr Copeland. I don't want to live here any more; it frightens me, and besides, it was wrong of Father to give it to me – I see that now.*

The second revelation was even more startling. Sadie Lawless hadn't been Edith's cousin. She had been her sister.

Rose had thought she had known her grandmother, but she had hardly known her at all. Edith had had a sister. Sadie Lawless had been her grandmother's sister. *Whatever the differences between us, Edith,* Sadie Lawless had written at the end of her letter, *you are my sister.*

Coming home in the early hours of the morning, Robert slipped into bed beside her, smelling of cigarettes and alcohol. 'A client,' he murmured when she asked him where he had been. 'Tommy Henderson. You know, owns Riley's in Gateshead. Tedious man.' He drew her to him, his palm settling on her breast, and then fell instantly and noisily asleep.

The next morning, returning to the house after taking Katherine and Eve to school, Rose found herself slipping her hand into the pockets of his raincoat, which was hanging on the stand in the hall. What was she looking for? Secrets. Everyone had secrets. Her grandmother had had plenty of secrets. Robert's might be betrayed by a note or a receipt or a lipstick-stained handkerchief. A couple of years ago, he had had a flirtation – he had sworn to her it was only a flirtation – with the wife of a friend. Rose was thinking about that now. The late nights, his air of distraction . . . There was something he wasn't telling her, she was sure of it.

His pockets were empty. She pushed the thoughts away,

ashamed of herself. What was a marriage without trust? Robert had problems with the business. He would sort it out; he always did. She should have faith in him.

She ground some coffee beans and put on the Cona, then settled down at the table with the orange-and-gold writing case. Sometime during the night, it had become clear to her that her grandmother had *meant* her to find Sadie's letters. Edith had been trying to tell her something. Or perhaps she had been asking her to *do* something. Something to do with the house, and Sadie, her sister.

The Cona bubbled away as Rose took out the letters and put them on the table. There were twenty-five in all, some written on the expensive-seeming heavy, cream paper, others on flimsier blue or white. Sadie had dated the heading of each letter. It took a while, arranging them in chronological order, breaking off to bring the Cona jug and a mug to the table and pour herself a coffee.

All the letters had been written in the first half of the 1930s. The earliest, dated October 1930, was the short, tetchy note Rose had glanced at in her grandmother's flat the previous day. Edith had been living in London, then. The date on Sadie's last letter, which had been posted to Edith's bungalow in Delhi, was 15 October 1934. There were no more letters after that. Why not? Why had Sadie stopped writing to her sister then? What had happened?

Rose reread the earliest letter. She noticed that it bore a Cambridge address. *I can't possibly see Philip Sprott every fortnight, Edith. It would be far too expensive, what with his fees and the train fare to London. And, anyway, I feel perfectly well now.*

Philip Sprott must have been a doctor. Sadie had been suffering from an illness and had consulted Dr Sprott, who, in those pre-NHS days, she would have had to pay. Rose read

21

on. The Meyricks have been so wonderfully kind. Toby gave up his study for me to sleep in and Constance hasn't let me do a thing. My health is much improved now. I take a walk round Midsummer Common every afternoon, no matter the weather. Then a few lines about novels read, a musical afternoon attended. Later on in the text:

Mabel, Horace and Rosalind are the most delightful children, naturally, but they leave one hardly capable of completing a thought. Not that many of my thoughts have been worth completing recently, I admit, but I know I shall feel fully recovered when I am able to work again. You mustn't think I'll hide away. I'm planning a timetable of improving activities that will give me no chance to brood. New surroundings and a new way of living will distract me from my memories.

Rose thought it likely that the memories Sadie had hoped to distract herself from were those of the death of her parents in the plane crash, only the previous year. Losing her own mother at the age of twenty had been a body blow, a wound that ached and which she suspected would never completely heal over. In the photograph, Sadie appeared to have been the younger of the two sisters. A rapid mental calculation — Edith had been eighty years of age at the time of her death — told her that Sadie's mother too might have died when Sadie was in her twenties. She had lost her father in the same terrible air accident.

Rose read the next letter, which was dated a week after the first.

So I'm here at last. The Egg is all furnished and looks perfectly charming. You should have seen the poor men carrying my etching press along that awful muddy path through the trees. They complained awfully, so I gave them cups of tea and enormous pieces of cake and they were much jollier after that. Mrs Thomsett, in the shop in Nutcombe, has been very helpful and directed me to Boxell's Garage,

22

where Mr Boxell himself promised to find me a second-hand bicycle.
Do you remember how entrancing the woods are in autumn, Edith?
You must come and visit me very soon.

The phone rang and Rose went to answer it. It was Robert, asking her whether she would mind if he brought home some dinner guests that evening. Her assent was automatic and she was aware of a sense of relief that he had chosen not to have another late night out. He was busy, that was all. Everything was fine.

She left the house. As she parked her Mini in the town centre, she ran through menus in her head. Melon for a starter, crêpes suzette for pudding. No, not crêpes; too much fussing around at the last minute. Lemon meringue pie then, which she could prepare in advance. The main course . . . not boeuf bourguignon; she hadn't time. Moussaka? No, too messy-looking. She settled on chicken à la king.

After she had whizzed round the shops, buying ingredients, Rose went to the public library. She looked up Sadie Lawless's name in the various London phone directories, and then, finding no trace of her, she looked up Philip Sprott. She had a hunch that he might have been a smart London doctor, with a practice in Harley Street, perhaps.

Her fingertip paused, running down the columns of the directory that included the Harley Street area. No Philip Sprott. When she widened her search, the name Dr P. Sprott sprang out at her. Not Harley Street, but Handel Street, in Bloomsbury. Rose noted down the number on a scrap of paper. As she left the library, it started to rain.

Back at the house, she made the pastry and put it in the fridge to rest before going to Robert's study and dialling the Handel Street number.

A woman's voice answered. 'Handel Street consulting rooms. Good afternoon.'

Rose asked to speak to Dr Philip Sprott. He was with a patient, the receptionist explained. Might she take a message?

She felt awkward, explaining her request. It sounded odd, even to her. The woman on the other end of the phone seemed to think so too.

'Nineteen thirty? That's forty years ago. We don't keep records going back that far.'

'I was hoping Dr Sprott might remember her.'

'I really don't think . . .'

'If you would just ask him, I'd be most grateful,' said Rose firmly. 'My great-aunt's name was Sadie Lawless.' She repeated her own name and phone number before thanking the receptionist.

After she had settled the girls in bed, Rose changed into a black maxi-dress made of silk-lined chiffon with trumpet sleeves and beading round the deep V neckline. She brushed her long, dark-brown hair, so that it lay flat and straight over her shoulders, and touched up her eye make-up.

Where was Robert? She glanced at her watch. Half past seven. Their guests were due at eight. She looked out of the bay window to the street, but saw only the cars rushing through the rain, litter washing along the gutters.

The phone rang and she hurried downstairs. She answered it, expecting it to be Robert, but the voice on the other end of the line was unfamiliar.

'Is that Mrs Martineau?'

'Yes; who is it, please?'

'My name's Philip Sprott. You left a message with my receptionist, asking about Sadie Lawless.'

24

Rose sat down in Robert's leather chair. 'Thank you for calling back, Dr Sprott. I appreciate it. I phoned you because Sadie Lawless was a patient of yours. I wondered whether you remembered her.'

'Yes, I do. When Carol gave me your message, it all came flooding back. May I ask why you're interested in her?'

'She's my great-aunt. I didn't know she existed until a few days ago, after my grandmother died and I found letters from her. I'm trying to trace her – apart from anything else, if Sadie's still alive, I should let her know that her sister has died. Your name was mentioned in one of the letters.'

'I'm afraid I'm not going to be able to help you very much.' Philip Sprott's voice was deep and sonorous. 'It must be decades since we had any contact. But some patients stand out, and, yes, I remember Sadie. She was vibrant, intelligent and charming. But bruised by loss.'

Through the study window, Rose saw the rain dancing on the paving stones. 'Because of her parents' death?'

A pause, and then Philip Sprott said, 'Mrs Martineau, are you aware that I'm a psychiatrist?'

A *psychiatrist*. 'No, I assumed . . .'

'I practise part-time now. Sadie was one of my first patients, when I was young and green. It was a long time ago, but I don't know that there's any limit on confidentiality.'

'I understand that, Dr Sprott.'

'You said your grandmother had died recently?'

'Yes.'

'Please accept my condolences for your loss. What can I tell you . . . ? I recall that the relationship between Sadie and her sister was difficult. There was a big age gap – ten years, I think.'

'And Sadie was the younger sister.'

25

'Yes, she was. She came to me after suffering a breakdown. She'd been jilted by her fiancé. The broken engagement, coming so soon after the loss of her parents . . . well, the human mind can only cope with so much.' Another silence, then Philip Sprott said, 'I can't remember the fiancé's name. I do recall thinking that he sounded an utter cad. He was an antique dealer, not that that's relevant. Sadie herself was a teacher.'

'And an artist.' Rose thought of the second letter. *You should have seen the poor men carrying my etching press along that awful muddy path through the trees.*

'Yes.' Amusement in his voice. 'Sadie used to draw during our appointments. She said it relaxed her. The fireplace . . . or the plane trees, through the window. Sometimes she drew me. She gave me a sketch. I probably still have it somewhere. I saw her for about a year, maybe eighteen months. She used to send me the occasional postcard after that, but then she stopped. She'd moved on, I assumed. I'm sorry I can't be more help, Mrs Martineau.'

Rose heard the front door slam. She thanked Dr Sprott and ended the call.

Robert was standing in the hallway, taking off his mackintosh. Moisture beaded his khaki shoulders.

'Where were you?' Rose said as she hurried out to him. 'They'll be here in five minutes.'

'I'm aware of that.' He sounded angry. His tone altered. 'Sorry. Sorry, darling. It's been a bit . . . Work — you know how it is. We lost the Gibson contract.'

'Robert, I'm so sorry.' She kissed him. 'How disappointing.'

'Plenty more fish in the sea.'

But his light words were at odds with the expression that washed across his face. Fear and anguish — and then it was

26

gone, so quickly that she might have thought she had imagined it.

'What is it?' she said gently. 'Tell me, love. Tell me what's wrong.'

'Nothing's wrong. I'm tired, that's all.' A smile that was no more than a stretching of the lips. 'Could do with a drink. Give me a couple of minutes; I'll go and get changed.'

The doorbell chimed. Rose checked her face in the hall mirror, put on a smile and opened the door.

'Hugh . . . Vivienne . . . How marvellous to see you. Do come in.'

Chapter Two

Sussex and Surrey — May 1970

The Sussex High Weald was an area of rolling hills between London and the south coast of England. Rose recalled long-ago school geography lessons in which she had coloured in the High Weald's geological features — brown for the low clay vales, orange for the high sandstone ridges, blue for the rivers that cut into deep, steep-sided valleys.

She had spread out the map on the passenger seat beside her and taped to the dashboard of her Mini the piece of paper on which she had written road numbers and the names of the towns and villages she must pass through. The heavy rain of the previous day had gone, replaced by sunshine, but puddles still washed across the road. She felt a lifting of the spirits as the car plunged through hills and valleys greening in the fine May weather. When she wound down the window, the scent of spring drifted to her.

She pulled into the verge and got out. Trees climbed up the slope, bluebells making an azure haze against the coppery floor beneath them. A stream rushed down the escarpment to a drain clogged with brown leaves. Rose ate an apple, drinking in the shrill of birdsong. Then a lorry drove by,

28

horn blaring, men wolf-whistling through the open window, and she got back into the Mini and drove on.

The roads narrowed and twisted as she headed deeper into the countryside. A thatched cottage, glimpsed between trees, and a mere, the blue of the sky mirrored in the water. Winter greyness was peeling away, replaced by flurries of blossom of startling hue.

The area of forested land surrounding the Egg was named Paley High Wood. Reaching Nutcombe village, Rose slowed the car and looked round. A pub, a shop, a small council estate and a run of redbrick bungalows. Thatched cottages were interspersed between several, more imposing buildings.

The road beside the church was narrow, little wider than the Mini, and led up a steep hill. As the branches of the trees to either side touched overhead, it became a tunnel, darkness at its core. Now and then, the sun flashed in bright leopard spots on the tarmac, dazzling her.

She drew up at a sharp turn in the road with a flat area to one side made of compacted earth and stones. She parked the Mini, then climbed out of the car and peered through the scrubby bushes. Was this the place her grandmother had described in her letter? If so, where was the path? At first, looking into the forest, she could see only trees. But then, beyond, she glimpsed a flicker of white, like a pale pebble in the bottom of a pond.

As she entered the woods she was showered with drops of rain from the bushes that ran round the perimeter. More rain dripped from the bright new leaves of the trees, and the mud was thick underfoot; she was glad she had thought to bring wellington boots. The damp, brown forest floor was illuminated by little clusters of flowers and she saw that there was a path, of sorts: a dark line sketched out beneath the tall, slender trees. Birdsong shrilled round her and a cuckoo's insistent two-note call darted, its location constantly moving, impossible to pinpoint. Above, branches criss-crossed, some in leaf, others bare and pierced by shards of light. The humid air seemed trapped between the canopy and the warm, wet ground.

The flashes of white assembled themselves into a house: Edith's house, once Sadie's home, and now hers. Though more than forty years had passed since Edward Lawless had created his masterpieces, the house appeared breathtakingly contemporary, incongruous in the ancient English woodland. You could have copied its construction with a set of children's building blocks: two square bricks piled on top of each other at the rear, a longer block laid on its side at the front. Its smooth concrete exterior made it egg-shaped – it was smaller than she had anticipated and nestled in a clearing.

As she drew closer, Rose saw that the two flat roofs were littered with dead leaves, as if the woodland was doing its best to erase the pale intruder. She circled the building. One side of the house, made almost entirely of glass, looked out on to a rectangular terrace. The paving slabs were dark with puddles and swirls of dead leaves. It seemed optimistic, a terrace. Had her great-grandfather imagined that the Egg's occupants would lounge in deckchairs, soaking up the sun? The trees must have grown since Edward Lawless had completed his legacy, because they now cast their shade all around.

Crossing the terrace, Rose peered inside. Her reflection in the window was made indistinct by the flickering images of trees, which appeared dense and devoid of light. Shadows overlaid the shapes contained in the interior – sofa, table, chair.

The front door was on the far side of the building. Rose unlocked it and stepped inside. When she flicked a switch, the ceiling light illuminated a narrow hallway and she blinked, looking round. The earthy scents of the forest were here masked by a musty aroma redolent of jumble sales and damp, stale linen. She shivered; the Egg had the chill of a place that has been uninhabited for too long.

Set into one side of the hall were three doors, made of a fine-grained, golden wood. The first opened into a cloakroom with wooden pegs and a high shelf, for hats and gloves, presumably. The second led into a cupboard containing a broom and stepladders, and the third door revealed a lavatory, where a threadbare towel hung from a hook and a sliver of green Lifebuoy soap deliquesced in a basin. The tap was dripping; she gave it a hard turn, but it continued to drip.

At the end of the hallway, an opening to her left gave into a neat kitchen area equipped with what were, Rose suspected, apart from the fridge and the oven, the original fittings. The streamlined fitted wooden units and three high circular windows made her think of a cabin in an ocean liner, as if the Egg was sailing through a watery forest.

Beyond was a sitting room, and here she found herself breathless, utterly entranced. The shadows cast by the trees through the great glass windows danced with the sunshine that washed over the pale floor-tiles. In this glistening white cube of a room, you would be able to sit in the warmth of the iron stove, watching rainstorms and gales. In hot weather, you would open the glass doors to the terrace and the cool of the woodland would drift indoors.

Standing at the window, Rose imagined coming to the house for weekends with Robert and the girls. Katherine and Eve could climb trees and make dens in the woods;

31

they would all go for family walks in the countryside. They would stay here overnight and wake up to sunlight and birdsong – how magical it would be! She would replace the furniture – the floral sofa, matching armchair and cheap pine bookcase, sideboard and table that must have belonged to Edith's deceased tenant, Mr Manners – with pieces that reflected the Egg's modernist roots.

She looked through the cupboards in the sitting room and kitchen, but found only a jigsaw puzzle, a stained mug and a packet of tea, some Vim and a stiffened grey floor-cloth. She was unsure what she had hoped to find – some evidence of Sadie, perhaps, some clue to why she had fled this house and given it to Edith. But this was not a place for secrets. Modest in size and almost monastically simple, it did not allow for clutter, for hidden caches of love letters or a secret diary stuffed beneath the floorboards. There were no dark corners; everything was exposed to the light.

She went upstairs. On the smaller, upper storey she found two bedrooms and a bathroom. The second bedroom, which faced out to the rear of the house, was empty of furniture. Some flies had met their deaths here and lay like a handful of currants, scattered on the sill. Looking out of the window, she saw an oblong slab of concrete – a septic tank, presumably – and, a short distance away, a track that ran down the hillside.

In the main bedroom, the bed was stripped of sheets and blankets, its mattress still dented by its memory of her grandmother's tenant. This room was level with the lower branches of the trees. Rose wondered whether this was why her great-grandfather had called the house the Egg: not because of its shape, but because of the way it seemed to nest precariously in the boughs.

Tall windows looked out on to the lower of the two flat roofs. In fine weather, Sadie might have used it as an impromptu sun terrace. Rose pictured her opening the window and stepping outside to lounge on a blanket rolled out on the asphalt, a cocktail to hand and wearing a modest thirties swimsuit – mint-green, perhaps, or shocking pink. Had Sadie Lawless been the sort of woman who would wear shocking pink?

She couldn't sell the Egg. This house was part of her family history, her heritage. Here, Sadie must have taken refuge from the disasters that had overtaken her life – the plane crash that had killed her parents, her fiancé's betrayal. And yet, four years later, she had walked away from it. *The Egg is now yours, Edith,* Sadie had written in her final letter. *I have posted the papers to Mr Copeland. I don't want to live here any more; it frightens me, and besides, it was wrong of Father to give it to me – I see that now.* In those phrases there was fear, yes, but there was also guilt. What could have frightened Sadie so much that she had given the house to Edith? The loneliness and isolation of the site, perhaps. And the sense of exposure you might feel, living behind this wall of glass.

Rose went downstairs. After wrestling with the lock of the glass doors in the sitting room, she stepped outside on to the terrace. No buildings could be seen from here – no roads, shops, villages or other signs of twentieth-century civilisation. Instead, ahead of her, an army of trees sloped upwards, light pouring between the boughs. Rose hauled the armchair out of the sitting room – the paving slabs were too wet to sit on – revelling in the warmth as she ate her sandwiches and drank coffee from her Thermos. She felt carefree, as if she were on holiday or a student once more, free of responsibilities.

But her mind drifted back to the events of the previous night and she felt unsettled again. She would have liked to have forgotten that sudden shaft of anguish she had glimpsed in Robert's eyes, but she couldn't. Robert was an optimist. His self-confidence was boundless. Events that plunged her into gloom washed off him. Difficulties with his businesses he viewed as a challenge, relishing the fight.

He was working at the airfield today. It was in an area of open country, not far from Weybridge. Rose thought she might drive there to meet him after picking up the girls from school. She used to do that quite often when Katherine and Eve were tiny, and then they would go on to a pub with a garden. She wasn't checking up on him, not really. Maybe she shouldn't go; maybe it was underhand of her. But she knew that she would.

She stepped off the terrace, then walked through the trees to the track she had glimpsed from the upper storey of the house. Brambles and weeds sprawled across the high earth banks on either side of it. The track lay several feet below the land that surrounded it, as if trodden down and compacted from centuries of usage. Water rushed over the stones and sand, last night's heavy rain making its way to the valley. When Rose looked back, she saw sections of the pale walls of the Egg between the trunks of the trees.

She wanted to see Edward Lawless's other house, the larger Gull's Wing, on the top of the ridge. As she climbed higher, the deciduous trees were replaced by conifers, well grown, blackish green and closely packed. The dry earth beneath them permitted few other plants to flourish and, in their shadow, she breathed in a resinous scent.

The road became visible through a mesh of dry, spiky branches. Emerging from the woodland felt like clambering

34

out of a cave and it took her a moment to get her bearings. On the opposite side of the road was a long brick wall, six or seven feet in height. Following it, Rose reached a wrought-iron gate. A name plate, set into the wall, told her that she had found the Gull's Wing.

Where the Egg charmed, the Gull's Wing dazzled. This house had none of the reticence of the Egg. Four or five times its size, it was a symphony of glass, wood and tile which proclaimed Edward Lawless's vision with a strong and assertive voice. The frontage was almost entirely of glass and the roof was supported by pale, slender columns which reminded Rose of a Greek temple.

A chain and padlock bound the gate to a post. Glimpsed between the iron railings, the front door had an impenetrable, defensive appearance, relieved only by a small, square window set at eye height. Curtains were drawn along the glass façade. Peering closer, Rose saw between them a fishlike twist of movement.

'Be careful, or she'll let them dogs out.'

Rose spun round. Behind her, a girl was freewheeling her bicycle to a halt. Mid-teens, striped cotton school frock, sandy hair in pigtails and pink National Health spectacles, she propped the bike against the wall and took a shopping bag of groceries out of the basket.

Rose said hello to her. 'Do you know the people who live here?'

'There's only Mrs Chiverton.' The girl balanced the bag against the gate. 'I fetch her shopping for her. She never talks to anyone. If she sees you, those dogs'll be out.' The girl climbed back on to her bicycle. 'I'd better get back. Bye,' she called out as she headed down the hill.

The front door of the Gull's Wing opened and two russet-

35

coloured hounds rushed down the path and leaped up at the gate. Rose stepped back. The dogs continued to bark and jump up as she walked along the road to the start of the track through the woods. As she headed down the sunken lane, the yips and whines faded to silence.

She was within half a dozen yards of the Egg when a shaft of sunlight made something glint on the forest floor: a shard of glass, or a coin, perhaps; she poked at the earth with a stick. Here, the dead leaves and topsoil had been washed away in the rivulets created by the previous day's rainstorm, baring the paler sandy soil beneath.

Crouching, Rose scrabbled in the dirt and prised out a small clod. As she rubbed away the earth, the metallic gleam became brighter and the shape of the object clearer.

She saw that she had found a ring. Gritted with soil, it looked unprepossessing – a cheap Woolworth's fake. She took it into the house and held it under the tap in the cloakroom.

Once she had washed it and polished it with a corner of her chiffon scarf, it shone, opulent and unmistakable. It wasn't a fake. She had found a gold ring lying in the dead leaves just a short distance from the Egg. In the brighter light of the hall, she examined it closely. Square stones that flashed green fire clustered in a criss-cross pattern on the front of the ring, and the band was ornamented with gems of a dense blackness. She turned the ring to catch the light.

She saw then that something was inscribed inside the band. Frowning, she held it up, struggling to make out the old-fashioned lettering.

In thee my choys I do rejoys.

The ring was a lover's token. Such a treasure to find on a sunny afternoon, she thought, as she slipped it into a zipped compartment of her bag and gathered up her belongings before leaving the Egg.

A memory jolted her as she made her way back along the path to her Mini. Philip Sprott had told her that Sadie had been engaged to an antique dealer. The ring she had found appeared to be very old. Perhaps it had been Sadie's. Perhaps it had been given to her by the fiancé who had jilted her and she had lost it here, forty years ago.

After she had picked up the girls from a friend's house, Rose drove to the airfield.

Robert had put Martineau Aviation in her name, which gave her a certain proprietorial feeling. When she had insisted on attending the first board meeting, he had told her that there was no need to and that her name was only there for tax reasons – which had only reinforced her determination to attend.

She liked the airfield and enjoyed seeing the planes – two Douglas DC-3s and a fat-bellied Armstrong Whitworth Argosy – taxi along the runway before gathering up speed and taking off elegantly into the air. Though she was familiar with the science of flight – her father had been in the RAF – there remained a touch of magic in that moment of lift from tarmac.

The board was small, just herself and Robert, who was the company secretary, and Robert's accountant, Clive Miller. Clive's wide-lapelled, pinstriped suits, snazzy shirts, Zapata moustache and smooth tongue gave him the air, Rose thought, of a successful second-hand car salesman. Robert conducted the meetings efficiently; his secretary, Lucy Holbrook, a pleasant woman of Rose's age, took the minutes.

At the most recent meeting, Martineau Aviation's operations manager, Ted Wilkinson, had joined them. Afterwards, he had caught up with her as she was leaving the office block. 'You don't need to waste your time with all this, Mrs Martineau,' he had drawled to her, derision in his eyes. 'Pretty little thing like you, I expect you'd rather be shopping or playing tennis or whatever it is that women like you waste their time on.' By the time she had thought of a suitable riposte, Wilkinson had walked away.

Rose parked a short distance from the single-storey building that contained the offices. The orange windsock leaped and thwacked; the airfield was at the top of a rise and always windy. She shepherded the girls across the tarmac. They all paused to watch a plane coming in to land.

The door to the office building opened and Dan Falconer, Wilkinson's junior and a recent recruit to the company, came out. The breeze caught at his fair, slightly curling hair.

'Hello, Dan.'

'Good afternoon, Mrs Martineau.' He turned to the girls. 'Hello, you two.'

'This is Katherine and this is Eve. Say hello, girls.'

Katherine was still squinting at the sky. 'It's the Argosy.'

'Well spotted,' said Dan. 'Ten minutes early. Headwind all the way from Marseilles.'

'When I flew in an aeroplane,' said Eve, 'I went over the clouds.'

'You've never flown in an aeroplane,' said Katherine scornfully.

'Yes, but pretend. Pretend I flew in an aeroplane. Pretend I flew to Bournemouth.'

Dan strode away. Watching his tall figure cross the tarmac, Rose suppressed a dash of irritation. She suspected that Dan Falconer thought his time too valuable to waste on a housewife like her. The girls were still arguing; she took their hands and hurried them into the building.

Dan stood near the runway, watching the aircraft land. He had come outside to get away from Ted Wilkinson, his immediate boss, who was looking for a fight. Wilkinson had instructed him to sign off half a dozen jobs and Dan had pointed out that they had not yet been properly costed, and then Wilkinson had called him a pompous little prick. The mechanics, Max and Gareth, who were both within earshot, had bent over their tasks, refusing to meet anyone's eye.

Dan had started working at Martineau Aviation four months ago. It would have been a decent little business were it not for two things: the operations manager was an idle and destructive drunk, and the owner, Robert Martineau, wasn't really interested in aeroplanes. Dan recognised the sort – the professional businessman who got into a new area to diversify his portfolio, or some such rubbish. That didn't work with aviation. You had to care about it, you had to love planes and everything that went with them. The aviation business broke hearts and spirits far more often than it made fortunes. Martineau had bought the business cheaply because it had been operating at a loss. Eighteen months later, it was still operating at a loss.

After leaving university, Dan had worked for a small engineering firm that made parts for motor cars. His second job had been with an air charter company based in Cardiff. Freight charter was risky and undependable; it operated on a knife edge, slipping easily into unprofitability if the hold was not full on each leg of the journey. All sorts of things could derail a business, things you had little control over – strikes, accidents and bad weather. And yet, deeply, unexpectedly and at great speed, he had fallen in love with it. It had taken him some time to accept his obsession. It was an aberration, a rocky island in a sea of reason.

The Cardiff company had failed when a Carvair, landing in poor visibility at Rotterdam airport, had gone down short of the runway and ploughed into a dyke. All five crew had been killed. Though the business had limped on for a while, the writing had been on the wall and Dan had moved across the country to take up the position at Martineau Aviation.

He had been appointed as deputy operations manager under Ted Wilkinson. Wilkinson – born in a back-to-back in Wakefield, left school at twelve, worked his way up from the bottom, 'Wasn't handed me on a plate, lad' – quickly made it clear to Dan – grammar-school boy, university educated – that he despised him. His first week at Martineau Aviation, there was salt in his tea, obscene pictures Sellotaped over his desk the day the boss and his wife looked round, and engine oil spilled on his jacket. But he had never in his life given up on something he really wanted, and Dan meant to have Wilkinson's job. Wilkinson was a drinker, a liar and a bully, and sooner or later he'd slip up so badly that even Martineau would notice.

The Argosy was taxiing along the runway. Dan's thoughts drifted to Rose Martineau. She was a good-looking woman, another of Martineau's trophies. Her slim figure in jeans and T-shirt, and her long, straight, dark hair, flicked about by the breeze, had caught Dan's attention as he left the office. Since joining the firm, he had become aware of the little tricks that Martineau and his accountant had adopted to evade paying tax. Sharp practice, you'd call it. Or corruption. Rose was one of them. Martineau had installed his wife on the

40

board to reduce his tax bill. Dan wondered whether she knew she was being used.

It was Friday, and he usually saw Celia on Fridays, but it was her sister's birthday, so they had changed their date to Saturday. They were to have a meal out at a restaurant in Kew before going to see a Hammer horror film. Dan thought horror films were ridiculous, but Celia had a weakness for them.

As Robert unlocked the front door, Rose said again, 'It's an amazing little house. Really special, Robert. You must come and see it. We could all stay there for a weekend.'

She watched him, noting his lack of reaction. At the airfield, she had left the girls with Lucy Holbrook before giving Robert's door a quick knock and going in. He had looked up, startled, then said into the phone, 'I have to go,' and replaced it on the cradle. Rose wondered who he had been talking to. And why he had cut off the call so brusquely.

They went into the house. Katherine and Eve dropped their satchels and school blazers on the floor. Rose was about to remind them to pick them up when Robert said in a low voice, 'Rose, there's something we need to talk about. Not with the girls here, but after they've gone to bed.'

'What?' She felt a stab of anxiety. 'What is it?'

He shook his head. 'No, not now. Later.'

As Rose lifted Eve from the bath and wrapped her up in a towel, the certainty that Robert was having an affair overwhelmed her. It would explain why he had been late home from work so often and why he seemed so distracted, and why he had cut off his phone call when she had opened the door to his office that afternoon. There was a warning, an intimation of danger, in her memory of him placing his

41

palm over the receiver to silence its voice. Who was he sleeping with? One of his clients . . . or Lucy Holbrook, his secretary, perhaps? Lucy was an attractive woman. Men often slept with their secretaries.

She held Eve close to her, pressing her face into her plump little body. No, he wouldn't; it was wrong of her even to think of it. What, then? Debts . . . irregularities . . . She pictured Clive devising another clever tax-avoidance scheme.

When the children were settled, she went downstairs. Robert was in the kitchen, a tumbler of whisky in his hand. He gave her a smile that didn't reach his eyes.

'Drink?'

'No, thanks. What was it you wanted to talk about?'

'I don't know where to start.' His gaze settled on her. 'The thing is . . . Rose, something bad is going to happen.'

'What?' she said. 'Tell me; you're frightening me.'

'Allegations about me are going to be made in the press.'

'Allegations?' she said blankly.

'On Sunday, I'm afraid.'

'Sunday?' Shock had reduced her to witless repetition.

'Yes. So you have to know.'

'What allegations?'

'About my private life. It's not true, of course.'

'What isn't? Robert, please . . .'

'The papers are going to say I was one of a group of men associated with a call girl.' His voice dripped with cold anger.

'What? That's ridiculous.' It was so preposterous, she almost felt relieved. 'Why would they think that?'

'They've made a mistake. Some of the men involved are friends of mine. Someone must have mentioned my name . . .' He pursed his lips. 'Accidentally.'

'Which friends?'

42

'Johnny . . . The press will make a big thing of it because of Johnny. I'll be a minor player, a footnote.'

Robert and Johnny Pakenham had been best friends at school. At the age of twenty-one, Johnny had inherited a seat in the House of Lords, along with rambling Wiltshire estates. Scandalous, impulsive, decadent; friend of pop stars, actresses and politicians; giver of drug-fuelled parties that lasted for three days and nights – the press adored Johnny Pakenham. Tall and elegantly gangly, he shared something of Mick Jagger's panther-like presence.

Rose had tried to like Johnny because he was one of Robert's oldest friends and had been his best man at their wedding. Though he was invariably charming to her, she sensed his dismissal of her. She suspected he thought her pretty enough, but too conventional, too square. When he looked at her, his red lips curved in amusement and his pale blue eyes held a glint of contempt. She wouldn't put it past Johnny to give the press Robert's name as a joke.

She said, 'This girl . . .'

'She's a cheap little tart. You know the sort.'

She didn't. People like that lived in a different world. She gave him a hard look. 'Do you know her?'

'No, certainly not.' A sour laugh. 'It's possible our paths may have crossed. I may have run into her somewhere, but, if so, I don't remember.'

'What's her name?'

'Rose, her name doesn't matter.'

'I'm going to find out soon enough, aren't I?'

Reluctantly, he said, 'She's called Debra Peters.'

But it made it worse, knowing her name. It made her real. 'You said you might have met her, Robert. Where?'

He made a gesture, palm up. 'Sometimes I have to take

43

clients to nightclubs. She was a nightclub hostess before . . .'
His mouth twisted. 'Before starting up a more lucrative career.'

'Not the sort of nightclub we go to, presumably.'

'Don't look at me like that. Don't . . . don't *judge* me, Rose.
Listen to me. Sometimes you have a business associate,
someone you're hoping to get something from at a good
price. Or maybe I'm buying raw materials from somewhere
up north – Bolton, say, or Bradford. You offer to take them
out for the night and they're looking for something different
from back home. A bit of glamour, the seedier the better.
So, yes, sometimes I take them to Soho, and, yes, some of
the places are strip clubs. I'm sorry my world isn't as nice
and spotless as yours, but that's how it is.' He dropped his
voice. 'Forgive me; it's not your fault. But it doesn't mean
anything.'

Didn't it? She couldn't tell. She thought for a while,
chewing her lip. 'You must tell them they've made a mistake.
Tell the press.'

'I have.'

'What did they say?'

'It doesn't work like that. They hear a rumour and build
it up into something scandalous.'

'Which newspaper is it?'

'The *News of the World*.' He swirled the last of the whisky in
his glass, then drank it. 'They're the worst kind of muckrakers.
They peddle salacious tripe and don't give a damn about the
truth.'

'And they're going to say . . . what? That you slept with
this woman?' She heard her voice rise, an uncontrolled
upward flip.

'Yes.' His face was a dark, furious red. 'And other things,
vile things.'

It was impossible to believe that, in a couple of days' time, a national newspaper would publicly accuse Robert of associating with a call girl. Everyone would know about it. Their friends . . . their families . . . Robert's parents, her father. She wasn't angry, just bewildered. How could this have happened?

He drew her to him, cradling her in his arms. 'Darling, I'm so sorry. I've tried so hard to spare you this; I thought I could choke it off at source, but it looks like the bastards are determined to go ahead with the story.'

She felt a rush of sympathy for him. 'It's so rotten, so rotten for you.'

He stroked her hair and they kissed. 'Let me get you a drink,' he said. He poured her a whisky.

She gave a little laugh. 'It's because of Johnny. They're damning you by association.'

'Yes, they are.'

'How long have you known about it?'

He added a splash of water to the glass and handed it to her. 'They phoned me this afternoon. They told me they're going to run the story on Sunday.'

She studied him. 'This isn't the first you've heard of it, though, is it?'

'I got wind of it a few weeks ago.'

She felt nauseous. She couldn't face cooking the plaice that lay, cream coloured and gleaming, on a plate on the counter.

'I didn't want to worry you.' He was opening a tin of olives. 'I hoped it would blow over.'

Rose had an odd little vision then of a cold wind screaming through Walton-on-Thames, catching up sweet wrappers and cigarette packets in its path. And the four of them, her little family whom she had believed safe, whirled up helplessly into the vortex. It hurt her that he hadn't told her, that he had kept it from her. It hurt more than the thought of their names splashed over the papers.

She took a mouthful of whisky. 'I thought we shared everything.'

'Rose, *please*. Try to understand . . . I didn't know what to do.'

'Perhaps she – that girl – has mixed you up with someone else.'

'Yes, perhaps. I'll sort it out, I promise. It'll be unpleasant for a while and then everyone will forget about it. But, before it blows up, I want you to take Katherine and Eve and go and stay somewhere – with my parents or your father, whichever you prefer.'

She shook her head. 'No, I won't do that.'

'Rose, Rose, you don't seem to understand!' His eyes were wild. 'The next few days are going to be pretty vile. Reporters on the doorstep, a lot of fuss and invasion of our privacy. Things like this, the press sees everyone as fair game – including you. As soon as the next scandal comes along, it'll all die down and they'll leave us alone, but it would be better for you and the girls if you went away.'

'We're staying here.' She put down her glass and took his hands in hers. 'We're staying together, whatever happens. How could you imagine even for a moment that I'd leave you to face this by yourself? We're a family. And, just think, how would it look if I left you? If we appeared to be living apart?'

His brows lowered and he let out a low groan. 'Yes. Yes, I suppose you're right.'

They embraced. The side of his jaw, roughened by stubble,

brushed against the top of her head. His arms held her tightly and she felt his heartbeat through his shirt, a strong, steady pounding.

'God,' he murmured. 'What a nightmare.'

'Can't Neil speak to them?' Neil Whittaker was Robert's lawyer. 'Can't he threaten to sue them? Robert, surely this is libellous . . . surely Neil can stop them!'

His hands slipped away from her; he turned aside. 'I've already spoken to Neil.'

'And?'

'He tried, but he didn't get anywhere. He said better to play it by ear, at least to start with.' His voice was flat.

Neil was a good lawyer, honest and straight as a die. Rose found it hard to understand why Neil felt reluctant to act. That Robert had confided in his lawyer before telling his wife dug in the knife. He had been trying to spare her, she told herself; he had hoped it might blow over without her needing to know.

But the ordinary days that only an hour ago had made ready to unfurl in front of her had been replaced by a future that was dark and unpredictable. When she recalled her recent dissatisfaction with life, her boredom and restlessness, she saw what a fool she had been. Just then, she would have given anything to return to her familiar routine, and the pleasant hours she had spent that morning, exploring the Egg and its surroundings, seemed a distant memory.

Chapter Three

Surrey – May–June 1970

The shrill of the doorbell cut through the Sunday morning quiet, jerking Rose awake. Robert must have been up for some time, because he was standing at the window, dressed in dark trousers and a crisp white shirt.

'Who is it?' she said sleepily.

'A reporter.'

Rose sat up, wide awake, and glanced at the clock. It was not yet seven.

'I'll deal with it.' Robert fastened a cufflink. 'Take the girls downstairs. Make sure you stay in the back of the house.' He left the room.

She heard the scrape and rattle of bolts and Yale. The chime stopped and in the silence the house seemed to vibrate. Eve came into the bedroom, her thumb in her mouth, and climbed into the double bed. Katherine padded after her. Standing at the window, she raised the corner of a curtain.

'What are those men doing?'

'Katherine, come away.'

'I'm only looking.'

'Come here, sweetheart.' She steered her daughter away from the window.

The phone rang. Robert called out, 'Stay there! I'll answer it!'

Rose drew back the bedroom curtain a few inches. Half a dozen men were standing on the far side of the road. Some had cameras slung round their necks, others were smoking. As she looked down, one of them glanced up at the house. There was a moment when their eyes met, and then a series of flashes. As if it had scorched her fingers, she dropped the curtain.

Her heart was pounding. She felt encircled, invaded, and it was horrible.

'Breakfast. Come on, you two.' She knotted the tie of her dressing gown. The girls ran downstairs.

They hadn't put up nets in the wide bay windows at the front of the house because they had thought them old-fashioned and suburban, which meant that the front rooms were visible from the street. The realisation dawned on her that, until the reporters gave up and went away, she must keep the curtains drawn and so half the house must remain in darkness.

In the kitchen, she put out cereal, sliced some bread for toast and switched on the kettle. She wasn't hungry and felt too edgy to sit down. The phone rang again and something thudded through the letterbox. She went to look.

Robert was in his office, talking on the telephone. A newspaper – not The Times, their usual paper, but a smaller tabloid – lay coiled like a snake on the doormat. She took it to the kitchen.

Standing at the work surface, her back to the children, her shoulders hunched, she read the front-page headline –

Peer in Vice-Ring Scandal — above a photo of Johnny and a girl. *Johnny Pakenham and blonde nineteen-year-old temptress, Debra Peters, leave the Dean Street nightclub.* Debra Peters was wearing a minidress and knee-high boots. Her light-coloured, shoulder-length hair was pulled back from her face and, though her hooded eyes met the camera, her full mouth was unsmiling. Pale lips, a lot of eyeliner. Pretty, though. Debra Peters' tip-tilted nose, high cheekbones and slanting eyes were a mingling of childishness and exoticism.

Nineteen . . . Good God; Johnny, like Robert, was thirty-four. Rose scanned the text. The story continued on an inner page, so she leafed through the paper. *The sexy blonde's clients include . . .* The name *Robert Martineau* leaped out at her, jarring, shocking.

'For God's sake, Rose, what the hell are you doing, reading that tripe?' Robert's voice was raised.

'It's here.'

'Of course it's there. I told you. Christ.'

'What's there?' said Katherine.

'It's my turn to have the card.' Eve's arm was up to the elbow in the Shredded Wheat packet.

'No, it's mine. The aeroplane cards are mine. You had the pop stars.' Katherine yanked the packet away from her sister and strands of cereal rained on the table.

'I don't like pop stars.' Eve began to cry.

'Stop it, you two.' Rose grabbed the box, put it in the larder, and ruffled Eve's dark curls.

The phone rang again. Robert answered it. *The sexy blonde's clients include old school-friend of Johnny Pakenham's, businessman Robert Martineau.* Rose made a pot of tea and put it on a tray with some toast and carried it to his study.

Robert's voice flowed through the open door, low and furiously sarcastic. 'Just at the moment, your reputation is

the least of my problems. Sorry; have to go – things to do.'
He slammed the receiver down.

Rose put the tray on his desk. 'Something to keep you
going. Who was that?'

'My dearest brother, who else? Helpful as ever.' He
grimaced. 'Have you spoken to your father?'

'No.'

'Do it before *they* have the pleasure of telling him.' A jerk
of his head in the direction of the road.

'Robert, can't we *do* something?'

'Not at the moment, no.' He raked a hand through his
hair. 'I'm sorry, darling; I'll give you the phone in a couple
of minutes, after I've rung Neil. Maybe he can think of
something to do about those bastards out there. He might
know someone who can pull some strings.'

Rose pictured herself phoning her father and telling him
that Robert had been publicly accused of consorting with a
prostitute. She couldn't recall ever saying the word 'prostitute'
in front of her father before. Indeed, it was almost inconceivable that she should.

She went upstairs to sort out the girls' clothes and have
a shower. She couldn't resist another peek out of the bedroom
window. Her next-door neighbour, a smartly dressed woman
in her forties, was crossing the road to speak to one of the
reporters. She imagined the conversation:

What are you doing here?

And then, *Haven't you seen the paper, love?*

The woman looked up at the Martineaus' house. Their
neighbours, thought Rose. Her friends and family. Everyone
who worked for Robert would gossip about them and laugh
and tell jokes. The tradesmen, her cleaner . . . Katherine and
Eve's teachers and the other mothers at the school gate.

Robert came into the room. 'You can have the phone now.'

'I might go and see Dad, talk to him face to face. It might be easier that way.'

'As soon as you leave the house, they'll be all over you like a pack of dogs.'

'We can't stay indoors all day,' she said angrily. 'I mean, the girls can't stay in all day. Think about it. They just can't.'

'Okay,' he said, frowning, rubbing his chin. 'I suppose it wouldn't be a bad idea. But the four of us, Rose. We'll all go out together.'

As they left the house, flashbulbs went off. Questions were shouted out as Robert opened the car door for the girls to climb in.

'Tell us about Johnny Pakenham and Debra Peters, Robert. How long have they been friends?'

Robert smiled, saying calmly, 'No comment, gentlemen,' then got into the car and slipped it into gear.

The Jaguar pulled away from the pavement. Robert's mouth was set, his eyes like granite. Eve's question, 'Daddy, why was that man taking a photo of us?' hung in the air, unanswered.

As they drove through Walton-on-Thames, some of Rose's tension seemed to slip away. They'd go home later that day and the reporters would have got bored and moved on to someone else – Johnny, probably. Robert was right: their real interest was in Johnny.

'Let's go to Bushy Park,' said Robert, raising his voice. 'You'd like that, wouldn't you, kids?'

'Can I have an ice cream, Daddy?'

'Eve, you've only just had breakfast. You're a piglet.' Robert made snorting sounds.

'I'm not; I'm a girl!'

'Of course you are, sweetheart.'

Rose said, 'The park for an hour, so they can run around. Then Dad's.'

'Okay.' Robert changed down a gear as they approached a junction. 'Neil thinks I should speak to the press,' he said.

Rose stared at him. 'Why?'

'To give my side of the story.'

'There is no story, so there's no *side* to give.'

'Rose, listen. We need to show them we're a happy family. Scotch the rumours.'

'"*We*"?'

'I need you to be at my side. It'll make a difference, Neil said.'

'I don't care what Neil said!'

She must have spoken louder than she had intended, because Katherine said, 'Mummy?'

'It's all right, love.' She dropped her voice. 'It's not up to Neil.'

'Darling, I know it'll be unpleasant, but it'll only take a few minutes. The idea is that, if I make a public statement, then they'll leave us alone. You won't need to say a word, just smile and let me do the talking.'

'A press conference . . .'

'Yes, if you like. The girls will need to be there as well.'

'No.' She didn't even have to think about that. 'No, absolutely not.'

'Rose, I understand how you feel, but we have to get the public on our side, and our best hope of doing that is by showing that Debra Peters is a cheap little tart, out to make money from smearing an innocent family.'

Rose looked back to where Katherine and Eve were sitting

in the back seat. She whispered, 'I don't want them to have any part in this.'

'Yes, I know, it's hateful, and I'm sorry.'

'You said it would blow over. You said that, as soon as the next scandal came along, they'd forget about us.'

'And, in the meantime, they could do me a lot of damage. Reputation counts for a great deal in business. A quick photo – that's all, Rose, I promise – and then you can take the girls indoors.'

She burned with resentment – against the press for invading their privacy, against Debra Peters for spreading lies, and against Robert himself, for demanding such a thing of her.

He squeezed her hand. 'Will you do it?'

'If I must.' She turned away from him, watching the flickering procession of houses and the people on the pavement.

'Thank you, darling. I said this afternoon.'

Her gaze swung back to him. 'What?'

'Best to nail this as soon as possible.'

'You've already agreed? Without asking me?'

'Rose, sweetheart.'

She tried to swallow down her shock and revulsion. This afternoon. But perhaps he was right, and perhaps it was better to get it over and done with. Perhaps she should think of it as one thought of an exam or an unpleasant medical procedure: something to be endured and then forgotten about.

'There's something else,' he said. He flicked an indicator before turning right. 'The press will ask me about Debra's notebook.'

'What notebook?'

'She kept a notebook with a list of her clients. Dates and

names, that sort of thing. She sold it to the *News of the World.* That's how they got my name.'

The cold sensation in the pit of her stomach, which had been there since Robert had spoken to her on Friday evening, solidified.

'I don't understand. How could your name be there?'

'God knows.' His eyes smouldered. 'She's trying to make money out of it, of course. The whole thing is a fabrication, don't you see? I didn't want you to be taken by surprise if they mention it. I'm so sorry to put you through this, darling, but I'll make it up to you later, I promise. We'll send the girls to my parents for the weekend and we'll go away somewhere wonderful – Paris or Rome.'

He parked the car and the girls raced out of the back. They walked through the park. Tiny beads of dew still clung to the grass beneath the trees, though it had burned off where the sun shone. In the grey distance, a deer put up its antlered head. It looked flat and unreal and was gone in an instant, and Rose wondered whether she had imagined it.

She kicked at the wet grass. Her daughters were to be paraded in front of the cameras like performing animals. That girl, Debra Peters, was claiming that Robert's name was in her damnable notebook. And all for money, for greed, without a thought to the harm she was inflicting. At that moment, Rose would happily have put a knife through Debra Peters' heart.

Celia said, 'Do you think he's telling the truth?'

Dan flipped over the steaks. 'Martineau? Not sure.'

It was Tuesday. On Tuesday evenings, Celia came to dinner at Dan's flat in Kew. Celia lived in a bedsit in Tufnell Park and wasn't much of a cook, so Dan did the cooking. Tonight, he was preparing steak, mushrooms and a green salad. Celia was watching her weight, so no potatoes.

Celia was perched on the edge of the table, a glass of wine in hand. She was small, barely five foot two, and had a delightfully neat figure, hazel eyes and silky, shoulder-length, light-brown hair. They had met eighteen months ago in a pub in Holborn when her date had failed to turn up and Dan's then girlfriend, a fiery brunette called Rebecca, had walked out on him. *Oh, for God's sake! You don't have a scrap of passion in you, do you?* had been her parting shot. Dan had been about to run out after her, but then Celia had appeared at his side. *You can buy me a drink, if you like,* she had said. He had been taken by her understated prettiness, and, anyway, Rebecca's accusation had stung. So he had bought Celia a gin and lime, and they had got talking and the evening hadn't been a disaster, after all.

Now and then, they spoke about living together, but Celia worked as the personal secretary to the director of a bank in the City and didn't fancy commuting from Surrey, and though Dan had suggested more than once that he sell his flat and move into central London, Celia hadn't been keen. It was a nice flat, she said, and, anyway, if they were going to move, they might as well wait until they could afford to buy a house. It *was* a nice flat, Dan was very fond of it, and what she said made sense, so, for the time being, they went on living apart.

She said, 'Those public-school types, they think they can get away with anything.'

The steaks had been cooking for six minutes, so Dan slid them out of the pan. 'Wilkinson had a field day, of course, going on about handcuffs and whips. Some of the others are more loyal. Lucy Holbrook felt sorry for Mrs Martineau.'

56

'Do you think she *knew*?'

He tossed her a copy of the *Sun*. There was a photo of Rose Martineau on the front page. She was wearing a light-coloured skirt and a frilly, short-sleeved blouse, and her long, dark hair was clipped back from her face. In that get-up, she looked oddly sexless, her prettiness negated. Martineau's daughters, in floral frocks, stood one on either side of their mother, who was holding their hands. The camera had caught Rose Martineau smiling as she looked at her husband, but her eyes were blank.

'You didn't waste money on that rubbish, did you, Dan?' said Celia. She was a great economiser.

'Someone brought it into the office. I thought you might like to see it.' He put the plates on the table. 'If she'd known about it, she'd have thrown him out, wouldn't she?'

Celia helped herself to salad. 'I wouldn't be so sure. How could you live with a man and not know? Honestly, you'd have to be a bit thick. Maybe she thinks it's worth it. I expect they have a big house and lots of holidays. Maybe she doesn't care and turns a blind eye.'

Dan found it hard to imagine how any woman could turn a blind eye to the father of her children visiting a very expensive call girl. But he had discovered a long time ago – during his childhood, in fact – that people were capable of all sorts of things that seemed to him beyond the pale.

Celia was looking at the photograph. 'She's quite attractive, isn't she? Awful frumpy clothes, though. I suppose she's trying to be sweetly pretty, but she can't really carry it off. She should have more pride.'

'She seems nice enough.'

'Honestly, Dan, you can be so soft.' Her voice had a sharp edge, so he let the subject drop. Celia had her jealous side.

They had dinner and then they went to bed and made love. Though Dan tried to persuade Celia to stay the night – he liked waking up in the morning beside her small, warm body – she hadn't got her toothbrush, she pointed out, and, anyway, her director, Paul, had an early meeting the next morning, for which she must be present. So he walked her to the station, where they kissed and parted.

On the way home, he mulled over their conversation. Had Robert Martineau paid that girl, Debra Peters, for sex? The newspapers seemed to think that he had. But you needed your head screwed on to be as successful as Martineau, so would he take such a risk? On the other hand, Martineau's purchase of the ailing aviation company in itself implied overconfidence, even arrogance, and, had his judgement been better, he would have sacked Ted Wilkinson months ago. Robert Martineau had had an enviable start in life, was from a good family, had been to the best schools. His family had probably given his business a useful injection of capital, early on in his career. Might that have made him rash? Might it have made him feel he could get away with anything?

Dan hadn't had an enviable start. His parents, if asked, would probably justify their follies by describing themselves as having been driven by passion. Dan would have said they were wayward. They had separated when Dan was four years old, his father to live with a hairdresser in Weymouth, his mother to start up a fashion shop that lost money with such rapidity that, within eighteen months, she had been forced to sell the family home to pay her debts. Dan had gone to stay with his father in Weymouth while his mother looked for somewhere for them to live. His stepmother hadn't liked him very much, and neither had his stepbrother, a sulky child called Terence, who liked to scribble on Dan's books and stamp on his Meccano constructions.

After six months, his stepmother had tired of him and sent him back to his mother, who was by then living in a bedsit in Green Lanes. She took a job in a haberdashery shop, which she gave up when she met Norman. Norman called himself an impresario, which meant that he drove a van for a jazz band. They got along for a while, the three of them going on the road with the jazz band, which was fun in the summer, but less so in winter. Dan missed a lot of school. His mother and Norman quarrelled and Dan ended up back in the Green Lanes bedsit. Meanwhile, his father wasn't living in Weymouth any more, but had moved to Cromer, in Norfolk, where he married a fat, blonde woman called Molly, who owned a chip shop.

And so on, and so on. If he ever related to anyone the complicated story of his childhood – which was very infrequently because something shameful clung to it, as if some tinge of their carelessness had attached to him – he always gave up at around the Molly stage. He knew his life story to be tedious and unenlightening. He had passed the eleven plus and been offered a place at a grammar school, where he had begun to see a way out for himself: collect a decent selection of O and A levels, get accepted for university and take a science degree, because that was where the steady jobs were for boys like him, boys without connections, without the solidity of a family. From the age of twelve, he had stayed in the bedsit by himself when his mother had gone off on one of her jaunts. He had kept out of trouble at school and had been fortunate to have teachers who recognised his ambition and nurtured his talent. At the age of eighteen, he had left London to study engineering at Sheffield University.

He visited his parents regularly but infrequently. His mother was living in a commune in the Lake District, while his father, who had some years ago separated from his third wife, had set up home in a caravan on the east coast. Dan's upbringing had taught him not to allow himself to get dragged down into the mire by the messy lives of those around him. The virtues he admired were those of common sense, steadfastness and trustworthiness. He didn't give a damn about whatever sexual shenanigans Robert Martineau got up to in his spare time, but he cared about his future in the company, and if the scandal looked as if it was going to bring it down, he'd be out of there like a shot and wouldn't look back.

On Wednesday, Robert dropped the girls off at school on the way to a business meeting. Rose left the house at ten to shop. Though she would have preferred to ignore the newspapers, she couldn't seem to find the resolution to do so. She bought a copy of the Sun and took it into a café. Bobby Moore's face smiled up at her from the front page. She ordered a coffee and, when the waitress had gone, leafed through the paper. Turning a page, she froze.

A voice said, 'Excuse me, do you mind awfully if I sit here? It's terribly busy.'

She looked up. A young woman – blonde, wearing jeans and a dusky pink T-shirt – was gesturing to the seat opposite her. 'No, of course not.'

'Thanks. It isn't usually so crowded.' The young woman sat down. Then, in a startled tone, she said, 'Goodness, is that you?'

She was staring at the photograph in the newspaper. It was of Rose against a background of trees that cast shadows over her light-coloured clothes.

Rose snatched the paper away and shoved it in her bag.

'I'm sorry.' The young woman looked embarrassed. 'I didn't mean to pry. If it's any consolation, it's a great photo. Whenever anyone takes a picture of me, I seem to have my eyes shut and look like an evil witch. You look stunning.'

Rose managed a smile. 'Thank you.'

'You sound like you're having a rough day. Here, have one of these.' The woman offered her a crumpled pack of Rothmans.

'Thanks, but I won't.'

'I know, it's a bad habit, but I can't seem to give them up. Weak willed, that's me. My name's Melanie Jones, by the way. Do you mind if I smoke?'

'Not at all.'

The lighter clicked. 'You okay?'

'Fine.' The coffees arrived. Rose stirred in a spoonful of sugar. She didn't usually take sugar, but the photo had shaken her.

Melanie Jones said, 'If you want to talk . . . I know we've only just met, but sometimes it helps.'

'I haven't worn that outfit since *Sunday*.' She hated that her voice quivered a little. 'We went to Bushy Park, me and my husband and our daughters. A photographer must have followed us.'

'What a bastard.'

'He must have been watching us all the time. It's such a horrible feeling.'

'You must feel very alone.' A puff of the cigarette.

'I do, yes.' She hadn't thought about that before. All those people who wouldn't let her be and yet she felt lonely.

'How old are your daughters?'

'Katherine's six and Eve is four.'

61

'Such pretty names.'

'Do you have children?'

A laugh. 'Haven't found a man mad enough to marry me yet. I'd love to, one day, though. I'd like girls, like you. Boys can be so rowdy.'

'Robert would have liked a son.'

'A man's man, is he, your husband?'

'He likes watching football and driving fast cars, so I suppose he must be. But he doesn't mind helping round the house and he's so sweet with the girls.'

'That's very touching, Rose. Nice that you see a different side to him.'

A warning bell rang. She gave Melanie Jones a close look. 'What did you say you did for a living?'

'I didn't. Do you go out to work yourself?'

'No, not now. You're a reporter, aren't you?'

'Yes, I am, but I'm not like those other ones.'

Rose stood up.

Melanie Jones said, 'I can help you.'

'No, you can't.' White-hot anger flared through her. 'Leave me alone.'

'I write for the women's page. Give me the rights to an exclusive article and I promise you it'll be sympathetic. Everyone'll see you in a favourable light. My readers will adore you. You're a beautiful woman and the mother to two delightful little girls. It would be the sensible thing to do, Rose. So far, we've only heard Debra Peters' side of the story. It would help Robert. You have to fight fire with fire, in this business.'

'No.' Fury made it hard for her to get the word out.

A hand grasped the sleeve of her jacket as she turned away. 'Debra Peters' boyfriend sold us her appointment book. I've seen it. Your husband's name is mentioned in it seven times. He's lying to you, Rose.'

'No, that's not true.' She pulled away.

'I'm afraid it is.' Melanie slipped her card into Rose's handbag as she clumsily fumbled for change to pay the waitress. 'If you change your mind, give me a ring. Most of the flak's been flying around Johnny Pakenham, but it may not always be that way. You've got to protect yourself, Rose. You've got to think of those two little girls.'

Walking home, she found herself glancing over her shoulder, wondering whether that man was following her or if that woman across the road might suddenly whip a camera out of her bag. What a fool she had been – what a naive, stupid fool. Robert had told her not to talk to anyone, but she had opened her mouth and gabbled away. Had she betrayed any intimate secrets? She did not think so. But she felt used, soiled and upset.

Melanie Jones had been lying about the appointment book. She must have been. She had been trying to sow a seed of doubt to divide her from Robert. Journalists often lied, to trick people into talking to them. She had proved herself to be a liar: if she hadn't actively told lies when introducing herself, she had nevertheless set out to deceive.

Yet the false charm had dropped away at the close of their conversation and the reporter's parting words had had an ominous ring: *seven times. He's lying to you, Rose.* The thing she was discovering about scandal was that its octopus limbs crept into every crevice of your life, and whether it was falsehood or truth didn't matter because it sucked in friends, relations and colleagues, and left nothing clean and undamaged. *Seven times.* Why did they prey on her so, those words? It was their specificity, she thought. It would have been easier to dismiss the reporter's claims had she said 'a few times', or 'half a dozen times'.

Robert, like Johnny, had a reckless side to his nature. Life ticking on in a comfortable way wasn't for him; he needed risk, found life flavourless without it. Rose wanted to stop picturing Robert and Johnny at some party or nightclub, but couldn't: Johnny narrowing his pale blue eyes and saying, *Go on, Robbie; what's the harm?* And Robert laughing and shrugging his shoulders. *Why not?*

Seven times. Robert wouldn't go with a prostitute *once.* He wasn't that sort of man. He was a kind, loving family man, the man who had swept her off her feet. He was her husband and her lover and her dearest friend and she trusted him completely.

And yet something had opened up these past awful days, displaying her marriage in a different, harsher light. Robert had kept so much from her. It had taken the imminent threat of exposure to force him to open up to her. What else might he have hidden from her? What secrets might he keep?

You must feel very alone. Friends had called, offering her comfort, consolation or a shoulder to cry on, but she had brushed them off. A powerful sense of humiliation isolated her and she had begun to see how loneliness and public disgrace might drive a wedge between her and Robert. She mustn't allow that to happen. She mustn't allow doubt and suspicion to spill into the cracks. She loved Robert and he loved her and that was all that mattered.

And yet, as she hurried past the handful of pressmen outside her house and ran up the steps and let herself indoors, she discerned a glimmer of doubt inside her. Debra Peters' boyfriend had sold the notebook to the newspaper. Melanie

Jones claimed to have seen it. Would she lie about that? Would she?

Her cleaner was off sick and the place was a mess, children's toys scattered, multicoloured, over the floors. The laundry basket was overflowing and her father was coming to tea. But as she vacuumed, mopped and ironed, the repetitive tasks failed to occupy her mind, which niggled and probed, finding no comforting place to rest.

Rose put the salt and pepper on the kitchen table. 'Something happened today.'

Robert, who had just come home, was shrugging off his jacket. 'What?'

She told him about Melanie Jones, about her duplicity.

'For God's sake,' he said. He sounded weary.

'This woman, this reporter, told me she'd seen that notebook. She told me that your name was listed in it seven times, Robert.'

He looked up, made to speak, but she cut him off.

'What I would mind most,' she said carefully, 'what I would find unforgiveable, would be if you lied to me.'

He shook his head. 'How can you even listen to someone like that?'

'Then swear to me. Swear to me that nothing ever happened between you and Debra Peters.'

'Nothing ever happened. I swear it, Rose.'

He took her in his arms and she felt weak with relief. She rested her head against his shoulder. Closing her eyes, she let out a breath as he stroked the nape of her neck.

'I love you,' he murmured. 'I love you so much.'

* * *

65

Next morning, Robert left the house while Rose was putting on her make-up. The sound of shouting from the street made her draw back the curtain and look outside. As she watched, Robert grabbed a journalist by his jacket lapels, wrenched the camera out of the man's grasp and threw it forcefully on to the pavement, where it shattered. Then he climbed into the Jaguar and drove away.

'The little shit deserved it,' was all he said that evening, when Rose asked him about the incident.

By Friday, the journalists had gone and the pavement was empty. On the front page of the *Sun*, an image of Robert, his face contorted with fury as he confronted the photographer, had toppled the World Cup from its recent perch. *In a display of violent temper, Martineau accused Miss Peters of being a gold-digger and a cheating, lying* b***h. Another article, inside the paper, claimed that Johnny Pakenham had admitted the truth of the allegations. 'I like a little variety in my life,' he was quoted as saying. 'Don't all men?' There was a different photo of Johnny and Debra Peters, climbing into a car. Johnny was smiling and the girl was hard-faced, as usual.

Rose's in-laws lived in Charlbury, in Oxfordshire, in a seventeenth-century manor house of soft gold Cotswold limestone. Three broad gables faced out to a sweeping gravel drive; the back of the house looked down on a garden of two acres, bordered by a stream.

Robert parked the car in the driveway and turned off the ignition. 'Christ, I could have done without this.'

Rose squeezed his hand. They could all have done without Robert's parents' ruby-wedding party, she reflected, as she let Katherine and Eve out of the car. She had never felt less like facing up to family and friends, to judgement and curiosity.

Inside the house, all was efficient bustle, hired waitresses hurrying about with trays of cutlery and glasses, and the hallway cleared of its customary clutter of umbrellas, fishing rods and waxed jackets. Lionel Martineau, a tall, gaunt man with a patrician manner, waved to them. Rose had always got on well with her in-laws, who were quiet, civilised and a little austere.

Lionel shook Robert's hand and planted a dry kiss on Rose's cheek. Congratulations were offered, thanks murmured.

'Your mother's doing the flowers,' Lionel said, and Robert swept the children away to their grandmother.

The French windows had been thrown open and tables spread with white cloths had been put up beneath the cedars on the lawn. Rose found Robert's elder brother, George, on the terrace, giving directions. George was taller, thinner and plainer than Robert. His nose was long and pointed, his jaw heavy. His eyes, which were a colour midway between blue and hazel and grey, tended to be beadily inquisitive.

Rose went to join him. 'Hello, George.'

'Rose.' They kissed.

'How are you?'

Her brother-in-law glanced with distaste at the tables on the lawn. 'I loathe eating outdoors. I've never seen the attraction of it.'

'It's what we do – the British. Picnic on the first day that passes for summer.'

He smiled. 'You're looking very summery, I must say.'

She was wearing a pink-and-cream sprigged silk frock and a string of pearls, given to her by Robert on her last birthday. 'Thank you. It's not too palace garden party?'

'Not at all; most appropriate. How are you bearing up?'

She was glad that her sunglasses sheltered her from his enquiring gaze. 'To tell the truth,' she said quietly, 'I hate it. I just hate it.'

'Poor Rose. You've had rather a week.'

'I have to admit that I'm glad it's over.' Rose took a deep breath and smiled as brightly as she could before changing the subject. 'The flowers are in the car.'

She had ordered two dozen yellow roses from a florist in Walton-on-Thames. George and Robert were to present them to her mother-in-law after the speeches.

They went to fetch them, skirting round the side of the house to the drive. 'The garden's looking good,' she said.

'Mummy has a new chap. Marvellous with the laburnums, apparently.'

She took the bouquet out of the car boot and showed them to him.

'Yes, not bad.' George examined the flowers. 'I prefer an apricot yellow, but needs must. Are you a red rose sort of woman?'

'I'm not all that keen on roses. Too stiff and gaudy. Ridiculous, I know, with my name.'

'I don't suppose buying roses has been your top priority, what with the press camping outside your house all week.'

The blue sky, the scents of spring and the prospect of a day away from home and the nightmare of the past week began to work their magic and she felt herself relax a little. She said, 'I'm hoping the worst might be over.'

'Are you?'

'The press have gone. There hasn't been anyone outside the house for the last couple of days. I think they've found better things to do.'

'Maybe you're right.'

She detected a hesitancy. 'George?'

'I hope you are. Truly, I do, Rose.'

'What are you saying?'

His high, broad forehead creased. 'I've always been fascinated by military strategy, as you know. All my biographies of Napoleon and Wellington . . . Robert likes to be disparaging. But a general never sends all his forces into battle at once. Never.'

She was disturbed to see in his eyes a glimmer of sympathy. She said sharply, 'Have you heard something, George?'

He smiled. 'Let's get these poor things into the house before they wilt, shall we?'

Robert came to join them in the hall. 'Mother looks as if she could do with a hand with the flowers.'

Rose went to the scullery, where Mary Martineau was stuffing tulips into vases.

'This was never my métier.' Her mother-in-law offered a cheek to be kissed. 'Give me a nice charity committee or hospital board any day. George told me I should have had a florist arrange them and I'm afraid he was right.'

'I'll have a go, if you like, Mary.'

Her mother-in-law began to clear away leaves and stubs of stem. She said, 'We don't read those sorts of newspapers, naturally, but you can't help hearing. It's all nonsense, isn't it, Rose?'

'Of course it is,' she said calmly.

A small exhalation of breath. 'I was sure it was.'

It was past ten in the evening by the time they returned home to Walton-on-Thames. The girls, worn out by games of French cricket and rides on the pony Mary Martineau kept for them in the paddock, fell asleep immediately. Rose had assumed she would do the same, but sleep evaded her, darting further from her reach the harder she chased it. Eventually, she looked at the clock and saw that it was almost two, and put on her dressing gown and went downstairs.

She made herself a cup of tea and a slice of toast, which she took into the front room. She hadn't eaten much at the party, had lost her appetite. She opened the curtains a few inches. The empty pavement and the quiet park on the far side of the road, motionless beneath the dark, dusty sky, soothed her. The shrub roses in the front garden were black and papery in the night, and a car hurried past, light from its headlamps spilling on the tarmac. Abandoning any conscious attempt to calm her mind, she let the events of the day reel over and over, like a television programme continually repeating itself.

Perhaps George had been trying to provoke, or perhaps he had merely been tactless, but she did not think so. He had been warning her. Of what, though? Her optimism – fragile, anyway – had not recovered from their conversation. Shortly afterwards, Lionel and Mary's friends and neighbours had begun to arrive at the house. While she had conversed with her fellow guests, Rose had felt separate from them; while she had eaten lunch and listened to the speeches, she had found herself watching Robert, her gaze darting up the table to where he sat beside his mother.

She was trying to reconcile her faith in Robert with a terror that Melanie Jones had been telling the truth about Debra Peters' notebook, but she had lost confidence in her judgement and her reasoning was marred by a jittery anxiety. The abyss of doubt into which she was helplessly tumbling showed up a lack of loyalty. And yet, as the day had gone on, her fears had solidified, settling around her like a shell, stiff and immoveable.

70

A sound; she looked up. Robert stood in the doorway.

'Rose, what's up?'

'Can't sleep.'

He took her in his arms. 'Come back to bed.'

'Soon. It's going to be all right, isn't it?' She looked up at his familiar features, daubed with shadow in the low light. 'It is, isn't it, Robert?'

'Of course it is.' He kissed her slowly, tenderly. 'I promise it is.'

She must have dozed off, lying on the sofa, because, when she woke, sunlight was filtering into the room. She went to the window and saw with sickening disappointment that the press had returned and were chatting and smoking and adjusting their cameras. A flash of bright hair: Melanie Jones was there too.

In the hallway, she put on a mackintosh and slid her feet into a pair of old shoes. Then she opened the door and went outside.

'Leave it a minute, boys.' Melanie Jones crossed the road to her.

'Go away.' It took an effort of will to speak quietly. 'Leave us alone.'

'Read it, Rose.' A newspaper was pressed into her hands.

She went back inside the house. She unfolded the paper and saw the headline: *Debra – The Truth.* In this photo, Debra Peters was laughing, pretty and young.

She read the article. When she had finished it, she went upstairs. Robert was stirring in bed; she dropped the newspaper on the pillow beside him. Then she went to the kitchen to make the girls' breakfast. The phone rang and someone knocked at the door. She made a cup of tea she couldn't drink.

Katherine and Eve were eating their cereal when Robert came into the kitchen.

'Rose,' he said.

'I'm taking the girls to my father's.'

'Rose, please . . .'

'Don't say anything.' Her gaze flicked from Katherine to Eve. 'Just don't.'

When the girls had finished breakfast, she took them upstairs and helped them get ready. Her Mini was parked in a side road that was accessible from the back garden. As she started up the engine, she heard a shout and saw men running from the corner of the street towards her. She stamped her foot on the accelerator and the Mini lurched, then sped away.

In the *News of the World* article, Debra Peters had stated that her relationship with Robert – was that the word? A man visiting a prostitute; could you call it a relationship? – had begun the previous autumn. There must have been a late night, an invented business dinner. Perhaps he had said to her, *Don't bother with this one, darling; it'll be pretty tedious.* She couldn't remember.

But, in October last year, there had been the first of seven assignations. Debra Peters had been merciless and explicit. Each rendezvous had been listed in her appointment book, dates and times noted alongside details of the client's sexual preferences and distinguishing marks. Robert's appendix scar and the mole on his breastbone, a penchant for leather and whips – all had been listed in Debra Peters' book.

Debra Peters had authorised today's article in response to – revenge for – Robert's comments in the newspaper the previous day. *Robert Martineau accused Debra of being a cheat and a liar – but it's wealthy businessman Martineau who's the lying cheat.* The story had been picked up by the BBC. Earlier that evening, as her father had occupied Katherine and Eve in another room, Rose had watched as images of both Robert and the call girl blazed across the screen.

She parked the car at the front of the house. A flashbulb flared, but she didn't care any more, except that it worsened her headache. As she shut the door behind her, Robert came out of his study.

He said, 'Where are the girls?'

'At my father's. I'm going back there as soon as I've got their things.'

'Can we talk?'

'No. I want you to leave.'

'Rose, I'm not expecting you to forgive me – I wouldn't; I know I don't deserve it – but could we please talk?'

She was standing by the coat stand, he by the open door of the study. When they had first moved into the house, she had scraped layers of green and brown paint from the door before covering it with a soft yellow. They had chosen the coat stand, an arts-and-crafts piece inset with blue-and-white delft tiles, together, in a thrift shop in Kingston-on-Thames.

She said, 'I'm packing a bag and then I'm going back to my father's. I expect you to be gone from here by the time I collect Katherine and Eve from school tomorrow.'

'Tomorrow . . .' he repeated.

Her precarious control snapped. 'This is my home! And I can't bear the sight of you! So, yes, Robert, tomorrow!' Her voice rose in a scream.

She stumbled upstairs. She had bought the suitcase she took out of the cupboard for their first trip to Italy: Umbria and Tuscany, hilltop towns and making love in hot, cheap

73

hotels. Perhaps Debra Peters had not been the first prostitute he had visited. Perhaps there had always been some lack he had needed to make up for. Perhaps she was dull in bed, unadventurous, supine, prim. *I like a little variety in my life. Don't all men?* She thought she had reached rock bottom, but there were darker depths beneath.

Packing school uniforms, hair brushes and toothbrushes for the girls, she remembered bringing Eve, as a newborn baby, home to this house. Robert's love for and pride in his daughters – she was sure of that, if nothing else, now. Where had it gone wrong? Where had *they* gone wrong?

Robert's betrayal had falsified every part of her life. He had spoiled everything. He had spoiled this house, which had been their family home, and everything they had chosen to put inside it. He had spoiled the clothes she wore and the jewellery he had given her. He had spoiled her friendships, because now her friends would look at her in a different way. He had spoiled her relationship with his family, because she would now look at them in a different way, wondering whether there was a corruptness inside them that they had passed on to Robert. He had spoiled the places they had been together, the pubs and restaurants, the holidays they had taken. He had spoiled her memories, because there was no moment of their life together that she was able to look back on with pleasure. Every word that had passed between them had covered up lies. Every touch had been a betrayal. She had been marked and shamed and must become a different person.

In the bedroom, collecting make-up from the dressing table, mascara and eyeliner fell from her hands as she sat down on the edge of the bed, overwhelmed by despair. Her head pulsed as if something was about to burst. She was made of glass and was brittle and worn to transparency.

Another cold breath would shatter her. Her marriage, her home and the life she had led were hollow and broken and without value. To think of Robert, to see his face and hear his voice, scratched deep scores across her heart. And yet she could think of nothing else.

Chapter Four

Surrey and Cambridge – June 1970

'When are we going home, Mummy?' asked Eve, as Rose tucked her daughters into bed.

'Soon,' said Rose.

'Thursday?'

'No, not Thursday.'

'She doesn't even know when Thursday is,' said Katherine.

'I do! Thursday's yesterday.'

Katherine laughed. 'Yesterday was Monday, silly. Is Daddy coming tomorrow?'

'No, love. I'll ask Grandad to come and kiss you goodnight.'

'I'm going to hide from Grandad!' Eve dived into Katherine's bed and pulled the blankets over her head. Katherine gave Rose a cool look. Eve might have swallowed the going-to-stay-with-Grandad-for-a-few-days story, but Katherine knew that something was wrong.

Rose went downstairs to the kitchen, where her father was washing up. 'They'd like you to say goodnight to them, Dad.'

Giles went upstairs. Rose dried up some plates and put them away. She was staying in her childhood home, but it seemed unfamiliar to her. Everything seemed unfamiliar now; nothing was right.

'Don't worry about that, love.' Giles came back into the room. 'Sit down and relax.'

She went into the sitting room, but didn't sit down and couldn't relax. The last few days, she had lurched between an uncontrollable nervous energy and exhausted lassitude. Her gaze drifted over the ornaments on the stone fire surround: a small bronze statue of Ganesh, the elephant god, remover of obstacles; a model of an Avro Lancaster, a plane her father had flown during the war; and a photograph of her mother, taken on their last family holiday in Scotland. In it, her mother was wearing a thick sweater the colour of heather blossom. Rose ran her fingertips across the glass and a wave of grief ran through her. She needed her mother to take her in her arms. She needed to press her face against the warm, knobbly texture of the sweater, and weep.

'Job done,' her father said, coming into the room.

She turned, blinking. 'Were they still in the same bed when you left them?'

'Best to leave them where they were, I thought. Eve's asleep already. I'll move her over later. Would you like a drink, Rose?'

'Please.'

Giles peered into the cabinet as if something other than the usual bottles of Glenfiddich and Tio Pepe might have crept in there.

'A sherry would be lovely, Dad,' she said, pre-empting his question. She had drunk too much whisky these last dreadful days and seemed to have a headache all the time. At least, she thought it was the whisky. Perhaps her headache was a consequence of the thoroughness of Robert's betrayal and her endless, deadening realisation of how little she must have meant to him.

Her father handed her a glass. 'It will get better, love,' he said gently.

'You can't know that.' The words burst out of her angrily.

'I remember what I felt like after your mother died.'

She wanted to say, *That wasn't the same; Mum hadn't lied to you over and over again*, but saw in time how obnoxious that would be. She pressed her hands round the glass, struggling to control her emotions.

She said quietly, 'I can't see how he can have done it. That's the thing, Dad. I try to, but I can't.'

'These things take time, Rose.'

'If only it would sink in. I manage to distract myself for a minute or two, but then I remember it all over again, and it's horrible – horrible.'

Her father patted her shoulder before sitting down in an armchair. 'After your mother died, I think I went on living more out of habit than anything else. I had to keep going, for your sake, just as you have to keep going for Katherine and Eve. I had to go on breathing and eating and speaking to people, though I didn't feel like doing so. And in time – and it took a long, long time – doing everyday things, even though I was just going through the motions, helped.'

'I can't face going back to the house.'

'I know. And you don't have to. You can stay here for as long as you like.'

She looked down at her glass. 'I don't know what to do with myself any more. It's all right when the girls are here, but when I'm on my own . . .'

'I can take a few days off, if you like, love; give you some company.'

She shook her head. 'No, Dad. I need to sort myself out.' She tucked her feet beneath her, pulling her cardigan round her. Though it was summer, she felt cold all the time. 'I don't know what to say to them. I can't tell them that their father did that. Why didn't he think of that, how impossible it would be? He might not have thought of me, but didn't he care about what he was doing to his children?'

She was crying again. She wiped her face with her fingers and waved her father away as he made to rise from his chair.

'I expect,' she heard Giles say, 'he acted on impulse.'

'Seven times?' She gave him a furious glare. 'Is it impulse if you do the same rotten, lousy thing seven times?'

'I'm not going to defend Robert's actions. I'm having a hard enough time preventing myself from throttling him.'

This, from a man who was so peaceable Rose had never even heard him swear, brought a weak smile to her face.

'Don't do that, Dad. It wouldn't help.'

'It would be momentarily satisfying, but, yes, I agree, it wouldn't.' Giles topped up her glass. 'Find things to do to fill the time till you can think straight, that's my advice. Read books, do the crossword, go out for a walk. Do anything, but do something. Leave the big decisions until you're ready to make them.'

The nights were the worst. After she had checked on the children and got ready for bed, Rose took a couple of aspirins and read for a while. Then she put off the light and curled up in bed.

Images crept into her mind: Robert drinking champagne with Debra Peters in some seedy nightclub; Robert in bed with Debra Peters, their naked bodies writhing, slick with sweat. Still, her strongest emotion was that of disbelief.

She felt permanently stunned. The shock resounded through her constantly, as if a string had been plucked and would not stop reverberating.

She turned on the bedside lamp and sat up in bed. A paperback lay beside the lamp: a Leon Uris, borrowed from her father's bookcase. The bookmark told her that she had read the first few chapters, but she couldn't remember the story at all.

Climbing out of bed, she opened a drawer and took out the ring she had found at the Egg. It lay in her palm, mysterious and ornate, guarding its secrets. She had found it just under a fortnight ago, though it seemed much longer. In that short space of time, her life had become unrecognisable to her. If the ring had belonged to Sadie, why had she kept it after her fiancé had broken off the engagement? Perhaps for the same reason she herself had not yet thrown down a drain her own diamond engagement ring, given to her by Robert, on a beach in Cornwall, nine years ago. Sadie's ring had represented too much. However much it hurt to look at it, getting rid of it might have felt like negating a precious part of her life. It might have made it seem as if that time of promise and happiness had never existed.

Rose tried the ring on. It was too small for the third finger of her left hand. She had found no more photographs of the sisters in her grandmother's flat, only the snapshot of the two in their coats and velvet hats. In that, Sadie had appeared to be smaller and slighter than Edith, yet she must have had strong hands, presumably, to operate an etching press. If the ring had belonged to Sadie, how had it ended up in the earth a few yards from the Egg?

Rose had rarely come up against failure before – and the failure of her marriage to Robert was so profound, and of such magnitude, that it tore away at her identity. She had lost belief in herself. She could no longer see a future. And yet, because of her daughters, she must keep going. She could not allow herself to fall apart.

She could not change what had happened, so somehow, anyhow, she must distract herself from it. What had her father said to her? *Do anything, but do something.* Rose knew that he was right. As her gaze settled on the ring, she knew what she was going to do. She was going to find Sadie. She was going to discover what had happened to her, and where she had gone after she had left the Egg, in October 1934. And what had frightened her so, there. If she filled her time by tracking down Sadie Lawless, then she wouldn't be able to think about how Robert must have woken in the mornings and thought, Perhaps I'll go and see that tart Debra tonight. And then I'll come home and play with my daughters and make love to my wife.

What did she know so far? That Sadie had been the younger and the prettier of the two sisters. That she and Edith had not got on. The psychiatrist, Philip Sprott, had said so and Sadie's last letter had confirmed it: *Whatever the differences between us, Edith . . .* Sadie had been an artist, a printmaker. According to Dr Sprott, she had been vibrant, intelligent and charming. It had been Sadie who had originally owned the Egg, so presumably her father must have left it to her. Why had he given the house to Sadie and not to Edith, the elder sister? Might that have been a source of friction between the two women?

Rose reread the first letter sent from the Egg. Sadie's cheerfulness seemed forced, now, as if she had been putting on a show. *The Egg is all furnished and looks perfectly charming . . . Do you remember how entrancing the woods are in autumn, Edith?*

She's trying to make the best of it. Time heals every-thing – countless well-meaning friends would have told her that. Sadie tells herself she must always face forward, never look back, and that, by moving into the Egg, she'll be able to concentrate on her art. If she needs inspiration, all she need do is look out of a window at the silver birches with their speckled white trunks, or the robin singing on a branch of red berries. She resolves to start her programme of self-improving activities first thing in the morning. She'll rise at seven and walk to the shop at Nutcombe, where she'll buy a bottle of milk, a loaf of bread and a newspaper. She'll tidy the house and chop kindling for the stove, and then she'll work on a print. In the afternoon, she'll go for a long walk, taking her sketchbook with her. She won't allow herself time to mourn what she's lost. She won't brood or think of what might have been.

The furniture – some inherited from her parents, other pieces her own flea-market finds – sits awkwardly in this plain white cube. As the night seeps through the great glass windows of the Egg, she's shot through with a yearning for London, for cafés and concerts, private views and bookshops. She didn't think this through. She moved in here on a whim, in response to a half-baked yearning for the simplicity of country life and a belief that the white purity of the Egg would enforce order on a disordered existence. But it isn't working; she's moved her turmoil in with her, has isolated herself with it. She feels cut off, adrift and desperately lonely.

She can't control the anguish that wells up inside her. She longs for the lover who has abandoned her. *I can't marry you; it doesn't feel right*, he told her. Or, *I've met someone else*. She dreads going to bed alone in the chilly little house because that's where she feels the absence of him most. She's becoming less than she once was; she's wearing away. She wonders whether, if she were to disappear off the face of the earth, anyone would notice.

Rose switched on the overhead light and opened Sadie's next letter, written in November 1930.

Mr Boxell at the garage has come up trumps! He has found me a splendid bicycle. I've painted it a very pretty holly green and it looks frightfully smart. I positively whizzed down the hill to the railway station a couple of mornings ago.

A humorous description of a tussle with the kitchen stove followed: Sadie's problems lighting it, a tin of soup eaten cold in consequence. The names of some of her friends were mentioned in the next paragraph. Sadie and a woman called Pearl had had tea at Jimmy's flat in Victoria. *Splinter,* whatever that was, wasn't making any money, so Jimmy was repairing bicycles to pay the rent. Jimmy had asked Sadie to do some etchings for *Splinter,* so presumably it must be a magazine or journal or book. *Something political,* Sadie wrote. *I shall have fun with that. Hearty peasant girls scything corn, perhaps.*

It occurred to Rose that she could track down Sadie through her friends. If only Sadie had given their surnames. She thumbed through more letters, skimming the text. Some differently coloured stamps caught her eye; squinting at them, she saw that several of Sadie's letters had been posted from France and Spain. Rose remembered the letter Sadie had sent from Cambridge, from her friend Constance's house, and took it out of its envelope. With a fleeting raising of the spirits, she read the heading, which gave Constance Meyrick's address as Maids Causeway, Cambridge.

She went back to reading the letter about the bicycle. Sadie's final paragraph said, *I haven't seen the Chivertons yet. I thought they might call. Maybe they are away. I imagine them leading very glamorous* lives. *We never met at the time they bought the house, but I would think that, if one ran into them in Nutcombe, they would be unmistakeable, wouldn't you?*

Rose lay back on the pillows, thinking. Images of the Egg, hidden in its forest, flashed through her mind. The sunken lane, rising to the ridgeway. The Gull's Wing, that glass palace, walled off from the road. And the girl in the striped frock leaving the bag of groceries by the gate.

There's only Mrs Chiverton . . . She never talks to anyone. If she sees you, those dogs'll be out.

As she headed back to her car after seeing Katherine and Eve into school, she passed a woman she knew slightly, Suzy Masters, the parent of a girl in Katherine's class. Rose forced a smile of greeting to her face.

Suzy looked at her blankly, then addressed another woman, standing beside her. 'I don't know how she can live with herself. Letting him get away with it like that. Such a bloody doormat.'

Her voice was clearly audible and some of the other parents stared, looking embarrassed. Rose wanted to say, *I didn't know*, but the words wouldn't come out. She hurried blindly back to the sanctuary of her car, her fingers fumbling as she unlocked the door. Then she sat down, her hands shaking as they rested on the steering wheel.

Was it always going to be like this? Was some new and horrible humiliation to take place every day? She took a deep breath, trying to calm herself, then started up the engine. She had arranged for her father to collect the girls from school today so that she could drive to Cambridge, where she hoped to find Sadie's friend, Constance Meyrick. She mustn't allow that judgemental little cow to upset her and send her scuttling back to hide in her father's house. And besides, she thought grimly, as she pulled away, heading for the North Circular, hadn't Suzy a point? She must have been stupid not to have noticed what was going on. Very, very stupid.

Rose parked on a side street and walked along the long, sloping Maids Causeway until she found the house. It was old and elegant, three storeys high. A flight of stone steps ran up to a black front door.

She rang the bell. The door was opened by a white-haired woman wearing a purple linen dress. 'I'm sorry to disturb you,' said Rose, 'but I'm looking for Constance Meyrick.'

'Then you've found her.' Mrs Meyrick peered at Rose through wire-rimmed glasses. 'Have we met?'

'No, never.' Rose introduced herself, then explained about the letters she had found in her grandmother's writing case. When she mentioned Sadie Lawless, Constance's blue eyes brightened.

'*Sadie.* It's years since I've heard that name. So you're her great-niece? You must come in, my dear.'

The wide hallway was lit by a stained-glass window that flung patches of yellow and blue light on to the floorboards. One wall was lined with bookshelves, the other covered with photographs, many of them of children.

'I'm looking after my grandson today,' Constance said. 'We've been playing in the garden.'

They went through a back room furnished with faded floral sofas to a terrace surrounded by ivy-covered walls. A rusty wrought-iron table and chairs were arranged in the shade and a small, dark-haired boy was putting plastic cars into a large cardboard box.

'Fergus, this is Rose,' said Constance. Fergus stared at her and then went back to his cars.

While Constance made tea, Fergus tried to climb into the box. Rose lifted him in and pushed him down the narrow brick path that ran between the flower beds, making car-engine noises, to the far end of the garden, where a tree bearing great white, waxy flowers cast its shade.

'You're admiring my magnolia,' Constance called out as she put a tea tray on the table. 'This house is far too big for me now. My children tell me I should move somewhere smaller. I tell them I need the bedrooms for when they come to stay, but the truth is I don't know how I could bear to leave my magnolia. Toby and I planted it the autumn after we moved in. Fergus, where's your hat? Come and have a drink, darling.'

Rose pushed the box and the boy back to the terrace.

'I've often wondered what happened to Sadie,' Constance said as she scooped the child on to her lap. 'She went away so suddenly.'

'Can you remember when you saw her last?'

'Sometime in the thirties. Thirty-four, I think. The autumn . . . yes, it must have been autumn, because I was expecting my fourth. Sadie had been living abroad. She'd sent me the occasional postcard, and then, suddenly, nothing. I wrote, of course, but received no reply.' Constance paused, frowning. 'I remember regretting, later, that I didn't do more. That I let our friendship fade away. Sadie and I had known each other for a long time. We met when we were at school in Hampstead. But I felt very unwell, that pregnancy, and then the baby had colic and didn't sleep, and it was hard to think of anything other than getting through the day. But, later — yes, I felt bad about it. I'd been fond of Sadie. She had no children, you know, and it troubled me to think that she may have felt I hadn't time for her.'

Rose took the ring out of her handbag and showed it to the older woman. 'I found this near her house in Sussex. I wondered whether it might have belonged to her – whether it could have been her engagement ring.'

Constance turned the ring over in her hand, then gave it back to Rose. 'I'm afraid I can't remember. It looks very old, doesn't it? It might be. It's the sort of showy thing he might have given her. Felix, I mean.'

'Sadie's fiancé?'

'Yes, the wretched man.' Fergus was settled with a drink and a cup of tea was placed in front of Rose. 'Of course, he was very handsome and charming, but it was obvious to me that he was completely undependable. Not the sort of man to settle down. Sadie couldn't see it. But then, we women are good at deceiving ourselves, when we choose to do so, aren't we?' Constance frowned. 'You would not have said Sadie was classically beautiful, but she had such life. Men found her very attractive.'

Had Rose been good at deceiving herself? She brushed the thought aside. 'I spoke to her psychiatrist, Philip Sprott,' she said. 'He told me that Sadie had had a breakdown.'

'She came here to convalesce after she left the nursing home. She stayed with us for a month or six weeks, something like that. She was very unwell at first, but I think it helped her, being here, among friends, and she slowly improved.'

'I wondered why she hadn't gone to stay with her sister.'

Constance offered Rose a plate of fig rolls. 'Sadie blamed Edith for putting her in the nursing home. She hated it there. Hospitals for the mentally ill weren't always kind places, back then. But perhaps Edith felt she had little alternative. As I said, Sadie was very ill.'

Fergus was sitting in the cardboard box again, drinking orange squash out of a beaker with a lid on. Constance adjusted his sunhat. 'Many women of our generation had to give up all hope of marriage and children. All those potential husbands, you see, lost or mutilated in the first war. Sadie had to live with that. She had a great many friends. I'm sure they were a comfort to her.'

'In her letters, she mentions someone called Jimmy and a woman called Pearl. Did you know them?'

Constance smiled. 'Jimmy was Jimmy Corrigan. Scots. Red haired. Sadie met Pearl at art college, at the Slade. I can't remember her surname, I'm afraid. She was Sadie's closest friend. Poor Jimmy was in love with Sadie, though I don't think she ever realised. As I say, we can be very blind.'

Fergus was shaking the contents of the beaker over the paving stones. Constance filled a miniature watering can from the tap on the wall and gave it to him.

'Some people called Chiverton were mentioned in the letters,' said Rose. 'They bought the Gull's Wing. I wondered whether you knew anything about them.'

'I do, yes.' Constance's gaze turned from the child to Rose. 'And so do you, I think, Rose. Sadie sold the house to Tom Chiverton.'

Rose stared her. 'Tom Chiverton? The poet, Tom Chiverton?'

'Yes.'

'Oh.' She was silent for a moment, absorbing this new information. 'How extraordinary,' she said. 'I had no idea.'

'You heard a lot about him, at that time. He used to give talks on the wireless.' Constance smiled. 'He was thought terribly glamorous.'

'We did some of his poems at school.' And a line that had latched itself in Rose's memory, from a poem learned by heart many years ago, sprang to the forefront of her mind: *There are two trees outside my window, one of silver, the other gold.*

Constance rose to fill the watering can. 'I remember feeling pleased that Tom and Diana Chiverton were living nearby. I hoped Sadie would make friends with them. After all, he was a poet and she was an artist, so I thought they'd have something in common. I worried about her, you see, living in that isolated place, all on her own. She'd lived in London before, and I'd visited her when I was in town. She'd rented digs or rooms in lodging houses. She had some money of her own, a small trust fund set up by her father, so she never had to stay in a hostel, like so many single women did back then, which was fortunate.'

A flutter of wind, a branch moved and a shadow fell over Constance's face. 'I tried to persuade Sadie to stay with us a little longer,' she said. 'She wouldn't, though. So, when she wrote to tell me that Diana Chiverton had invited her to supper, I felt relieved.'

Chapter Five

Sussex and London – October 1930

Sadie was scrubbing ink-stained rags in a bucket on the terrace of the Egg. There was a flurry of barking and she saw a flash of movement between the trees that bordered the sunken lane. Two russet-gold dogs, lithe as antelopes, snaked between hornbeam and oak.

A voice called out, 'Ilonka! Gizi!'

A tall woman strode through the stretch of woodland between the sunken lane and the Egg. She was wearing a long, fur-trimmed black coat and a scarlet Cossack-style cap, from which locks of dark hair escaped. The temperature had fallen that day, gusts of cold wind stripping the leaves from the trees, and the woman's pale face was flushed pink along her high cheekbones. It was a strong face, dominated by flashing dark eyes which were framed by bold black brows. Sadie thought her startlingly beautiful.

She pointed to a tunnel through the undergrowth. 'They went that way.'

'Such rascals.' The woman tapped her palm against her thigh. 'Ilonka! Come here now!'

'Like children, I suppose.'

The woman seemed to look at her properly for the first time. 'Oh, much more fun than children. Have you moved in here?'

'I'm Sadie Lawless.' Sadie felt herself being appraised by the stranger. 'Forgive me for not offering you my hand, but I'm afraid it's rather inky.'

'My name's Diana Chiverton.'

So this was Tom Chiverton's wife. 'Then you must live at the Gull's Wing.'

'I do, yes. I'm pleased to meet you, Miss Lawless. We haven't met before, have we? You must forgive my asking, but Tom and I were frightfully busy at the time of the house purchase. The publication of *Lunar*, you see.'

'My solicitor handled the sale,' said Sadie. 'No, we never met.'

The two dogs raced back through the box bushes. 'This is Gizi and this is Ilonka.' Diana Chiverton fondled their muscular necks. 'They are Vizslas, a Hungarian breed. They are hunting dogs.'

'They're beautiful,' said Sadie, sensing that this was expected of her.

'They are *exquisite*. And terribly loyal. I admire loyalty, don't you? I consider it the most essential quality. Why do you have inky hands, Miss Lawless?'

Sadie tipped the dirty water on to the earth. 'I've been making a lino print.'

'Do you know Stanley Chute? He does the most marvellous woodcuts.'

'Only by reputation.'

'He's a friend of ours. Perhaps I may introduce you.' Diana's gaze moved to the Egg. 'Tom and I wondered whether you would sell the house. It's been empty so long.'

91

'I'll never sell it.' Loyalty was, as Diana Chiverton had said, an admirable quality and, for Sadie, the Egg would always be bound up with memories of her father and their shared affection for the project.

'I'll tell Tom that the house is occupied at last,' said Diana. 'He likes to run through the woods in the early mornings.'

Again, Sadie felt that some response was required of her. She owned the woodland that surrounded the house – was Diana Chiverton asking her permission?

'I hope he'll continue to do so,' she said pleasantly. 'If I see him, I'll wave to him.'

'We often go for a ramble here with our guests. The trees are so glorious.'

No, Diana Chiverton wasn't asking permission; she was staking a claim. But no one could ever really own Paley High Wood. She herself was merely its custodian for a time.

Diana turned to go, the dogs at her heels. 'I mustn't keep you, Miss Lawless, I'm sure you have a great deal to do. Goodbye.'

Sadie murmured a farewell, but did not watch her leave as she spread out the rags to dry on the terrace. She felt she had given her visitor enough of her attention. Diana Chiverton had demanded attention from the moment she strode through the forest with her pack of dogs at her heels, like Artemis . . . or the goddess Diana. The image was carefully thought out, Sadie suspected, and designed to impress, even intimidate. She wondered whether Diana's appearance at the Egg had been as fortuitous as she had implied; perhaps the Chivertons had seen her when she had walked along the ridgeway past the Gull's Wing a few days ago, or perhaps word that the Egg was inhabited had drifted up from the tradespeople of Nutcombe.

Diana Chiverton had controlled the conversation. Sadie had been dismissed with a wintry little smile, along with exactly the same phrase – 'I mustn't keep you' – that her own mother had used to detach herself from unwanted callers or the sort of people who did not know how to end a conversation. Had Diana's intimation that she might have met her, but forgotten her, been intentionally insulting? It was hard to tell. *The publication of* Lunar, *you see.* She had been referring to Tom Chiverton's latest collection of poems. It had received great praise in the review pages of the newspapers.

The daylight was fading, so she went indoors and set about lighting the stove. The house cooled quickly – those wide windows and flat roof. It seemed unlikely she would have much to do with the Chivertons, which was a relief, she told herself. Diana's suggestion that she introduce her to Stanley Chute had been half-hearted. Sadie, who was wearing her customary work clothes of paint-stained overalls and a jersey with holes in the elbows, suspected Diana would think her not their sort.

But, when she rose the next morning, she found a note pushed through the letter box, inviting her to the Gull's Wing that evening. It was warmly worded: *a small, informal supper, and I understand if you must refuse because I've given you such short notice, but Tom and I would be so delighted if you were able to attend.*

Sadie pictured Tom dashing down the sunken lane on his morning constitutional and posting the letter through her door. Perhaps she had misjudged Diana, had leaped to conclusions. Unhappiness and loneliness were taking their toll on her, making her mean spirited. It would be all too easy, she acknowledged, to resent Tom and Diana, who were living in the house her own parents had intended to make their home.

She must not blame them for events that were not of their making. In a way, Tom Chiverton had been her saviour. He had paid a fair price for a house that had attracted a great deal of interest, but few offers. Prospective purchasers had been put off by the unconventional construction of the Gull's Wing, but Tom had had the vision to see its beauty.

At six o'clock that evening, Sadie looked through her wardrobe, deciding what to wear. Her black wool frock would be a safe option, but she sensed that Diana was the sort of woman who would despise those who played safe, so she reached for an olive-green velvet dress with an embroidered neckline. Self-consciously bohemian, perhaps, but she loved it. She swept her hair behind her ears and clipped on diamond earrings. A slick of lipstick and a dusting of powder. She put on her rubber boots and her mackintosh and left the house.

The torch lit her way as she walked up the road. The Gull's Wing had been her father's masterpiece. He had built it to show what he could do. He had designed the Egg with a different purpose, seeking to demonstrate that even a modest building, somewhere ordinary folk could afford to live, could be beautiful and extraordinary. He had planned to create houses for all sorts of people, not only the wealthy, and had imagined a whole village of houses like the Egg. He had had the idea for the Egg first, before the Gull's Wing. Sadie remembered the evening he had shown her and her mother the initial drawings. It was a seed of an idea, he claimed. Sadie had said it was more like an egg, about to hatch, and somehow the name had stuck.

Nearing the house, she saw that lights had been strung between the pillars along its frontage, giving it a festive air. However often she saw the Gull's Wing, it still astounded.

How could it not? It had been designed to astonish and delight, to take the breath away. Though the house had been open to the road when her father had built it, the Chivertons had added a low fence that ran the length of the property.

A maid answered her ring of the doorbell, a pretty girl, very young, fifteen or sixteen.

'If you'll let me have your boots, miss, I'll get that mud off for you.'

'Thank you. What's your name?'

'Ivy, miss.'

'Then thank you, Ivy.'

The layout of the house was unconventional. To one side of the hall was the kitchen and cloakroom, to the other were studios, service areas and servants' quarters. A staircase led up to a large open-plan sitting and dining area on the first floor. The bedrooms and a bathroom were above, on the second floor.

The Chivertons had decorated the long, generous entrance hall with three large, bold, colourful paintings. A wooden carving, five feet in height, a stylised image of a couple embracing, stood by the door that led out to the garden. On a shelf were stacks of letters, books and magazines, along with two skulls – that of a horse and an owl.

The buzz of conversation from the first floor became audible as she ascended the staircase. Ivy opened the double doors and Sadie found herself among guests who sat or stood in small groups, smoking, drinking, smiling and roaring with laughter.

A long, rectangular dining table, which must have comfortably sat twenty people, ran along one side of the room. Three large sofas, upholstered in claret and burnt orange, formed a horseshoe round the wood-burning stove, in front of which the Vizslas, Ilonka and Gizi, slept on a rug. A grand piano stood at the other end of the room. Red- and orange-striped curtains had been drawn over the windows. Sadie had no curtains in the Egg – her father had despised curtains, regarding them as unnecessary and dustily lower middle class – and she wondered whether Tom and Diana thought them essential to guard their privacy from the curious. Perhaps Tom found himself pestered by autograph hunters.

Fragments of conversation reached her ears:

'. . . a meditation on memory, he said to me . . .'

'. . . the welcome was warm enough, but I'm certain there were *icicles* . . .'

'. . . droned on, à la Roger Fry, for simply hours . . .'

So not such a simple supper, after all. The noise and brightness were a shock to Sadie after a fortnight of her own company.

Diana Chiverton, wearing a long, pale-grey gown, swept towards her. Her dark hair was brushed back from her forehead and tumbled in a smooth, polished fall to her shoulders.

'Miss Lawless, how marvellous that you could join us. Tom!' Diana's voice lifted above the hubbub. 'Tom, you must come and say hello.'

A man holding court in the middle of a circle of guests turned and raised a hand in acknowledgement. Tom Chiverton must have been the tallest man in the room. His broad shoulders and alert, attentive pose gave him a leonine air. Photographs in newspapers showed him to be notably good-looking; in person, he was arrestingly handsome. A lock of dark hair fell over his high forehead and his profile displayed to advantage his strong features – Roman nose, square jaw and curling upper lip.

He crossed the room to join them. 'Miss Lawless – Sadie –

I'm so pleased to make your acquaintance. Diana has told me all about you.' A squeeze of the fingers, rather than a handshake. Dark brown eyes, flecked with gold, focused on her.

He smiled. 'It's high time our paths ceased crossing in a merely theoretical sense and we got to know each other – don't you agree, Sadie? Had you turned us down, I would have invited you again tomorrow night. I would have begged you on bended knee until you surrendered to me.'

'Tom, you must stop it,' scolded Diana. 'You're making poor Sadie blush.'

Supper was shepherd's pie, leeks and carrots. The vegetables, Diana announced, had been grown by Tom.

'Poetic leeks,' said someone. 'You should write a verse, Tom.'

'Tom never writes *verse*,' said Diana coldly.

'That's you told, Miles,' said a girl in a peasant blouse.

'I beg your pardon.' Miles bowed his head in Diana's direction.

The man seated beside Sadie – young, copper hair, green eyes and a thin, sculptured face – murmured, 'Miles will have to say his mea culpas or he won't be invited again. *Verse* . . . Oh dear.' He smiled at her. 'I'm Rufus Vaughan.'

'Sadie Lawless,' she said. 'How do you know the Chivertons? Are you a poet, like Tom?'

'No, I'm a dancer and choreographer with a ballet company. Tom and I are thinking of collaborating on a new work. Dance and the spoken word. I went to school with Diana's brother. My people were in India, so sometimes I used to stay with his people – Diana's people, that is.'

His gaze settled on Diana, at the far end of the table. Sadie wondered whether he was in love with her. It wouldn't have surprised her if a lot of men in the room were in love with Diana Chiverton.

'That was kind of them.'

'It was; they were kind people. I haven't seen you here before.'

'I'm a neighbour.'

'I didn't think Tom and Di had neighbours. I thought that was the point of this house – its glorious isolation.' Rufus scanned the room. 'It's an extraordinary place, but there's something *aloof* about it.'

'My father built it.'

'Oh. Are you kidding? No, plainly not. I'm sorry to be so crass.'

'Please, don't apologise. It's the sort of building people either love or hate.'

They talked about Rufus's work until the maid, Ivy, cleared away the supper plates. A chink of fork against wine glass made the room fall silent. Rising to her feet, Diana said, 'I can see you're all delightfully settled, but you know the Chiverton custom.'

Rufus Vaughan stood up. 'All change now. Enjoyed talking to you, Sadie.'

The guests were shuffling out of their seats and gathering up napkins and wine glasses. Only Tom Chiverton remained in his chair at the head of the table. Diana stood behind him, directing her guests. One long, pale hand rested on her husband's shoulder and the other stroked his dark curls.

To her surprise, Sadie found herself instructed to sit next to Tom.

'I hear you make prints,' he said, as the pudding, an apple crumble, was served.

'I do, yes. Lino cuts, mostly.'

'You're serious about your work, I presume.' He gave her a fierce look. 'Can't bear people who dabble and call themselves artists.'

'I'm not a dabbler. I haven't done as much as I would have liked during the last few years because I've been teaching – to earn money, you see.' She said this proudly, unashamed of having had to earn a living. She suspected many people in the room did not have to think about such practicalities.

Tom said, surprising her, 'I put in a few years myself, teaching English and Latin. I enjoyed my years in the classroom. It's an honourable profession. Are you still teaching?'

'No, I gave it up.'

'Why was that?'

'I was engaged to be married to someone.'

Why had she told him that? She would have hardly needed to lie – only to gloss over the truth – but something about Tom Chiverton demanded honesty. She suspected that, if he detected evasiveness, he would despise it. She was both drawn to him and wary of him. And yet she was enjoying herself, she realised, her old pleasure in company and conversation returning.

He said, 'But you didn't marry the someone.'

'No.' With a twist of pain, she thought of Felix, her beautiful Felix. 'It didn't work out. He's with someone else now.' She wondered whether the someone else was still silly, spiteful Dahlia Knight, or whether he had moved on. With Felix, there would always be someone.

'You may detest me for saying it, but I'm sure that these things happen for a purpose.' In the dark depths of Tom's eyes, she detected understanding. 'I'm a great believer in fate.

Something watches over our lives and knows what's right for us, though we may not realise it at the time.'

'God, you mean?' She could not keep the scorn from her voice.

'Not in the conventional sense, no. A life force . . . a unity. You think I'm talking twaddle, don't you?'

She did, though she did not say so. Instead, she said, 'Felix would have made a rotten husband – I do see that now.'

'I'm afraid a great many men make rotten husbands.' The corners of his mouth curled in a smile. 'Yet I sometimes think we're the sort women prefer.'

She found it odd that Tom appeared to number himself among the rotten husbands. And his generalisation irked her. Too many men seemed to think they knew what women wanted, and they were so often mistaken.

'I don't see how you can say that,' she said. 'What one woman wants – babies, a family – another woman may loathe the idea of.'

'I meant that the difficulty is that men and women don't want the same things. A woman is searching for the man who will make her complete. Men, on the other hand, are driven by restlessness and dissatisfaction. It hardly makes for happiness.'

'What are you two talking about? You look very deep in conversation.'

Sadie looked up. Diana had come to stand beside them.

'We're talking about marriage, my dearest,' said Tom.

'I hope you're not boring poor Sadie. Other people's love affairs are so desperately yawn-making.' Diana ran the backs of her fingers caressingly down Tom's cheek, then said, 'Your father's death was a great loss to architecture, Sadie. It must be strange, coming back to this house under such circumstances. It must seem so different. I hope you don't hate it.'

'This room looks delightfully warm and eye-catching. I like it.'

'Diana chose everything,' said Tom. 'I always leave all that to her. She has an incomparable sense of colour.'

They talked about the work of Le Corbusier and Peter Behrens, contemporaries of Edward Lawless, and then coffee was served and Tom turned away and began to converse with the woman seated on his other side. Sadie found it both a relief and a disappointment to be out of the headlamp glare of his attention.

Her other neighbour introduced himself as Roger Eriksson. His handsomeness was of the florid, fleshy sort. 'I'm afraid you must put up with me now,' he said. 'I'm a mere jobbing novelist. Rather a comedown after our illustrious poet, but there you are. My wife, Helen, is my passport to this sparkling company. There she is, in the pink frock. Hello, sweetie-pie.'

He waved to an attractive, fair-haired young woman. Sadie recognised the name of Helen Eriksson as belonging to a rising star of the opera.

'I'm only here under sufferance,' Roger went on. 'I doubt if Tom and Di are great readers of murder mysteries.' He poked at the remains of his pudding. 'It always amuses me – they consider themselves sophisticates and yet one's obliged to eat boarding-school food. One can't help wondering if the perfect Diana has a failing: she can't actually cook.'

'Doesn't she employ a cook?'

Roger's eyes glinted. 'Oh, there *was* a cook, but apparently she walked out this morning. The Chivertons' servants fall into two categories: the ones who fall in love with them and stay with them for ever, and the ones who turn and run as soon as they have the opportunity.' His gaze settled on Sadie. 'You're the late substitute, aren't you?'

101

'What do you mean?'

'Poppy Seaforth has the flu and had to drop out at the last minute. Diana won't have an uneven number at the table. Neither will Tom, actually. For an intelligent man, he can be frightfully superstitious.'

The information that she had been invited to avoid an awkward number of guests took away some of Sadie's pleasure in the evening. Soon, people began to drift away from the table and cigarette cases were opened and passed round. Tom stood at the sideboard, pouring brandies. He broke off to take Diana in his arms. They kissed and murmured to each other, their low words inaudible. They were so perfectly suited, Sadie thought, both tall, dark and handsome, almost a cliché of the ideal couple.

The other guests, she sensed, were settling in for a long session of drinking and talking, in which she did not wish to take part. When she had drunk her coffee and smoked a cigarette, she thanked the Chivertons for their hospitality and prepared to leave.

'Are you sure you'll be all right, walking home by yourself?' Diana asked, as she saw her to the front door, but Sadie sensed her hostess impatient to get back to her guests and quickly reassured her.

She decided to return to the Egg through the woods instead of by the road. The way was shorter and it wouldn't matter now if she got mud on her stockings. She needed to test herself. Until two weeks ago, she had spent her entire life living in cities. She did not like to think herself frightened of the countryside at night.

The torchlight bobbed ahead of her, catching on dense black conifers and coppiced hazels. Away from the Gull's Wing, she felt herself relax. The thin, sandy gully that ran down the centre of the sunken lane gleamed wet in the moonlight. Halfway along, she stopped and turned off her torch. As her eyes grew accustomed to the darkness, she saw that the woods at night were not featureless at all. Tree trunks, undergrowth, dips and hillocks were sketched in by the beams of the full moon. An owl hooted and something small and scared scurried for shelter. The thin, silvery light that fell slanting from the sky was transformative, revealing to her an enchanted and mysterious world that resonated with life, that was contained within her own world, but until then unknown to her.

Maybe Roger Eriksson had been right; maybe Tom and Diana had invited her to make up the numbers. But that might not have been the only reason. As she left the house, Diana had said, 'Do drop in and see us whenever you're passing.' Diana was not the sort of woman who would tolerate the bore or the vulgar, and would not have encouraged her to visit again if she had not proved up to scratch. So, if there had been a test, she had passed it.

'The truth is,' said Sadie, 'Edith's ashamed of me. Lawlesses don't have nervous breakdowns.'

Sadie and her two dearest friends, Pearl Foster and Jimmy Corrigan, were in Jimmy's rooms near Victoria Station, from where Sadie was to catch her train back to Sussex. Jimmy, who came from Glasgow, was tall, skinny, red haired and bony. He was the proprietor of a journal called *Splinter*. The work was poorly remunerated, so, a keen cyclist, he supplemented his salary by doing bike repairs. Three bicycles, somewhat dismantled, cluttered up the small, dark room. Though the furnishings were spartan – Jimmy didn't own any sofas or armchairs – there were a great many books, newspapers and periodicals piled on shelves or stacked on the floor.

'Perhaps Edith's worried about you,' said Pearl.

Pearl had inherited her heavy black hair and large dark eyes from her Indian grandmother. She and Sadie had been friends since their first day at the Slade. During her portraiture phase, she had often painted Pearl.

The room was cold and Sadie had kept her coat on. She had had an appointment with Philip Sprott that morning and then lunch at Edith's house.

She made a scathing sound. 'I embarrass her – I always have. Whenever we talk about my "illness", as she calls it, she sends Louisa away. It's as if I'm infectious. Everything has to be hidden away with Edith. Just think how quickly she bundled me off to that ghastly nursing home.'

'It was a God-awful place,' said Jimmy.

Pearl squeezed Sadie's hand. 'We were all so worried about you.'

The fortnight she had spent in the nursing home had been one of the most horrible of Sadie's life. She was unable to recall the events that had taken place there – her complete loss of will, independence and privacy – without profound humiliation. She had not forgiven Edith for organising her incarceration. Sisters should look out for each other, they should take care of each other. When she had most needed Edith, what had she done? She had locked her away, out of sight.

They had parted affectionately enough today, though, both making an effort, Edith suggesting she come to stay with them for Christmas, Sadie accepting her fate and thanking her.

She said, 'She's still insisting I see a wretched psychiatrist.'

'Yes, but the divine Philip . . .' Pearl smiled dreamily. 'I wouldn't mind lying on a couch, talking about myself to Philip Sprott.'

Sadie had chosen Philip as her analyst because he was a friend of a friend. And because he was young and approachable and kind, and did not make her feel small and foolish and degraded, as the psychiatrist in the nursing home had. It made analysis, which she found invasive, less of an ordeal. But he *was* rather distractingly handsome.

'Take another, hen.' Jimmy thrust a plate of teacakes at her. 'You look thin.'

'We're longing to hear about Tom Chiverton,' said Pearl. 'In the photographs, he looks rather frightening. *Brooding*.'

'He's perfectly pleasant.' Sadie was aware of an evasion, saying this. *Pleasant* was not the right word for Tom Chiverton, who had exuded intensity. She tried again. 'I can't imagine having a light conversation with him – not like we have.'

'I'm bloody insulted.' Jimmy lit a Gold Flake and slid the pack across the table to Pearl. 'Are you implying that Tom Chiverton is deeper than we are? Or cleverer?'

'Do shut up, Jimmy,' said Pearl.

'We talked about terribly serious things. Work and religion and marriage.'

'*Marriage?*' Jimmy gave her a look. 'The old goat was making eyes at you.'

'Of course he wasn't.' Sadie leaned forward so that Jimmy could light her cigarette. 'He wouldn't.'

'Rot. All men would, if they had the chance.'

'No, you're wrong.' She breathed out a thin column of smoke. 'Tom and Diana are so madly in love, you can't imagine.'

Conversation turned to Pearl's difficulties with her married lover, Ralph, who taught part-time at the Slade. They hardly ever had more than an hour together, said Pearl with a sigh. She lived with her mother, so couldn't invite Ralph to her house; he, of course, had his wife and children. Sadie offered Pearl the use of the Egg for a weekend – she would go and stay with a friend – and Pearl thanked her, but lowered her eyelashes and said regretfully that she didn't think Ralph would be able to find the time. Then she kissed them both goodbye and hurried home to her mother.

After seeing her out, Jimmy came back into the room. 'I can't quite bring myself to tell the poor wee thing that wretched Ralph is stringing her along. I think the penny will drop eventually.'

Sadie wasn't so sure. Sometimes it was easier to believe what you wanted to believe. She said, 'Have you seen Felix?'

'At the Porters' party.'

'Was he . . . ?' She shouldn't ask, but couldn't stop herself. 'Was he with anyone?'

Jimmy said gently, 'You should let it alone, hen.'

'Was he?'

'He was with that girl, Dahlia Thing.'

'Did you speak to him?'

'No, because I'd have ended up hitting him if I had. Didn't seem a good plan.'

'Edith, of course, still can't leave it alone.' Sadie mimicked her sister's voice: '"I always knew he was a bad lot."'

'But he was, Sadie.' Jimmy's bright blue eyes focused on her. 'Your sister's right – he truly was.'

Felix had been at the back of her mind all day. Visits to London did this to her. Today, she had fought the memories off, had resisted going to the places she and he had frequented, and had successfully struggled against the compulsion to call at his flat in Kensington. She felt drained by the effort.

On the train, speeding out of London, she still felt cold. The heating in the compartment did not seem to be working and she rubbed her hands together to warm them. She ran her thumb over the ring that Felix had given her, which she now wore on her right hand. She supposed she should get rid of it somehow, but could not seem to find the will. The words inscribed on the inside of the band, In thee my choys I do rejoys, reminded her that she had been loved once.

She opened the copy of Lunar, Tom Chiverton's latest collection of poetry, which she had bought in Hatchards, and tried to read, but her attention drifted, so she put it away and looked out of the window instead. Why did the view of street lamps and lit houses tonight seem so oppressive, so sad? The futility and regret she tried constantly to resist washed over her. So many thoughts, so many memories – she gave herself up to them.

She had met Felix Rudd in October 1929, at a wedding in the West End. Her parents had been dead for over eight months, but she was still trapped in a black tunnel of grief. The bride had been a dear friend and, to oblige her, she had accepted the invitation.

Felix had caught her looking at him across the hotel dining room. Their gazes had entangled and a hot blush had flooded through her, yet she had not looked away. As the wedding breakfast had gone on, she had to force herself not to stare at him. Later, in the ballroom, she had turned, and there he was beside her. In that moment, her life had changed. Felix was an excellent dancer, nimble on his feet, with the knack of guiding a girl through the slight pressure of his hand.

After the evening ended, he asked her out for dinner. A fortnight later, they were lovers.

Felix Rudd was quick and bright and darting. He had black curls and slanting coal-black eyes, and was slender, speedy of movement and sharp of wit. He was the same age as Sadie and thus had narrowly escaped the slaughter of the war. She had fallen in love with him so quickly and thoroughly that the grief, which had been her constant companion since the plane crash that had killed her parents, slipped aside as if she had shed a heavy black coat. Love and desire had coursed through her with the force of an electric shock, jolting her back into life.

Felix lived in Kensington Church Street, in a flat above his antiques business. He had inherited, from his grandparents, two flats in Maida Vale, which he rented out. He had an eye for beauty and for what was of value, and a list of exclusive and wealthy clients. He was adored by his parents and was well read and claimed to have left-wing leanings. Sometimes Sadie went with him to political meetings, more often to the cinema. He could be touchy and moody and they had some spectacular quarrels that involved plate throwing and storming off. Afterwards, the making up was always wonderful. He was self-centred – Sadie put it down to his being an only child – but he compensated for it with a beguiling flair, charm and energy. He was a passionate lover and made her ache for him.

He was a creature of the night, most at ease in scruffy little Soho nightclubs where the doorman let you in only if he knew your face, and where the music was raucous and seductive and the three-piece band was hazed by a fug of cigarette smoke. The nightclubs were often windowless and dimly lit. Sadie remembered thinking that, if light had penetrated those sombre interiors, everything inside them would have turned to dust.

She had thought of herself as unconventional, but Felix had taken her to places she had never been before. There was the police raid when they escaped from the nightclub through a bathroom window — she wriggling through the aperture, he catching her in his arms before they ran down an alleyway, struggling to stifle their laughter. There was the all-night party on a boat on the Thames, where someone slipped the ropes tying them to the wharf and they found themselves floating down the river, towards the estuary, before a coastguard vessel towed them back to land. There were the reefers, bought from a musician in the band, which they smoked, lying in a quiet, grassy spot in Hyde Park. And there was the cocaine she had tried only once, because, after the elation had dissipated, an intense depression had washed over her and remained with her for days.

She hadn't told Philip Sprott about that. Philip never judged, never disapproved. Instead, he made you see yourself clearly, which was, in Sadie's opinion, worse. Crash and burn, Sadie, crash and burn. At the beginning of 1929, the plane in which her parents had crossed the Channel had crashed and burst into flames. Eighteen months later, love had torn her to pieces, had thrown her on to the fire, and she had crashed and burned in a spectacular, all-consuming fashion.

When, at the end of February, Felix had asked her to marry him, she had accepted without hesitation. His family were delighted by the engagement, Edith less so. When Sadie and Felix had gone to tea at Edith's house, her sister's disapproval had been almost palpable. Even Felix, usually so good in company, wilted, and, in the gloomy sub-Victorian atmosphere of the Fullers' home, his wit and vivacity turned into misjudged prolixity.

Three weeks before the wedding, he had come to her rooms and asked her to release him from the engagement. 'I've realised I'm not a marrying sort of man,' he said. 'It wouldn't be fair to you, Sadie; you deserve better.' He was twisting his hands together and had a tortured expression. 'I thought I could go through with it; I thought you were the right one. But I'm not sure there is a right one, not for me. When I think of marrying, that it's for ever, I feel as if I'm choking. It's a terrible failing in me. It's like an illness.'

The train drew into East Grinstead Station. The air tasted of soot and frost, of winter, and she hurried to the platform where the little steam engine that ran up and down the branch line to Nutcombe was waiting. She found an empty compartment and slammed the door shut. A whistle, and smoke clouded up against the window as they pulled out of the station.

Reaching Nutcombe, the cold settled round her as she crossed the platform and collected her bicycle. The frail circle of light from the headlamp illuminated her route up the hillside. She cycled fast, standing on the pedals, through silent woods, where frost was forming. You take a risk, flying so high. Had Felix been bad for her? Yes, he had – she saw that now. But a part of her continued to miss the glory of the affair. She could not regret loving him, though it hurt beyond anything. Her thoughts turned to a day they had spent in Brittany. It had been during the school holidays, so she had accompanied him on a buying trip across the Channel. They had driven to the coast, where they had bathed and picnicked and made love in a secret little cove of fine, silky sand. In her recollection, it remained a day of incom-

110

parable perfection. However old she was, however lonely or unhappy, she would always have the memory of the shifting sea and the saltiness of his skin and the warmth of the sun on their naked bodies.

The branches were bare charcoal lines against a dense white sky and only the beeches clung on to their ruff of brown, papery leaves. Sadie walked each afternoon because walking made her feel better and sleep more soundly at night, and because she had a hunch that it might do her more good than psychoanalysis.

The girl, Winnie Thomsett, served her in the village shop. Sadie complimented her on her hairstyle, a tortured arrangement of pin curls, and bought a bun and an apple. Then she walked a short stretch out of the village before a footpath took her off the road and up a steep, grassy slope topped by a stand of elms, where she sat down on a tree stump and ate her lunch. When she had finished, she sketched first the elms with their rookery, and then Nutcombe, tumbled like a child's building blocks along the river valley below.

Her path onwards took her through a patchwork of field, hedge and copse. The rain thickened, drumming into mustard-coloured puddles, and Sadie put up the hood of her mackintosh as she turned along the long, straight lane that would take her back to Paley High Wood. Mud clung to her boots.

In the dense hazel thicket that walled one side of the lane, she caught sight of an owl, perched on a branch, its feathers fluffed out in the cold. Before she had time to reach for her camera, it rose with a flare of wings and flew off, low over the fields. Sadie scrabbled in the rucksack for pencil and paper, anxious to capture the image before it slipped from her mind. Her fingers slid on the wet pencil, but she was not displeased with her sketch: the lifting of the wings, the extension of the body.

Hearing a sound from behind her, she turned, looking back in the direction from which she had just walked. A horse and rider were heading along the lane towards her. She flattened herself against the hazels to allow them to pass.

Through the curtain of rain, she recognised Tom Chiverton. He was wearing an oilskin coat and his thick, curling hair was moulded wetly to his head. His rugged good looks were made for days like this, for hill and wind and rain.

He reined in his horse. 'Sadie, well met, good afternoon! What are you drawing? May I see?'

She showed him the owl. 'They perch on the roof of our house at night and hoot to each other,' he said. 'Diana tells me they keep her awake. It's a fine little sketch. I'll give you a lift back to the Egg, if you like.'

'On the horse?' she said foolishly.

He laughed. 'Naturally, on the horse. You mustn't be frightened; I know how to control him. And Roman's easily strong enough for two. Anyway, you're as light as a feather, I can tell that.'

'It's kind of you, Tom, but I won't, thank you. I enjoy walking in the rain.'

'Good for you.' He raised his hand in a salute. 'Good day, then.'

Tom rode on, but, after a short distance, looked back over his shoulder and called out, 'Come to lunch tomorrow! Twelve-ish. No arguments, Sadie – I insist!' Then he put his heels to the sides of his mount, and soon horse and rider were veiled by the rain.

In spite of the cold weather and the trickle of water

running down her nose, Sadie's face felt hot. Why had she refused Tom's offer? She was chilled to the bone and soaked to the skin and longed to be home. Was it because she had never learned to ride and found the large, muscular animal daunting?

No, it was Tom himself and the prospect of being in such close proximity to him that had made her hesitate. Perhaps he had felt a mingling of contempt and pity for her – the strong, virile man, scornful of the spinster who shrank from physical intimacy. If so, he had misinterpreted her reluctance. And that was an excellent thing, she told herself, as she hurried for the shelter of the trees. Better that he should despise her than detect what she herself had only just acknowledged: how powerfully she was attracted to him.

Chapter Six

Surrey and London – July 1970

Walton-on-Thames was dusty in the summer heat. Rose stripped off her jacket as she left the employment bureau.

'If anything comes up, Mrs Martineau, we'll let you know.' The parting words of her interviewer, Miss Pritchard (fifty-ish, hand-knitted, short-sleeved sweater, pussycat spectacles) remained with her as she walked away, their tone conveying to Rose how improbable it was that any position suited to her skills, or lack of them, might arise. 'If only your typing was more proficient,' Miss Pritchard had said as her fingertip, encased in bristly rubber, leafed through Rose's skimpy curriculum vitae. 'Or you had more experience.'

She had plenty of experience, she thought savagely, as she queued at a greengrocer's shop to buy fruit and vegetables, and plenty of skills. She knew how to care for a sick baby and help an anxious six-year-old through her first piano exam. She knew how to cook a three-course meal for eight and keep a large house so that it ran comfortably and efficiently. She was a good organiser and had a knack for putting people at their ease. But none of this seemed to count. 'Most of my clients expect shorthand, Mrs Martineau. I may be able to find you a position as a filing clerk.'

Rose paid for her items and left the shop. Sunlight blistered the pavement. Perhaps she should consider teaching. She might be able to find a private school that would appreciate her physics degree and be prepared to overlook her lack of a teaching certificate. But she knew that she did not have the patience. Maybe she had had it once, but not any more. The bewilderment and stupefaction that had been her initial response to Robert's betrayal had burned away, replaced by a rage that coursed through her veins from when she woke in the morning to the moment when, tormented by insomnia, she fell asleep at night.

She walked home. She had stayed with her father for a week, then she and the girls had returned to Walton-on-Thames. Yet she did not feel at ease there, as though the ruin of her marriage had made a physical alteration to her home. The rooms looked unnaturally ordered and a little bleak, like stage sets for a gloomy play about marital discord or a deserted wife.

But Robert hadn't deserted her; she had thrown him out. She had only to say and he would come back. Then she wouldn't have to find a job or see her daughters made unhappy by the absence of their father. She had only to forgive him. Only. Forgiveness was inconceivable. Robert didn't deserve it and Rose couldn't imagine how to begin to forgive him. She didn't *want* to forgive him, and yet a part of her was always listening for his key in the door or the slither of his mackintosh, slung untidily on the coat stand, as it slipped to the floor. The study was still his. She shared the bedroom with her memories of him. She supposed she should move the furniture round, try to make the rooms look different somehow, but she hadn't the heart.

115

The house squeezed the breath out of her. She hadn't slept properly in the weeks that had passed since the publication of the article, 'Debra – The Truth'. The tossing and turning, the pummelling of her pillow and the search for a cool place on the sheet as sleep eluded her had become a familiar misery. On the edges of her thoughts, clamouring to take centre stage, were her tormentors: Debra Peters, Johnny Pakenham and Robert himself.

She tried to distract herself, but only found other worries – her anxieties about the children, her own financial dependency and her loneliness. My God, she was lonely. She had gone from weekly boarding to a student hall to a shared flat and then marriage. She had never before been the only adult in a household. She had fantasies about Debra Peters, though not the sort that Robert presumably had. She imagined talking to her, forcing her to understand the consequences of her greed and immorality. She liked to imagine Debra weeping and begging her forgiveness, but it never convinced for long. There was always a moment when the imaginary Debra gave a contemptuous laugh and walked away, her pert, nineteen-year-old, miniskirted rump swaying provocatively. Rose's impotence fed her rage.

Even her search for Sadie had ground to a halt. By now, she had read through all the letters. Sadie had an irritating habit of referring to her friends only by their Christian names – Lachlan, Madge, Roger and Helen, Alma, and her best friend, Pearl – which made them hard to trace. Constance Meyrick, Sadie's friend in Cambridge, had supplied Jimmy Corrigan's surname, but an attempt to track him down through the telephone directories had so far proved unsuccessful. None of the J. Corrigans Rose had got through to had been the right one; others hadn't picked up the phone.

She had written to the J. Corrigans she had been unable to rule out, asking whether they had known Sadie.

But Jimmy might have emigrated to Australia. He might be dead. There was a sketch of him in one of the letters that Sadie had sent from Spain, showing a tall, thin man in baggy thirties trousers and open-necked white shirt, standing beside an old-fashioned car. The letter, which was dated June 1933, told Rose that Sadie and Jimmy had travelled around villages on the Castilian plain that summer, before ending up in Madrid. *I bought some olive oil for poor Jimmy's sunburn*, Sadie had written. *He's as red as a lobster.*

As for Tom Chiverton, he too appeared to be a dead end. Rose had written to Diana Chiverton, at the Gull's Wing, to ask her whether she remembered Sadie, but had received no reply.

The phone rang. She went into the study.

'Hello?'

'Rose, it's me.'

'Robert.' She couldn't bring herself to say *Hello* or *How are you?* It would have made it easier for him. Childish, but there you are.

'I'm calling because I need you to sign some papers. I was wondering whether I could come round with them today.' He spoke in an offhand manner, as if nothing had changed between them.

'What papers?'

'I'm selling the air-freight business.'

'I'm afraid I'm rather busy.' A lie.

'Rose, this won't take you a moment.' A rise of annoyance in his voice and she felt a flicker of triumph in having provoked him.

'Send the documents round. I'll post them back to you

when I've dealt with them. Goodbye, Robert.' She put down the phone.

But the pleasure she had taken in needling him faded, and was quickly overtaken by flatness and misery. It would have been easier never to have spoken to him again, but that was impossible because he was the father of their daughters and he paid for the upkeep of the house. Robert, who had lied to her so comprehensively, was still paying her bills. They still shared a bank account. She couldn't put her grand-mother's flat on the market because probate had not yet been granted. Until she sold it, she was dependent on Robert. She needed to find a job because she needed to earn money. The disappointment of the morning's interview washed over her again.

In the kitchen, she made herself a mug of coffee and a cheese and pickle sandwich. She took her lunch outside to the terrace, along with the book she had ordered and had collected from the public library that morning. It was a biography of Tom Chiverton, entitled *Poet of the Downs*.

She curled up on a wicker chair. The sun pounded down as she searched the index for references to Sadie Lawless. There was a paragraph about Sadie's father, the architect Edward Lawless, discussing the construction of the Gull's Wing, but Sadie wasn't mentioned at all. Constance Meyrick, in Cambridge, had told her that Sadie had known Tom and Diana Chiverton, so her absence from the biography was puzzling and frustrating – and yet another dead end. It was disappointing that so many illustrious names should figure in the index, but not Sadie's. Perhaps she wasn't famous enough; perhaps the biographer, Geoffrey Cranham, had not thought a minor female artist merited a place among all those celebrated men.

The book fell open at a photograph of Tom Chiverton. The caption told Rose that the portrait had been taken on the South Downs. It must have been winter, because the poet was framed by storm clouds and bare-branched trees. His hands were thrust into the pockets of his long overcoat, his boots were muddy and an unseen wind tugged at his dishevelled locks of dark hair. His brow was wide and clear, and his deep-set, hooded eyes challenged the onlooker, latching hungrily on to her, defying her to turn away. It registered with Rose that Tom Chiverton had been a remarkably attractive man.

She read a few pages about Chiverton's Hampshire childhood. The paragraphs were lifeless and stodgily written, a dreary listing of the occupations of the poet's forebears — gamekeepers, blacksmiths — and the men who had taught him at school. She flicked through to the chapter that dealt with his death. Tom Chiverton had died in 1957, of lung cancer, at home at the Gull's Wing. His wife, Diana, had nursed him during the final months of his life.

Which meant that Diana had lived on for another thirteen years, alone in the house. The Chivertons had had no children. In the centre of the book was a photo of Diana, taken in the 1930s. A pair of dogs, which appeared to be a similar breed to the red-brown creatures that had leaped up at the gate of the Gull's Wing, stood beside her. *Diana with her beloved Hungarian Vizslas, Ilonka and Gizi.* Diana Chiverton looked slim, beautiful and vital, effortlessly stylish in her dark slacks and white blouse. Rose imagined her striding down the sunken lane through the woods, Ilonka and Gizi running ahead of her.

The sun shone; Rose closed the book and shut her eyes. Waking with a jolt an hour later, she rescued the library book from where it had fallen, splayed on the paving stones, then glanced at her watch, yelped, and, grabbing her bag and keys, dashed out of the house. Jogging along the road to the girls' school, her mind felt cloudy from the heat and her afternoon nap.

She reached the school as the infant class was being let out the front door. She kissed Eve and checked that she had her belongings. Katherine came out of the building a few minutes later.

'Good day, darling?'

'All right,' Katherine said sulkily, crossly.

The unhappiness in her elder daughter's eyes made Rose's heart ache. 'Tell me what's bothering you, Katie-Lou,' she said gently.

'Mum, don't.' Katherine turned away. 'And don't call me that. It's silly.'

'Was the work too hard?'

'No, don't be stupid.'

Normally, Rose would have reprimanded her daughter for rudeness; today, she let it pass.

'Has someone said something unkind to you?'

'No.'

They walked on, Katherine dragging the toes of her sandals on the pavement in a way designed to irritate. Rose ignored it for a while, then said sharply, 'Don't do that; you'll ruin your sandals.'

Katherine sighed loudly.

Eve skipped beside them, singing to herself.

'Shut up, you nitwit,' said Katherine, and gave her a slap.

'Katherine, no,' said Rose sharply.

Eve, used to her sister's moods, moved out of reach, and sang more loudly. Rose took Katherine's hand. There was a token tugging away, but then her fingers relaxed and she leaned her head against Rose's arm.

Inside the house, a buff envelope was lying on the front doormat. While the girls drank their milk and ate their biscuits, Rose checked through the documents Robert had sent over, noting the pencil crosses and comments he had scrawled to indicate where she should place her signature.

She used to tease him about his writing, which was poorly formed and schoolboyish, and something inside her curled up painfully at the sight of it. Still, five weeks after their separation, she could be overwhelmed by a sense of unreality. That he was selling the aviation business was a regret to add to all her other regrets. She had enjoyed the meetings she attended there, had felt something more than a mother and a housewife. She picked up a pen, smoothed out the first sheet, then felt a hot surge of fury at Robert's high-handed attitude. After everything he had done, he still expected her to be at his beck and call. She put the pen down. Let him wait.

She put the papers in the study to be looked at later, and listened to Eve's reading and helped Katherine with her homework – a miserable, snarling half-hour of spellings; not her daughter's strong point. By the time they had finished, they were all tired and frazzled, so she let the girls watch some TV while she made tea, which she ate with them: fish, new potatoes and a salad. She picked at her food, having little appetite. After tea, they played a game in the garden, then bath and bed.

This was the time of day when Robert's absence felt most palpable. There was no one to pretend, with a histrionic flapping of fingers, to drop the ball during a game of French cricket, and no monster creeping upstairs to make Eve shriek with delighted horror when he put his head round the bathroom door and roared. Rose tried, but this had never been her role and she knew herself to be unconvincing.

When the girls were settled in bed, she went to the kitchen and poured herself a glass of wine, drank a large glug of it and felt a little better. Her gaze settled on the library book, on the kitchen table. *Poet of the Downs* was proving of little help in her search for Sadie. She needed to try a different approach.

Fetching her address book, she searched for her friend Tony Marsh's telephone number. She had first met Tony at a party in a basement in Bristol ten years ago, when she had been a student. He worked in the antiques trade. Perhaps he would be able to tell her something about the ring that might or might not have belonged to Sadie Lawless.

She dialled the number. Tony answered, and Rose greeted him and asked him how he was.

'Well, I've broken my foot,' he said. 'Dropped a wardrobe on it.'

'Oh, Tony, you poor thing.'

'It's bloody boring, laid up with my foot on a stool. It's good to hear from you, Rose. How are things?'

'Fine,' she said evasively.

'Really?'

She sighed. 'Actually, it's been awful. Just awful. I'm trying to take my mind off everything. And I wondered . . . are you up to going out somewhere for lunch, Tony? Tomorrow, maybe?'

Tony Marsh was not her usual sort of friend. His background was rural and impoverished, and he had left school at fifteen to join the navy; his left forearm still bore the scars from an engine-room fire. Rose had never been sure how old he was – probably forty or fifty by now, something like that. He had the short, slight build of a racecourse jockey, and the springy stance and wiry muscles of a professional boxer, and he was resolutely unhandsome, his pinched features yellowed and wizened-looking, perhaps from too many years working with the chemicals he used for sprucing up furniture. But he was funny and honest and loyal, and during the dark time when her mother had been ill, he often kept her company, supplying a drink and a cigarette and, when she wasn't up to conversation, quiet companionship. He had an eye for the unusual and valuable, a knack of ferreting out the treasure among the rubbish in a house clearance or jumble sale, and when she had been choosing pieces to furnish the Walton-on-Thames house, they had spent several happy afternoons together, driving round the countryside, sifting through antique shops and junk shops.

Meeting him in a dark, smoky little London pub, not far from Waterloo Station, she found Tony already seated at a corner table. He was wearing his usual garb of olive-green moleskin trousers and an ancient dust-coloured tweed jacket with frayed cuffs, and a yellow muffler. His long, thin, greying hair was tied back with, Rose thought, a shoelace.

They hugged. He smelled of peppermints and cigarettes. 'I tried to phone you,' he said. 'But you're a hard person to get hold of, Rose.'

'I had to take the phone off the hook.' She sat down at the scarred table. 'People pester you. Journalists, that sort of thing.'

And acquaintances poking their noses into her business, and friends – she had thought them friends – barely able to hide their curiosity and pleasure in her misfortune. And the

123

odd heavy breather; she had had to make her number ex-directory. The company of even her true friends, women who had faithful husbands and happy families, she now found hard to endure. It was easier to be with someone like Tony, who had been through the mill as well.

He limped to the bar to fetch her a vodka and lemonade. Sitting down again, he slid a pack of Player's No. 6 across the table to her.

'No, thanks.'

Tony lit a cigarette. 'Do you want to talk about it?'

'Not really, no.' She shrugged. 'My husband was having sex with a very expensive prostitute. What's there to say?'

'I always thought he was a self-centred prick.'

'Then you were right.' She studied his thin, lined face. 'You never married, did you, Tony?'

'There was a girl once. She went off with another bloke. My fault; I was in a bit of bother with the cops.' He tapped ash from his cigarette. 'Marriage isn't for me. I like to be free and easy.'

'I found a ring.' Rose took it out of her bag. 'I wondered whether you could tell me anything about it.'

Tony took a magnifying glass out of his pocket, screwing up his face as he looked at the ring. 'When you say you found it . . .'

'It was in some woodland, near a house I've inherited from my grandmother.'

'It's pretty,' he said. 'And very old, I think.'

'How old?'

'I'm no expert on antique jewellery, Rose, but I'd say, from the inscription, Elizabethan or Jacobean.'

'Do you know what the stones are?'

'The green ones are emeralds; I'm pretty sure of that. I

don't know about these.' Tony frowned as he indicated the black gems on the shoulders of the ring. 'I can show it to someone, if you don't mind leaving it with me. Shouldn't take too long.'

'Would you? Thanks, Tony. I'm wondering whether it might have belonged to my great-aunt. She used to live in the house, back in the early thirties. I'm trying to trace her, but not having much luck.'

Their ploughman's lunches arrived. Rose bought another couple of drinks. They talked about the ups and downs of the antique business, and about Kevin, Tony's teenage son by a past lover; the boy was a tearaway, as Tony himself had once been, Rose imagined. 'Turns his nose up at the work I offer him,' said Tony gloomily. 'Thinks himself too good for hauling furniture around and a bit of French polishing.'

Rose left an hour later to catch the train back to Walton-on-Thames. She had tucked the biography of Tom Chiverton into her bag and opened it as the train pulled out of Waterloo. She was reading the chapters that dealt with Tom's early successes, the poetry collections *Lunar* and *Ellipse*, published in the late 1920s and early 1930s, which should have been exciting, but had been reduced by the biographer to lists of awards won and lectures and after-dinner speeches given.

But even Geoffrey Cranham's leaden prose could not disguise the fact that Tom Chiverton's rise, during the years that Sadie had been living at the Egg, had been meteoric. The Chivertons – and the Gull's Wing – appeared to have been at the centre of an artistic circle; a quick trawl through the index revealed the names of poets Louis MacNeice and Geoffrey Grigson, and the composer Constant Lambert. Had Sadie been invited to those evenings at the Gull's Wing, made glittering by the rising stars of the arts world, or had Tom, the celebrated poet, looked down on Sadie, the artist who had never achieved fame?

It occurred to her that she might be able to track Sadie Lawless down using a different route. Perhaps Sadie had sold her prints; perhaps she had exhibited at art galleries. She decided to speak to her brother-in-law, George, who knew about art. She should phone George, anyway; she hadn't spoken to him since her in-laws' ruby wedding party and she didn't want him to think that she was avoiding him, or hating him because she hated Robert. The Martineaus had phoned her a couple of days after Debra Peters' exposé had been published. There had been a stiff and difficult conversation, Mary on the verge of tears and Lionel openly disgusted by his son's behaviour. The ramifications of the scandal seemed to Rose endless, like bacteria multiplying on rotten meat, infecting so many lives.

Sadie Lawless had been a single woman, living alone. Constance Meyrick had said that she had lived in digs and lodgings, and the psychiatrist Philip Sprott had told her that Sadie had worked as a teacher – an art teacher, presumably. So she had supported herself. Sadie had used her time and talents to carve out a career. Rose felt a flicker of envy. After graduating from the Slade, Sadie's direction must have seemed clear to her.

Rose could see no obvious route for herself, no job that might both satisfy her and allow her financial independence. Her thoughts roamed unhappily. She had hardly used her physics degree, had not worked outside the home for almost eight years, unless you counted the meetings she had attended at Martineau Aviation. She wished she could have become more involved with the company, and regretted not having had the chance to understand it, instead of merely rubber-

126

stamping decisions taken by Robert. And now he was selling it, so even that small participation was lost to her.

As the train pulled in to Walton-on-Thames and she took her ticket out of her bag, a thought occurred to her. What would happen if she didn't sign the documents Robert had posted to her? She rose from her seat and made her way to the carriage door, an idea beginning to form in the back of her mind. When she brushed too close to it, she almost shied away from it. It frightened her, and yet it attracted and excited her at the same time. Could she do it? Was she capable of it? *Dare* she?

She thought of her interview with Miss Pritchard at the employment bureau, and of the dependency she had come to loathe, and of the days which stretched ahead of her, formless and without challenge and purpose. She, like Sadie, needed to start again. She needed to slough off her feelings of misery and worthlessness and find out what she was capable of.

Because Robert had put the company in her name, the sale of Martineau Aviation could not go through without her signature. If she did not sign, he could not sell. Perhaps she had found a way of giving herself and her family a future.

Rose said, 'I haven't signed it.'

Robert groaned. 'Christ, Rose, how long can it *take*? What else have you had to do?'

A roar of resentment inside her head; she stifled it. She must stay cool and rational and not give in to her emotions. They went into the study and she shut the door behind them.

'Why do you want to sell the company, Robert?'

'Because it's not making enough money.' She sensed his unwillingness to admit failure as he went on, reluctantly, 'I

didn't expect it to take so long to pull round. It's a special-
ised business, freight aviation. I'd rather put the capital into
something else.'

'You're not selling because you think it *can't* make money?'

'No . . . Look, Rose, it's not how I work, that's all. If a
business isn't making a decent profit within a couple of
years, I keep any parts of it that are doing well and then I
ditch the rest. It's how I've always operated.' He frowned,
looking at her. 'Why do you want to know?'

'Because I want you to give it to me. Properly, not just in
name.' Robert started to speak; she interrupted him. 'I want
to work there; I want to run it. I want it to be mine.'

He gave a crack of laughter. 'Rose . . .'

'Don't laugh at me, Robert.' This time, she was unable to
suppress her fury. 'I need a job, I need a way of supporting
the girls, so don't you dare laugh at me.'

'I'm sorry.' He looked down at the papers on the desk. 'I
didn't mean . . . It was a shock, that's all. Look, Rose, it's an
aviation company.'

'I'm aware of that.'

'You don't know the first thing about aviation.'

That wasn't true. Hers had been an RAF family, until her
father left the forces to work in industry, in the early fifties.
There were photos of planes and models of planes in the house
in which she had been brought up. Her father had taught her
from the earliest age to distinguish the aircraft she saw in the
sky by their shape. She understood the science of flight, how
the difference in pressure on either side of the wings of an
aeroplane creates the force that lifts it into the air.

She let it pass. 'I can learn.'

'You can't just walk into something like that. It's not like
running a home.'

'I didn't imagine for a moment that it was. I'm not fooling around, Robert. I'm serious about this.'

Robert had a short fuse. His shock was visible, along with the conscious effort he was making to control his temper. He said, his voice low and level, 'It's admirable that you think you want to try, but it won't work.'

'Why not?' She had stayed awake throughout the previous night, making notes, drawing up plans. As soon as the idea had popped into her head, she had felt herself changing. Her lassitude had vanished and she felt charged with energy.

'You could say that I'm more qualified to run a charter-aviation company than you are, Robert. At least I have a degree in a relevant subject.'

Robert had abandoned his university course at the end of his first year. He liked to say that he had chosen to take his degree in the university of life, and was proud of this, seeing it as adventurous, dashing and go-getting. Rose had once shared his pride, but now she thought it showed a lack of grit, an inability to stick at things. It should have warned her that he might take the same casual attitude to other aspects of his life. To marriage, for instance. Or to love.

He shook his head. 'No, Rose. This is a crazy idea. It's ridiculous.'

She had to turn away from him then, to look out of the window to the terrace. From the adjacent room came the hum of the television programme that the girls were watching. If Rose and Robert started hurling insults at each other, Katherine and Eve would hear. You heard about the emotional damage estranged parents inflicted on their children; she was desperate to avoid that.

She turned back to him. 'Why is it crazy?' she said quietly.

'I should have thought that was obvious.' Robert, too, was

making an effort to control his feelings. 'You've no experience of running a business.'

'Nor had you, when you bought the garage.'

'And it was bloody hard. I made mistake after mistake.'

'But you learned from it. I can learn too.'

His forefinger stabbed at the desk top. 'Listen. You have to understand the money side of it — okay, you could do that, I know you could — but there's flair, too, a nose for what's going to sell and what won't work. Do you honestly think you've got that? And—' He held up a hand, cutting off her interruption. 'You've got to win the men's respect. That takes time; you have to earn it. Men, like the pilots, Eric and Roy — or Ted Wilkinson — you can't just assume they'll accept you.'

'I doubt if I'd keep Wilkinson.'

'Then there's your first tricky task: giving a man the sack. You'll have to take difficult decisions all the time. You'll have to tell the workforce things they don't want to hear. Sometimes you'll have to get rid of good men, men you like and admire, to keep the wages bill down.'

'I know it wouldn't be easy, but I'd do it, and I'd get better at it with practice.' She kept her voice low and calm. If she couldn't manage this conversation with Robert, what made her think she could manage the men and women who worked at Martineau Aviation?

She leaned back against the edge of the desk. 'I think what you're saying is that the staff might not be happy if the firm was run by a woman.'

'Yes, I am saying that. You can be as liberated as you like, Rose, but aviation's a man's business and you'd find it damned hard to fit in.'

Frowning, she said, 'People have been saying the same

thing – men have been saying the same thing – over the last hundred years or so about pretty well every worthwhile career. Being a doctor was once a man's business. A university lecturer . . . a barrister. If we women had waited until we fitted in, we'd still be teachers and nurses and not much else.'

He let out a breath. 'I'm just telling you, I've been to a fair few other airfields and not one of them has been run by a woman.'

'Then perhaps it's time they were.'

He moved away, shrugging his shoulders, and was silent for a moment. Then he said, 'If I hand over the business to you, what's in it for me? A damned hefty loss, that's what. I need the money; I've plans for it. So why would I do that?'

Because you owe me, she thought. Because of what you did. I'm hurting you in your pocket, Robert, where you'll notice it most. I'm going to make you pay.

But she managed not to say any of that. To start a new life built on resentment and a desire to wound wouldn't work; she knew that in her heart. And it was not the truth. In asking him to give her Martineau Aviation, she wasn't looking for revenge; instead, she was trying to fill a gap that had been there, almost without her noticing it, for a long time.

She tried again. 'What sort of lives do you want Katherine and Eve to have?'

He blinked. 'Happy ones, of course.'

'How do we help them achieve that?'

'By making them feel loved and secure . . .' He grimaced and a look of shame crossed his face. 'You don't have to point it out, Rose.'

'I wasn't. A good education's important too, isn't it, if we want them to have a decent future?'

'Yes. We've always agreed on that.'

'And what's the point of an education if, when they look around them, all they see are the limits that are placed on women's lives? What do I say when Katherine asks me why I studied science at school, but ended up at home, doing the ironing and making cakes? I need to have an answer for her, Robert. A good answer.'

Frowning, she wrapped her arms round herself. She felt weary, and she wanted him to go, because being with him made the pain rise to the surface again. Not that it was ever far away.

'You hurt me,' she said quietly. 'I can't begin to convey how much these last couple of months have hurt. At the moment, I can't imagine ever feeling happy again. I'm still waiting to wake up in the morning and not feel nauseous as soon as I remember what's happened. When I leave the house, I think people are looking at me, talking about me. I *need* this job; I need to be something other than the wife you cheated on; I need people to see me for what I do and what I am, not for what you did to me. But I need it for our daughters' sake, too.'

He dipped his head. 'Perhaps I'm trying to protect you, Rose. Perhaps I don't want you to fail.'

'I don't intend to fail. And if I do, then it won't be for want of trying, so fair enough. Listen, Robert, I know I'm asking a lot. I know it'll cost you and maybe that'll make difficulties for you. I had an idea, though, that might help. You can sell the house. That would raise some money. I know it won't go the whole way to recompensing you, but even if it made things a bit easier . . .'

His eyes had narrowed. 'Sell this house? Are you serious?'

'Yes.'

'I'm not going to sell the house. Where would you and the girls live?'

'In Granny's flat.' This was another thought that had occurred to her in the middle of the night. Her grandmother's flat was large and comfortable, if old fashioned; more importantly, it was conveniently near the airfield, which lay to one side of Weybridge.

'Edith's flat? *Jesus*,' he said angrily, turning away. 'You've got it all worked out, haven't you? We're not going to sell this house, Rose. It's our *home*.'

'I hate it.' Her voice was small and quiet.

'How can you say that?'

'How can you screw a nineteen-year-old prostitute? It is how it is.' The words burst out of her and she looked away, pressing her fingers against her mouth.

A long moment passed before he spoke again. 'What do you want, Rose? For me to say that I'm sorry? Well, I am, every second of every damnable day. I was a fool; I behaved badly, shockingly badly, and I'll never stop regretting it. I threw away what was most important to me, and for nothing, for a thrill. I wish I could turn back time, I dearly do, but I can't.'

'You lied to me.' Her voice was cold.

'Yes.'

Was that shame she saw in his eyes? It bloody well should be. 'You thought you'd get away with it. I wonder what else you kept from me.'

'That's unfair.'

'Is it?'

His fists clenched. 'I can't change the past. If you'd only give me another chance.'

'No, Robert. Please, I don't want to speak about it now.'

He made to say something, but then broke off, raising his

palms in a gesture that conveyed either bitterness or hope-lessness, or perhaps a mixture of the two. Her shoulders ached with tension. In the silence, she heard the low rumble of a neighbour's lawnmower and the squawk of a transistor radio.

He said, 'And if I don't do as you ask?'

'Then I'll know what you think of me,' she said slowly. 'That I am worthless and useless. And that would settle a few things in my mind.'

'What are you talking about?'

'I'd consult a solicitor about getting a divorce.'

A slow shake of the head. 'I didn't know you could be so ruthless.'

'Am I ruthless?' She met his gaze. 'Whenever I look at you, Robert, whenever I think of you, I feel small and ugly and humiliated. *That's* how I feel.'

'*Rose.*' Pain washed across his face and his eyes dropped. 'Please don't,' he said softly. 'Not because of me. I'm not worth it.'

He sat down in the leather chair. Neither of them spoke. She felt drained and exhausted, and almost regretted initiating the conversation. The cost, the rending and tearing of her heart, was too dear.

But eventually he said, 'Okay. Fair enough. You can have it.' He looked up at her. 'It won't be easy, but I wish you luck with it.'

Relief rushed through her. 'Thank you.'

'I'll have to talk to Neil. And to Clive.'

'I don't want Clive on the board.'

'Then you'll need to find another accountant.'

'Yes.'

He stood up. 'I'll get the girls.' He had promised to take

them to tea at a Wimpy. 'I'll speak to Neil. He can draw up the paperwork. I'll let you know when it's ready.'

He frowned, looking back at her as he opened the door.

'You may not have all that long to turn the company round,' he said. 'There are loans that need to be repaid, I'm afraid. Three to six months at most, I'd say, Rose.'

After Robert and the girls had gone out, when the house was quiet and empty, Rose leaned against the kitchen work surface, closed her eyes and took a deep breath. She couldn't go back now. She was going to do it. She was going to run a freight-aviation company.

She didn't know where to start. And she hated flying.

She found herself wondering, as she took the laundry basket upstairs and began to collect clothes for washing, whether Sadie, in going to live at the Egg, had been making a new beginning, whether she had hoped, as she shut herself off from society, to make pictures that were brilliant and beautiful, and whether the leap into the dark had frightened her, too.

Chapter Seven

Sussex – November 1930

Half a dozen guests were lounging on the orange-and claret-coloured sofas in the sitting room of the Gull's Wing. Tom Chiverton's lips brushed dryly against Sadie's cheek as he welcomed her to the house.

'Hello, darling.' Roger Eriksson, the murder-mystery writer, gave her a languid wave. His wife, Helen, smiled at her.

A woman in a mustard-coloured frock, with large black buttons sewn down the front, patted the seat beside her. She was, Sadie guessed, a decade or so older than her and good-looking in a striking rather than conventional manner. Her straight, fine brown hair was cut in a bob and her grey eyes danced just below the fringe.

'Come and sit next to me, Sadie.'

'Thank you.' She sat down.

'I'm Alma Rathbone,' the woman said. A slender, crimson-nailed hand, adorned with chunky rings, was offered to Sadie. 'We saw you at Tom and Di's supper, but I don't think we spoke. That scoundrel over there in the armchair, the handsome one, is my husband, Martin.'

136

Hearing his name, Martin looked round. Sadie thought him indeed very handsome. His features were quite wonderfully symmetrical, his blue eyes piercing, and his thin, shapely mouth had a disdainful, almost cruel slant. She recognised him from somewhere . . . A theatre poster, she thought.

He said, 'So you've passed the test, Sadie.'

'Martin,' said Alma. 'Do shut up.'

Martin continued as if his wife had not spoken: 'We're the crème de la crème, d'you see? Tom and Di's inner circle.'

'Honestly, Martin, put a sock in it. He's so unbearably conceited,' continued Alma affably. 'Diana told me you're an artist, Sadie. Are you an oil painter? Or perhaps a watercolourist?'

They talked about their work. Alma was a fashion designer who created individual pieces sold through a small, exclusive shop in Knightsbridge. She had designed the mustard-coloured frock she was wearing.

'I've created a couple of frocks for Diana,' Alma told her. 'She is, of course, the perfect woman to design for: tall and slim and with such a marvellous upright posture. That orange silk blouse suits her so well, don't you think?'

Their conversation was interrupted by Diana instructing them to sit down at the table. Sadie found herself seated between Alma Rathbone and Roger Eriksson.

Tom poured out claret and Ivy brought in a pie. Served alongside it were dauphinoise potatoes, buttered carrots, roast turnips and creamed leeks. Sadie supposed that Diana had engaged a new cook.

As the maid handed round the plates, Diana related to them an amusing incident that had taken place during Tom's most recent stay in London: a dog escaping its owner in Green Park, Tom diving into the Mall to rescue it from the traffic, and the owner, who chanced to have a copy of *Lunar* in her pocket, recognising him.

'And then,' she finished, 'with all the horns blaring, she asked him to autograph it!'

Everyone laughed. Tom said, 'At least she didn't chase me up the road, like that girl in Foyles.'

'I had to have a sharp word,' said Diana. 'Such pests, some of these women.'

'It's always the women, is it, Tom?' said Martin dryly. 'What a bore.'

'You must miss all the excitement, out here,' said Roger.

'Not in the least.'

'Oh, come on, Di. The theatres . . . the cinemas. I find it hard to believe that you don't, on a dark winter's evening, hanker after a decent restaurant.'

'Not at all.' Diana's tone was chilly.

'London's a cesspit,' said Tom. 'Here, we can breathe.'

Roger smiled. 'You keep a flat in the cesspit, Tom.'

'Needs must. I'd be happy to stay here all the time, but my publisher and readers require me to show my face now and then. Surely you must find the same?'

'I can't say it's too much of a problem. The London press aren't exactly queuing up to interview me. It must be tough, Tom. Still, the price of fame and all that.'

'I consider a talk on the wireless to be a chance to share with others what I most care about. I spoke about this place, what we're trying to make of it, why we bought it, our plans for the future. I've made a start on the outbuildings.'

A bespectacled man called Lewis Emory, looking out at the rain, said, 'I hope they're not going to be washed away, Tom.'

Helen Eriksson sighed as she glanced out of the window. 'Do you think it's going to rain for ever?'

'It's clearing.' Tom topped up their glasses.

'Rot,' said Roger. 'It's set in for the rest of the day.'

'No, it's clearing,' said Tom.

The talk moved to the newly commissioned opera in which Helen was to take a leading role, an interpretation of the Leda and the Swan myth, before veering off to the recent research undertaken by Lewis and his wife, Polly, who were archaeologists. It was the sort of conversation Sadie had taken part in almost since birth. Her parents' friends, who had come from all over Europe, had often discussed and argued late into the night. They had been dear, kind people, earnest and intellectual, socialists or sometimes communists. They had paid little attention to fashion, the men shedding strands of pipe tobacco like dandelion clocks over their worn tweeds, while locks of brittle grey hair had escaped from the women's plaits and buns, and the lace on their high-collared, old-fashioned blouses had sometimes been a little grubby.

But, as the intellectual exploration at the Chiverton lunch table continued, Sadie noticed that something was absent. The Lawlesses and their friends might have debated for hours the opinions of a French philosopher, but they had also asked after each other's children and grandchildren. Photos had been admired and passed round the lunch table and anecdotes about a grandchild's musical or academic prowess were listened to with affectionate indulgence. Family was not mentioned once in the Chivertons' house. Tom and Diana were childless. Sadie wondered whether the other couples in the room were also.

At the end of the meal, they rose from the table and arranged themselves on sofas and chairs. Diana poured coffee and Helen Eriksson was implored to go to the grand piano. Alma turned the pages of the music for Helen as she sang an arrangement of 'Full Fathom Five'. Tom took the men downstairs to show them the shotgun he had recently acquired for killing the rats that infested the barn.

Sadie went to stand at the window. Tom had been right; the rain had stopped and sunlight was flashing on the wet cobbles in the courtyard. A tin can had been set up on a fence at the far end of the garden and Martin Rathbone was taking aim at it. Sadie's gaze moved from Martin to Tom, who was standing by the stable door. The breeze whipped at his dark, curling hair; he had not, like the others, put on a coat to go out in the chill air, but was still in his shirt and jacket. His stance, which resembled that of a hare about to spring, was made tense by his barely contained energy. His smile, she guessed, showed his pleasure in leaving the house for the outdoors.

'Look at them. They won't stand a chance against Tom.'

Sadie turned to see Diana, who had come to stand beside her. 'Is he a good shot?'

'Whatever Tom chooses to do, he does it brilliantly. Have I told you how we met? It was at my cousin's house, in Northumberland. It was a cold day in May, but half a dozen of us went swimming in the river. Tom was like an otter, sleek and dark, rushing through the water. None of the other men could keep up with him.' Diana's eyes slid away from the view to come to rest on Sadie. 'I knew then I would marry him. I was twenty years old.'

'How romantic.'

'Romantic?' Diana laughed. 'Tom would be amused to hear you say that. If you knew him better, you would think him the least romantic man alive. He never sends me flowers or takes me for a candlelit dinner. Not that I'd want him to. Passion is the only thing that matters, not tawdry little romantic gestures. Tom and I think exactly the same about that. But then we think the same about everything.'

Sadie couldn't help thinking that must restrict conversation. What would you talk about if you always agreed? But she said, 'You must feel so proud of him.'

'We're proud of each other. Tom always says that he couldn't have achieved anything without me.' Diana made a little inward breath and pressed her palms together, leaning towards the window. 'Isn't he glorious?' she murmured.

As Sadie watched, Tom set the tin can up on a more distant support, took his position and raised the gun. A shot rang out, echoing against the trees, and the can leaped and tumbled to the ground. Diana gave a little inward smile and then went back to the coffee pot.

At four o'clock, Sadie left the Gull's Wing. The light was almost gone and the dense, opaque, green and black branches still dripped with rain. As she headed home, she scoured the path to either side of her, gathering leaves and twigs, a feather or two, and some fragile, pale toadstools, like ivory buttons on thread.

Back in the Egg, she went upstairs to her studio. The owl sketch she had made the previous afternoon still lay on the windowsill. She tore it to pieces, then took a large square of card and began to paste the torn fragments on to it. Then she set out on the table the natural objects she had gathered on her walk home, moving them around the collage until she had found the right place for them.

She worked on into the evening. An owl hooted and the wind carved out its path through the trees. At nine o'clock, she went downstairs and heated up some soup. She carried the mug into the living room and stood at the windows. For the first time, she found herself minding the absence of curtains. She felt exposed, too easily seen through the glass that divided her from the woodland, too visible and available.

'"Last night I walked beneath a sky of beaten metal" . . .' She murmured aloud the line from Lunar's title poem. A footnote in the book had told her that Tom had composed it during a midnight walk in woodland. The words, chosen as meticulously as one would select pearls to string on a necklace, had fixed themselves in her memory, hard and clear and cold. She wondered whether the woodland Tom had been walking in had been this one, Paley High Wood, and if so, whether he had ever stopped to look through the great glass windows of the Egg. And she thought of him as she had seen him that afternoon, standing in the courtyard, the gun braced against his powerful shoulder, and the mastery of his shot.

It occurred to her that Diana, with her eulogy to her perfect marriage, might have been warning her off, but it seemed unlikely and was certainly unnecessary. Sadie thought she understood what sort of woman Diana Chiverton was, her life driven and shaped by the love of a man. She had been that sort of woman once, and she felt a flare of envy, because Diana possessed what she was teaching herself to do without: union with the man she loved, freedom from loneliness and an outlet for desire.

A week later, Roger Eriksson, rather red faced, knocked on the door of the Egg.

'Sadie, you must save me,' he announced, histrionically.

She let him into the house. 'What from?'

'The Sunday walk.' He mopped his brow with his handkerchief and smoothed back his dishevelled hair. 'I've told

142

Tom and Di I have a prior engagement. I'm exhausted; I'm not built for these great expeditions. I'd go the pub, but they may end up there. Seven miles round some bloody windswept hill yesterday; I thought I was going to die. Tom, of course, keeps up the pace like a slave-driver. If they call for you, you must tell them you're working.'

'I *am* working. Come and see.'

They went upstairs to her studio. In the woods one afternoon she had come across a jumble of pigeon feathers strewn beneath a group of elms, scraps of flesh still adhering to the pinions of a wing. She had sketched the branches in charcoal, black scars across the white base, like cracks in ice, and then attached the fragments of torn wing. The image was monochrome apart from a drip of red: a depiction not of violence itself, but of the consequences of violence. Evidence of owl, she thought, rather than actual owl.

'It's rather *fierce*,' he said.

'I wanted it to be fierce. Nature is fierce, isn't it?'

'Oh, don't you start.' Roger collapsed into a chair. 'If I hear another word about nature's virility, I shall *weep*.'

'Are you hungry? I was about to make lunch.'

'Starving.' He added gloomily, 'They're planning a picnic. In *November*.'

'I'll make us a sandwich.'

In the kitchen, she took out a loaf of bread. Roger looked nosily around, then said, 'I don't know how you bear it here. I'd end up talking to myself. May I have this?' He pointed to a crust of bread, and then leaned against the counter, munching, and said, with the air of one imparting secrets, 'Tom insisted on moving out to Sussex, you know. Diana wasn't keen at first.'

'They seem very happy here.'

143

'Oh, they put on a good show. The Chivertons couldn't possibly be seen to have made a mistake, could they? But does anyone really enjoy living in a muddy field in the middle of winter? Diana went along with it because she worships him.'

'It's a good enough reason, Roger.'

'I'm not so sure it's good for Tom, always getting his own way.' His expression was one of private amusement. 'But then, whatever Tom wants, he invariably gets.'

Sadie put a sandwich on a plate for him; Roger thanked her.

'I'm not saying he isn't madly in love with her. Diana's an extremely attractive woman. And you never hear them having those little spats most married couples indulge in. I can't help hoping they fight like cat and dog when no one else is around. May I have some mustard, Sadie?'

She handed him a jar and a knife, and he daubed it thickly on the bread. Through a mouthful of sandwich, he said, 'Of course, their only true loyalty is to themselves. They are complete egotists; you must have noticed that. Frightfully amusing and clever – at least, he is clever; I'm not so sure about her – but utterly self-centred.'

'If you dislike them, why do you visit them?'

'I didn't say I disliked them. They have their redeeming features. They're good fun and Tom is extremely well read. I'm afraid there are only a few people I like unreservedly. Helen and my daughter and my mother, and that's about it.' He shrugged. 'It's my nature.'

'I didn't know you had a daughter, Roger.'

He opened his wallet, took out a photograph and showed it to her. 'That's my Kathleen. She's four years old.'

The photo was of a little girl with blond pigtails and a wide smile. 'She's adorable,' said Sadie.

'She takes after Helen, thank goodness. The nanny's looking after her this weekend.'

'The Chivertons don't have children, do they?'

He shook his head. 'Neither of them are keen. Tom thinks they'd get in the way of his work and Diana prefers dogs and horses. Anyway, it would mean thinking about someone other than themselves.' Roger prised a chunk of bread from his teeth. 'They're having frightfully deep discussions about the new opera. Tom's writing the libretto, did you know? He's taking on all sorts of things, these days, because he's in a bit of a stew financially,' he added indiscreetly.

'But he's awfully successful,' Sadie said, surprised.

'Poetry doesn't pay. Tom's having to do collaborative work to make some cash – special editions and anthologies, that sort of thing. He likes to spread his wings. I sometimes think that, at heart, he's a dilettante. Or maybe he has a hard time doing justice to all his talents, he's so burdened with them.'

Sadie wondered whether Roger's cynical remarks were motivated by the jealousy of the less successful writer for the one with the golden touch. She put on the kettle to make tea. 'But Tom and Diana live so well.'

'I don't mean as a miner, for example, or a street sweeper or typist would be short of money. But neither of them has independent means.' He strolled into the sitting room to peer out of the window warily, as if Tom might catch sight of him and pounce. 'I suppose this is the perfect place to get over a broken heart,' he said.

She gave him a sharp glance. 'Tom told you?'

'No, Tom told Diana; they tell each other everything. And Diana told Helen, and Helen told me.'

'Oh.'

Foolish of her, she thought, to mind that Tom had discussed her private affairs. She had not forbidden him to.

'I'm here to work, Roger,' she said briskly. 'Not to mope.'

'Oh, I'm sure you are.' His tone altered, becoming hesitant. 'Would you mind me saying something? A word of advice?'

She suspected he would have his say whether she minded or not, so shook her head.

'Don't count on them.' He held up a finger, silencing her. 'And don't always be at their beck and call. Tom and Diana are very beguiling and they know how to dish out the charm, but they can pick one up and put one down with remarkable rapidity.'

'What do you mean?'

'They have a way of dropping people like a *stone*. They'd have finished with me months ago if it wasn't for Helen. Tom's the sort of chap who's invited to every dinner table worth sitting at. He mixes with the great and the good, and makes sure everyone knows about it. I'm not saying it's an affectation – not at all. Tom sees it as being part of the job, of what it is to be Tom Chiverton, and no doubt he's right. But what you have to realise is that Tom and Di view themselves as an art form in their own right – as an *undertaking*. They need to be admired, but they like their privacy too, and woe betide anyone who gets in the way of that. I doubt if they're capable of *loving* anyone but themselves. I've met perfectly pleasant, likeable guests at the Gull's Wing, and they've been all over them, but then you never see them again. It's a question of whether you fit in with what they want at the time. You may be in favour because you're amusing or you have connections or you look decorative at a dinner table, but you shouldn't assume it'll last. And if you cross them, well . . . neither are the forgiving sort.'

Roger took another bite of his sandwich and said, between chews, 'I like you, Sadie. Even a cynical old bastard like me can see that you have a sweet nature. Don't depend on them; that's all I'm saying. Enjoy Tom and Di for what they are, but don't get in too deep.'

The frost that greyed the grass in the shade of the trees had not thawed for days and her breath made little white puffs. An intense cold had penetrated the forest, crisping every fallen leaf, and the air that filled her lungs was sharp and cold and piny.

As Sadie neared the top of the ridge, a harsh explosion of sound split the air. Coming out of the woodland, on to the road, she saw that Diana was standing in the courtyard of the Gull's Wing, shooting crows. She was wearing her long black coat, and her wild black hair was flailing in the wind as she aimed the shotgun. Another blast and something dark tumbled through the sky. One of the dogs ran to scoop it up.

Diana lowered the shotgun and waved to Sadie. 'The wretched crows foul the courtyard,' she called out. 'Such a nuisance. I thought I'd have a crack at them while it was still light. Do come in, Sadie.'

'I don't want to disturb you.'

'Oh, you mustn't worry about that.' Diana, warm and affable, ushered her into the house. 'You haven't seen a Delage motor car on your walk, have you?'

'I'm afraid not.'

'Do, please, go upstairs. My brother, Maurice, is somewhere around. I'll make some tea.'

Sadie thanked her and went upstairs. A tall, slim, dark-haired man, in his twenties, she guessed, and recognisably Diana's brother, stood up as she came into the room.

'Hello. I thought you were Elizabeth.'

'No, I'm Sadie – Sadie Lawless. Are you Maurice?'

'Maurice Hever; pleased to meet you.' They shook hands. He looked a little disconsolate. 'Di said that Elizabeth was coming.'

'I don't know her, I'm afraid.'

'She's such an awfully good sport. I say, have you seen Tom? His face is a frightful mess. He got into a fight with a trespasser – some oaf who was taking photos of the house. He hit Tom with his camera.'

'Is he all right?'

Maurice guffawed. 'The other chap got the worst of it; Tom saw to that. Apparently, the blighter could hardly walk.'

'Where is he?'

He made a vague gesture to the lower part of the house. 'His editor's here. They're having a frightfully deep powwow about something.' Hands in pockets, he strode to the window. 'Did you walk here?'

'Yes; I live half a mile away.'

'You didn't notice a black motor car on the road, did you?'

'I'm afraid not.'

He peered outside. 'Some friends of mine are dropping by. They're late; I think they must have had a puncture. We're motoring down to Cornwall. I'm ravenous, aren't you? I'll go and see if I can rustle up something to eat.'

He left the room. Sadie looked out of the window. The sky gleamed palely. She sat down on a sofa and leafed through a magazine while she waited for Maurice to return or Diana to appear with the tea. From the lower floor of the house, she heard a rumble of voices.

A toot of a horn brought her to her feet. She looked out the window. A large, black motor car had drawn up at the side of the road. She watched as Maurice slung a case into the boot and then climbed in, waving and calling out fare-wells. The car drove away at speed.

I shouldn't be here, Sadie thought. Tom and Diana were busy and she was in the way. She decided to leave it another five minutes before making some excuse and leaving. Uneasily, she circled the room. Papers were heaped on a small table, the typing scribbled over with black ink. A phrase caught her eye: *The absolution of desire*. She thought she under-stood it, but would have found it hard to explain what it meant.

Empty cups and glasses cluttered the occasional tables and a large stoneware vase had been filled with conifer and holly branches. The scent of the fir needles was strong and medic-inal. Sadie had the odd notion that the woodland was creeping inside the house, chilling and dampening the air.

Five minutes passed. She went downstairs to the ground floor. Voices drew her to their source.

'The same old thing,' a man – not Tom – was saying. 'The tired English pastoral. Is that all we're capable of?'

'I wouldn't say that it was *tired*.'

'But is it relevant? That's the question.'

'The pastoral's constantly being reinterpreted through the prism of the present day.'

'Rural idylls are never as charming as they're made out to be.'

'What would you know about that?' Tom spoke for the first time, his tone lacerating, and Sadie paused in the corridor. 'People like you, Rex, think Hampstead is in the depths of the countryside. Were you afraid you'd be gobbled up by wolves, walking here from the station? If you're left a heap of bones by the roadside, I promise I'll write you a nice obituary.'

'Tom, I only meant to suggest—'

'I *am* the English pastoral. It's *here.*' Sadie pictured Tom thumping his ribcage in the region of his heart. 'This is what I love. There's nothing I love more, and if you can't see that, or if you think it valueless, then perhaps you should leave.'

'Tom, there's no question of us not valuing your work. Please understand that. But, for an American audience—'

'Damn the bloody Americans! And damn you too, for your pig-headed ignorance!'

A door slammed; hearing footsteps, Sadie retreated up the stairs.

She caught Diana's voice, saying, 'Tom, dearest . . .'

'My work is everything to me,' he said furiously. 'Why can't anyone seem to understand that?'

'I do, my darling. And you are everything to me.'

'Oh, for God's sake! Leave me be! *Christ.*'

Another door slammed. Tom had lost his temper. Men were prone to losing their tempers. The discussions in the house were today freighted with emotions Sadie was not party to and disputes that she, an interloper, should not have overheard. Perhaps she should speak to Diana and make sure she was all right. She had never before heard Tom address her so roughly. But, no; she felt certain that Diana would hate to know that anyone had witnessed the exchange. Better to pretend ignorance.

She went back upstairs to the sitting room. Glancing out of the window, she watched the pigs snuffling in the mud and the buff and brown hens pecking at the ground and settling in a rise and fall of feathers beneath a hedge. Tom had gone outside and was standing by the barn, smoking a cigarette. She could see, even from this distance, that one side of his face was mottled with purple bruises.

150

Diana came in with a tray of tea things.

'I should go,' Sadie said. 'I can see you're all very busy.'

'Nonsense.' As she put the tray on the table, Diana's voice was hard and brisk. 'Of course you must stay. Tom would be so disappointed if he missed seeing you.'

Sadie doubted that, but she sat down. Two men came into the sitting room; Diana introduced them as Rex and Edwin, from Tom's publishers. Rex was a plump young man, wearing a lovat-green tweed jacket and a crimson cravat. Edwin was older and distinguished-looking.

'Sadie.' Tom's voice, from the doorway, made her glance up. 'How charming you look today.' He turned to address the two men sitting on the claret-coloured sofa. 'Sadie's a very talented artist. I once came across her in the middle of a rainstorm, making a fine little sketch of an owl. I hope you've framed it, Sadie.'

'I'm afraid I tore it up and used it in a collage.'

He laughed as he sat down beside Diana. 'How appropriately modernist.'

Diana handed around tea, sandwiches and cake. As the conversation moved on, Sadie gathered that Edwin and Rex had come to the Gull's Wing to discuss with Tom a planned American reading tour. Rex, who looked uncomfortably hot in his seat by the fire and pulled now and then at his silk cravat, seemed to annoy Tom, who persistently disagreed with the poor man. He reminded Sadie of a great, hungry beast, toying with some small, vulnerable creature. He made no attempt to disguise his mood, reacting with anger or biting sarcasm to whatever displeased him. When the men's argument became particularly heated, Diana brought Sadie into the conversation. Sadie wondered whether that was why Diana had been so keen that she stay, to act as a buffer between Tom and the two men.

The discussion drifted to the subject of ley lines. Tom was an enthusiastic advocate of Alfred Watkins' work on the subject.

'I met Watkins once,' he said. 'Fascinating chap. Fine photographer, too.'

'This part of England is littered with historical sites,' said Rex, unwisely. 'Join any two points of interest and you'd get a straight line.'

Tom said coldly, 'I believe the ridge road to be a Neolithic track. The Gull's Wing itself is built on a ley line. Perhaps you should open your mind, Rex.' He leaned forward in his seat, every muscle in his big, powerful body taut. 'Not everything can be pinned down and neatly proved. You can't pin down *love*, for instance. Or longing or jealousy or hatred or any of the other emotions that make us human. Does that mean they don't exist?'

'I don't think it's quite the same. You feel the *effect* of love; you feel an emotion.'

'Thank you for pointing that out to me. You'd almost think I hadn't spent the last twenty years trying to write the odd thing about love.' Tom's voice dripped scorn.

'I had no intention . . . I didn't mean to imply—'

'Then don't be such a bloody idiot,' Tom snapped.

During the past half-hour, darkness had fallen. Diana rose to draw the curtains. On her way back to her seat, she stopped to fondle Tom's curly head in a way that reminded Sadie of her gentleness with the Vizslas. 'Oh, I think one can quite easily find proof of love,' she said. 'Wouldn't you agree, Sadie?'

Sadie paused before replying, partly because she didn't want to say something foolish and annoy Tom further, and partly because she had exiled herself to the Egg because of love. She had spent the last few months struggling to manage its consequences and would not make some glib, dishonest reply.

'I think that love has a shadow, a reflection,' she said. 'I think that, if we truly experience it, some of that reflection will always remain with us.' She found herself touching the ring she wore on her right hand, running her fingertips over the clustered emeralds. She remembered Diana saying to her that passion was the only thing that mattered. Was that true? There was truth in it, she decided, but passion could be selfish and destructive too.

There was a general nodding and agreement, but she hardly paid attention. What she had come to accept during her time at the Egg was that, though she had loved, Felix had not. No shadow had fallen over him; if he had looked into a glass, his image would have been unaltered. The phrase etched into the ring he had given her, *In thee my choys I do rejoys*, had, for him, referred to only a fleeting passion. He had not once tried to get in touch with her since her breakdown, not even to check how she was. He did not love her, had never truly loved her. It was a hard thing to accept and her heart ached with it, but she was just about there.

The occasion, sticky and halting as it was, appeared to be reaching a conclusion. Sadie excused herself to visit the bathroom on the ground floor. Her reflection stared back at her from the mirror, pink cheeked from the heat of the fire and rather tousle-haired. She splashed cold water on her face and tidied her hair with her hands.

When she came out, Tom was in the hall. 'Stanley's sent me the first set of woodcuts. Would you like to see them?'

'Yes, very much.'

They went to Tom's study. An electric lamp illuminated the floor-to-ceiling bookshelves that covered two walls. This room was at the front of the house; in summer, the pillared overhang must give shelter from the sunlight. A board, pinned with cuttings, photographs, leaves and feathers – like her, Tom collected scraps from the forest – stood above a circular table stacked with letters and notebooks. A small desk, scarred and rickety-looking, bore pens, ink and pencils, and a block of thick white paper.

Tom spread out some illustrations for her to look at. 'They're very fine, don't you think?'

Stanley Chute had made three small oval woodcuts: a hare leaping on grass, a fox loping across a field and a badger emerging from its sett. Each woodcut was accompanied by a couplet, handwritten in italics.

'They're exquisite,' she said. 'So lifelike.'

'Yet, at the same time, mystical and emblematic. They concentrate the essence of the animal, don't you think?'

'Marvellously, yes. What are you using them for?'

'Edwin wants to publish a special edition of *Lunar*. Original artwork, nicely produced, always sells a book. Forgive me, Sadie.'

She glanced at him, startled. 'What for?'

'For my foul mood this afternoon.' His mouth clenched. 'That ass, Rex – I'm having a hard time stopping myself punching him. This American tour couldn't have come at a worse time.'

'Couldn't you postpone it?'

'They tell me not.' He said with sudden passion, 'The tour . . . the special edition . . . they force me to work not on what I long to do, but on what will sell. It's wretched, utterly wretched!'

'Must it be a great deal more work for you?'

'Edwin insists I include three or four poems that haven't

been published elsewhere. So, either I break off from what I've been working on for the past six months, and at a point when I'm beginning to discover a new voice, or I work up a couple of old pieces I know to be second rate. I resent being put in this position. It's a sort of enslavement.'

'Can't you refuse?'

In the dim light, his eyes were black and burning. 'No, I'm afraid not. The upkeep of this place has cost more than I'd bargained for.'

Sadie remembered what Roger had said about the Chivertons being short of money. So it was true.

'When the others come,' Tom went on, 'it'll be easier. I'll have to charge some sort of rent, though I'd hoped to avoid that.'

'Others?'

'It's always been my intention to share the Gull's Wing with kindred souls – writers and artists, people who share my vision for the land. We planned from the start to reno-vate the barn, to make it habitable. I've started work repairing the roof. It's a big project and it'll take me a while.'

'But,' she said, 'won't that take you away from writing? Wouldn't it be better to engage a workman to mend the roof? Though, I suppose it would be expensive.'

'I like to work with my hands, Sadie. I need to be close to stone and wood and soil. I *need* physical work, to be out in the elements.' He clenched his fists. 'I need something solid to pit myself against.'

'Sometimes it's good to tire yourself out.'

'Exactly. One feels restless otherwise. Anyway, I hope to finish the roof by summer, so that the first members of our little community will be able to move in.'

'Are you sure it won't disturb you, having other people around?'

'I hope not.' Absently, Tom riffled through the drawings on the desk. 'There was a time when a poem would come into my head as I walked across the Downs. I put one foot in front of the other and the lines formed. It was as if they were there, waiting for me to find them. I'm afraid I've lost that facility, that *ease*. Sometimes, my head's full of chatter, most of it such *drivel*, and I find myself wishing everyone would leave me alone. I admire you, Sadie. You shut yourself away and concentrate on your work.'

She said, surprised, 'If you knew how measly the results have been these past few months, you wouldn't say that.'

'But you keep trying. And after considerable personal difficulties.'

'As you said, perhaps that gives me something to draw on. And . . .' She paused, gathering her thoughts. 'Maybe what I am now is what I truly am. Maybe that other woman, the Sadie who was going to marry Felix, wasn't the real me.'

He gave her one of his quick, magnetic smiles. 'I must say, you don't strike me as one of those young women who see marriage as the be-all and end-all of existence.'

'Until I met Felix, I'd no expectations of marrying.'

'You're a free spirit, like me. I've reservations about the institution myself.'

Again, his comment struck her forcibly. Tom and Diana seemed so perfectly suited, so happily married.

'I have doubts about the artificial restrictions marriage imposes,' he added. 'Diana and I talked about it long and hard before we decided to wed. But my work requires us both to be in the public eye and I would hate her to be the subject of gossip.'

'Yes, I see that. You wanted to protect her from the sorts of comments people make.'

'I don't see myself as the marrying type.'

He spoke in the present tense, as if that was how he still felt. It seemed a strange thing to say when his beautiful wife was upstairs, soothing the ruffled feathers of his colleagues.

'Do you think it's possible to be completely free?' she asked him. 'Don't you think that there are always boundaries, Tom, places we can't tread?'

'Come, that's not worthy of you, Sadie.' His head was cocked to one side as he studied her, his gaze touched with a mixture of reproach and amusement. 'I don't see you as a woman who looks for an excuse to flee the true intensity of life.'

A tension had crept into the room and it crossed her mind that she should return upstairs, or at least change the direction of the conversation. But she was reluctant to break the mood. The pleasure of expressing herself frankly, of feeling listened to as an equal by someone as vital and original as Tom, was hard to walk away from.

And, anyway, he was still speaking.

'The first time I saw you, Sadie, you were at your house in the woods. I was running through the trees and there you were, in the clearing, chopping firewood. You didn't see me and I stopped to watch for a while. You were wearing a green coat and your hair was wild and golden, and you looked like something out of a fairy story. An enchantress or an elf. Yes, that's the word that springs to my mind when I think of you – "elfin". Your fine, bright hair . . . your blue-green eyes . . . your high cheekbones and pointed chin.'

As he described her, he touched her. A palm stroking her hair. A fingertip drifting along her cheek. She stood motionless, enchanted indeed.

'You're such an ethereal little thing,' he said in a low murmur. 'You must think of me as some great, hard rock. You and I, Sadie, we're like the hills and the rain. We touch and then we part, but we've left a mark on each other.'

His lips pressed against hers and she closed her eyes, lost in his kiss. His tongue explored her mouth and she felt his body, warm against her, hard and hungry for touch. Outside, the wind howled and the trees made a rushing sound as they swayed to and fro.

Footsteps on the stairs; his clasp slackened and she took a pace back, horrified at herself. What had she been thinking of, kissing Tom Chiverton while Diana was on the floor above, pouring out the tea? Shaken, she hurried out of the room.

Ilonka and Gizi were lounging in the hall. They gave each other startled glances. Sadie went upstairs and sat down on the sofa. Diana asked her if she would like more tea and she shook her head. Her heart was pounding and her mouth was dry and she did not think she would hold the cup steady. Rex returned from the bathroom, sat down, and began to talk about a film he had seen. A few minutes later, Tom came back into the room. His fingers kneaded his wife's neck as he joined in the conversation about the film.

Shortly afterwards, Sadie regained her composure sufficiently to rise and thank her hosts. Tom's smile, and the farewell kiss that brushed against her cheek, was that of a charming friend.

Chapter Eight

Surrey and London – August 1970

As Martineau Aviation's workforce filed out of the meeting room that Friday morning, Dan Falconer heard Ted Wilkinson make a remark that was crude, even by his standards. He didn't trouble to lower his voice and followed up his comment with loud laughter at his own wit. Though Mrs Martineau gave no indication that she had overheard the comment, Dan suspected that she had.

In the hangar, Wilkinson slapped his fleshy hands together and said, 'That's this dump down the pan, then, with that bitch in charge. You and me, Max, we're going to have a housewife telling us what to do. What do you think of that? Time for a drink, I'd say.'

The mechanic said, 'I should have a look at that wheel.'

'I don't think Miss Fancy-Pants is going to notice if you don't do your homework, lad.' Wilkinson's lip curled as he turned to Dan. 'Are you coming?'

'No.'

'Don't be a prissy little swot. I say you should come.'

Wilkinson was standing in front of him, uncomfortably close. His forefinger prodded Dan's chest and his pale blue eyes betrayed a barely suppressed violence. Tall and heavyset, his muscles running to fat, Wilkinson liked to make a threat of his powerful physical presence.

Max looked away, but Dan didn't flinch. 'I'm staying here,' he said.

'Nancy. Bleedin' soft little nancy. Suit yourself, then.'

Wilkinson grabbed his jacket and he and Max left the hangar. Dan gave them a few minutes; by the time he too went outside, Wilkinson's Vauxhall was heading, at speed, down the concrete pathway that led to the road and the nearest pub. In two or three hours' time, he'd be back, incapable of walking in a straight line without Max's supporting arm. Dan had told the lad he should turn down Wilkinson's requests for a drinking companion, but Max was afraid for his job. Wilkinson could be a vindictive bastard, when he chose.

Dan walked to the edge of the grass, where a cool breeze washed over the flat hilltop on which the airfield lay. A DC-3, Martineau Aviation's most venerable plane, was standing on the runway. If the company folded, they'd have to sell the poor old girl. Wilkinson was right about one thing: if Mrs Martineau didn't get off to a good start, the business wouldn't last long. They all knew the books were dipping into the red.

Dan returned to the small office he shared with Wilkinson. It was the job of the operations manager to prepare charter quotes, assess sites, arrange flight plans and keep up to date with information about cargoes. The company was failing because they weren't getting enough business in, and so the planes were too often on the ground, rather than in the air.

If you looked at it rationally, the chances of Rose Martineau succeeding where her husband had failed were remote. If she wasn't able to turn the company round, Dan would have to leave. Since Robert Martineau's involvement in the Debra Peters' scandal had been made public, Celia had been encouraging him to keep an eye on the job market.

It seemed rough not to give her a chance, though. Dan put on his jacket and went down the corridor. Lucy Holbrook was sitting at her desk, typing.

'Is Mrs Martineau in?' He nodded at the closed door of the office.

'Yes. Dan, what is it?'

Without answering Lucy's question, Dan knocked, then went into the office. Rose was standing at the desk, files and notebooks open in front of her. She looked up.

'Forgive me for interrupting you,' he said. 'May I speak to you?'

She gave him a smile. 'Go ahead, Dan.'

'If you want to have any hope of making this place survive, then you should think about getting rid of Ted Wilkinson.'

She didn't say anything, so he ploughed on. 'He's lazy and careless, and he's a bully. He poisons the atmosphere in the workshops and hangar. It doesn't bother me, but it does bother the younger men. He pushes them around. Ted's a drinker; he has four or five pints every lunchtime and sleeps it off in the afternoons. That's where he is at the moment – at the pub, with Max. Max went with him because he's scared of Ted. He's a good worker, but he does what Ted tells him to.'

She clipped shut a box file. 'So, you're telling me that Wilkinson isn't up to the job.'

'Yes, Mrs Martineau.'

'Rose, please; there's no need for formality.'

'Perhaps he was good at it once, but he isn't now.'

She frowned, then said, 'Sit down. I wanted to talk to you,

161

anyway. I'm trying to work out what we need to do to survive.'

Dan sat opposite her.

She tapped one manicured fingernail on the desktop. 'If you were me,' she said, 'where would you start?'

'By identifying the worst aspects of our situation. List them, then work out the best solutions.'

She glanced at a piece of paper on the desk. 'What's getting in the way of us making money?'

'Costs, first.'

She nodded. 'Staff costs, fuel costs, the maintenance of the aircraft. The lease of the buildings, utility bills. Can we cut down on staffing costs?'

Dan saw that one of the papers on the desk was a list of employees. There were notes pencilled against the names. All their jobs were on the line – including, he suspected, his own.

She said, 'Does the operation manager's role really need two people?'

'It shouldn't. One man could do it, if he put his mind to it. I could do it.'

She looked back at the list. 'We're paying two mechanics.'

'You need two as a minimum. We ought to have three. A plane's delayed, you still need to have a mechanic at the airfield when it lands. Max and Gareth are both good workers. Same with the pilots and co-pilots – they're ex-RAF; you won't find better. You can't economise on flight crew or mechanics. You need a loadmaster too, to stow the cargo and keep track of it.'

'Our fuel costs seem very high. Could we find someone to supply us at a cheaper price? If we offered to pay cash, for instance?'

'I'll look into it.'

'Thank you. And the lease on the buildings – I was wondering if we should renegotiate it.'

'Mr Martineau tried, but they wouldn't budge.'

Once again, she made a note.

Dan said, 'We've more space than we need. One possibility would be to try to sublet the spare offices, to claw back a part of the rent. Would you like me to look into that as well?'

'Please, Dan. And the aircraft – do we really need three? Are we doing enough business to justify keeping three planes in the air?'

'We could be, if we put our minds to it.' He hated to think that the older of the two DC-3s might be mothballed in a corner of the hangar. Or, worse, sold off.

'And . . .' She leafed over a page. 'Might we be setting our prices too low?'

'Some routes, it's possible. It depends how much competition there is. Popular routes, you need to be careful you're not going to be undercut.'

'Marseilles appears to be losing us money. Should we drop it?'

'I don't think so. There's money to be made there. The problem is that it's not ending up in our pockets.'

'Why is that?'

'Too often, the hold's not full both ways. If it's empty on the return flight, we still have to pay for fuel and an air crew, but we don't earn a penny. Marseilles is one of our longer hauls, so fuel costs are high. Empty planes cost money.'

'Why are they empty?'

'Because Mr Martineau didn't get in enough new business.' Dan saw no point in beating about the bush.

She didn't blink. 'How would I go about remedying that?'

'You'd talk to the import–export agents and persuade them to give us more contracts. You might want to think of finding a new agent in Marseilles. We're small fry to the man we're with at the moment, so he's going to give the best jobs to his more important customers. Look for someone who's starting up, who's hungry for new business and won't charge too high a commission. It would help, of course, if you spoke good French.'

'I do.'

Of course she did. Rose Martineau would have had that sort of education and those sorts of summer holidays.

He said, 'You'll need to be prepared to walk away, if the terms aren't good enough.'

Her eyebrows raised slightly as she studied him. He wondered whether she thought he had overstepped the mark. But she gave an almost imperceptible nod, and said, 'I think that's all for now. Thank you, Dan.'

As he rose to leave, she said, 'For the time being, I'd like you to take over the role of operations manager.'

'From when?'

'From now. Three months' trial. Oh, and when Mr Wilkinson comes back to work, tell him that I'd like to see him.'

At five o'clock that afternoon, Rose packed her papers into her bag. The school term had ended the previous week and her father had volunteered to take the day off work to look after Katherine and Eve. On her way out of the building to collect them, she stopped by Lucy Holbrook's work station.

'I have to go now, Lucy.' She put a sheaf of documents on the secretary's desk. 'Could you deal with these urgently, please?'

'Of course.' Lucy looked up from her typewriter. 'Are you okay, Rose?'

'Fine, thanks.'

'I learned early on always to have my back to the wall when I was in the same room as Ted Wilkinson. Funny how those sorts of men, men who don't like women, are so often bottom pinchers.'

Rose's interview with Wilkinson had been unpleasant. He had been drunk and crudely insulting. She had paid him a month's salary in lieu of notice and had him escorted from the premises by the caretaker, who was ex-army.

'I don't think he'd have been happy,' she said, 'working for a woman.'

Lucy, who was uncapping a plum-coloured lipstick, sniggered. 'Bloody hell. That's the understatement of the century.'

Rose felt the release of tension. 'And you, Lucy? You don't mind working for me?' She remembered Robert's secretary once telling her that she felt her status came from the man she worked for: important man, important job.

'Why should I? I think we'll get on fine.' Outlining her lips, Lucy gave her a sideways glance. 'So, is my job safe?'

'It's as safe as any of our jobs are,' Rose said honestly.

Driving out of the airfield, her predominant emotion was relief at having survived her first day. She had interviewed each member of staff in turn. It had not been necessary for Dan Falconer to tell her to get rid of Wilkinson; if she had had any doubts, his crude remark at the morning meeting would have hardened her resolve: *So now the wife's cracking the whip.* No, she had fired Wilkinson with no regrets and was confident that Dan would do a better job.

Dan Falconer was a good-looking man. He had all the ingredients. You couldn't sit across a desk from him and not notice that he was tall and athletic-looking, or that his dark gold hair, cornflower-blue eyes and regular features made a winning combination. Not that she found him attractive. Looks mattered, but personality, in Rose's view, mattered more, and Dan was a cold fish. He hadn't smiled once during their conversation and nor had he made any expression of friend-liness or encouragement. No *Welcome to the company* or *If there's anything I can do*. He had been closed and guarded, and she had come away from the half-hour with the impression that he had been interviewing her, rather than the other way round.

Nor had Dan batted a beautifully shaped eyelid when she had promoted him. His attention had been focused solely on the business of getting Martineau Aviation back into profit, and for that she was thankful. She needed someone like him to help her find her way through the morass of freight aviation, with its pitfalls and sink holes. If he was cool to the point of iciness, then he should be all the better at the job. An operations manager had to know when to walk away from a deal that might not pay off and when to doggedly pursue a contract that might not, at first, seem possible to win. And Dan Falconer, she guessed, was just her man.

And, anyway, she had not, since the scandal had broken, felt the slightest interest in men, in sex. Robert's betrayal appeared to have killed off that part of her. And thank God for that, because she hadn't a scrap of attention to spare. All her energies must be concentrated on Martineau Aviation and on making sure the children were not upset by the enormous changes taking place in their lives.

They were to move into her grandmother's flat in Weybridge in just over a week. She was meeting Tony Marsh at the flat at nine o'clock on Saturday morning; he had offered to sell her grandmother's effects for her. As soon as possible, she must engage a nanny or mother's help to look after Katherine and Eve, rather than relying on piecemeal arrangements with her father and friends. She must find the girls a new school, because, with the airfield on the other side of Weybridge, she wouldn't have time to drive them to their school in Walton-on-Thames before going to work.

She could not afford to be the sort of boss who came in late and went home early because of family commitments, because that would only reinforce the men's fears and prejudices about working for a woman. Though Robert had often been an absent boss, she must be in the office each day, learning about every part of the business so that she could get it back on track. There were bills to be paid and loans to be serviced, and it was up to her to find a way of making Martineau Aviation survive long enough to turn it round. She had gone through the figures meticulously and they were not encouraging.

After talking to Dan, Rose had telephoned the agent who was handling the lease of the buildings at the airfield. He had promised to call his client and find out whether a reduction in the cost of the lease could be negotiated. Their refusal had been relayed to her an hour later. She had no leverage, Rose concluded. She might have threatened to move to a different site, but what if the leaseholders had called her bluff? Any move would involve costs that Martineau Aviation was unable to pay. The level of upheaval involved would inevitably affect their income stream, which, as Dan had pointed out, was inadequate already. They must stay where they were and find savings elsewhere.

She had cut the wages bill by firing Ted Wilkinson, but it was hard to see further scope for economy. Lucy Holbrook was invaluable and knew the business inside out, and, as

Dan had said, you couldn't economise on air crew or mechanics. The only other employees were Reggie, the caretaker, and Fred, the nightwatchman – both essential on a site which stored valuable goods and equipment and was miles from anywhere.

A close inspection of the company's finances had led to the discovery of all sorts of dismaying things. Robert's golf-club membership had been put through the business, as had his membership of various London clubs. Fees had been paid to various advisers, some of whose names Rose recognised as Robert's cronies. They were paying an agent in Rome who hadn't generated a single contract in more than a year, but who had taken Robert on skiing trips. Martineau Aviation might even have paid for his nights out at the club where he met Debra Peters.

These things tarnished her by association. She had fired Ted Wilkinson for abusing his position, and yet she herself, while nominally in charge of the company, had presided over corrupt business practices. Those expenses would be taken off the books straight away, but she had been left feeling stained by complicity.

In Rose's father's house, Giles and Katherine were halfway through a game of chess. Eve was kneeling at the coffee table, cutting out paper shapes with a pair of plastic scissors. She squawked, seeing Rose come into the room, scrambled to her feet and threw herself into her mother's arms.

Katherine looked up. 'We don't have to go yet, do we, Mum? We're in the middle of a game.'

'There's some shepherd's pie in the oven, keeping warm,' said Giles. 'Why don't you sit down, love, and eat that, while I beat this granddaughter of mine.'

'Grandad!' Katherine glared at him. 'You're not going to win – I am.'

Rose went into the kitchen with Eve balanced on her hip. She ate the shepherd's pie out of the casserole dish, sitting at the table, with her daughter on her knee. Eve's account of her day was sketchy, and mostly relayed in baby language.

Twenty minutes later, as they left the house, Rose murmured, 'Thanks, Dad.'

'We enjoyed ourselves. What will you do with them tomorrow?'

'Abbie's mother offered to take them for the day.' Abbie was Katherine's best friend. 'Robert will pick them up as soon as he's finished work.'

'Let me know if there's anything I can do to help.'

She smiled at him. 'Just put up with me. And let me know if I'm about to do something completely mad.'

Giles, too, smiled. 'Such as proposing to run an aviation business, you mean? I'm so proud of you, Rose.'

She hugged him. 'Thanks, Dad. I was going to ask you if you'd think about coming on the board, but then I thought, not yet.'

'It smacks of nepotism.'

'Yes. And some of the things Robert was doing flew pretty close to the wind. I can't be like that.'

'No, of course not; I see that. But informal advice I may be able to give, if I can and if it's wanted. Anyway, you know where I am, love. You can do this, Rose. I have absolute faith in you.'

They drove back to Walton-on-Thames. Rose had begun to pack for the move to Weybridge and the rooms had taken on a transient, dislocated air, the shelves emptied and pictures gone from the walls, cardboard boxes piled in corners.

Though she had told Robert that she had come to hate the house, leaving her home of the last five years was a heart-breaking business.

She gave the girls a bath, then put Eve to bed and listened to Katherine, in pyjamas and dressing gown, play through her piano pieces. After Katherine went to bed, Rose looked over the notes she had made at work. She was running through the list Lucy had given her of the company's foreign agents when she heard a crash, followed by a loud wail.

She ran upstairs. Eve was standing on the bedroom rug, screaming. Fragments of the shattered ceramic base of her bedside lamp were strewn around her.

'Darling, what happened?' Rose scooped her daughter up in her arms and sat down on the bed.

'I fell off!' Eve was sobbing bitterly.

'Sweetie, what did you fall off?'

'This.' Eve gave the bedside table a punitive kick. 'I wanted to see out of the window. But it was too high, so I climbed on that thing! And I fell off!'

Rose made soothing noises and stroked Eve's dark, curly head. 'Evie, why did you want to look out of the window?'

'I wanted to see if Daddy was coming. I wanted him to say goodnight to me.'

'Oh, darling . . .' All sorts of horrors came into her mind: Eve might have managed to climb on to the sill. She might have opened the window to look for Robert and then fallen out. She might have torn the flex out of the lamp and electrocuted herself.

She got a grip and said gently, 'You'll see Daddy tomorrow. He's coming to take you out to tea and then you're going back to his flat. You'll like that, won't you?'

'I liked it when he *lived* here!'

'I know, sweetheart.'

She cuddled her daughter until she fell asleep in her arms and then tucked her into bed. After she had cleared up the broken fragments of lamp, Rose poured herself a large gin and tonic. Good God, what was she doing? Why on earth had she thought that she would be able to run an aviation company at the same time as looking after two young children? *And* move house?

She went upstairs. She would leave packing up the kitchen and the girls' rooms until last, but she could tackle her own bedroom now. Driven by a mixture of anger and anxiety, she began to sort through her clothes, piling winter coats, jerseys, heavy skirts, boots and jackets into carrier bags and boxes.

The phone rang and she hurried downstairs. She picked up the receiver. It was George, Robert's elder brother.

'Sorry it's taken me a while to get back to you, Rose,' he said. 'I've asked round a few people I know, about Sadie Lawless.'

'That's good of you, George. Did you find anything out?'

'I did, actually. She was a printmaker and a painter. She used to be represented by an art gallery in Jermyn Street.'

Rose sat down on the edge of the desk. 'So she was a proper artist?'

'Yes, very much so. The woman who originally took her on was called Madge Danford. Sadie Lawless was a client of hers, back in the nineteen thirties. Miss Danford died in nineteen sixty-two. She left the business to Nerissa Taylor, who still runs the gallery. It was Miss Taylor that I spoke to. She never met your great-aunt, but apparently Miss Danford often talked about her. And, by the way, Rose, she owns a couple of Sadie Lawless's paintings. I'm more of a nineteenth-century-watercolours man, but I thought they were rather fine. I said you'd call in and have a chat with her.'

'Thank you so much, George.'

''S a pleasure.'

A looseness in his speech made her say, 'George? Are you all right?'

'I'm fine, perfectly fine.'

As Rose pictured her brother-in-law in his flat in Charles Street – volumes of hardback history books on the shelves, brown leather armchairs grouped round a fireplace decorated with delft tiles – Robert's voice echoed: *It looks like a particularly fusty gentlemen's club, somewhere you'd go to die, or if you were half dead already.*

'George,' she said gently, 'are you drunk?' She knew he was a drinker, but he didn't usually let it show.

'Not *drunk*,' he said thoughtfully. 'But not entirely sober. You?'

'Oh, you know.' Her glass was empty. 'Taking the edge off the day. What's wrong?'

'Nothing's wrong.'

George Martineau was an intensely private man. Rose could not recall ever having had a personal conversation with him. They talked about *things*, she and her brother-in-law: an opera he had seen, a book she had read.

'George? Honestly?'

He gave an embarrassed laugh. 'It's terribly mundane, I'm afraid. A broken heart, that's all.'

She tried to disguise her surprise. 'I'm so sorry. I didn't know you had a girlfriend.'

'Oh, Rose, I don't. Never have.'

She must have been more tired than she realised, because it took her a second or two to understand, and then she said, 'Oh.'

'Precisely. Oh.'

'George, I'm sorry; how stupid of me. I didn't know.'

'Why should you? I've been assiduous in keeping my, um, proclivities to myself.'

'Why? It's not against the law now.'

'I dislike being the subject of gossip. It irks me.' A sigh. 'I know you think me a pompous and tiresome fellow.'

'Only sometimes. I'm rather fond of you, actually.'

'Thank you,' he said quietly, adding, 'That means a lot to me.' And then, after a moment, 'But the truth is that I'm afraid I'm far too pompous to subject myself to the sort of comments people make. Though homosexuality may no longer be illegal, that doesn't mean it doesn't still meet with a certain amount of disgust and mockery. Robert, for instance . . . Good old heterosexual, rampaging Robert . . . He'd have a field day.'

'Robert isn't completely insensitive.' For all his faults, Robert was neither a bigot nor a boor. 'I expect he'd make a few silly remarks and then he'd be understanding.'

'You see, I'm not sure I could bear the silly remarks.'

'George, you're not the only one to have kept secrets.'

'No.' His crack of laughter lasted too long. 'It's funny, isn't it? Robert and his prostitute . . . Me and Peter . . . But I know which Father would find easier to bear.' A silence, then he said, 'So, if you wouldn't mind keeping this between the two of us . . . It isn't only family; some of my acquaintances would cut me dead, if they knew.'

Are they acquaintances worth having? she wanted to say, but said, instead, 'Were you together long, you and your friend?'

'Six years.'

As she absorbed this, he went on, 'Peter's the sweetest man. Cultured and intelligent and kind. Not some glamorous, greedy little rent boy, if that's what you were imagining.'

'I wasn't.'

'No. Sorry.' A sigh. 'You must forgive me. He's married, you see. Wife and child. It becomes a strain, living a double life, and . . .' Another silence. 'He decided he couldn't see me any more. I begged him not to do it.' His voice ached with sadness.

'Oh, George, you poor man.'

'I never thought myself capable of self-abnegation, but there you are – one finds these things out. I daresay it'll get better in time. That's what people always say, isn't it?'

'They certainly do.'

'You always were a strong woman, Rose.'

'Was I?' Sometimes she found it hard to remember what she had been before the scandal had broken, before her life had cracked into pieces, leaving her struggling to stick them back together. 'It's easy to be strong if you're not tested.'

'I've always admired your composure. There, that's an unfashionable quality, isn't it? But still, it's one I appreciate.' Over the telephone line, a small, dry laugh. 'What's so galling is that, in spite of everything, one goes on longing for love. Is it over for good between you and Robert?'

'I don't know.' She twisted the telephone flex round her hand. 'Robert doesn't want it to be. It's such a mess, George. Often, I hate him.'

'But not always.'

'No.' The word was a sigh. 'Not always.'

They ended the phone call shortly afterwards. The day's heat had settled within the walls of the house; in the hot, stuffy kitchen she ran herself a glass of water and made another gin and tonic. Then she went back upstairs and checked on the girls.

Eve was sound asleep, one arm wrapped round her toy

174

panda. Rose wondered whether the baby language her daughter had been using earlier indicated that she felt insecure. A hot wave of panic spread over her at the thought of the enormous tasks she had set herself and the disruption she was bringing into her children's lives. But what was the alternative? Give up, give in, remain dependent on Robert, or settle for a job that bored and dissatisfied her.

She wanted her daughters to know that there were options for women other than marriage and motherhood. She wanted them to grow up capable, skilled and independent, both financially and emotionally. She was doing this for herself, yes, but she was doing it for Katherine and Eve too.

She must make yet another list: finish the packing; clear out and clean her grandmother's flat before moving in the furniture from the Walton-on-Thames house; go to the bank and ask them to extend the loans; find a new agent in Marseilles; interview nannies; check out the schools.

'You can do this.' She murmured her father's words aloud. She had to go on believing that. She mustn't ever lose faith. If she didn't believe in herself, why on earth should anyone else?

And yet her panic was quickly followed by the discovery that, in spite of all her concerns, in spite of the awful figures and Ted Wilkinson trying to make a fool of her and the intransigence of the leasehold company, she had enjoyed herself today. Boredom and a sense of futility had evaporated, replaced by excitement at the challenge she had taken on. For the first time in weeks – or months, or even years – she felt truly alive.

She sorted out Katherine's tangle of bedclothes and picked up a book that had fallen to the floor: her daughter's much-loved copy of The Observer's Book of Aircraft. Then she went to

175

her own room and sat down on the bed. Did she hate Robert, as she had said to George? She took a large swallow of gin. Yes, often she did. But the all-consuming anger that had gripped her during the immediate aftermath of the newspaper exposé had begun to fade and was sometimes replaced by sadness. She had lost so much – they had lost so much. It was not even as if she could regret having married him. Marriage had given her Katherine and Eve, who were the best things that had ever happened to her.

She and Robert had been good for a while, she thought. But she hadn't noticed when they had stopped being good. When she looked back, she saw that she had ignored the signals, had gone on far too long kidding herself that everything was fine. And when the sparks had finally burst into flames, the safe, secure existence she had believed to be hers had turned to ashes.

Maybe you were never safe. Maybe what you thought was security was only ever a finely balanced walk along a knife edge. Rose opened the drawers of her bedside table and began to sort through the contents: items to be packed now, items to be packed at the last minute, an old notebook and a stub of ChapStick to be thrown away.

The orange-and-gold folder that contained Sadie Lawless's letters was in the bottom drawer. Her conversation with George rang through her head as she opened it: *some of my acquaintances would cut me dead, if they knew*, he had said. A suspicion, based on her memory of the contents of letters, was forming in her mind. She began to reread them to check it out. *I haven't seen the Chivertons yet. I thought they might call*, Sadie wrote to Edith in her first letter, sent from the Egg, dated October 1930. *Maybe they are away. I imagine them leading very glamorous lives.*

In her next letter, Sadie described a supper at the Gull's Wing: *The sitting room is hardly recognisable. Diana Chiverton seems awfully fond of bright colours. You'd think orange and claret would clash, but it looks rather marvellous.*

In another, written a week later, Sadie appeared to be responding to a criticism of Edith's:

Living at the Egg has forced me to get used to solitude, and isn't that a good thing, as I shall probably live the rest of my life alone? It's all right, Edith; I know I mustn't hide away too much; I know I mustn't become a hermit. But I have to find a purpose. It's possible that I've already done my best work. It happens, you know, to artists. Perhaps whatever I had has burned out and perhaps I need to think of something else to do, something I'll enjoy and find worthwhile. Because, you see, I can't trudge through the remainder of my life with no light or love or passion.

And then, over the page:

I went to lunch at the Gull's Wing again yesterday. It was such fun. Tom and Diana are unconventional, but Diana is a warm and welcoming hostess, and the conversation is never dull when Tom is around. Do you remember the farce we saw at the Aldwych Theatre? The man who played the part of the tennis coach came to lunch. We played charades and he and Tom were frightfully good.

Sadie's next letter described a supper with Tom and Diana Chiverton: *Just me and the Erikssons; a delightful evening. Did you hear Tom's talk on the wireless? It was on Friday evening. I missed it because there's no reception at the Egg. I asked Mr Boxell at the garage, but he says there are too many trees.*

A couple of weeks later, an entire two pages were taken

up with a description of a hike on the Downs with Tom and Diana and another couple, Alma and Martin: *On the way back, it poured!* Sadie finished. *I'd forgotten my hat, but thankfully Tom lent me his sou'wester or I think I'd have drowned. When we reached the Gull's Wing, we all sat round the fire and Ivy brought us jugs of cocoa to warm ourselves up.*

Then there was a gap. It seemed that Sadie had not written again to Edith until 12 December:

> I must tell you about my pupils. Mrs Greene is married to a retired colonel and they live in Nutcombe. She collects different species of snowdrop and hopes to learn to paint them. Then there's Colin Ferrers, who is seventeen years old and cycles over from Crowborough. He wants to go to art college and I hope that he will, because he's really rather talented. I also have my three little girls, Iris, who is eight, and her twin five-year-old sisters, Holly and Heather. They are such fun, but awfully rampaging. I suspect that their mother breathes a sigh of relief as she drives away after leaving them for their art lesson. Ronald Lee is a widower. He's a farmer and a keen ornithologist. He lost his right hand in the war and is trying to learn to draw with his left. My last pupil was quite unexpected. Winnie Thomsett has asked me if she may have art lessons. I'm going to suggest that she and Colin Ferrers share, so I can offer them reduced rates.

And, finally, a few lines about Christmas, which Sadie was to spend with Edith, and an offer that she, Sadie, bring with her some holly branches to decorate the Fullers' house.

Another long gap, this time a month, passed before Sadie wrote to Edith again. There was no reference to Tom and Diana Chiverton in this letter, which was dated 15 January. Nor in the next, nor the one after that. Quickly, Rose skimmed through the remaining letters in the case.

178

Her memory had been correct. Half a dozen letters in which Sadie wrote about little other than her interactions with the Chivertons, and then suddenly they were not mentioned at all. Half a dozen letters in which Sadie gave every impression of looking on Tom and Diana as her new best friends.

And then silence. Why?

'Not a bad market for Indian furniture, right now,' Tony Marsh said, running a hand over the doors of the padouk cabinet. 'Someone'll snap this up.' He flicked his ratty, grey-brown hair out of his eyes as he turned back to Rose. 'I'll take the lot, if you want – the furniture and the decorative objects.'

Rose and Tony were in Edith's flat. Tony and his son, Kevin, were to spend the day clearing it out.

She felt a weight falling from her shoulders. 'Seriously? Even the tiger-skin rug? And that hideous clock?'

'Especially the clock. I'm going to stick it in the shop window. Bet you it'll be gone in a day.' His gaze ran round the room. 'People use these things in boutiques and hotels, for atmosphere. Is there anything you'd like to keep for yourself, Rose?'

'I thought the china. Goodness knows what I'll do with it, but it's rather lovely and it'll remind me of her – our lunches, and Granny telling me stories about India.'

'Kevin will pack it up for you. Then, if you end up storing it, it's already boxed.'

She said with heartfelt gratitude, 'Tony, I can't thank you enough.'

'I've something for you. Kevin!' Tony addressed his son, who was wrapping a pair of soapstone candlesticks in tissue paper. 'Get that lot out to the van.'

Kevin, who was as short and wiry as his father, heaved up an enormous box and carted it out of the room. His footsteps in the corridor faded away.

Tony gave her back the ring she had found at the Egg, along with a scrap of paper.

'I showed it, first, to a guy I know in Hatton Garden,' he said. 'And then I thought of Clara Partridge. It's taken me a while to track her down, because she moves around a lot – can't pay the rent and does a moonlight flit every few months. What Clara doesn't know about antique jewellery could be written on the back of a postage stamp. She was very taken with it. She's written some notes for you.'

Rose opened the piece of paper. The handwriting was large and ill formed.

'She has arthritis,' explained Tony. 'Takes me a while to work out what she's on about.'

Rose read the note. *What do you already know about your ring?* Miss Partridge had written. *That it is very beautiful and very old, I should think. I believe it to date from the late sixteenth century. I'm afraid I can't tell you the name of the jeweller who made it; however, I can tell you about the stones. The bezel is a quincunx of rectangular emeralds.*

'Bezel?' said Rose, looking up at Tony. 'Quincunx?'

'The bezel's this bit.' Tony ran a callused fingertip over the cluster on the front of the ring. 'A quincunx means five stones arranged in that sort of pattern.'

Rose read on. *The hoop is plain gold, approximately nine carats, flat in section and set with nine black diamonds.*

'Diamonds . . .'

'Yeah, black diamonds. Quite unusual.'

'I didn't know there were such things.' She held the ring up to the light. 'They don't sparkle. They're rather beautiful, though, aren't they?'

Rose deciphered the last few sentences of the letter. *There is no more romantic piece of jewellery than a ring*, Clara Partridge had written. *They all have stories to tell, and I'm sure that this one, with its charming and passionate inscription, would, if it could speak, relate a remarkable tale.*

Kevin came back into the room. Rose put the ring on her finger and the note in her bag and hugged Tony. 'Thanks so much. May I pay Miss Partridge for her trouble?'

'How about I find her something she might like here? If that's okay with you. I expect she'd prefer that. This'll take us most of the day. I'll put the keys through your letter box when we've finished, shall I?'

'Please.' She thanked Tony and Kevin and said goodbye, and then made for the railway station.

Katherine and Eve had stayed overnight with Robert in the Chelsea flat in which he was now living. Rose was to collect them later. In the meantime, she was heading for Jermyn Street and the Danford art gallery, which had represented Sadie Lawless during the 1930s.

She took a bus from Waterloo to Piccadilly Circus and then walked the short distance to Jermyn Street. On a Saturday morning, London was hot, dusty and busy. Red double-decker buses ploughed slowly down Piccadilly, belching out black fumes, and the sky was a hard blue, hazed with heat above the tallest buildings.

The elegant grey-and-white exterior of the Danford Gallery slotted neatly into its surroundings, bracketed by a smart restaurant on one side and a menswear shop on the other. Inside, the gallery was a clean, white, airy oblong. A series of works by Graham Sutherland hung on the walls – swirls of grey and black, green and chartreuse.

A very young and very beautiful girl slouched behind a desk. She looked up briefly at Rose before returning to thumbing through her magazine. Approaching the desk, Rose asked to speak to Nerissa Taylor. The girl swiped her long hair out of her eyes, picked up a phone and said, sulkily and inaccurately, 'Nerissa, there's a Mrs Martin to see you.'

A woman in her forties, whose striking, narrow, angular face was framed by thick brown curls, appeared through the rear door of the gallery. She was wearing a sleeveless midi-dress of chestnut-coloured crêpe.

'Hello; I'm Nerissa Taylor. May I help you?'

'My name's Rose Martineau.' Rose offered her hand. 'My brother-in-law, George Martineau, spoke to you the other day. He came here on my behalf. I'm Sadie Lawless's great-niece.'

Nerissa Taylor's hazel eyes sparkled. 'Then you're very welcome. I'm delighted to meet you, Mrs Martineau.'

'Rose, please. I've been trying to find out whatever I can about Sadie. George told me that your gallery used to represent her.'

'Back in the thirties, yes. May I offer you a coffee?' Nerissa addressed the girl at the desk. 'Heidi, two coffees, please.' She turned back to Rose. 'I never met Sadie Lawless. She was years before my time. Madge thought her a very fine artist, though. Sadie was one of the first clients she took on, back in the early days.'

'Do you know exactly when that was?'

'Madge represented Sadie from nineteen thirty-one . . . maybe thirty-two. She thought her awfully underrated.' An open-handed gesture: *You know how it is.* 'It was hard for women, back then. I could name you half a dozen very talented female artists who were similarly overlooked. And

182

then, of course, her body of work is limited. An artist may have to work for a decade to build up a reputation.'

'And Sadie didn't?'

'I'm afraid not. The Danford Gallery put on a couple of exhibitions for her. The first was in November nineteen thirty-three, the second in October nineteen thirty-four, which is an extraordinary burst of creativity, if you think about it. Several of the artists we represent show once every five years — a few, once in a decade. To have produced such a volume of high-calibre work in less than a year is impressive. But then, afterwards, there was nothing more.'

'Why not?'

Heidi came back with a tray and put it on the desk. Nerissa poured out two coffees and handed one to Rose. 'Do help yourself to sugar and cream,' she said. 'You don't know, then?'

'About what?'

'About Sadie failing to turn up for her second exhibition.'

Rose added cream to a small blue ceramic cup. 'I didn't know she existed until a few months ago. My grandmother died and I inherited her flat, and when I was sorting her things out, I found some letters from Sadie. Up till then, I didn't even know my grandmother had a sister. She never mentioned her.'

Nerissa made another little sweeping gesture. 'Families . . .'

'I think they must have quarrelled.'

Sadie, the baby of the family, might have been her father's favourite. It wasn't hard to imagine prickly, oversensitive Edith succumbing to jealousy and falling out with her younger sister. Several of Sadie's letters hinted at a disagreement between them.

She said, 'How d'you mean, she didn't turn up for the exhibition?'

'Madge used to like to put on a private view, a day or two before an exhibition opened – by invitation only, for critics and reviewers, and friends and relations, of course. Well, everyone came except Sadie.'

Rose stared at her. 'She didn't turn up for her own private view?'

Nerissa took a sip of coffee. 'You can imagine how tricky that was. The star of the show, failing to turn up.'

'Do you know why?'

Nerissa shook her head. 'Madge never found out.'

'I don't understand. Did she get cold feet?'

'Sadie had no reason to be nervous. The reviews were good.'

Rose thought hard. Why would a talented young woman, who must have fought hard to have her work taken seriously, not come to her own private view?

'Might she have moved to another gallery?'

'I don't think so. Our business is a small world. Everyone knows everyone and I'm sure that, if Sadie had gone else-where, Madge would have heard about it.'

'But she must have said *something* . . .'

'Madge never saw or heard from her again. No phone call, no letter, no explanation. It was the end of their relationship. Sadie simply broke off all contact.'

'How extraordinary.' And troubling, Rose reflected.

'Madge wondered whether it had all been too much for her and she couldn't cope. Success brings its own problems. Madge always worried that she'd put too much pressure on her. She thought Sadie might have fallen ill again.'

Nerissa was hinting that Sadie may have had another breakdown. Was that what had happened to her, back in October 1934? Might she have suffered a recurrence of her illness and been incarcerated in some dire institution, and then hidden away and forgotten about, because, at that time, mental illness had been considered shameful. If so, what an awful fate.

Rose said, 'Do you know what date the private view was held?'

'It was the sixteenth of October. Madge kept a catalogue.' Nerissa tucked a brown curl behind her ear. 'As an artist, Sadie Lawless is largely forgotten now. I've always thought that rather a tragedy. I own two of her paintings. Madge left them to me. Would you like to see them?'

'Yes, very much.'

Nerissa addressed the young woman at the desk. 'Heidi, I'm going up to the flat. If Jonathan turns up, let me know straight away.'

A door in the corridor behind the gallery led to a narrow flight of stairs. The high-ceilinged rooms of the flat above the gallery, with their ornate cornices and architraves, were attractively furnished in soft rose-pinks and dull greens.

'This is where Madge used to live,' said Nerissa. 'I haven't changed much; she had such marvellous taste.' She indicated two paintings that hung on the wall opposite the large sash windows. 'They're oils,' she said. 'Sadie Lawless was better known as a printmaker, but she was a very fine landscape painter as well. I've always thought the most remarkable aspect of her work was her use of colour. She was a wonderful colourist, capable of a very varied palette.'

The disturbance Rose experienced, looking at the paintings, was because she felt for the first time that she was seeing the real Sadie Lawless. Before, Sadie had existed theoretically – a puzzle to be solved, a mystery to be unravelled. These pictures spoke to Rose as if Sadie herself had stepped into the room and tapped her on the shoulder.

185

Both paintings were landscapes. The first, the more abstract, was made up of bands of intense colour, yellows and purples and indigos, which made Rose think of sunlit fields beneath a sky of pounding blue. It pulsed with life. The other painting depicted a hot, dry terrain, baked to red dust by the sun, the earth the colour of fire: a landscape on the verge of bursting into flames. The mountains that rose grey-violet in the distance were a dream of coolness and shade. Or they were a mirage, a false promise conjured up by the relentless heat.

Nerissa indicated the first landscape. 'This one, *Lavender Fields*, was painted in Provence. The other's my favourite, though. It's beautiful, but ominous, don't you think? It's one of Sadie's Spanish paintings. It dates from nineteen thirty-three.'

Among the rust-coloured rocks and plains of the second painting, Rose made out a dash of black and white. Might it be a figure? If so, who was it? A companion of Sadie's? Or a lover? Or even a self-portrait? When she moved closer, the image dissolved into dabs and streaks, meaningless and fragmentary.

Rose asked Nerissa another question. 'Did Madge ever mention Tom and Diana Chiverton?'

Nerissa raised her eyebrows. 'Tom Chiverton, the poet?'

'Yes. They lived near Sadie, in Sussex.'

'No, not that I remember.'

A voice called up the stairs. 'Nerissa, Jonathan's here!'

'I'm so sorry; I have a customer. I'm afraid you must excuse me, Rose.'

Rose took a card out of her handbag. 'If you remember anything else, anything at all, please phone me. And thank you so much for your time, Nerissa. It's been so helpful.'

186

Out in the street, the glare of the sun seemed to burn her eyes after the cool interior of the gallery, and she scrabbled in her bag for her sunglasses. She considered what Nerissa Taylor had told her. Sadie had been a talented artist and yet she had failed to turn up for her second exhibition. Madge Danford had neither seen nor heard of her protégée afterwards and had wondered whether Sadie had suffered another breakdown. A phrase from Sadie's last letter to Edith rang in Rose's memory: *I don't want to live here any more; it frightens me, and besides, it was wrong of Father to give it to me — I see that now.* What had Sadie become afraid of, living at the Egg? Had her fear had a rational cause?

Sadie's private view had been held on 16 October 1934, but Sadie herself had not attended it. The last of the letters to Edith had been written the day before, on 15 October. Constance Meyrick, in Cambridge, had said that she lost touch with Sadie at much the same time.

A pattern had formed, one that perplexed and baffled Rose, and in spite of the hot, close day, she felt a chill inside her and found herself running her thumb over the bezel of the emerald ring as she headed off towards Robert's flat in Chelsea.

Chapter Nine

A strong wind had blown the last of the leaves from the trees that surrounded the Egg, and now they butted up against Sadie's bedroom window. The broom rasped against the asphalt as Sadie, who was standing on the lower of the two roofs, swept them into a heap. Gold and brown, crimson and russet, they tumbled over the edge before being caught up by a gust of wind, dancing like a flock of sparrows, then floating to the ground.

More than a week had passed since Tom had kissed her. She had seen neither of the Chivertons since, had only, once or twice, heard the clop of a horse's hooves on the sunken lane and glimpsed a red-gold dog snaking through box and hawthorn. By now, Tom would be regretting the kiss or he would have forgotten it. It had been the product of his rage and frustration at the obstacles that kept him from doing the work he loved. He had kissed her because he had been angry and he was the sort of man who liked to translate anger into action.

As for her, she must keep busy, must suppress the memory of Tom's mouth on hers and his hand on the small of her

188

back as he pressed her body against his. She must contemplate the guilt that accompanied her memories and crush the desire. It was hard, though. The mind scolded while the body yearned.

She stepped back into the bedroom, closing the glass doors behind her. As the afternoon darkened to evening, the storm intensified and, now and then, a branch struck the flat roof of the Egg, its impact echoing through the sitting room. Rain beat against the windows, blurring and distorting the shapes of the trees.

It was, at first, hard to distinguish the hammering on the front door from the clamour of the wind and rain, but finally she hurried into the hall and opened it.

Tom Chiverton was swathed in a mackintosh and his features were shadowed by the brim of his sou'wester. Behind him, the bare branches of the trees flailed.

'May I come in, Sadie?'

What could she say? *No, Tom, you must stand on the doorstep, getting wet.* As she let him into the house, her stomach clenched.

He stripped off his hat and rainwater trailed from his flattened black curls. 'The damned train was late leaving Victoria,' he said impatiently. 'I thought it would be quicker to walk up the sunken lane, but it's like a quagmire. Diana's taken the car. She's in Devon, with Maurice, at the nursing home.'

Sadie remembered Maurice, Diana's brother, the dark-haired boy who had driven away in the Delage motor car. 'Is Maurice ill?'

Tom scowled. 'We haven't told you, have we? Maurice was in a motor accident. He was rather smashed up.'

'Tom, I'm so sorry,' she said, shocked. She took his dripping mackintosh and hung it on a peg. 'How awful. Is he terribly hurt?'

'He's broken his leg and a rib or two. It was his fault; he

drives like a madman. Diana is administering chocolate and grapes. I had some books sent down from Foyles.'

It seemed gracious and necessary for her to say, 'Come and dry yourself by the fire.'

He took a package out of his mackintosh pocket and offered it to her. 'I hope you'll accept this, Sadie, along with my apologies.'

As she unpeeled the brown paper, her face burned. She saw that Tom had given her a bottle of French brandy.

'Tom, there was no need.'

'I'd hate to think there was any bad feeling between us. Have you forgiven me, Sadie?'

'Please, forget it. But thank you; this is kind of you.'

He followed her into the sitting room. 'What a week. My God, I could do with a drink.'

His figure seemed brooding and monumental in the small room, as if he had brought in with him the blackness of the stormy night outside. The scarcely contained emotion she had glimpsed in the hall, he expressed in the clenching and unclenching of his fists.

'There hasn't been a moment,' he said, 'what with Diana so worried about Maurice and all the wretched meetings with my publishers because of the American tour.'

'You're going ahead with it?'

'Yes.' A shake of his shaggy, wet, leonine head. 'Edwin believes it will make my reputation in the States.'

'When will you leave?'

'We sail in the middle of January.' A quick, angry gesture, raking back the hair that had flopped over his forehead. 'Six weeks out of my life, damn it.'

Sadie fetched two glasses. When she came back into the room, Tom was still standing at the window.

'It's a fine room,' he said. For the first time, he smiled. 'Your view surpasses even ours, Sadie. I have a confession to make. I was walking in the woods one day and I couldn't resist having a look inside the house. It was a long time ago, before you came to live here. A housebreaker once taught me how to turn a lock with a hairpin, and I was curious to see inside. I feel a certain connection to it. I think of the Egg as the little sister to the Gull's Wing.'

He spoke casually, as if what he had told her was of no import, and yet the discovery that Tom had been in the Egg without her knowing disturbed her. His actions seemed rash, his confession equally so, almost as if he was claiming an intimacy – or possession.

'Housebreaking, Tom,' she said with a touch of irony. 'You have so many talents. But there's not much of a view here. From the Gull's Wing, you can see for miles.'

'The Egg is a part of the forest. You might be living in a burrow or a foxhole. It's quite marvellously primeval.'

'Primitive,' she said dryly, 'might be a better word. When I've run out of paraffin or the electricity cuts out, all I care about is keeping warm and having enough light to get by.'

He sat down beside her. She was aware of his proximity; he brought with him the scent of rainwater and fresh air.

'I'd happily spend a month becoming acquainted with a single acre of land,' he said. 'I despise those artists and writers who feel they have to travel the world in search of inspiration. One should learn to understand one's own landscape first. I believe we lack vigour – masculinity, even – when we end up moving constantly from place to place. If we lose our connection with the land and the soil, we lose our past.' He laughed, tipping back his head to display his thick, muscular throat. 'You must forgive me again, Sadie. Diana calls it my back-to-the-land speech.'

'You were born here, weren't you?'

'On the Hampshire side of the Downs, yes. Nationality – homeland – matters. Not in a narrow or small-minded sense, but a man's love of his own soil is bred into him.' He reached for the brandy bottle and filled their glasses. 'Be honest with me. You feel the same, don't you?'

'I was born in Hampstead. Hardly a rural paradise.'

'The Heath has a certain grandeur, though. Has this land been in your family for long?'

'No, not at all.' As she related the story of how Edward Lawless had bought the land in Paley High Wood, the knot of tension beneath her ribs remained. 'My father was driving back to London one day when he saw the for-sale sign. He told me that he parked the car and walked round the wood and, before an hour had passed, he'd decided to buy the land and build the two houses.'

'I don't suppose you'd ever be able to sell this place.'

'No, never.'

'I'll take care of the Gull's Wing for you, Sadie – I promise.'

When he looked at her in that way, when his fathomless eyes seemed to contain her with him in their darkness, the core of detachment and resistance melted inside her. She murmured something, afraid that his effect on her might be evident to him.

'The house is my sanctuary, my citadel,' he said. 'Before we bought the Gull's Wing, Diana and I were living in London, in Holborn, and it was destroying me. I hadn't written anything decent for months. The noise of the city, the stench of smoke and petrol, and, of course, the people, who won't leave you alone, who insist on having a piece of

192

you – it was impossible. And then I came here and walked in the woods each night, and in less than three months I had all the poems for *Lunar.*'

Sadie tucked a leg beneath her. 'I wish it would work its magic on me. My output's been dismally meagre. Most of what I've done has ended up in the fire.'

'We all go through lean periods.'

She hunched her shoulders. 'I'd rather you two had the house than anyone else. I can tell that you understand its magic. And Diana's made it look so beautiful.'

'The bright colours reflect her personality. Diana's a strong, passionate woman, and I admire that, although it can be . . . it can be . . .'

He did not finish his sentence and his look of desolation disconcerted her. She touched his arm. 'Tom, what is it?'

'It can be claustrophobic.' The clink of bottle spout on glass, then the rasp of a match being struck. 'But I hate myself for saying that,' he said softly. 'I hate myself even for thinking it. Without Diana, I would be nothing. She's the guardian of my peace and privacy, and she's indispensable to my career.'

She said hesitantly, 'I've never been married, but isn't there always a tension between our needs for freedom and companionship?'

He expelled a plume of smoke. 'Our marriage has always been a very public one. When my readers think of me, they think of Diana too. When a newspaper or journal writes about me, they write about her too. We sit beside each other at the dinner table and we dance in each other's arms at parties. My public may love me, but they also love Diana. She is capable of a depth of passion and intensity that I've rarely encountered in anyone else. For her, it's simple. She and I are one.'

Perhaps she shouldn't say it. Perhaps she should turn the conversation to less intimate matters – the weather, or the teetering British economy. Yes, that was what she should do.

Yet she said, 'But it's not so simple for you, Tom.'

'No.' His mouth gave a rueful twist. He was looking out of the window, his handsome profile backlit by the glow of the table lamp. When he spoke, it was so quietly, Sadie had to lean towards him to hear. 'Sometimes I can't breathe.'

'You love Diana,' she said gently. 'I can tell that you do.'

He pressed the heels of his hands against his forehead. 'But not *exclusively*. I'm incapable of that. I can't bind myself, Sadie. That's how it is with women, and that's how it is with my work. Poetry will always be my first love, and yet not to experience the exhilaration of attempting other forms would drive me insane. I demand to experiment and explore, because I shall die if I don't. Is that wrong of me?'

'No, no.' Who was she to condemn – she, who was thirty years old and had not yet settled to either a marriage or a career? 'Not at all.'

'I hoped you'd understand.'

What a relief it was to converse with a man who comprehended the conflicts and trickeries of the heart! What a pleasure to know that she might confess her own missteps and humiliations to this man, knowing that she would be understood, and not judged. Tom Chiverton made a living from writing about the terrible risks of love, and the irrationality of it.

'I thought I'd found the man I'd love for the rest of my life,' she said. 'I was wrong, though.'

'Did you love him, Sadie?'

'Oh, immensely.'

'Then you must never regret it. There are a great many

people who go through their entire lives without feeling real love even once.'

As he spoke, he gripped her hand. She felt the warmth of his fingers, rough skinned – those of a man who worked the land. She did not pull away, had not the strength of will. Her body, starved of human contact for so long, ached for his touch. She wanted him to take her in his arms; she wanted it so much it was unbearable.

But it was Tom who drew away. He picked up his glass. 'Here, we should drink the whole damned bottle.'

He sloshed more brandy into their glasses, then fumbled in his jacket pocket for his packet of Gold Leaf. He offered it to her and Sadie took a cigarette. As she leaned towards him so that he could light it, he gave a groan and stroked back the curtain of hair from her face. At his caress, a violent shiver ran through her and she tilted up her mouth to kiss him.

She had forgotten how desire could rush through you like an electrical charge, making the senses possess a greater acuity than ever before. The scent of his hair and skin as he unbuttoned her blouse was heady and intoxicating, and the taste of him – salt and tobacco and the lingering sweetness and fieriness of the brandy – acted like a narcotic, so that she forgot everything else. She was kicking off her shoes and he was tugging off her skirt and there was a fleeting moment when she remembered the uncurtained window and felt exposed and shamed, but as his voice coaxed her, murmuring soft endearments, inhibition fell away and, as he moved against her, she rose up to meet him. Then he was inside her and she could think of nothing but the pleasure that burned and expanded, filling her body until she cried out for more. Beneath skin, muscle and bone, his heart beat against hers, and as she drew in breath, he did also. There came a moment when she closed her eyes, seized by a delight so intense it was almost intolerable. Outside, the storm still howled, but she no longer heard it.

Sometime in the night, Tom must have risen and fetched a blanket from the bedroom; waking the next morning, Sadie felt its weight on her – and the heat of his body, and his encircling arm, and his palm, cradling her breast.

When, eventually, they had fallen asleep, they had lain together on the sofa. For the first time since she had come to live at the Egg, she had slept through the night without waking.

She opened her eyes. The glass, framing the trees. The branches limp now, the storm blown out. The terrace discoloured and blighted by fallen leaves and twigs. Their clothes, scattered on the tiles. The brandy bottle, almost empty, and the glasses, with their sticky residue.

And a sour taste in her mouth. Her head ached. What had she done? Desire had dwindled, and now not a flicker of it was recoverable. Instead, she felt only regret and shame. She did not love him. She did not even like him all the time.

She shuffled to a sitting position, pulling up the blanket to cover her breasts. She heard him chuckle. 'Awake at last, little Sadie. I've been watching you for an age. I didn't want to disturb you.'

He kissed the nape of her neck, then rose and went to stand at the window, facing out. She realised that he was studying his reflection in the window, admiring the duplication of his naked body against the dripping trees. A hand ran over a haunch, then he raised his arms above his head, stretching his muscles, puffing out his chest.

It was his flaunting pose as much as what he said next that made her regret magnify and burn till it scorched her.

'I could never leave Diana. It would ruin my career.'

His words were jarring and ugly, and her automatic response – 'Tom, I would never expect you to' – was received, she saw, with relief. There was no good slant she could put on his statement, no way of convincing herself that what he had said was not self-serving, that he had not meant what she knew he had meant: though he might choose to give, she must never demand.

'I knew you'd understand,' he said. 'Darling Sadie.' He bestowed on her the full power of his smile.

The assumptions he was making, the rules he was spelling out, and the vision she guessed him to be imagining of her role in his future, scoured her. Why had she not seen the truth about this preening, naked man in her sitting room before? Why had it taken her so catastrophically long? What a fool she had been – what a naive, greedy little fool. She rose from the sofa.

'What are you doing?' he said.

'Getting dressed.' Her fingers fumbled, picking up her underclothes.

'Diana's away. We have all day.'

'Tom, you have to go.'

'Don't be a silly girl,' he said indulgently.

She moved away, putting the sofa between them, buttoning up her skirt. 'Tom, you need to go. Anyone might come by. Anyone might see us.'

He laughed. 'You shouldn't be afraid.'

'I'm not afraid.' Though she was. 'I want you to go.' She looked up, meeting his gaze. 'Surely you see how wrong it was?'

197

'I don't believe in denying passion. I assumed you felt the same.' There was irritation in his voice, as if he thought she was being unreasonable.

She had buttoned up her blouse the wrong way; she started again, but her hands fell away, the fiddly pearl buttons half fastened.

She looked up at him. 'You're making it sound as if desire excuses everything, Tom. As if it overrides all those important, essential things, like faithfulness and loyalty and devotion. But it doesn't. Passion is just something we feel, like hunger or thirst or the cold. It's not a . . . a *pretext* that makes it all right to hurt people.'

'I've no intention of hurting anyone. I thought I'd made that clear.'

'But we will — surely you see that?' She swiped back her tangled hair from her face. 'In a moment, you're going to say that it'll be absolutely fine, as long as we're careful. But I don't want *that* . . . what you seem to think I want. I don't want some furtive hole-in-the-corner affair. That's what women like me get offered, but, actually, I've realised that I don't want it. So, put on your clothes, Tom, and just go.'

'I hadn't thought you a prude.'

'I'm not. Or, if I am, I don't care. Actually, I'm appalled at myself. Yes, that's about it. Appalled.'

'Why are you spouting this claptrap?' He flung out his hands.

His form, majestic on horseback or running through the woods, had become to her ridiculous in the mundane domestic situation of her sitting room.

'It's what I believe,' she said quietly.

'You love as I love. I know that you do.'

She recognised his tone of voice — low, throbbing and

emotional. She had heard him apply it when reading a verse of a poem.

She said coolly, 'No, I don't think I do.'

'Rot. I simply don't believe that you're not attracted to me.'

His conceit, his unlimited self-assurance, made her laugh aloud. Anger flared across his face and it was then that he began to pull on his shirt. She almost felt sorry for him – had any woman ever punctured his vanity before? She suspected not.

She was fully dressed now, except for her stockings – ridiculous limp, black objects that had unaccountably taken up residence beneath the table, like oversized slugs. She stuffed them in her pocket; they embarrassed her.

'If I love again,' she said quietly, 'I want it to be with a man who feels as I do, who cares about love as I do. I want it to be with a man who'll treat love carefully and kindly and understand how it can sear. Love isn't just passion, Tom. There's respect and there's admiration and gentleness and generosity. There's no place for self-esteem, nor for self-preservation.'

'Do you think I don't know that?' He was dressed now, his jacket slung over a shoulder, his features contorted by feeling. 'What right do you have to set yourself up as my judge and jury? What you think you want isn't what you truly want, Sadie. I know you better than you know yourself. I saw the real Sadie last night; I saw the yearning, passionate woman and not this cruel, merciless creature you pretend to be.' Then he strode out of the room.

Moments later, the door slammed and Sadie was on her own again. She moved around, plumping a cushion here, straightening a pile of books there, as if by doing so she could tidy away the events of the previous night and make them neat and orderly. But her movements felt clumsy and ill coordinated. She had invited Tom Chiverton into her house and had drunk his brandy, when she had known what he was. She had let one thing lead to another, when she had known how wrong it was and how utterly she was betraying Diana, who had been kind to her.

What she had done made her as shallow and thoughtless as Felix, as Dahlia Knight, and she knew that the ramifications of what had taken place the night before might be unstoppable. What if Diana were somehow to find out what had happened? The possibility was too awful to contemplate. Tom might be practised at covering his tracks – she suspected he was – but even if Diana were to remain ignorant of their coupling, another punishment was in store for her. Every time she looked out of a window, she would do so knowing that she might see Tom or Diana walking down the track. Every footstep she heard, every sound of a voice in the trees, might belong to the man she had slept with or the woman she had betrayed. Every invitation to the Gull's Wing, every smile, would bring with it a burden of guilt.

For him, it would be easier, she suspected. She was not stupid enough to think she had been Tom Chiverton's first lover. All the women she had met at the Gull's Wing had been young and good-looking. The old and the unattractive weren't welcome there. Someone like Tom, who was handsome, talented and famous, could have his pick of pretty girls. He had spoken to her of his doubts about marriage and the artificial constraints it imposed – how much plainer could he have been?

His celebrity must give him opportunity. It was easy to imagine Tom at a book signing, scrawling his name on the title page of *Lunar*, then looking up and allowing his female readers to luxuriate in the warmth of his smile. They, like her, would make the mistake of believing that the man they found in the pages of *Lunar* was the man they saw before them. But he was not, and, to be fair, he had never pretended otherwise.

Diana's tragedy was that she would never be first in Tom's heart. He loved Diana, in his way, but it was a divided love, tormented, torn and ambiguous, because, for Tom, his work would always come first. Sadie might have found some comfort in this, because it meant that she had only ever taken up a small fraction of his attention, had that sort of reasoning not inclined her to dislike herself even more.

In the kitchen, putting on the kettle to make tea, she recalled the phrase she had glimpsed scribbled on a scrap of paper in the Gull's Wing: *The absolution of desire.* Tom was wrong, though. Desire did not absolve you from its consequences; responsibility remained. You always knew what you were doing. You only chose to ignore the voice that told you to turn away.

One possible consequence of the night haunted her: she might be pregnant. She didn't think she was; she thought the timings were wrong, though her knowledge of such things was hazy. She heated up water in the geyser and ran as deep a bath as she could. Then she pulled off her clothes again and soaked for an hour, hoping to dislodge anything that might have gained a hold inside her.

Shame and guilt could not be dislodged, however. Her generation had had to shape their own morality in response to the carnage of the Great War. Everyone needed love and you found it where you could. So, some of her friends had married men who were crippled or blinded, and others loved

201

women and found happiness there. Others still had adopted a child that needed a home. Some, like Pearl, had affairs with married men. Sadie herself had slept with married men in the past, the sort who complained that their wives were unfaithful to them or were only interested in their children. She might have felt justified in having a little piece – a little, borrowed piece – of what other women took for granted. She might have felt angry and vengeful – why shouldn't she, she who had been denied the lasting comforts of husband and children, at least know pleasure?

But nothing excused what she had just done, she thought, as she lay hot and anxious in the soapy water. Nothing made it even the littlest bit all right. Tom and Diana had invited her into their home and she had dined at their table. In stealing what belonged to her hostess, she had betrayed an ancient rule of hospitality. She did not, now that she thought it over, feel that Diana had ever much liked her – but then she had seen Diana betray few signs of true warmth towards the other women who came to the Gull's Wing. Diana loved Tom. All her deep feelings were for Tom. Other women – the young, beautiful women who were her guests in the house – threatened her.

Tom had come to Sadie's house to seduce her and she had allowed herself to be seduced. She had made it easy for him, had taken him, literally, in her open arms.

You love as I love, he had said, but that was not true. Diana would accompany Tom to the States next month; on the surface, the Chivertons' perfect marriage, in all its hidden complexities, would go on as before.

Emotion had destabilised her in the past. With Felix, she had experienced the fierce power of love, how it can shift you from grief to joy and plunge you back into grief again.

202

She had chosen to shut herself away in the Egg because she had become afraid of the person, peeled and raw, that she was. As she climbed out of the cooling water, she knew that she needed to change, to make herself into something different, or she would be fated to go on making the same old mistakes for ever. She must find a way of living at peace with both her head and her heart, however difficult and lonely that might be.

If she ever loved a man again, she must respect and admire him wholeheartedly. He must be honest, principled and generous, and capable of putting other people before himself. Better to die a spinster, scraping a living from her art, than to settle for less. Better to put all her energies into what she could influence and change, into what she could create. Do something, do anything, but force herself through whatever barriers were preventing her from making anything of worth.

She dried herself and dressed. She took her sketch pad and pencils outside and sat on the terrace, drawing the twigs and lengths of ivy that the wind had slung on the boards. When she had completed a dozen sketches, she went back to her studio and began to cut out the first block for a new print. By the time the light was too poor to see clearly, she knew that, though it wasn't good yet, there was at least the possibility that it might become so.

Snowflakes danced, as small as pearl buttons, so light they seemed incapable of sinking through the air. As the day lengthened, the snow thickened, clumps of it as puffy as thistledown. There was a strange stillness, and the birds had hidden themselves away, so that only the fast-falling snow-flakes moved, blotting out the sections of sky trapped between the branches.

Waking one morning, she found her bedroom plunged into a chilly gloom. A crust of snow, several inches deep, butted against the windows of the house and curved from the eaves. She wrapped a blanket round her shoulders and went to stand at the window. The snow had spread itself, smooth as wedding-cake icing, over the flat roof. She pushed the glass door open, forcing back the compacted snow, and stepped outside. Her bare feet stung as they sketched a frozen path across the crystalline surface.

She heard voices. People were walking down the sunken lane, the cold muffling their chatter and laughter. From her perch, she saw, through the branches of the trees, the Vizslas, swooping and darting. They had the look of wolves, she thought. She wondered whether someone would call in, and she stood, half expecting Diana to emerge from the trees. But the sounds faded, and she went back into the house.

A few days later, a thaw set in. As Sadie emerged from the path on to the road, the woodland was alive with the drip-drip of melting snow. That morning, she was to catch the train to London, and Edith's house. She was to stay with her sister for just under a fortnight, until after New Year.

The sound of a motor car heading towards her made her look up. Recognising the Chivertons' Wolseley, she stepped on to the bank and raised a hand in greeting.

The car sped past her. She watched it disappear round the bend. Tom had been at the wheel, Diana in the passenger seat. They could not have failed to see her; they must have seen her and her suitcase and her shopping bag of holly on the verge beside her. Yet they had not stopped to offer her a lift. They had not even acknowledged her.

So, she had been dropped; she had suspected it already.

She picked up her case and walked down the hill. Perhaps Diana had found out what had happened. Perhaps someone, some servant of the Chivertons, had been passing that night and had looked through the window and seen them. Or perhaps Tom had taken offence at her rejection of him and had confessed to Diana, some slanted version. The Chivertons might have an arrangement: Tom played the field, Diana put up with it – something like that. Men had it their own way, by and large, and it was possible that Diana, who loved Tom above everything, had come to the conclusion that putting up with her husband's infidelities was a price worth paying. Though there was a simpler explanation: that she had bored them, that she had not come up to scratch.

Hearing the train's whistle, she hurried the remainder of the way to the station. It occurred to her, as she waved to the station master and rushed into the ticket office, that she, too, had had her reservations. They had not been made for each other, she and Tom and Diana, and any attraction between them had been fleeting. She regretted the ease with which she had given herself to them and the neediness that had made her lose her judgement so absolutely. As the train pulled out of the station, she was aware of an intense relief, knowing that she would soon be back in the city.

Sadie went to a New Year party in Garratt Lane, a long street that meandered through Tooting, Earlsfield and Wandsworth, in south London. Tobacconists and pharmacists jostled against advertising hoardings and cheap boarding houses offering beds at a shilling a night. A cloth-capped cats'-meat man pushed his barrow up and down the road, calling out his wares.

Sadie was looking for a flat belonging to Dulcie Clarke, a

friend of Pearl's, whose party it was. She found it above a funeral parlour, the window of which was decorated with dusty-looking artificial lilies and a photograph of a hearse pulled by four black-plumed horses.

She rang the bell. When there was no reply, she tried the door and found it open.

A voice from above called out, 'Do come up!' so she climbed the stairs. The landing door gave into a modestly sized room. Guests were chatting and laughing; in a corner, people were dancing to the music of a piano, played by a young woman wearing a jade-green turban. There were far more women in the room than men.

A fair-haired young woman in a blue paisley smock approached Sadie. 'Hello; who are you?'

'I'm Sadie Lawless, Pearl Foster's friend. She invited me.'

The fair-haired woman scanned the room. 'I don't think Pearl's here yet. My name's Vee Evans.'

They shook hands and Vee offered her a glass of cider.

'Thanks. Perhaps I should say hello to Miss Clarke. Could you tell me who she is?'

'That's her, in the grey dress.' Vee's gaze slid to the far side of the room, to a petite woman whose dark hair was tied back with a scarlet scarf. 'She's in an awfully bad mood because she's quarrelled with Hugh. And when Dulcie's in a huff, everyone knows about it. So I should chat to us, if I were you.'

'I didn't see you at the meeting, Vee.' A thin, pale man came to stand at Vee's shoulder. He wore spectacles; behind them, his eyes shone with unnatural brilliance.

'I had to sit with Mum.' Vee explained to Sadie, 'She's bedridden. Me and my sisters, we take turns. How did it go?'

'Wal Hannington spoke.'

'Oh, typical; trust me to miss him!'

'It's a shame you couldn't come. He had it spot on, as usual. The financiers and profiteers who caused the crash are going on doing what they've always done, piling up the shekels, while the unemployed pay for their mistakes. Children are going shoeless and hungry, while the wealthy dine at the Ritz.' The burning gaze focused on Sadie. 'Who's this?'

'I'm Sadie Lawless.'

'I haven't seen you here before.'

'She's a friend of Pearl's, Arthur,' said Vee, rubbing his arm. 'She's not a police spy. We're communists,' she explained to Sadie. 'They put poor Arthur in prison, so he thinks everyone is a police spy.'

'I'm not, honestly,' said Sadie.

Arthur took a pipe from his pocket, stuffed tobacco into the bowl, and then coughed horribly for a long time. When he could speak again, he said, 'Vee's talking nonsense. But we have to be careful. They keep us under surveillance.'

A couple joined them and a heated discussion ensued about the organisation of the next hunger march. The girl in the jade-green turban was playing the tango, 'Jalousie', and two women were dancing together, their movements measured and exquisite. Some guests seated near Sadie were talking in an animated way about their jobs working for a magazine, telling funny stories about their colleagues.

Perched on the arm of a chair, drinking cider, Sadie felt relieved at having escaped the formality of Edith's home. Christmas with Edith and Cyril had been a strain; she had felt it, and so had Edith, Sadie suspected. These were her people, these waifs and strays and misfits; this was where she belonged.

Seeing Pearl at the door, she went to greet her.

'Sadie, I'm so sorry I'm late.' Pearl looked as beautiful and elegant as always, but her eyes were red rimmed and there were black shadows beneath them. Concerned, Sadie asked her what was wrong.

Pearl murmured, 'I have to talk to you. Not here – I can't bear it.'

'We'll go, then.'

'You don't mind?'

'Not at all.'

Sadie put on her coat and they left the party.

As they walked along darkened pavements, through the sooty streets of Tooting, Pearl said suddenly, 'I think I'm expecting a baby.'

Sadie looked at her friend in horror. 'Are you sure?'

'No, no, not at all. But I really think I might be. And Ralph thinks so too, and he should know, because of Miriam. I can't go to the doctor; he's known me since I was teeny and, anyway, he and Mummy are friends.'

Pearl's voice was weary. Sadie linked her arm through her friend's as they passed a coal merchant's, where black dust glittered over the pavement. There was the sweet smell of manure from the stables.

'What did Ralph say when you told him?'

'He was furious.' Pearl's tone was bleak.

Sadie was furious with Ralph, but before she could say anything, Pearl gave a sigh. 'He was furious about everything. About our situation. And our rotten luck. He's always so careful.'

Not careful enough, Sadie couldn't help thinking. Yet, what right had she to judge Ralph? She hadn't even thought about preventing a baby when she and Tom Chiverton had made love. Her discovery that her monthly bleed had begun at its expected time had almost prompted her to let out a cheer in Edith's bathroom.

Pearl went on, 'Miriam is expecting again. Ralph doesn't even want that baby, let alone mine, if I'm having one. He says they can't afford it.'

'You poor thing.' Sadie squeezed Pearl's arm. 'What an awful worry. What will you do?'

'I don't know. I can't even think about that yet. It was dreadful, simply dreadful, telling Ralph.'

They walked for a while, stepping carefully round a ragged man sleeping in a shop doorway.

'I had to tell you,' Pearl went on. 'There's no one else I can talk to. I can't possibly tell Mummy; it would kill her.'

Sadie's heart ached for Pearl, caught in the trap so many women feared. She had met Pearl's mother a number of times. Mrs Foster was a softly spoken, genteel lady, immensely proud of and fond of her beautiful and talented daughter.

'Ralph must help you decide what to do,' said Sadie. 'He can't just walk away from this.'

Pearl gave her a hard look. 'You know perfectly well he could, if he chose. But I can't.'

'Do you think he will?'

'No, I'm sure he won't.'

There was a pub, the Magpie, across the road – a small, shabby place; Sadie suggested they go in for a drink. In the ladies' bar, a coal fire burned in the grate and they were served glasses of viscid, bluish gin. The only other inhabitant of the small room was a very old woman, sitting beside the fire. She was wearing a long black skirt and a blouse of a high-necked, Edwardian style beneath several knitted shawls and a threadbare coat, and was drinking a glass of stout.

Pearl said quietly, 'Ralph will never leave Miriam. And I wouldn't want him to, and that's the truth, Sadie. I met his little boys once and they were so sweet.' A tear slid down Pearl's cheek and she dashed it away.

An idea sprang into Sadie's head. 'You could come and live with me. Why not? I've plenty of room. We could bring up the baby together. It would have two mothers and that would be almost as good as a mother and father, wouldn't it? Think how glorious it would be to have a little baby to look after!'

For a while, they happily pictured it: the two of them sharing the upbringing of Pearl's baby, surviving meagrely but feasibly on Sadie's small inheritance and their earnings from their art, and the child running free in the forest.

But it wouldn't do and the pleasant dream crumbled. 'Sadie, I can't,' said Pearl sadly.

'Why not?'

'Because of Mummy, for one thing. Her widow's pension's tiny. She wouldn't be able to pay the rent if I couldn't work at the shop. And she'd miss me and I'd miss her. And I'd miss Ralph, too.' Pearl's huge, dark eyes met Sadie's. 'I know you don't like him awfully, but I do love him, you see, so very much. He's not perfect, he can be quite selfish, I'm not blind to that, and I know I'll only ever have a tiny piece of him, but, to me, that's better than nothing. So much better than nothing.'

Sadie thought, for the hundredth time, of that night at the Egg. 'I'm not judging you. How could I? I can hardly claim moral superiority.' Then she put her hands over her face and whispered, 'Pearl, I've done a terrible thing.'

'Sadie? Sadie, what is it?'

'Something happened. Something very wrong.' At least

Pearl loved Ralph. If passion did not absolve, perhaps love did, a little.

She said, 'You know that Tom Chiverton is my neighbour.'

'Yes, darling.'

'I went to bed with him. And I really, really wish I hadn't.'

'Are you in love with him?'

'No. For a while, I thought I was, but then I realised I wasn't, not one bit. I just *wanted* him. So much.'

'That's the trouble,' said Pearl with a sigh. 'Wanting them. It's not only desire, though, that's so irresistible, but one wants to be loved, too.'

'I feel so ashamed. His wife adores him. She'd hate me, if she knew. It was only once, but that's enough, isn't it?'

Pearl went to the bar to buy more drinks. When she came back to the table, she said, 'I feel guilty about Miriam all the time, I honestly do. I know it's wrong, but I don't stop. When I've had an awful day at work, when it's the middle of winter and Mrs Kennedy tells us we're to keep the shop door open and I get so frozen I can't feel my toes any more, or if Maud is unwell and I don't get my lunch break and I feel faint with hunger, I tell myself that soon I'll see Ralph. He makes me happy, you see.' Her expression darkened. 'Some of the time, he makes me happy.'

'I haven't your excuse. I'm lucky; I don't have to go out to work.'

'But Sadie – Felix. I saw what he did to you, how much he hurt you. No one could blame you for trying to find a little happiness. Don't get into a mess like me, that's all.' Pearl blinked, then blew her nose.

To lighten the mood, Sadie said, 'When I told Tom to leave, can you guess what he said?'

'I can't imagine.'

'He said, "I don't believe you're not attracted to me".'

Pearl tipped back her face and cackled. 'You are a thirty-year-old spinster, dearest, so you'd just have to be in love with Tom Chiverton.'

'How could I resist him?'

'In fact, Sadie, you should be grateful.'

They laughed together, their mockery sharpening with each phrase, and the old woman sitting by the fire gave them an indulgent smile. But then, in an instant, like the turn of a page, the laughter left Sadie and she felt ashamed of herself, and a little frightened.

Chapter Ten

Sussex and Suffolk – October 1970

Since Rose's last visit to the Egg, moss had crawled up the shaded walls, staining the concrete green. The air was heavy with an overripe, earthy fungal smell and the site seemed more overgrown and dank smelling than she remembered, as if the trees were working hard to reclaim the land, sending up saplings and blanketing the earth with dead leaves.

The last time she had driven to the Egg was five months ago. It had been late spring and she had still been Robert's wife. Her days had been taken up with looking after her children, running the Walton-on-Thames house and entertaining her husband's friends. Her distractions had been the *Times* crossword and the first drink of the evening. The last time she had driven to the Egg had been the day Robert had told her about Debra Peters.

Now she was separated from Robert and she and the girls were living in the flat in Weybridge that had once belonged to her grandmother. And she was running an air-freight business.

She and Dan had spent the day at an airfield near Hayward's Heath. Dan had driven, so that she could read through papers in the car. The airfield was on an exposed site, where steely clouds rushed overhead and puddles gleamed on the tarmac. They had spent the day in lengthy, sometimes heated, discussions with the managing director of the company, Kevin Goode, whom Dan had worked with during his Cardiff days. Kevin had since set up his own air-freight business, Westfield Air. Dan had suggested Martineau Aviation approach Westfield Air with the proposal of putting together a joint bid for a contract, as neither firm had the capability to carry out all the work on its own.

Kevin Goode was a short, broad-shouldered man with a thick neck, crinkled forehead and hard blue eyes. He had proved to be a tough negotiator and the discussions had gone on for most of the day.

Rose had decided to take a detour to the Egg on their way home because she had woken in the middle of the previous night, worrying about the house her grandmother had left her. And about a lot of other things besides: the children, the business, money, the future. Though the boxes were unpacked and the furniture had been arranged in the Weybridge flat, the rooms seemed disordered – objects going missing, things not in the right place. She and the girls were finding it hard to sleep at night; sometimes they all ended up huddled together in the same bed. She hoped she would love living there one day, but she didn't yet. Though she had longed to leave the house in Walton-on-Thames, on the day they moved out, she had stood in an empty room and felt a desolation so powerful she found it hard to breathe. The scuffs and scratches on the skirting boards and the thumbprints on the door handles had all seemed a final, faint writing of her life with Robert.

Her marriage in tatters. Love that she had thought would

last a lifetime reduced to bitterness and recriminations. There had been an ache in her heart as she locked the front door for the last time and drove to the estate agent to hand in the keys. It was still there: a low, throbbing pulse.

Rain scythed between the branches of the trees and gathered in the shallow declivity of the path. She had asked Dan to wait in his car, anticipating that it would take only five minutes to check out the house. She had felt, during the last couple of hours, a frazzled irritation rising inside her, and needed time to herself.

An odour of damp and decay reached her nostrils as she unlocked the front door. She saw the inch of dirty water muddying the tiles in the hall.

'Damn,' she said furiously. 'Oh, damn.'

She looked up at the ceiling. A thick brown streak cascaded from a corner, showing her where rainwater had made ingress to the house. When she poked at the stained plaster with a fingertip, a chunk came away.

'Damn, damn, damn,' she repeated, as she splashed along the hallway.

Dan was sitting in his Cortina, waiting for Rose. Raindrops danced against the windscreen. He and Celia had had an argument the previous night – or what passed for an argument; they were not a plate-throwing couple.

Dan had cooked dinner and Celia was clearing up. He had suggested they go to Paris for a weekend to celebrate her thirtieth birthday. 'Paris,' she said, as she scraped the plates into the bin, and then, 'And where's the money coming from?'

Startled and a little offended, he said, 'I'll pay, of course. It's your birthday.'

215

She had become huffily accusing: 'If you've got that sort of money to throw around, perhaps you should be putting more by for the house.'

And Dan had discovered an unexpectedly deep well of resentment inside himself, and said, 'For God's sake, are we never to enjoy ourselves?'

And so it had continued, Celia accusing him of profligacy, he finding her attitude increasingly grating. They had not raised their voices, but nor had they made it up in bed. Celia had not stayed the night and, though he walked her to the station, she turned her face away as he kissed her goodbye, so that his lips only brushed her cheek.

Sitting in his car, waiting for Rose to return from whatever it was she was doing, he acknowledged that, yesterday evening, he had seen something in Celia that he disliked; he sensed she had felt the same about him. The blank, painful sense that something irrevocable had taken place had dogged him throughout the day, confronting him whenever he had a moment to reflect.

He glanced at his watch. Rose had been gone for fifteen minutes – where the hell was she? Restless, he climbed out of the car and looked round. He was surrounded by woodland that spread up- and downhill and to either side of him. Rose had said something about a house. He supposed he should go and check that she was all right.

He took off his tie, rolled it up and dropped it in his jacket pocket, and set off along a path that snaked through the trees. With each step, more mud clung to his shoes. The wind tugged the dead leaves from the branches and stirred up the soggy brown leaves on the forest floor.

A house flickered between a dark mesh of tree trunks. Dan had expected a cottage – beams, thatch, quaintly welcoming – but it wasn't like that at all. It was surprising to find such a building in such a situation: white, blocky, uncompromisingly modern. Standing at the foot of a terrace, he peered up at the two glass walls, one on top of the other, but the interiors were obscured by reflections.

Rose was kneeling on the lower roof, poking at something. When he called out to her, she stood up.

'The roof's leaking,' she shouted back. 'Rainwater's getting in. I'm trying to find out where it's coming from.'

'I'll come up,' he offered. 'Give you a hand.'

'The door's round the side.'

Dan went inside the house. He could see it must be a bad leak, because the hall was awash. He took off his shoes at the foot of the stairs and carried them, putting them back on after he had stepped out of the bedroom window on to the roof.

'Didn't want to spoil the carpet,' he explained, knotting the laces.

'Thoughtful of you, Dan, but probably pointless. I'm afraid the whole building's about to collapse.'

Rose, who usually exuded an air of calm purposefulness, was looking harassed. She sat back on her heels and waved at the sill, which was visibly rotting. 'I keep thinking the roof's going to give way and I'll find myself in the kitchen.' She scowled, pushing her hair, which had escaped from the day's neat arrangement, behind her ears. 'I was wondering if I could find some way of keeping it dry until I manage to get hold of a builder.'

'I'll have a look round for something waterproof,' he offered.

The best thing he could find was the old groundsheet he used to keep the boot of his car clean. On his way back to

217

the house, he collected stones to weight it down. Back on the roof, they cobbled together a makeshift waterproofing.

Dan swept the water out of the door while Rose checked the other rooms, and then they walked back to the car. It was almost dark; he had forgotten how intensely black woodland can be at nightfall.

He thought that Rose seemed low and tried to reassure her. 'Once you get that sill fixed, it'll soon dry out.'

'I suppose so. Dear Lord, my shoes.'

They reached the car. Dan opened the passenger door and Rose got into the front seat. She said, 'There's a shop in the village. I might call in there, see if they can recommend a local builder. If you're not in a hurry, that is.'

'I'm not.' He thought of his flat – tidy and quiet – and Celia's things there: her toothpaste and face cream in the bathroom, her spare mac hanging on a peg.

Light from the Cortina's headlamps glazed the winding road to Nutcombe. Dan parked outside the village shop – J. *Thomsett Grocer & Baker* – and Rose went inside. A Lyons Maid sign flapped in the wind – not many takers today, Dan suspected. Next to the front door was a basket of speckled windfall apples and bags of Coalite and kindling.

There was a phone kiosk, too; he could give Celia a ring. But he decided not to and went for a stroll instead. The village was built in a valley, and he caught the rank and watery smells of the river before he saw it. Street lamps illuminated small cottages with weeds growing through the thatch and he passed only a few larger houses, one of which was a vicarage where ivy had scrambled over the gate post, half obscuring the name plate. Lights flashed from the windows of a pub and Dan realised that he was ravenous. Lunch had been a plate of skimpily filled sandwiches and a cup of watery coffee while negotiations continued. He wouldn't put it past Kevin to have kept them hungry deliberately, to wear them down.

His disagreement with Celia had been about more than money, he thought. It had been about practicality and passion. Until yesterday, he would have put himself on the practical side of the equation. It was sobering to realise he had limits.

He heard Rose call out to him, and turned and went to meet her.

'Any luck?'

'Yes, the woman in the shop was very helpful. She gave me a couple of names. I'll phone them tomorrow.'

'You don't fancy a drink, do you?' he said.

He had surprised her. She stumbled: 'Oh . . . I don't know . . .'

He said quickly, 'You're in a hurry. You need to get home to your children.'

'No – it's Friday; they're staying with Robert.' She scooped a hank of dark hair out of her eyes. 'Why not? We could have something to eat. I'm famished.'

Dan was standing, his back to her, at the bar, ordering two ploughman's and drinks. Rose's gaze ran from his fair hair, ruffled by the rain, to his broad shoulders, then down his spine to his narrow waist and hips. A pleasurable flutter of appreciation, then she scolded herself: *Stop it, Rose.* She tried to distract herself by examining her shoes – fawn suede, from Ravel – now covered in mud and never to be the same again. Then her thoughts moved to the Egg's roof. What on earth would the repair cost? It couldn't have come at a worse time.

Dan came back to the table with his half of bitter and her

gin and tonic. He split open a bag of crisps for them to share while they waited for the food.

Rose took a crisp. 'Is Kevin always like that?'

Dan threw her a smile. 'That was him on his best behaviour, especially for you, Rose. He has a temper. He can let fly, when he feels like it. He's been touchier since his divorce.'

'You like him, though?'

'Yes, I do. He can be difficult, but he's as straight as a die. Never tries to cut corners.'

'Some of their conditions are unreasonable. They're trying to charge us through the nose for using their airfield. I'm not going to leap at it.'

'Let him sweat for a few days? Good idea. My guess is that Kevin needs the deal as much as we do.'

'I doubt that,' she said bluntly. 'If I can't get my hands on a substantial sum of money in the next couple of months, we won't be able to pay the next instalment of the bank loan.'

Dan frowned. 'I was hoping that, with all the new business coming in, things would have picked up.'

'No one pays up front, that's the trouble. Plenty of our customers are in the same position as we are, trying to stave off payment for as long as possible.'

Rose and Dan were working flat out to cut costs and bring in new customers and retain old ones. During the dock workers' strike in July, businesses had turned to air freight to deliver their goods, giving Martineau Aviation a boost. Since the unions had returned to work, some clients had stayed with them, but others had gone back to using cheaper sea freight.

'Have you spoken to the bank?' Dan asked her. 'Seen if they'll extend the loan?'

The waitress brought their food to the table. Rose opened the gold-wrapped pat of butter. 'Yes, I did. They turned me down.'

'Why? The business is fundamentally solid.'

Her interview with the bank manager, Mr Nash, had been brief and humiliating. 'I don't think it was the business that was the problem.'

'What, then?'

'It was me. Mr Nash said I was untried and inexperienced – which is true. So I pointed out to him that I'm a quick learner.'

'And?'

'And he said I couldn't expect a bank to hand out money to every little girl who thinks she can run a business.'

His eyes widened. 'And you told him he could stuff his loan?'

'No. I maintained my dignity, shook his hand and thanked him for his time. Then screamed quietly to myself as soon as I was out in the street.'

'How restrained of you.'

'I've phoned a couple of other banks and they said much the same. One of men I spoke to laughed at me, Dan. He actually laughed.' She shrugged. 'That isn't important. But I do have to find that money.'

'I think I've found a firm who wants to rent the vacant office. That should help a bit.' The larger of the two empty offices had already been sublet to a company that repaired sewing machines. The agreement was bringing in a useful sum each month. 'And I've been talking to a supplier who'll let us have a cheaper source of fuel.' The pub, which was heated by an open fire, was hot; he took off his jacket. 'The problem is we'd have to pay cash. From what you're saying, it doesn't sound as if we have any.'

'Pretty much, yes.'

'Has Vic any thoughts?' Vic was the accountant Rose had engaged to replace Clive Miller, who had worked for Robert.

'Not so far.' Rose occupied herself with scraping the butter off the gold paper. 'He doesn't go in for the sort of creative accounting Clive did. I'll think of something, though. I'll beg, borrow or steal.' She looked at him. 'Dan, I'm joking. About the stealing bit, anyway.'

'Assuming the deal with Kevin goes through, it won't raise the money in time.'

'No, I'm afraid not. Mr Nash made it perfectly clear that he was prepared to foreclose if we can't pay.'

With noticeable reluctance, Dan said, 'You could sell the older of the DC-3s. You won't get a lot for it, but you would get something. It's not in use all of the time.'

She tore off a chunk of bread. 'I'd only do that as a last resort. It'd look a bit desperate, don't you think? The staff might worry about their jobs and think of moving on somewhere else. They're good people and I don't want to lose them.'

'You won't, Rose.' He spoke with certainty. 'There's a much better atmosphere in the place now. With Wilkinson gone and, well, sorry to be blunt, but with your husband no longer in charge, people know where they are now. Everyone's happier.'

Since she had begun to work at the firm, Rose had learned to rely on Dan for his knowledge of the aviation business, his judgement and his calm response to a crisis. You asked him to do something and he did it, quickly and efficiently, without a fuss. He was good at coming up with solutions to problems and had more than once stopped her making a silly mistake. And she was discovering, beneath his cool exterior, both humour and kindness.

'Does that include you, Dan?' she said. 'I'm not going to lose you, am I?'

'Not unless you choose to.'

'I couldn't manage without you,' she said frankly.

'You could, Rose. You honestly could. But I've no intention of going anywhere.'

Her relief was heartfelt; she smiled at him. 'I'd give you a pay rise, if I had any money.' She contemplated her pickled onion, which was the size and shape of a brownish eyeball, and decided against eating it. 'It's a good thing I love the work, or I wouldn't think it worth the sleepless nights.'

'There are easier businesses to work in. Ones that don't collapse as soon as the weather changes. But I like aeroplanes – always have. You can know everything about the science of flight, yet still find it magical.'

'Did you ever think of training to be a pilot?'

'Wasn't an option. Lousy eyesight. I have severe astigmatism.'

She had noticed that he wore glasses to drive. She found herself peering into his eyes, which were a mid-blue with just a hint of green, as if she might be able to see their imperfection, but then she looked away and concentrated on finishing her supper.

When they had finished, they left the pub to walk back to where Dan had parked the car. The rain had cleared and the moon cast a silvery light on the wet street.

He said, 'Tell me about the house. Is it yours?'

'I inherited it from my grandmother. Her father, an architect called Edward Lawless, designed it. He left it to my great-aunt, Sadie, and she gave it to my grandmother.' Briefly, she sketched out to him the discoveries and frustrations of her search for Sadie.

'I'm wondering whether she went to live abroad,' she

finished, looking round the darkened village. 'Some of her letters were sent from Europe. But, if so, why doesn't anyone seem to know where she went? By all accounts, she had a lot of friends.'

'You said she went missing in the mid-thirties?'

'Yes.'

'Europe was a mess then, and heading for far worse. Maybe Sadie thought she'd have a better future in the States. Or Australia — anywhere. Or maybe she stayed in Europe and got caught up in one war or another.'

'I still think she'd have written,' Rose said stubbornly. 'I still think that, if she'd gone to live abroad, she'd have told her friends. She wouldn't have just gone off, Dan; I know she wouldn't.'

I know Sadie, she thought. Sadie cared about her friends. They were important to her and she wouldn't have walked away from them without a backward glance.

She said, as they approached the car, 'The truly frustrating thing is that someone who knew Sadie back in the thirties, when she was staying at the Egg, is living only a mile and a half away.'

'Have you spoken to him?'

'Her. It's Diana Chiverton, the widow of Tom Chiverton, the poet. Tom died over ten years ago, but Diana's still living in the house they owned when Sadie was here. My great-grandfather built that house, too.' She scraped a ridge of mud from her shoe on to the grass. 'It's called the Gull's Wing. It's up on the ridgeway and it's spectacular, Dan. But she refuses to talk to me. It's so bloody annoying. I've written to her several times and she doesn't reply. You can't even knock on the door, because the gate's padlocked. She let her dogs out when I was just standing outside, looking.'

Dan unlocked the car. Rose was about to get in when she said suddenly, 'You idiot. Oh, you idiot.' And then, seeing his startled glance, 'Not you, Dan – *me*. It was right under my nose.'

A street lamp on the far side of the road illuminated the sign above the village shop: *J. Thomsett Grocer & Baker*. Sadie's letters had spoken of the helpfulness of a Mrs Thomsett, at the shop in Nutcombe. Sadie had given art lessons to a Winnie Thomsett. Might Winnie still live in Nutcombe? If so, might she remember Sadie? Could she even be the slight woman in her fifties whom Rose had spoken to only an hour ago in the shop, the woman who had recommended a builder to repair the roof?

But the shop was in darkness now, so she would have to wait. They headed out of the village and were soon driving through the black, wooded hills of the Weald. She had always enjoyed watching a man drive well, and she found herself glancing at Dan now and then, the direction of her gaze concealed by the darkness in the car.

Dan had to take his car to the garage, because it needed two new front tyres fitted, so, on Saturday, he caught the train from Liverpool Street Station, changing at Ipswich.

His father met him at Darsham railway station. They shook hands and headed to a Morris Minor van with a lacework of rust eating away the wheel arches.

Mick patted the bonnet affectionately. 'Got her for a song. I'll do her up, then sell her on. Thinking of starting up a business. People queue up to buy these vans.'

Dan murmured something non-committal. His father's life history was littered with businesses enthusiastically set up, projects begun and abandoned. He had learned to avoid being dragged into his world, an unwilling collaborator in a fantasy.

On the drive to the caravan park near Southwold, Mick continued to talk about his plans. 'As soon as I've got enough cash in the bank, I'm going to move back to London. In summer, the coast's the best place in the world, but you can feel a bit out on a limb come wintertime. I've got contacts in London, you know, in the used-car business.'

'That's great, Dad.'

'What are you driving, these days, son?'

'A Cortina.'

'A Cortina!'

A packet of Embassy cigarettes was waved under Dan's nose. He shook his head. Mick Falconer executed a series of complicated manoeuvres, extracting a cigarette and lighting it, while steering through winding country roads.

'A Cortina!' he repeated with a chuckle. 'Would have thought you'd go for a Capri, at least. At your age, you should have something sporty.'

Dan let his father ramble on about cars. It was what passed for conversation between them. There were too many subjects that could not be touched upon, too many spaces that could not be filled.

They were driving through the outskirts of Southwold when Mick said, 'Have you seen your mother? Is she still living in that place in the Lake District?'

'Yes, she's still in the commune. I saw her a month ago. She's okay.'

Dan visited a parent each month, alternating them. It was as often as he could stand. His mother wasn't okay – she was thin and ill-looking – but he saw no point in telling his father that. His parents had stopped communicating years ago. His mother blamed his father for the disasters that had overtaken her life, while his father had always lived in a world of his own invention, in which the lucky break was just round the corner.

'And your girlfriend?' Mick said, as they drove along a low road with marshland to one side and sand dunes to the other. 'Sheila, wasn't it?'

'Celia.'

'I'd like to meet her, son. You should bring her with you next time.'

Into Dan's head came an image of Celia in the damp, chilly caravan. She would keep her coat on. She would try to avoid sitting on the chairs, with their stained orange cushions. He said nothing.

'Time you two got married,' persisted his father, as, with a creaky change down of gear, the van slowed to turn into the entrance to the caravan park. 'I don't know what you're waiting for. You should tell her, from me, she doesn't know how lucky she is, having a chap like you running round after her.'

Mixed with irritation at his father's dogged pursuit of the subject was a more difficult emotion. Mick Falconer had always regarded his son's educational achievements and career with awe. Dan had, in the past, had to endure his father boring his friends in the pub: *A degree in engineering . . . Sends those planes all over Europe . . . Always had a head for figures.* Simple, uncomplicated admiration was harder to process than neglect.

In the caravan, Mick made tea. It was roomy enough, but felt fragile, perched between marshland and the grey North Sea. Dan never noticed the cold, but he worried that his father, who was in his late fifties, would soon begin to struggle in the chill Suffolk winters.

227

They walked into town. Dan offered to buy lunch in a café, but Mick said he would prefer fish and chips, and then insisted on paying. They ate their lunch sitting on a bench on the seafront, coat collars up in a wind that turned Mick's nose blue. His coat was a thin, grubby, navy anorak; the sight of it made Dan feel depressed. They faced out to waves that gathered themselves up before battering down in a translucent, grey-green curve, then shrank back again, leaving ragged white trails of foam on the sand and shingle.

Dan talked about planes and the new business Martineau Aviation had taken on, importing olives and lemons from Italy and oysters from Marseilles.

'Oysters!' said his father admiringly. 'And that feller . . . The chap who was paying the tart . . .'

'Robert Martineau? Haven't seen him for months. His wife's running the business now. I told you, Dad.'

'And how do you like working for a woman?'

'It's fine.'

'Is she a looker?'

'I suppose so, yes,' he said stiffly.

Heading off his father's inevitable bad jokes and mildly sexist comments, Dan turned the conversation to the safer topic of football. Then, overriding Mick's protests, he bought him a couple of bags of groceries and, afterwards, they headed back to the caravan. Over tea and Mr Kipling French Fancies, his father reminisced about a past he had reconstructed and which was now unrecognisable to Dan.

After an hour or so, Dan rose and said that he had to go; his father protested, telling him he should stay the night. Gently, Dan refused, and they got back into the Morris Minor and drove to Darsham Station. On the platform, his father's conversation petered out and he looked tired and old. The train appeared round a corner of the track and Mick offered his hand to be shaken. Dan ignored it and hugged him instead.

'Look after yourself, Dad. I'll see you soon.'

Invariably, on the journey home from Suffolk, a black gloom would descend on him: a mixture of guilt that he could not give his father what he wanted, along with resentment that he presumed to demand anything of him at all. After a while, the train left the shifting, unreliable landscape of the Suffolk coast behind. Inland, the view through the window was of fields and pleasant villages. They seemed to Dan to reflect a neatness he struggled to find in his personal life.

The train reached the outskirts of Ipswich, with its brick terraces and small factories and gasworks, and drew to a halt at the station. Dan got out of the carriage and changed for the London platform. An icy wind blew across the tracks and sidings, and many of the passengers huddled in the waiting room, but Dan stood outside, not noticing the weather.

Chapter Eleven

Surrey, Sussex and London – November 1970

R ose was putting on her make-up, getting ready to leave the flat to go to work. She heard shouts from the kitchen.

'Leave it alone!' Katherine's voice.

'I want some!' Eve, now.

'You don't even like Rice Krispies. You said you didn't like them; you just said they go soggy.'

'I want them now. You're not allowed to stop me.'

'Leave it alone, you silly little girl.'

Rose hurried into the kitchen, mascara brush in hand, in time to see Eve yank the cereal box from Katherine's hand and Rice Krispies spray like confetti over the table and floor.

'Stop it, you two! What on earth do you think you're doing?'

'She won't let me have any Rice Krispies!'

'I don't want to see her stupid fat face when I'm eating my breakfast.'

'Katherine, that's enough,' said Rose sharply. She dismantled the wall of cereal boxes Katherine had constructed around her on the table, putting them away in the cupboard.

'Mum,' moaned Katherine.

'Don't be so silly. Look at the mess you've both made.' She glanced at the clock. 'We need to go in a couple of minutes. Hurry up and finish your breakfast.'

Eve said, 'Are you taking us to school, Mummy?'

'No, not today; you're going with Nadine.'

Nadine Kent was the nanny Rose had engaged to help with the children during the week. She had a five-year-old son, Jonathan, who attended the same school as Katherine and Eve, and a baby daughter, Martha. The school Rose had moved the girls to was a bright, well-run establishment, with a good reputation. Robert was paying the fees. Rose could not pay them herself because, until the company was on its feet, she was taking only a minimal salary.

She dropped the children off at Nadine's house at quarter past eight in the mornings, which meant she could be at work shortly after half past. Then Nadine picked the girls up from school, at three thirty, and took them to her own house, from where Rose – or Robert, on Fridays – collected them after finishing work.

It was particularly important that she get to the airfield promptly today, because she was driving to Westfield Air that afternoon to discuss some last-minute details of the joint contract with Kevin Goode. Afterwards, she was to meet a builder at the Egg, to discuss the repairs to the roof.

Eve said, 'I want you to take us, Mummy.' Tears were spilling down her cheeks.

Rose hugged her and wiped away the tears. 'I'll pick you up from school tomorrow, darling; how about that?' She felt panicked as she made her promise. It would mean missing a meeting, and she had so much work to get through.

'I hate that school,' grumbled Katherine. 'My old school was much nicer. Why do we have to go there?'

Rose put the milk in the fridge and the cereal bowls and mugs in the sink and ran hot water on them. 'Why don't you like it?'

'I miss *Abbie.*' Abbie had been Katherine's best friend at her previous school.

'I know, darling.' She stroked Katherine's head. 'But you'll make new friends; truly, you will.' She checked the clock again and fetched her bag and briefcase. 'Go and get your things; we have to go.'

She hurried her daughters out over a floor still crunching with Rice Krispies. She dropped off Katherine and Eve at Nadine's, giving them a kiss and a hug before heading for the airfield. She had a horrible suspicion that she had mascara on only one set of eyelashes and couldn't remember whether she'd put her cosmetics bag in her handbag. When she saw the Mini's speedometer hit sixty-five on the narrow, winding country road, she braked and made a conscious effort to relax.

After a busy morning, she left a list of tasks for Lucy and Dan to complete, and then set off, cross-country, to Westfield Air. Kevin was more affable this time, almost charming, and the final details of the contract were eventually argued out to their mutual satisfaction.

A light rain was misting the air by the time she drove to the Egg. The builder, Mr Jackson, was already parked at the bend in the road. Rose let him into the house and showed him the stain on the wall, and then they went upstairs and out on to the roof. There was a lot of teeth-sucking and tutting as he unpeeled the makeshift covering she and Dan had put over the rotten window frame.

He poked at the wood with a biro for such a long time that Rose, unable to bear the suspense, said, 'Will you need to replace the entire frame?'

'Oh, no. Only this section of it, love. See, it's fine here.'
More poking.

Then he pulled back the asphalt covering and inspected the roof. That, too, was pronounced salvageable. After giving Mr Jackson her address, so that he could send her an estimate, Rose's heart felt lighter.

'I'll get a tarpaulin on that roof, first thing tomorrow,' the builder promised. 'Keep it dry till the work's done.'

Rose thanked him, and they shook hands and said goodbye. Then she had a quick check round the rest of the house and swept some more fallen leaves from the roof. She remembered her most recent visit to the Egg, standing on the roof and looking down at Dan – how the wind had ruffled his fair hair and how shadows from the dying light had emphasised the planes and hollows of his face.

She locked up, then walked back to the Mini. The sky was darkening, the thin drizzle blurring the outlines of the trees, and soon the houses of Nutcombe village emerged, softened and subdued by the wet, grey light.

Rose parked at the side of the road and went into the shop. Behind the counter was the same slight, thin-faced woman with a silvery bob that she had spoken to on her previous visit, who had recommended Mr Jackson to her. A lad in a parka and oil-stained jeans – long, dark hair slicked back, pencil behind one ear, acne scars – was buying cigarettes and a KitKat. Three people in the small space made it seem crowded. The pleasant, homely odour of apples, bread and sugary cakes, and the sweet jars containing bitter lemons, humbugs, pear drops and barley sugar, reminded Rose of the grocery shops of her childhood.

The lad paid and left the shop. Rose picked out some bacon and cabbage, and three cakes as a teatime treat, then thanked the woman behind the counter for recommending Mr Jackson.

'Larry's a good sort,' she said, as she rang up the purchases. She gave Rose a curious look and Rose noticed that her eyes were a clear, pale greyish-blue. 'There hasn't been anyone up at the house for months. I thought they'd get another tenant in. Are you from the lettings agency?'

'No; I own the house now. My name's Rose Martineau. I inherited the Egg from my grandmother, who was given it by her sister, Sadie Lawless.'

The light eyes widened. 'Now, there's a name I haven't heard for a while. So you're Sadie's niece – no, great-niece. Well I never. You don't look like her . . . though, there's something about the eyes . . .'

Rose's heart speeded up. 'Are you, by any chance, Winnie Thomsett?'

'I *was* Winnie Thomsett. I've been Winnie Ferrers for more than thirty-five years, now.'

The name Ferrers rang a bell, but Rose couldn't immediately place it. She said, 'So, you knew Sadie, when she was living here.'

'I did, yes.'

'Have you a moment? Could I possibly talk to you about her?'

The doorbell chimed, announcing the arrival of a customer, a woman with two little boys. Winnie weighed out three pounds of potatoes and carefully wrapped a section of dimpled cardboard that contained a dozen eggs.

When they were alone again, she said, 'What was it you wanted to know about her?'

'Anything, really. What she was like, what sort of person she was . . . How she fitted into the village.'

A snort. Winnie wiped potato dust from the bowl of the

234

scales. 'She didn't. Some of them used to make fun of her for her strange clothes and odd ways, and because she lived on her own. But she was a sweet, kind lady. She never put on airs. She cycled down to the shop most mornings and always passed the time of day with me. She was never the sort just to pass you by, as if you were beneath her notice, like some I could mention.'

A shiver ran down Rose's spine. She imagined Sadie standing where she herself stood now, buying bread and milk, and getting stared at because she was wearing some garment that might be considered, in the quiet, remote little village, outlandish. She might have shocked the inhabitants of Nutcombe by wearing trousers, for instance.

With little pats of her hands, Winnie Ferrers was tidying up the newspapers and magazines on the counter. 'You never knew her, then?' she asked Rose.

'I didn't know of her existence until after my grandmother died.' This had become her frequent refrain. The more often she said it, the more extraordinary it seemed; to have a sister and keep her secret implied, Rose felt, a lot of anger or a lot of guilt. Or maybe both. She thought of Katherine and Eve, squabbling over the breakfast cereal. You assumed that childhood resentments and jealousies would be erased by time, but sometimes they weren't – sometimes they festered.

'I found some letters from Sadie in my grandmother's house,' she explained. 'In one of them, she said that she'd taught you to draw.'

'She did.' Winnie smiled to herself. 'I never had much of a gift for it, but Colin did.'

Winnie Thomsett has asked me if she may have art lessons, Sadie had written to Edith. *I'm going to suggest that she and Colin Ferrers share, so I can offer them reduced rates.*

235

'You married Colin Ferrers?'

'That's right. That was where we met, up at Sadie's house.'

'Does he remember her?'

'Colin was killed at the D-Day landings, dear.'

'I'm so sorry.' The formulaic words felt inadequate to Rose. 'How awful.'

The bowl was replaced on the scales and Winnie brushed her hands clean on her pink overall. 'Colin was fond of Sadie too. I remember him saying that she was the best teacher he'd ever had – and he went to art school. Sadie could draw and paint anything. She'd draw a bird and it'd look like it was about to fly away. She tried to teach us to see things properly, like she did.'

'Do you remember when you last saw her?'

Winnie frowned. 'It was about six weeks or so before we married. The wedding was on the eighth of December nineteen thirty-four, so that would make it October. I wanted a winter wedding – I fancied myself in one of those little capes with fur round the hood. Sadie and I had a chat here, in the shop. She was going to come to the wedding, but she never did. I felt sad about that, sad that we'd just lost touch, like it didn't matter. I'd thought of her as a friend. Anyway, in the New Year, Colin and I went to live in Manchester and I found out I was expecting William, and I suppose I had other things to think about then.'

'You wouldn't remember, would you, whether the last time you saw her was before or after her show at the gallery?'

'It was before.' A copy of *Woman and Home* was carefully aligned. 'The day before. I remember Sadie telling me she was going to London the next day.'

'How did she seem? Was she nervous . . . agitated?'

'Nervy as a kitten. She'd come to the shop to buy string

and brown paper. She dropped her purse on the floor. Coins everywhere. I tried to calm her down. Nothing's that important, is it? Nothing's worth getting yourself into such a state.'

'She'd had a breakdown before she came to live here.'

'Had she? I didn't know. The poor thing. She was always the nervy type.' Winnie ran a duster over the sweet jars. 'I used to take her groceries up to the house. I'd call in and we'd have a little chat and a cup of tea. Sometimes she'd show me what she was working on. She worked so hard. I remember her glowering over that old press of hers, hardly saying a word.' She frowned. 'A funny thing . . . One day I went up to the studio and she'd put a mattress on the floor in there. Pillow and blanket and everything. She said she didn't like sleeping in the bedroom because she was afraid someone might look in at her.'

Sadie's bedroom had been on the first floor of the Egg, up in the branches of the trees. 'I don't understand,' Rose said. 'How could anyone have looked in?'

'Doesn't make any sense, does it? As I said, Sadie was the nervy type. Mind you, you'd feel like you were on show all the time, living in that place, with all those windows, wouldn't you?'

The phone rang and Winnie answered it. As she lectured whoever was on the other end of the line about a late delivery, Rose considered what she had discovered. Sadie had told Winnie that she was going to London the next day, for the private view. But she had never appeared at the Danford Gallery. What had happened to her in the intervening twenty-four hours? Where had she gone?

Winnie put down the phone, then smoothed out the creased top page of a Beano. 'During the war, it was hard to travel and I was working all hours and looking after the kids.

And then I lost my poor Colin. We came back to Nutcombe after that. I hadn't the heart to stay up there. Manchester's such a damp, grey city and I never got used to it. I'm a country girl; I belong here. I thought Sadie might have come back, too, but she never did. There were RAF officers living in the Egg, then. They were a rowdy lot, but they cleared out quite soon. The house was let out, after that.'

The door opened and a lad came in with a bundle of evening newspapers. Winnie thanked him and slit the twine that bound them with a knife. She began to scribble names and numbers on the tops of the newspapers.

She said, 'Sadie used to go abroad, for months at a time. Sometimes she'd lend out the house to her friends.' She smiled. 'One weekend, there was quite a party. I don't know how they all fitted in. I suppose it meant someone was keeping an eye on the place. They were a nice lot; they did their shopping here – not like that crowd at the Gull's Wing, always driving over to Crowborough for this and that fancy thing.'

'The Chivertons, you mean?'

Winnie stacked the newspapers into a neat pile, for the paper boy, Rose assumed. 'Mrs Chiverton didn't come in here more than once a month,' Winnie said. 'Thought herself too good for us, back then, I reckon. It's a different story now. I still see her, now and then, walking those dogs. My grand-daughter, Janice, takes her groceries up the hill for her.'

'A girl with sandy hair and glasses?'

'Yes, that's my Janice.' Winnie smiled. 'She's a good girl.'

'I met her once when I went to have a look at the Gull's Wing. I've been hoping to speak to Mrs Chiverton.'

Another snort. 'You won't get far, there. Keeps herself to herself, that one.'

238

'And Tom Chiverton? Did you know him? Did Sadie know him?'

'Oh, Sadie knew him, all right.' Suddenly, Winnie's voice was run through with contempt. 'She used to go to his house, when she first came to the village. Parties and suchlike. But, by the time she was giving me and Colin lessons, she wasn't having anything more to do with him, and thank the Lord for that.'

'Why do you say that?'

The doorbell sounded as another customer, a middle-aged woman, came into the shop. 'Hello, Carol,' Winnie called out. 'Your magazine's in.' She took a knitting magazine from a shelf and set it on the counter.

While Carol browsed the shop, Winnie lowered her voice to speak to Rose. 'Sadie was young and pretty. And him, well, he was one for the girls, the old goat. He had wandering hands, if you know what I mean – used to make free of himself with the housemaids. There was a girl in the village – Ivy Long. Ivy and I were at school together. She worked as a maid, up at the Gull's Wing. She stuck it out as long as she could, because it was hard to get work, then, with the farms in such a bad way, and there wasn't much for a girl round here but to go into service. Ivy's mother wasn't well, so she wanted to stay at home with her. She was glad of the job to begin with. But, in the end, she gave in her notice and went into service in London.'

'Because of Tom Chiverton?'

Carol paid for the magazine and a bar of Dairy Milk. Winnie enquired after Carol's dog and Carol told her he was much better, then she said goodbye and left the shop.

Winnie's gaze had fixed on the street outside. 'What's past is past,' she said quietly, 'and I've never believed in speaking ill of the dead. But Tom Chiverton was a nasty piece of work. I saw him have a go at Sadie, once.' She nodded in the direction of the window, towards where Rose had parked her car. 'Out there, in broad daylight. He was shouting at her. It was like he'd lost his head. She was yelling at him, too, telling him to leave her alone. I was going to go out and tell him to push off, famous poet or no, but then she cycled away.'

'Do you know what they were arguing about?'

Winnie shook her head.

Rose glanced at the clock on the wall. 'I have to go,' she said. 'Thank you so much, Winnie. Thank you for talking to me about Sadie.'

The older woman's expression softened. 'It's years since I've thought about her. It seems so long ago. It was a shame she went away. She would have remembered Colin. It would have been nice to talk to her about him. Wherever she went, I hope she was happy. She deserved to be happy, but we don't always get what we deserve, do we?'

The council workers had been on strike for weeks now and heaps of rubbish had piled up on the pavements, tumbling from rotting, odorous mountains on to London's streets and squares. As Dan came out of Camden Town Underground station, the stench of decay reached him.

Celia was seated at a table in the Indian restaurant when he arrived. They had patched up their disagreement and had compromised by celebrating her thirtieth birthday with a night at a hotel in Bath. But something had changed, and Dan found himself noticing things that hadn't bothered him before. Or perhaps they had, and he had let it blow over.

They were at the poppadom-and-mango-chutney stage, and

were telling each other about the events of their week, when Celia said, 'Roberta's leaving to get married. Mr Simmonds' secretary – you remember, Dan.' Mr Simmonds was the managing director of the City bank that Celia worked for.

'Are you going to apply for her job?'

'I'm thinking about it. Roberta's always doing her nails or chatting to a friend on the phone when I go into her office. It makes me fed up that she does half the work I do, for more money.'

'So let them know you're interested.'

Celia dipped a shard of poppadom in the chutney. 'You don't mind, then? If I take this job, I'll have to stay in Tufnell Park.'

Celia was referring to the discussions they had periodically about buying a house and living together, as a tryout before marriage. Because her job was in London and his in Surrey, they could never agree where to live, so nothing ever came of the conversations.

'Go for it,' he said.

'I will, then. You could always look for something more central, you know, Dan.'

'All the airfields are out in the country.'

'You don't have to work at an airfield. I thought you might be getting fed up with it by now.'

'Fed up with what?'

'Working for that woman.'

For some reason, Celia never referred to Rose by name. Swallowing his irritation, Dan said, 'I enjoy working for Rose.'

'There are lots of other things you could do, with your degree.'

The waiter cleared their plates away. When they were alone

241

again, Dan said, 'There is something else I'd like to do. I'd like to have my own air-freight business.'

Celia gave a brittle little laugh. 'Goodness me! Where did that come from?'

'I've had it at the back of my mind for some time.'

'It's the first I've heard of it.'

Ambitions – dreams – he had discovered, emerged when you had time and space to create them. For the first twenty-five years or so of his life, he had concentrated on survival, on finding an even keel. It was only in the last few years that he had allowed himself to dream.

'I suppose I didn't think it was feasible,' he said.

'Running your own business . . . It's too risky. People lose everything. Look at Andy.' Andy was Celia's elder brother, a largely supine, pot-smoking layabout, who had ploughed a big chunk of his parents' savings into a half-hearted record business that had fizzled into bankruptcy within a couple of years.

'I'm not Andy,' he said. 'Think of Rose, instead – how she just went for it. You've got to admire her. No experience, not much in the way of financial back-up, only hard work and grit.'

'But you're not like her, Dan.' A frown pleated itself between Celia's eyebrows. 'If it all goes wrong for her, someone else will pick up the pieces.'

'You don't know that.'

'Dan, people like her always have it easy.'

Celia's attitude, the way she made assumptions about people, irked him. 'I don't think Rose has had it easy at all,' he said.

She made a scornful outward breath. He looked away, focusing his gaze on the representations of Hindu deities on the orange walls. As the silence between them lengthened, the waiter returned to the table, bearing warming trays and dishes of food.

Kevin Goode was another example of someone who had just gone for it. Kevin was from north London, had been to a secondary modern, had no family money and had struggled, just as Dan had struggled, and now he owned an air-freight business. Often, thinking of Kevin, Dan wondered what on earth he was waiting for.

'Look,' he coaxed, 'it doesn't have to be risky. I'll take my time. I'm not talking about going off and buying a plane tomorrow morning.'

'I should hope not!'

'But, in two years . . . five, if I have to wait that long . . . When I'm ready.'

Celia looked at him through narrowed, resentful eyes. 'Buying a *plane* . . .'

'Buy one or charter one. It's tricky to run an air-freight business without one.'

'Don't be sarcastic.'

'Sorry.' Again, he made an effort. When he had envisaged broaching the subject of starting up his own business to Celia, she had, in his imagined conversation, been supportive, encouraging, interested.

'I know how to keep the initial costs down,' he said. 'I'd start small. I'd buy or charter an old plane in decent condition and rent a strip of airfield. I know the business inside out, by now; I know what makes money and what doesn't, and I've a good idea of what'll make money in the future. It'll cost something, but maybe not so much as you think.'

She seized on his last sentence. 'And where's the money coming from?'

'I've some put by.'

'That's for our house, Dan.'

'I thought we'd just agreed that, if you went for this new job, we wouldn't be looking for a house quite yet.' In spite of his best intentions, his voice hardened.

'That doesn't mean you can just go and spend our money on a *plane*.'

Celia was pink with anger; her small eyes sparked. She poked a tablespoon at one of the dishes, then put it down. They glowered at each other over the untouched rice and chicken madras.

'I don't know what's come over you,' she said stiffly. 'You've changed. You never used to be like this – all these *ideas*.'

And he heard himself say, 'If that's true, then I don't think much of myself. You and I, Celia, we're too cautious. Sometimes you have to take a chance.'

'You're not taking a chance with our money! We're not like that, you and I, Dan! We're not extravagant . . . We're not *irrational*!'

'No, you're right, we're not.' He saw, suddenly and with horrible clarity, what they were. 'We're dull . . . We're unadventurous. Perhaps we're worse than that. I'm afraid that we are – we've become – mean and small-minded.'

She flushed. 'I'm not mean. That's a horrible thing to say.'

'You weren't when we first met, but you are now. And so am I, I daresay. I'm as much to blame as you are – more, perhaps. We've made each other small and mean. We play safe. We've brought out the worst in each other. I don't think we're good for each other.'

These were not things he had planned to say, and he saw her shock at his words written on her face. In the silence that ensued, while her eyes glittered with tears,

244

half a dozen men, tanked up on alcohol, crashed through the door of the restaurant, demanding curries. There was raucous laughter and a tinkling of cutlery as one of them fell against a table.

Celia blinked back her tears, drew herself upright and said, in a small, dignified voice, 'Then perhaps it's time to call it a day. I'm sorry if I've disappointed you, Dan.'

'Celia, please.' He felt awful. 'I'm sorry.'

'But it's what you think, isn't it?'

He saw the courage it had taken her to ask the question and knew he had to answer honestly. 'Yes.'

Her head dipped.

He said, 'It's my fault, not yours. It's me.'

She stumbled to her feet, knocking her handbag off the banquette, and he picked it up and gave it to her.

'Celia . . .'

'No, I don't want you to say anything. I can't bear it.'

'Let me walk you to the station.'

Celia shook her head, biting her lip, then picked up her coat and bag and left the restaurant. The diners on the adjacent table were watching, fascinated. Dan gave them a savage glare and they looked away. Then he took some notes out of his wallet, tucked them beside the uneaten food and left the restaurant too.

There was a pub a short way up the road; he went into it and bought a double whisky. The tables were busy, so he propped himself against a wall and drank till he had blurred the edges of his black mood. He knew that he had hurt her and he was not proud of the way they had parted.

But their parting had been inevitable. He had not loved Celia, had never loved her, and nor had she loved him. They had seen in each other a practical solution to the problem

245

of living: they had been an evasion of passion, rather than a celebration of it.

He wondered whether to refill his glass, decided against it and left the pub. The streets were dark, the tarmac wet and sheeny, and the rain was turning the newspapers and cardboard dumped on the pavements to a papier-mâché pulp. Now and then, a car drove by, sending up curls of water. Lights blurred in the drizzle, smudging the signage of the shops and cafés. On the far side of the road, a girl in plat-form shoes stumbled as she picked her way between the rubbish. Her boyfriend tugged at her hand, hurrying her along, while, in the distance, a siren wailed and blue lights flashed between buildings.

A sense that the world he knew was slipping into chaos, that all he knew and valued was disintegrating, washed over him. The rifts that were tearing apart the fabric of society showed in the frequent clashes between the unions, the bosses and the government, and in the repeated disruption to daily life. His personal life was a mess. Yet another long-term relationship had ended. There was a pattern, his choices dictated by a desire for safety, and his sense of suffocation rising as the safe choice stifled.

Rose had invited her father to supper. They had eaten and were clearing up. While Giles dried the dishes, Rose talked to him about Martineau Aviation's financial predicament.

'It's always hard, getting your feet off the ground,' he said. 'If you can survive the first couple of years, you'll probably survive the next ten. Shall we have a drink?'

'I'd better not, Dad. I've work to do. You go ahead.'

'Why don't I make us some coffee, then?'

Rose took a tray of coffee things into the sitting room.

She put a cup on the table beside her father. Eve curled up on Rose's lap while Katherine knelt on the sitting-room floor, drawing an aeroplane. Katherine's nose almost touched the paper; she must get her eyes tested, thought Rose — another task to add to the list.

Giles said, 'How much do you need to keep the bank quiet?'

Rose made a face. 'Fifteen hundred pounds, I'm afraid.'

'I'll lend it you.'

Her hand, stroking Eve's curls, paused. 'Dad, you can't. It's a huge sum of money. Far too much.'

'It's a huge sum of money that's sitting in my bank account doing nothing. What have I to spend it on? A few rounds of golf . . . The odd book or record. It'll give you a breathing space, love. You can pay me back, when you can.'

Eve squirmed against Rose — a warm, comforting weight. 'Dad . . .'

'Discussion over. You're my daughter; I want to help. Let me know who to make the cheque out to.'

Eve's eyes were closing. She slept, Rose thought, like a baby animal curled up in a nest. She kissed her daughter's head.

'Thanks, Dad. You won't regret it.'

'I know that.'

Her father left shortly afterwards and Rose carried Eve to her bed. She did not wake up as she was changed into her pyjamas. Eve still insisted on sharing a bedroom with Katherine, though there were three bedrooms in the flat. Katherine complained, but without much conviction, which made Rose suspect that she was glad of the company. They were all still struggling to settle. Perhaps they weren't used to living on a first floor, something like that, or perhaps something of Edith Fuller's former post-colonial gloominess lingered on.

Katherine went to bed too and Rose opened her briefcase and took out the new proposal Dan had left on her desk that afternoon. Her father's generosity would relieve the immediate pressure on Martineau Aviation. By the time spring came, the payments from the new business she and Dan were bringing in would have put the company's finances on a more even keel. Her confidence was returning, along with her belief in herself. She imagined telling Dan that they were off the hook, how pleased he would be. She almost picked up the phone and called him – but he might be busy and she didn't want to interrupt him. He might be with his girlfriend. She knew nothing of his private life.

She put aside the proposal and poured herself a drink, after all. She was out of lemons and the icebox in the fridge had seized up because no one had defrosted it. More items for the list she always carried around in her head. Sipping her vodka and tonic, she opened the collection of Tom Chiverton's poems she had bought from a bookseller in Weybridge. Turning a page, some lines caught her eye:

The owls have come back,
I hear them calling to each other in the woods
Remnants in the dead leaves, a feather, bones, a claw
She has made herself into a ghost to haunt me.

The poem, which was called 'Retribution', was not considered to be one of Chiverton's best. It lacked, the critic said, in the footnotes, the lyricism of much of his earlier work.

Rose thought it revealing, though. *She has made herself into a ghost to haunt me*. Tom Chiverton's ghost had been female. He

248

had invested her with intention – to reduce him to a scattering of feathers, bones and claws. But who had been the hunter and who the hunted?

What sort of man had Tom Chiverton been? The poet painted in the biography, *Poet of the Downs*, had been an exemplar who stood head and shoulders above his contemporaries, a genius driven by his love of language and the Sussex countryside. Nowhere in the six hundred pages that Rose had ploughed through had there been any hint that Tom might have been unfaithful to his wife – or that he had, in Winnie Ferrers' phrase, made free of himself with the housemaids.

Which had been the real Tom Chiverton – Winnie Ferrers' self-centred philanderer or the biographer Geoffrey Cranham's literary prodigy? It was possible that he was both. A man could be a great poet as well as a womaniser. Back then, when Sadie Lawless had been living at the Egg, it would have been easy for Tom Chiverton to keep his secrets. Times had been different. Nutcombe village would have been more isolated from the outside world, its inhabitants divided not only by class, but by gender. If the maid, Ivy, had complained, who would have believed her? The prejudices Rose had encountered – the bank manager who laughed at her, the clients who, hearing her voice when she answered the telephone, assumed she must be the secretary and asked to speak to the boss, love – must have been far more deeply ingrained then. Tom Chiverton might have thought himself entitled to grope the housemaid. *It was only a bit of fun.* Men said things like that, didn't they? Entitlement led to resentment and eventually to justification. *She was a tease. She was leading me on. I could tell by the way she was dressed.*

Rose thought of Sadie, alone in the Egg, surrounded by

all those windows. And of Tom Chiverton, *a nasty piece of work*, living just half a mile away.

Sadie's fallen out with him. There was a time when she enjoyed his company, but now she doesn't like the way he looks at her. His dark eyes follow her as she walks through the woods. She keeps away from the ridge road and the Gull's Wing, but, even so, their paths cross; it's inevitable in so small a place. On the station platform, as the train comes in, she looks up and sees him crossing the footbridge. When she comes out of the shop with her pint of milk and copy of The Times, she glances across the road and sees him, standing beside her green bicycle.

Chapter Twelve

London and Sussex — April–August 1931

Sadie was staying with Edith, in her London home. She had been invited to the dinner that Edith and Cyril were giving to celebrate Edith's forty-first birthday, on 5 April. At the centre of the dinner table was an arrangement of white narcissi that enhanced the splendour and purity of the silverware and the cream-coloured dinner service.

'Isn't it fortunate that you have your sister staying to help you out?' said one of the guests, a Mrs Campbell, the wife of a colleague of Cyril's. A small, dark, bushy-eyebrowed woman in her forties, she was wearing a brown velvet evening frock and a diamanté headband.

'Yes, frightfully,' Edith said, without enthusiasm.

'She's such a darling.' Mrs Campbell beamed at Sadie across the dinner table.

The occasion had gone wrong before it had even begun. Cyril had been called out to his mother's bedside only minutes before the first of the dinner guests arrived. As he dashed out to hail a cab, he jokingly remarked that he hoped to be back in time for pudding.

Edith had stood, flustered, after the front door had closed

behind him, scarlet with anxiety and from the heat of the kitchen. 'It's too late to telephone,' she said to Sadie. 'Should I send them away? But that would look so dreadfully impolite, wouldn't it? What would I do with all the food? And it's not as if Gertrude is dying. She's done this sort of thing before.'

The Campbells and the Macmillans had arrived, drinks had been served in the drawing room and then they had all trooped into the dining room. The evening, sticky from the first, did not take off. They missed Cyril's easy good humour, thought Sadie, his knack of making an occasion flow happily along. Edith looked on edge. Sadie assumed she was worried about both Cyril and her mother-in-law, and she tried to fill the gaps in the conversation herself. To entertain the guests and to help Edith out, she made herself out to be a little more bohemian than she actually was, and so they raised their eyebrows, pleasurably shocked and amused. Roland Macmillan, who was something important in the India Office, twirled his moustaches.

Bernadette came in with the roast beef, and Sadie, knowing how Edith loathed carving, said, 'David, do you think you might do the honours?'

David Campbell, sitting beside her, said, 'Ho! Delighted, my dear. Just hand the beast my way,' and he brandished the carving knife, while Edith fanned herself with her napkin.

The evening ground on. Cyril was not back in time for pudding. Sadie told the story of her first night at the Egg, failing to light the stove and having to eat cold soup out of a tin because her box of china had gone missing in the move. The Campbells and the Macmillans roared with laughter. Compliments for the food were supplied and Edith was sympathised with yet again over Cyril's absence. Sadie was asked questions about her home, her profession. David

Campbell claimed to have never met a real, live artist before — as if she was some rare and extraordinary creature, such as a unicorn or a griffin, she couldn't help thinking.

The guests left at midnight, replete with food and wine, kissing Sadie's cheek and thanking Edith. Cyril returned, looking exhausted, shortly afterwards. 'Poor Mama isn't at all well,' he said. 'The doctor is afraid the cough may have turned to pneumonia. Quite distressing.' He squeezed Sadie's shoulder and kissed Edith. 'Thank you, my dearest girls. So good of you both to hold the fort.' Edith sent him up to bed with the promise of hot buttered rum.

'I'll make it, if you like,' offered Sadie.

'No, thank you. I know how Cyril likes his drinks.' Edith gave her a frosty look. 'Is the hem of your frock supposed to be like that?'

'Well, yes.'

Sadie loved her new frock, which Pearl had helped her sew. The panels of black and bronze art silk formed an asymmetric skirt that swept down one side, almost to the ankles.

'How odd,' said Edith.

Sadie hoped that her sister, who was clearly in a bad mood, was going to leave it at that. But, as she made to go to the kitchen, Edith looked back at her. The words burst out, bitter and rancorous: 'People always make allowances for you, don't they, Sadie? Your odd clothes, your unguarded conversation. If I were to do as you do, they would laugh at me behind my back, but you . . . I don't know how you do it. I've never known how you do it. It seems so unfair.'

Sadie went up to bed. The effort of telling funny stories, of being sparkling and amusing for the entertainment of strangers with whom she had little in common, had worn her out. She sat down on her bed in Edith's spare room.

Though she had tried to help Edith, she had clearly annoyed her. It was hard to know what exactly she had done wrong. As she unclipped her earrings, she was aware of a feeling of resentment and a longing for tomorrow – no, it was already today – when she would return to the Egg.

The early-evening train was ten minutes late coming into East Grinstead, so Sadie had to run along the platform to where the two-carriage, up-and-down service that rattled along the branch line to Nutcombe was waiting. She flung herself into an empty compartment.

A billow of smoke blocked out her view of the station and the whistle howled. Sadie curled up in a corner seat and opened her book. Then the door to the compartment opened and she looked up and saw Tom Chiverton.

He shut the door behind him and sat down on the middle seat of the opposite row. 'Hello, Sadie.' He laughed. 'You look like a startled deer.'

She pulled her coat round her. 'You shouldn't be here, Tom.'

He waved a stub of cardboard ticket at her. 'I'm perfectly entitled.' Then he held up the flat of his hand in a gesture of appeasement. 'I won't tease you, promise.'

She made a small gesture: it *doesn't matter; we're grown-ups; we can cope with this.* There was a silence, during which she could feel his gaze on her, like the heat from a pan of boiling water.

To have spent the fifteen-minute journey without either of them saying another word would have been unbearable. The atmosphere throbbed with tension. Better to keep it light, she thought, make conversation, pretend nothing had happened.

'I didn't know you were back from America.'

'Yes, over a month ago. Diana and I have been in the south of France since then.'

'Did the tour go well?'

'Very. It's an extraordinary country. Sometimes I fell in love with it and sometimes I loathed it. The scenery is magnificent.' He put his head against the back of the seat and swung out his long legs in front of him, so that they acted as a barrier between Sadie and the door. 'There was talk of a visiting professorship in New England, but I turned it down.'

Sadie made a vague, murmured response.

Tom leaned forward. 'Aren't you going to ask me why?'

'I wouldn't presume.'

'I couldn't *write* there. And, besides, you're here.'

'That should make no difference to you,' she said coldly.

'Is that what you think? I thought of you a great deal while we were away.'

Bored by his fooling around, she made to rise; he waved a hand. 'No, no, don't let me frighten you off.'

'I'm not *frightened*. Just fed up with this . . . this *silliness*.'

'If you prefer, I won't say another word.' His smile was that of a wolf, contemplating its prey. 'I'll content myself with drinking in your beauty.'

She let out a sigh. 'Tom, please stop it; you're being ridiculous.'

The train rattled along. From beyond the compartment, a shriek as a pair of little boys in school caps and blazers ran along the corridor.

She said, suddenly, 'Does Diana know?'

'About us? No, I don't think so.'

'I wondered . . .' It was her turn to feel ridiculous; he might think her offended by being left off the Chivertons' guest list.

And he seemed to follow her thoughts, because he said, 'She decided that you weren't our sort.'

Odd how the insult piqued her. She wanted to laugh at herself.

He added, 'It would have been awkward, you must admit – you continuing to come to the Gull's Wing, when you consider everything there is between us.'

'Tom, there's nothing between us,' she said tiredly. 'I thought I'd made that clear. It was a mistake and I regret it bitterly. And so should you.'

'I can't do that, Sadie.'

'Why not?'

'Because I love you.'

'No, you don't,' she said sharply, leaning forward and scowling at him. 'Maybe you're attracted to me – or maybe you're infatuated with me – or maybe your vanity's offended because I'm not claiming to worship you madly, like all the other women do. But you don't *love* me.'

'I do. Whatever you think of me, that's the truth.'

She gave him a furious glare, expecting to see in his eyes mockery and self-satisfaction. But there was neither; instead, pretence and artifice had fallen away, and she thought that, for once, she was seeing the real Tom Chiverton, shorn of self-satisfaction and pride – vulnerable, even. It shook her, and she looked out of the window to where shadows fell from the oaks and elms, blue-black on fields just greening.

The train slowed as it drew into Nutcombe, and she rose and buttoned up her coat. She said, 'Tom, you're a married man. Diana adores you, she worships you, her whole life revolves around you. *That's* love, and I'm sure you know it. Not some stupid fumble between two people who were too drunk to know what they were doing.'

She reached up to take her overnight bag down from the rack, but he, a foot taller, was there first. As he handed it to her, he said, his voice low, 'I can't forget you, Sadie. You shouldn't ask me to. Every time I run through the woods, I think of you. When I see your house in the woods, I wonder what you're doing and whether you're thinking of me. I'll always be there. I'm your shadow. I'm the leaves moving in the trees.'

She tugged the bag off him in an exasperated movement and hurried out into the corridor. When the train drew to a halt, she opened the door and rushed across the platform without looking back.

As she collected her bicycle from where she had left it outside the shop and flung her overnight bag into the basket, she heard the sound of a motor-car engine starting up. On the other side of the street, Tom was climbing into the passenger seat of the Wolseley. Diana's dark head was visible over the steering wheel as they drove away.

As she pedalled furiously uphill, Sadie imagined sharing Tom's pretension with Pearl — *I'm your shadow. I'm the leaves moving in the trees* — but she knew, in the next instant, that she would never do so, because what he had said had unnerved her too much. She felt a crushing disappointment. In the Chivertons' long absence, she had persuaded herself that she could put what had happened behind her, that she should thank her lucky stars that the consequences of her liaison with Tom had not been more severe, and forget about it, move on. The deed had been momentous, and yet, at the same time, so fleeting and without meaning.

Now, she was not so sure. Though she would have liked to believe that Tom had been teasing her, it was not impossible that he imagined he was in love with her. And that was deeply troubling.

During her absence, the Egg had taken on the cold quiet of the woodland that surrounded it. As she unlocked the front door, the light of her torch illuminated a trail of muddy footprints on the white tiles. She must have made them as she left the house a few days ago, hurrying to catch her train.

She switched on the light. She had an urge to measure her own boot against one of the footprints, to ensure they were the same size, but told herself not to be silly. She carried her overnight case upstairs. The door to her studio was open and the light from the landing washed across her collage, which was propped up on the trestle table. The branches, like cracks in ice, and the pigeon feathers.

In the bedroom, she put on the bedside lamp. Shadows pooled in the corners of the room, underlining several dressing-table drawers that were standing out unevenly, as if someone had opened and closed them in a hurry. She hadn't worn Felix's ring to London because she had known that Edith would disapprove. She opened a drawer and checked that the ring was still there. Of course it was. She slipped it back on her finger.

The night seeped into the room and she felt its dark pressure on the nape of her neck as she took her evening frock out of the case and hung it in the wardrobe. She was about to go downstairs and make herself something to eat when a movement beyond the window caught her eye. She stood, her palm on the glass, looking out at the flat roof with its swirl of dead leaves. *I'm your shadow. I'm the leaves moving in the trees.*

She went downstairs. Cracking eggs and grating cheese to make an omelette, she reflected on their conversation. How dare Tom say those things to her? Why couldn't he have pretended, as she was prepared to pretend, that nothing had ever happened?

He dared, she thought soberly, because, back on that stormy night, she had given herself to him. She had made it easy for him. That was the sort of woman he thought she was: *easy*.

A pale gold light slanted through acid-green leaves and spilled and flickered on the beech mast. Birdsong thrilled in the tree canopy and, from the wet branches, blobs of rain tumbled on to starry celandines and wood anemones.

Sadie had set up her easel on the far side of the sunken lane, from where she could see the fall of the Downs to the valley, bathed in the spring afternoon's champagne light. She worked for a couple of hours, reducing sky, hill, copse and river to bands of blue, green and ochre. Sunlight sparkled, caressing the hills and refracting on the river.

A flash of white, down in the dark curve of the hill, where the trees grew thickly. Sadie turned back to her painting, trying to rediscover the quiet space of her concentration. When she looked again, she saw it more clearly, bleached against the tree trunks. Now and then, you saw a fallow deer in Paley High Wood. Focus, Sadie. Her hand paused, making the sweep of the hill, so round and solid she could cup it in her palm.

The flash of white coalesced into a man running through the trees. Dark trousers, white singlet, black hair. Would he see her? The brush, touching the canvas, trembled, and she had to fight the urge to bundle her paints and brushes back into the box, to collapse the easel and hurry away to the safety of the house.

When she looked back again, he had gone. But she had lost her concentration and, after another half-hour, she gathered up her belongings and headed home. Approaching the Egg, she glimpsed its white shell as disassociated fragments between the trunks and branches, pieces of a house in the process of being swallowed up by the forest.

Sadie and her youngest pupils, the little girls Iris, Hazel and Heather, were painting the bluebells that flowered beneath the beech trees. She set up a small folding table in a clearing and put out paper and a pot of chalky pastels. She was trying to teach them first how to look, to see the colour of the flowers as it truly was, and then how to mix the shade that was somewhere between blue and purple.

They bent over the table, chubby hands scribbling layers of pastel. Sadie heard the clip of horses' hooves and glanced up. Two riders were heading along the edge of the field. Diana Chiverton rode ahead. She was wearing jodhpurs and an open-necked white shirt, and her dark hair was neatly coiled on her shoulders. Tom followed behind her on his great black horse. Their voices drifted over.

Tom was saying, 'It will mean being away for several weeks.'

And Diana: 'I'll write to the hotels in advance, as usual.'

'For God's sake, there's no need for that; I don't need a nanny.'

'Tom, my love, I know you like to be comfortable.'

'No, I don't; I don't give a damn. I'd sleep out on the hills, if it gave me some peace. It's not as if I'll be able to work, away from here.'

'Then cancel it.'

'I can't; I've made a commitment. It means a lot to me, that my work reaches ordinary people.'

'They could always visit a public library.'

Tom, tetchy again: 'It's not so simple. You don't know. How could you, when life has always been so easy for you? I don't think you should come. It will bore you.'

The voices faded. Hazel's pastel broke and she began to cry. Sadie knelt down beside her on the dead leaves and talked to her gently. When she looked up, the Chivertons had passed out of sight, and were hidden behind the solid grey trunks of the beech trees.

London smelled of rainswept pavements and wet gaberdine. Office workers were dashing out to lunch, their umbrellas bobbing like jellyfish in a rain-spattered sea. Motor cars flung up curls of water from puddles in which cigarette stubs bobbed; a cyclist, collar up, head down and hat jammed low over his forehead, zoomed past Sadie as she crossed the road, missing her by a whisker.

Sadie was spending the day with Lachlan Brodie, who rented a studio in Chelsea. They had met at the Slade, where Lachlan was a part-time teacher. Scots, black bearded, thickset and square shouldered, he opened the door to her and hugged her.

'So, you're living in Sussex,' he said, when they were upstairs in his studio and Sadie had draped her wet things over the back of a chair. 'I suppose you've become a vegetarian and taken up folk dancing as well.'

'I may do, Lachlan.'

He filled the kettle and lit the spirit stove that sat in a corner of the room. The clutter of paper and inks and squashed-up tubes and cleaning rags, stiff and dark with layers of colour, felt like home to Sadie. Raindrops pattered on the high dormer windows and dripped through the rotting corner of a frame into a rusty Oxo tin on the floor.

Lachlan was printing a new edition and Sadie had offered to give him a hand. The first print, which was to be called *Rain*, was a swirling design of teal, pink and black hats, umbrellas and faces. There were to be three more in the series: *Snow*, *Fog* and *Wind*.

The print was finished towards the end of the afternoon and pronounced a success. They celebrated by dining on fish and chips, and then spent an enjoyable few hours in the pub, discussing the artistic failings of several acquaintances.

Parting at the Underground station, Lachlan said to her, 'Thank you for your help, my dear girl. It wouldn't have gone half so well without you. You'll give me a hand with the others, won't you? If you ever decide to give up Sussex and vegetarianism, Sadie, there'll always be work for you here, if you want it.'

Summer approached, at first in fits and starts, and then, settling down at last, in a wash of heat and light. One warm afternoon, Sadie changed into her bathing costume and stepped out of the bedroom window on to the flat roof. Lying on her stomach on a rolled-out towel, she felt the rays of sun press through her skin to muscle and bone, warming, softening. She slipped down the straps to brown her shoulders, picturing herself as if from a bird's-eye view: her black costume, the rectangular white towel, the asphalt roof.

She was on the verge of dozing off when she heard the crack of a broken branch. A pheasant rose up into the sky with a whirr of wings.

Sadie sat up, clutching her swimsuit to her chest as she stared out into the trees. All day, the foliage had hung limp in the hot, humid atmosphere. And yet now a ripple was

262

passing through sweet chestnut and elm. The leaves should not have moved, she thought. The day was windless.

Someone was out there, she was sure of it. As she stood up, she saw a shadow slide, liquid, beneath the branches and then vanish. The soft tread of footsteps was audible above the wild beating of her heart. Whoever was out there was moving through the undergrowth that surrounded the Egg.

'Tom? Is that you?' she called out. 'Are you there?'

No answer.

'Tom?' she shouted, angry now. 'You're there, I know it!'

In the bedroom, she pulled on a robe and hurried downstairs. She had opened the glass doors in the sitting room wide to let in air. Sunlight, pouring through the glass wall, flickered and flashed with the shadows of the trees on the white tiles.

She went out on to the terrace. The feeling that she was being watched was a powerful sensation, physical and intrusive. 'Tom?' she called again. 'Tom?'

No answer. Scouring the trees, it occurred to her that, though they protected the house, they also hid whatever lay beyond it. She went back inside and closed the glass doors, sealing the heat in with her.

She changed out of her bathing costume in the bathroom, which had only a small, frosted window. She told herself that perhaps a fallow deer had made the branches sway, or one of the villagers had been looking for fungi in the woodland. Or Ivy, the maid at the Gull's Wing, might have been taking a shortcut home and, shocked by the sight of a half-naked woman on the roof, had scurried away. She had no evidence, no evidence at all, that Tom had been there.

All those people who had warned her not to isolate herself

at the Egg had been right. It wasn't good for a person to be too much on their own. You ended up imagining things.

Sadie was in an art gallery in Jermyn Street. Lachlan Brodie was a friend of the owner, Madge Danford, and had spoken to her on Sadie's behalf about the possibility of her taking Sadie on as a client. Madge wore her dark hair in sleek curls that lay flat round her face. Her make-up was discreet, apart from her dark red lips, and her mint-green frock was cut fashionably on the cross and clung to her hips. She had only recently established the gallery, Lachlan had explained to Sadie, and was actively looking for new young artists.

It felt, Sadie thought, as Madge leafed silently through her portfolio, as if her children were about to be appraised and criticised and found wanting. She forced her features into a state of pleasant expectation and tried to quiet the thudding of her heart.

'This I like,' said Madge, studying a print of the ploughed fields, ridged like corduroy. She moved the paper aside to look at a stand of elms on the hillside, green and gold in the spring. 'And this I like very much. Oh, yes.'

Madge glanced at Sadie and gave a light laugh. 'Don't look so worried. I adore them. You have a gift for colour. You shouldn't bother with the black and whites –' an etching was placed dismissively to one side – 'but these, yes. Have you much else?'

'Some.' She added, honestly, 'Not a great deal; I've been through rather a dry period. But I've been working a lot better recently.'

Madge looked thoughtful. 'I won't take you on now, Sadie,' she said. 'You haven't enough material and I sense that you're in the process of, shall we say, a metamorphosis. But work hard and keep in touch. Come and see me again in six months, a year – whenever you're ready – and we'll talk again.' She gave Sadie a bright, encouraging smile. 'I can hardly wait to see what you will become.'

Heading along Piccadilly to meet Pearl outside the dress shop where she worked, her portfolio tucked under her arm, Sadie felt exhilarated. Miss Danford had admired her work. *I can hardly wait to see what you will become.* Life seemed suddenly full of glorious possibility. She was turning a corner, at last.

She and Pearl had supper together at a Lyons' tea shop. Pearl was no longer seeing Ralph. Their relationship had not survived the pregnancy scare, which had ended in a miscarriage. Over sardines on toast, followed by fruit salad, Pearl told Sadie that she had given in her notice at the dress shop and would be taking up a position as an art teacher at a girls' school in Hertfordshire in the autumn.

'I feel as if I'm about to enter a nunnery, Sadie, darling,' she said. 'But I have to get out of London, I simply have to.'

They parted with kisses and hugs, and Pearl promising to visit the Egg soon. At Victoria Station, Sadie caught the train to East Grinstead by the skin of her teeth, flinging herself into the first compartment with vacant seats. As it drew away from the platform, she felt the stare of the man in trilby and grubby raincoat, sitting opposite her, and tugged down her skirt over her knees.

'You were in a tearing hurry, missy,' he said.

'I didn't want to miss the train. My husband's waiting for me at the station.' She had gloves on, so he could not see that she was not wearing a ring.

He leaned forward to offer her a packet of fruit gums. 'If I was your husband, I wouldn't let a pretty little thing like you go wandering about on her own.'

'No, thanks,' she said frostily, and looked away. She decided that, if he tried to draw down the blinds, she would find a seat in another compartment. She took her book out of her bag and began pointedly to read.

It was dark by the time she turned off the hill for the path through Paley High Wood. She propped her bicycle against the wall and put her key in the lock of the Egg's front door. It would not turn. When she tried the door, she discovered with a shock that it was already open.

She stepped into the hall and switched on the electric light. There was the impulse to call out, to ask whether anyone was there – but if a voice were to answer her, what on earth should she do? Her fear intensified as she caught sight of footprints on the tiles. She placed her foot beside one; that the print was the same size as her own reassured her.

She had forgotten to lock the door when she left the house in the morning, that was all. She had been excited about her appointment with Madge Danford and, in a rush to catch the train, had been careless. She had nothing to worry about; the inhabitants of Nutcombe village probably never locked their doors.

And yet, as she turned on the lights in the sitting room, she felt it again: the disturbing sensation that she was being watched. She looked round, checking that everything was where it should be. The cup, saucer and plate she had used at breakfast that morning were on the draining board by the sink. A bottle of milk stood in a pail of water to keep cold. Her books, newspapers, pens and paper littered the table in the sitting room, just as they always did.

She went upstairs. Her bed was rumpled because she hadn't had time to make it in the morning. Several items of clothing were draped over a chair, and her jewellery and the purse in which she kept her payments from her pupils were safe in a drawer. The book she was reading lay open on the bedside table and a silk scarf had slithered to the floor beneath the dressing table. She retrieved it, winding it round her hand.

She went into the studio. She had a good visual memory and, as her gaze swung over the room, her unease returned. Surely that tube of paint was not where she had left it? Surely she had not left the sketches for her new print so carelessly in disarray?

She saw then that someone had daubed great drips of red on to the collage that was propped on the trestle table. Instead of the single streak of scarlet that she had painted, slashes of the colour now obliterated the pale pigeon-feathers and charcoal branches. Stripes of red criss-crossed the image over and over again, as if some unseen hand had violated it in what appeared to be a paroxysm of rage, turning the monochrome scene blood red.

Unable to sleep in the bedroom, Sadie dragged a comfortable chair into the kitchen and curled up in it, wrapping a blanket round her. Dawn was seeping through the windows when she eventually dozed off. Waking, a couple of hours later, some of her terrors of the night seemed irrational. She had not been robbed, and nor had she been murdered in her bed. The only damage had been to a work of art, and not a very good one at that.

She knew who had broken into her house. *I'll always be there*, he had said to her. *I'm your shadow.* Tom Chiverton had claimed to love her and had vowed to haunt her. He knew how to pick a lock. He had broken into the house before. He had defaced the collage because he had been angry with her for rejecting him. The furious, attention-seeking splashes of red paint were his message to her: *I'm still here, Sadie. Don't forget me.*

She found the tube of cadmium red, squashed flat and missing its lid, beneath the etching press. She carried the collage downstairs and hacked it to pieces with an axe, then shoved it into the stove to burn.

In the afternoon, she caught the train to East Grinstead, where she bought, from a draper's, yards of cream-coloured glazed cotton fabric. Cutting out her curtains on the sitting-room floor that evening, she hoped he was watching. *You won't be able to see me any more,* she was saying. *I'm shutting you out of my life, Tom.*

August brought with it a heatwave. One morning, Sadie met Edith at Nutcombe railway station. The train on which her elder sister had just arrived screeched and belched smoke to announce that it was setting off on its shuttle back to East Grinstead.

Light slanted through the branches of the trees, falling in kaleidoscope fragments on the platform, and on Edith, in her straw hat and fawn linen summer travelling coat. She was carrying only a parasol and a small leather clutch.

'Where's your case?' asked Sadie.

'My case?' Edith wrinkled up her nose in the way she did when someone had said something silly.

'Your overnight case.'

'I haven't brought an overnight case.'

'But I thought you were staying.'

'I was quite clear in my letter that I couldn't possibly spare more than a day.'

'But you said . . .' With an effort, Sadie let her sentence tail off. She was sure that Edith had agreed that she would stay the night at the Egg. Or, at least, she had not made it clear that she would not.

Edith showed her ticket to the guard and they left the station. As they climbed up the hill, Edith puffing a little, Sadie found it hard to put aside her disappointment. She had planned a walk and a picnic. She had tidied and cleaned the house. She had intended to give Edith her bedroom, while she slept on the sofa, and had purchased new, pretty bed linen. She had emptied out two of her drawers and arranged a mirror, water jug, glass, basin and a vase of wild flowers on the dressing table. She had not realised how deeply she longed not to be alone in the Egg for a night until Edith had told her she would not be staying.

So now the day would be rushed and unsatisfactory. She tried to keep the whine from her voice as she said, 'We've been saying for ages that you should come for a weekend. It seems such a long way to travel and quite a tiresome journey for so short a time.'

Edith, red with heat and exertion, patted her face with a small embroidered hankie. 'The train sat for quarter of an hour at East Grinstead and the window was jammed – I couldn't open it. I didn't dare leave the carriage to buy myself a cold drink from the refreshment room in case it set off.'

Sadie's irritation faded and she felt sorry for Edith. 'We're almost there. I'll run you a glass of lovely cold water as soon as we're home.'

They turned off from the road to take the path beneath the trees, Edith picking through the earth in her white kid shoes and muttering how a little gravel might improve the approach. A harsh light fell on the forest floor in spots and drifts.

As they neared the house, Edith exclaimed, 'But it's all so overgrown! I remember the house being in a clearing!'

'Trees are in the habit of growing,' said Sadie dryly.

'There's no need to be sarcastic.'

'I wasn't being sarcastic.' Though perhaps she had been, a little. She added, 'I can't hack them back myself. But you're right, I must find someone to lop them. I'm afraid it will be frightfully expensive, though.'

They reached the house. Edith sat down heavily on one of the canvas chairs Sadie had arranged on the terrace, anticipating that they might sit outside if the evening was fine.

In the kitchen, she ran two tumblers of water and took them into the sitting room. She opened the glass doors. 'Come indoors, Edith. It's cooler in here.'

Edith sat on the sofa and drank the water while Sadie made tea and arranged some biscuits on a plate. She carried the tray into the sitting room.

'How is Louisa?'

'She's very well. She sends her love.'

'Please give my best love to her. I wondered whether she might come with you.'

'Oh, no, she's staying with a friend in Whitstable.'

'A schoolfriend?'

'Yes. A girl called Marjorie Lester. Mr Lester is a barrister and Mrs Lester is a very pleasant woman. She's the women's captain at the tennis club. Louisa has become very keen on tennis this summer. She has a marvellous backhand. Mrs Lester wrote to ask my permission to let her attend the summer party at the club. She has promised to chaperone the girls very carefully. I made her an evening dress of pink tussore silk. She looks so sweet in it.'

'And Cyril? How is he? Is he well?'

'Apart from his dyspepsia, yes.'

Sadie sensed, in Edith's alternating garrulousness and terseness, an evasion, something not said. They drank their tea and talked of a lunch Edith had had at Peter Jones with an old friend of their parents.

Afterwards, Sadie offered to show her sister round the house.

'I'd forgotten how small it was,' Edith said, following her into the kitchen.

'It's the perfect size for me.'

'I don't know how you manage without a gas stove.'

'Oh, I'm a dab hand at laying a coal fire.'

Why did she find herself slipping into Girl Guide-ish cheeriness in Edith's company? She must surely annoy Edith and certainly irritated herself. It was because her sister's remarks seemed barbed, stabbing little hooks of criticism. You could let them sink in or try to brush them off.

She said, 'A supper party might be tricky, I admit. Cyril must come with you, the next time you visit, and I shall try to manage it.'

'Cyril has been offered a post in India,' said Edith.

'India.' Sadie stared at her.

'Yes.' Edith was folding a tea towel, smoothing it with her palm. 'It's a wonderful opportunity. The permanent under-secretary thinks very highly of him.'

A thought popped into Sadie's head: that this was why Edith had come to the Egg today, not for her long-overdue visit, but to tell her about Cyril and India.

'And you?'

'I shall go with him, naturally. You know he's always wanted to travel. And now that Gertrude is gone and we have no ties, we're free to go where we like. I mean . . .' Edith looked flustered.

271

Sadie watched her try to reassemble her clumsy remark. *We couldn't leave the country while Cyril's mother was still alive, but it doesn't matter about you.* Another barb hooked itself beneath her skin and remained there, imparting its poison.

'I meant, it would have been cruel to go while poor Gertrude was so unwell,' Edith finished.

Sadie gave her a thoughtful look. 'Are you telling me that Cyril is considering taking the post, or that he's already decided?'

'He accepted it. Sadie, he had no choice.' Edith looked cross and guilty, as if caught in a misdemeanour. 'He couldn't possibly have refused. He has to think of his career. I'm sorry it will put such a great distance between us, but I shall make home visits, and, of course, I'll write.'

Cyril must pursue his ambitions. Edith, her only sister, must accompany him halfway across the world. Plenty of people who knew her might have thought she wouldn't mind. *We don't really get on . . .* How many times had she said that when talking about Edith to her friends? And yet she felt floored, shocked to the core, and the thought occurred to her that soon she would be completely alone.

'How long are you going for?'

'We don't know yet.'

'Months or years?'

Edith flushed. 'Years, I should think.'

Years. 'When are you leaving?'

'October. The fifth of October.'

October. Less than two months away and, from the sound of it, the passage already booked, the suitcases almost packed and labelled. *Oh, I'd better mention it to Sadie,* she imagined Edith murmuring to Cyril, between sorting out shipping agents and ordering sola topis from the Army & Navy. She felt so desolate she could have wept, knowing herself so unimportant to her sister.

Edith said, 'We sail a week after seeing Louisa back to school.'

'You're not taking her with you?'

'Sadie, I can't. She must complete her schooling. If we wait until she finishes . . .' Again, Edith sounded distressed. 'Cyril was very fortunate to be offered this opportunity. He may not have another one.'

'I don't know how you can bear it, leaving your own daughter.' The words snapped out of her, flint hard and sparking.

'Do you imagine that it's easy?' said Edith, equally sharply. 'Do you imagine I haven't lain awake, night after night, wondering whether I'm doing the right thing?'

Sadie looked up to the three round windows, like a ship's portholes, that pierced the kitchen wall. In the strong sunlight, the silhouettes of the trees were a dull and lifeless black.

'Sorry,' she murmured.

'Don't let's quarrel. Who knows how long it will be till we see each other again? Perhaps I should have written to warn you . . . Yes, perhaps I should. Though, you're not exactly a good correspondent yourself, Sadie.'

'I always reply to your letters.'

'Oh, yes, you *reply* . . . but it would be nice if sometimes you took the initiative . . . A visit . . . A coffee in town on the days you're seeing Dr Sprott.'

Why must Edith always try to make out that any fault lay with her? Why must she justify her own failings by shifting the blame to someone else? And yet Sadie was aware of an unpleasant, creeping guilt, and her mind sprung back reluc-

273

tantly to London trips where she had chosen to pay calls on
Pearl, Jimmy or Lachlan – anyone but her sister.

Edith gave the tea towel a final vigorous pat, and then,
having gained the upper hand, said briskly, 'I realise this
must all be rather a shock. Why don't you show me what
you've done to the rest of the house? We can talk about it
later.'

Offhandedly, Sadie said, 'If you like.'

Heat had gathered in the windowless passageway and stairs.
They plodded to the upper floor, not speaking. The day had
taken on an air of futility – it was, Sadie sensed, already
unsalvageable. Edith was going to live in India. Years and
years might pass before they saw each other again. Her family,
ripped apart by the death of their parents, had been shredded
to nothing.

In Sadie's bedroom, the direction of Edith's gaze moved
outside, to the flat roof and the trees. 'You've put up curtains,'
she said.

'Yes. I know Father disliked them, but—'

'"Bourgeois and ugly".' Edith was quoting their father.

Sadie smiled. 'I couldn't sleep,' she said. Before she put
up the curtains, there had been nights when she dragged
the mattress into her workroom and slept there, away from
the open gaze of the window.

'It can't be good for you, living here on your own,' Edith
said.

'I've no choice but to live on my own.'

'How long do you mean to stay here?'

She imagined Edith discussing her with Cyril: *We must think
what to do about Sadie.* 'I don't know,' she said sullenly.

'You could always rent it out and live somewhere else.'

'I'm happy here.'

'I *worry* about you.'

'Not enough to live in the same country as me.'

'Sadie! That's so unfair!'

Perhaps it was, she thought bitterly. Perhaps, in this instance, Edith was right. But not in the past.

'You weren't worried enough to stay with me when I most needed you.'

And there, it was out, the hurt she had nurtured for more than a year, and she felt a heady, delicious delight in saying it, the sort of pleasure one takes in thwacking a stick at a bank of cow parsley and watching the tall stems snap and break.

'What are you talking about?' The red had risen again to Edith's cheeks.

'You, shutting me away in that awful place. That nursing home.'

'The nursing home? It was the best nursing home I could find! Dr Chisholm recommended it!' There were two coins of scarlet on Edith's cheeks and her fringe drooped lankly over her high forehead.

'It was a horrible, vile bloody place, and you know it was.'

'Please don't use that language.'

Sadie gave a croak of laughter. 'Oh, for pity's sake, Edith; they're only words. Deserting someone – abandoning them when they're going through an awful time . . . isn't that far worse?'

'I didn't *abandon* you. Don't be ridiculous.'

'I needed someone who cared about me. I needed your support. I needed my *family*. But you couldn't bear to be near me.'

'That's not true . . .' The words came out in a gasp.

'You sent me away because you were ashamed of me.'

Sadie felt a wild exultation in saying aloud what she had believed for a long time to be true.

'Ashamed?' Edith, usually controlled, allowed her voice to rise in a shriek. '*Ashamed?* I was out of my mind with worry! I tried! I tried my best, heaven knows – but with you it's just one thing after another! First, that wretched man – and I *warned* you about him! And then, in spite of all advice, you would insist on carrying on teaching, even though you were plainly exhausted!'

Pearl, too, had tried to encourage her to take time off work, but she had refused. Sadie pushed the memory away.

'I had to earn a living,' she said. 'You wouldn't know about that, would you, Edith?' Her sister had never done a day's work in her life. 'It's all very well for you; you have Cyril, but I have to rely on myself.'

'You had what you inherited from Father. You had that. You had both the houses.'

There was a depth of resentment in Edith's voice that caught Sadie by surprise. She felt herself teetering on the edge of a chasm. Something dark and unpleasant was opening up and she might, if she was not careful, slip into it.

Before Sadie could respond, Edith, making a sweeping movement with her palms, said, 'Father gave you *everything*. And yet you sold the Gull's Wing. He loved that house.'

'Edith . . .' At her sister's unexpected attack, Sadie felt winded. 'I had no choice but to sell it.'

'Rot. There were plenty of other things you could have done. You could have let it out, for instance.'

'No, I couldn't; I told you that. I explained to you, but you obviously didn't listen. There was an enormous mortgage. I couldn't possibly pay it off.'

'I'm sure you could have found a way. I always loved that

276

house. You *ought* to have kept the Gull's Wing in the family. Father would have *wanted* you to.'

That hurt. Sadie recalled the evenings she and her father had pored over bills that had showed up in relentless detail the rising expenses of the project. The Gull's Wing had gobbled up money, the costs surpassing the budget Edward Lawless had set aside before the house was even halfway complete. How dare Edith, in her ignorance and arrogance, blame her for having sold it?

She said coldly, 'You have no idea how much effort Papa had to put in to see the houses through to completion. You've no idea of the time he spent – or how exhausted he was. You didn't see how he had to fight every step of the way – to buy the land, to obtain the permissions and to find builders capable of carrying out the work. You weren't there. You were married to Cyril by then. You know nothing about what the Gull's Wing cost him. *Nothing.*'

'Yes, you're right.' Edith's features had contorted in a grimace and she looked ugly. 'What would I know? You two, you always shut me out.'

'That's not true.'

'It is, and you know it, Sadie.'

Sadie fumbled to take a cigarette from the packet on the bookcase. Her hand trembled as she struck the match.

'You shut yourself out, Edith,' she said quietly. 'It's what you do. You close yourself off from people. You have a hard little heart and there's never been room in it for me.'

'That's a wicked thing to say!'

Sadie pursed her lips, letting out a stream of smoke. 'Is it? I thought we were telling the truth. You've always resented me. You've never loved me at all.'

The phrases came out, tumbling and uncontrollable, in

vicious, fiery little puffs. But, as soon as she said them, her exhilaration vanished and she felt depleted, as if the words had extracted the oxygen from her lungs.

Edith sat down on the bed. She shut her eyes; she, too, looked drained and drawn about the mouth. With a stiff, clumsy movement, she reached up to tuck a lock of damp hair behind her ear. On the edge of Sadie's consciousness flickered the beginnings of regret, an awareness that there were words that should never be said – words that, once released into the atmosphere, remained there, impossible to shift.

When she spoke, Edith's voice was low and grainy. 'Perhaps you're right; perhaps I've never loved you. What chance did we ever have, you and I, to love each other as sisters should? I'm not a fool; I could see how it was. From the day you were born, you were Father's favourite. Mother should have comforted me, she should have made up for it, but she didn't. She lived in her own world. He was the sun and she bathed in his warmth and whatever he did was right. The worst thing – I think it is the worst thing – is that I could always see why he loved you more. You were prettier, cleverer and more charming than me. But he shouldn't have. It wasn't right. I'm a mother and I know that.' When she looked up, Sadie recognised a cold judgement in her eyes. 'Your trouble, Sadie, is that you don't think the normal rules of society apply to you. You think you can do exactly as you please and everyone will change to suit you. Father was the same, of course. And then, when the money runs out or the cad goes off with another girl, you're shocked and disappointed, and you stand there, expecting other people to pick up the pieces. I've tried to protect you, but it's impossible. Well, not any more. Not any more.'

Edith rose and left the room. Nausea washed through Sadie and she wrestled with the catch to open the window. The air that wafted inside the room was solid and hot. She leaned against the frame, rubbing a palm from wrist to elbow. Odd that, in this heat, she should suddenly feel cold.

She went downstairs. In the hall, she registered that Edith's coat and hat were no longer on the peg. She looked into the kitchen, then the sitting room, but they were empty, as she had known they would be. On the terrace, she turned her gaze to the path that led to the road, as if it might contain some evidence of Edith's fleeing form – an impression of a shoe, a handkerchief dropped in the dead leaves – but there was nothing.

She should go after her, she thought. If she cycled, she could catch up with her sister before she reached the station. But she did not; it was already too late and nothing could be retrieved, and, after a while, she turned back into the house.

In the afternoon, having run out of cigarettes, Sadie cycled to the shop. The day was unbearably warm and a trickle of sweat ran down her neck as she propped her bicycle against a fence. The ache in her heart urged her to walk to the station and look along the platform, as if she might still find Edith there, but she crushed the impulse. She would have left hours ago, but even if by some chance all the trains had been delayed, what could Sadie say to her? Some of Edith's accusations had been justified. Their father had not been even-handed with his two daughters. Acknowledging this intensified the distress she felt, because it meant acknowledging that the man she had adored had been imperfect.

She went into the shop to buy cigarettes from Winnie

Thomsett, who was serving behind the counter. Half a dozen farm labourers, shirts and trousers dusty with chaff from the harvest, were purchasing tobacco and matches and bottles of pop, crowding the small space.

Outside, she stood in the shade and lit a cigarette. Looking up, she saw that Tom Chiverton was standing on the opposite side of the road, beside her bicycle. The fury generated by her quarrel with Edith resurfaced and found a new mark.

She crossed the road to him. 'Leave me alone!' she hissed.

He had the nerve to look surprised. 'What?'

'You have to stop it, Tom.'

'Stop what?'

'You. Hiding outside my house. *Watching* me.'

'Sadie, I would never do that.'

'Tell the truth. You were spying on me when I was sunbathing. You were, weren't you? Admit it.'

He was incapable of shame, but there was, in his sideways glance, an admission of guilt. 'I wasn't *spying*,' he said. 'I happened to be walking there and I saw you. You shouldn't blame me.'

'And I suppose you *happened* to break into my house?'

'What are you talking about?'

'Oh, come *on*!' she cried scornfully.

'I haven't been in your house since that night.' He didn't seem to care who might overhear his remark and did not lower his voice.

'I don't believe you. You *wanted* me to know. Why else would you have done it?'

'Done what?' He looked offended. 'Yes, I've glanced through the window once or twice. Yes, I see you in the woods now and then. There's nothing wrong in that.'

'There's something wrong in daubing paint over my picture!'

He gave her a puzzled look. 'Paint?'

'Red paint! All over my collage!' Her anger boiled up. 'As you know perfectly well!'

'It wasn't me!' He sounded furious too. 'What are you talking about?'

'I'm talking about you, Tom, breaking into my house and damaging my collage. Don't try to pretend it wasn't you.'

'Sadie, I wouldn't do that.' He was shouting. 'How can you think that of me?'

He was such a liar. Enraged, she said, 'Tom, I *know*. My God, why can't you just leave me alone?'

He stilled, frowning deeply. 'Red paint on a picture . . . ?'

'*Yes*.' A hiss.

He shook his head. 'You have to believe me, Sadie. I've never touched any of your work. I wouldn't. It would be like defacing a poem. I wouldn't do that.'

His air of wounded seriousness, coming so soon after her quarrel with Edith, made Sadie realise the utter impossibility of ever getting through to him. She pushed past him, grabbing her bicycle, and, as she pedalled away, she shouted back at him, 'Leave me alone, Tom! Just leave me alone!'

Such a good liar, she thought again, as she started the steep ascent. From anyone else, his denial would have been convincing. But who else would do such a thing?

Halfway up the hill, an answer occurred to her. And, in spite of the heat and exercise, icy fingers seemed to lay themselves on her shoulder.

Diana.

Chapter Thirteen

Suffolk – December 1970

Dan's father was recovering from bronchitis and hadn't wanted to make the journey to London, so, a couple of days after Christmas, Dan drove up to Southwold. They exchanged presents – he had bought Mick a new anorak, which was exclaimed over and admired, and Mick gave him a set of tools.

'I remember you hammering away at a piece of wood with a nail in it when you were a tiny kid, just three or four,' he said. 'You used to like helping me make things when you were a little lad. Carpentering, you called it.' His father laughed and shook his head wonderingly. 'Carpentering.'

It was hard to work out what made him feel more depressed, Dan reflected: that he already had a set of tools, and of better quality than those his father had given him, or that he had no memory at all of doing woodwork with his father as a small child and found himself questioning whether Mick had made his story up.

They ate some cold chicken, left over from his father's dinner the previous day, along with the salad and cake that Dan had brought with him. Dan tried to refuse Mick's suggestion of a walk, pointing out that the raw air would be bad for his cough, but his father insisted. The wind slapped them in the face and Mick began to hack as they left the caravan. The site was muddy and churned up after recent rains, and Dan hovered by his father, ready to support him if he slipped.

They headed along an unmade road to the harbour. There was a chorus of tinkling and chiming from the rigging of the boats as they passed a clutter of huts, some ramshackle, others spruce with black paint. His father had already asked after his mother and made sympathetic noises about Celia, and they had talked about cars and football, so all topics of conversation had been exhausted. Mick seemed quieter than usual, which Dan put down to his ill health, and the screaming wind filled in the silence.

They found a cosy table beside an open fire in the Harbour Inn, and Dan bought two pints of beer. They toasted the season and then Mick drained a third of his glass before saying, 'I've lost my job. They were getting rid of people. I daresay they picked on me because of my age. They kept on that old girl, Alice Welton, because she was a cousin or something. I'd like to see her hauling those heavy boxes about.' He sounded bitter.

Dan's mood lowered further. His father had been working for two and a half days a week in a general store in Southwold. The money he earned supplemented the small pension he had from a previous employer and enabled him to live his meagre lifestyle.

'I'm sorry, Dad,' he said. 'How are you managing?'

'Fine.' Mick gave him a cheerful smile. He wiped the foam from his mouth with the back of his hand. 'I'm thinking of setting up on my own. Doesn't matter how old you are, then, or who you're related to, does it? I got talking to this

283

fellow in the Nelson. He's got a nice little business selling cleaning materials – washing-up liquid, polish for floors, that sort of thing – and he said I could buy into it. You get the stuff in bulk, dirt cheap, and then you sell it on to the customer at a fifty per cent markup. No, listen, son.' He raised his palm, cutting off Dan's interruption. 'You don't need a shop or any sort of premises, that's the beauty of it. You go to people's houses and put on a little show. I can do that. You know I've always been able to do the patter.'

'How much do you have to put down, to buy the materials?'

'Fifty quid, that's all,' said his father triumphantly. He shoved a hand into the crisp packet, spilling the contents on to the table.

'Got it in savings, have you, Dad?' As he asked the question, he knew that he was being cruel.

'No, but I thought I could sell the van.'

'Oh, for pity's sake . . .' Frustration bubbled up inside him. 'No one's going to give you fifty quid for the van. And, even if they did, how would you manage without it? And how long do you think it would take you to earn your fifty pounds back? The people at the bottom of the heap, the people doing the selling, never make any money out of these schemes. The only ones who do are the guys selling them their rubbish for fifty pounds a time.'

Mick started to speak, then fell silent. A long moment passed before he said, 'Selling to gullible chumps like me, you mean?'

'Dad . . .'

'You're right, Dan. Yes, of course, I see, you're right.'

Again, the silence stretched out, punctuated by the cries of the gulls that wheeled in the sky outside the pub. He was usually gentler with his father, but the thought of him digging

284

his way deeper into poverty had enraged him. He wanted to leave, he wanted to get into his car and drive home to London, where there was sanity, order and rationality.

'You've always had a head for figures, Dan,' Mick said. His voice sounded hoarse. 'I've always been proud of you. Your brains must have come from your mum, not from me. Something'll come up. I'll ask round the pubs. I've done bar work often enough. They'll snap me up, you'll see.'

Dan dug a fingernail into the ball of his thumb until it hurt. 'Yes, Dad. But let me give you a hand, in the meantime.'

'No, I wouldn't dream of it. I'm fine. You'll have another one, won't you?'

'Just a half.'

His father went to the bar. Dan sat in a state of rigid suspension, trying not to think of anything, because there was nothing he could think of that didn't hurt or anger him. The hurt was worse than the anger, but then it always had been. He was hurt for his father, that he had lost yet another job, and yet he knew, because he knew his father, that he would never have put his heart and soul into his work. He would have thought it beneath him, would have complained about the long hours and early starts and back-breaking hefting of boxes of goods. He would have resented his superiors, believing himself to be cleverer and more skilled than them. He would have taken a few minutes extra on all his fag breaks and lunch breaks, would have come in late, more often than not, with some story about a puncture or other delay. What he could have got away with when he was young, handsome and charming, he couldn't get away with any more, and yet he was incapable of seeing that. Dan had often thought how much easier life must be if you had a set of independent, solvent, capable parents. But there was

285

also a pervading sense of shame that he had never been able to rid himself of, as if he himself was somehow to blame for his parents' inadequacies.

Mick came back to the table. He looked dejected, which made Dan feel angry and frustrated all over again. It would have been easier not to say anything, to let him go on throwing good money after bad, but then what?

'I wanted to go back to your mother,' his father said.

Dan's gaze jerked in his direction. 'Did you? When?'

'After Cheryl threw me out.' Cheryl had been the hair-dresser in Weymouth. 'I didn't have the guts. Didn't have the guts to talk to her, to tell her I'd made a mistake. I've always regretted that. I should have tried. I should have been there for you.'

He ought, Dan thought, to put his hand on his father's shoulder and tell him it didn't matter, water under the bridge, all that. But he couldn't say the words. Instead, they finished their drinks in silence and walked back to the caravan.

They had a cup of tea and another piece of cake. While his father was in the toilet, Dan tucked a couple of ten-pound notes under the tea caddy. Then he invented an urgent appointment in London and they said goodbye.

But the thought of his empty flat was uninviting, and on impulse, a few miles into the drive home, he took a turning down the narrow road to Dunwich, hoping to exorcise his hurt and rage by a brisk walk along the beach.

He was familiar with the history of the town, and knew how the waves and currents that battered this coast had over centuries reduced a thriving port to a hamlet. By the time he parked the car on the roadside and walked to the shingle beach, it was growing dark, and the bulky, granite-coloured sky was much the same shade as the sea. Asphalt-grey waves reared and crashed magnificently against the pebbles. A town, with churches and houses, lay drowned beneath that sea, a history obliterated. Dan's own history weighed on his back as he tramped along the shore.

Cold, salty drops of water flecked his face and he thought about Rose. He had thought a lot about Rose since the Martineau Aviation Christmas party, three weeks ago, and it was better to think about Rose than about Mick.

The freezing-cold aircraft hangar, a cassette player turned up full blast, sausage rolls and crisps in plastic boxes, and the staff bawling out the chorus of 'Yellow River'. Coloured streamers and a Christmas tree decorated with baubles. The emergency generator had been to hand in case the electricity cut off – it had been the power workers' turn to be on strike then. Rose had danced with everyone that evening – with the pilots, co-pilots and caretaker, and the loadmaster, who had two left feet. Everyone had danced, including Dan himself, because otherwise they would have died of cold in the vast, perishing expanse of the hangar.

Throughout the evening, he had watched her, admiring her energy and the whirl of her long, dark hair and the laughter in her bright eyes. He had thought how beautiful she looked – how completely, perfectly beautiful – and, as the plaintive introduction to 'Yesterday' soared into the empty space, he had asked her to dance. They slipped easily into the rhythm of the music. He breathed in the scent of her perfume. Her hair brushed against his cheek and he felt, beneath his fingertips, her soft, pliant body.

He would have had to have been blind not to notice that Rose was an attractive woman, and yet his attraction to her was not only physical. He liked her and he admired and respected her. He had an idea of the determination and grit it must have taken to scrape herself up and start again after the body blow of the scandal. He applauded the success she was making of a business in a sphere that was dominated by men.

He had no reason to believe that Rose thought of him as anything more than a capable operations manager. She did not seem to dislike his company and they had always worked well together. But that was all. She was, after all, still married. If he were to tell her how he felt about her, he would risk putting so much that he cared about in jeopardy – his job, his future and his financial security.

And how could he match her? She seemed in every way superior to him, not only because she was his boss at Martineau Aviation, but also in character, class and background. Today, alone in this Christmas season, on an empty beach, the familiar sense of failure clung to him, touching his shoulder now and then to remind him that it was there and always would be. It was almost, he thought, as he turned to face out to sea, an old friend. You chased promotion and success, you saved money in the bank, you kept your flat spotlessly clean and tidy, and yet it was always there, a suspicion that you were holding on by your fingertips to everything you had scrabbled so hard to earn.

Walking along the shore, witnessing the push and pull of the sea, he felt ashamed at having hurt his father, and yet, at the same time, he railed against his situation. Though he tried to blank out his memory of Mick humbly accepting the tongue-lashing he had given him in the pub, his attempt wasn't successful. Which angered him. It was hard to see why he, who had always been conscientious, hard-working and financially solvent, should have to tiptoe tactfully around Mick Falconer's hopeless affairs.

And yet something that his father had said to him echoed: *I didn't have the guts to talk to her.* Perhaps he wasn't so different from his father, after all. He hadn't the guts to tell Rose how he felt about her. He was playing safe, as usual, avoiding risk, doing anything but put his neck on the line.

There was a point, invisible and unnoticed until it had passed, when the sky darkened into night. Walking back along the beach, with the sea to one side of him and the cliff to the other, he had to return to the car by memory. He understood, just then, why you might cut and run, as his father had, why you might walk away from the mess and burden of living, and keep on heading into the dark.

Chapter Fourteen

London — August 1931

It was the last day of August. Sadie was in the American Bar of the Savoy, where Alma Rathbone and her friends were celebrating Alma's forty-fifth birthday with White Lady cocktails. Greeting Sadie, Alma twirled so that the skirt of her silver lamé frock spun out. 'It's not subtle, darling, is it? But who wants to be subtle on their birthday?'

The women's jewellery, their diamonds and pearls and Venetian glass beads, reflected in the burnished gold rail of the bar. In the array of bottles and glasses, in the polished tabletops and the mirrors of the women's powder compacts as they checked their faces, you caught fragments: a length of pale blue watered silk, a fringed Chinese stole, the gold strap of a Cartier watch. An enamelled case flicked open to offer pink, blue and yellow cocktail cigarettes. Sadie caught a waft of perfume, heavy with tuberose.

The beads on a tiny evening bag slung on the back of a chair rustled, scratching against the floor as its owner, a thin, hollow-eyed, dissatisfied-looking girl, tipped the chair back at a dangerous angle.

'I hate these things, don't you?'

'Birthday parties, do you mean?' said Sadie.

The girl waggled her long, slender fingers. 'I mean, we'll trail around, going to this and that, and I daresay I'll get frightfully plastered, I always do, and then I'll feel awful tomorrow, and I have to go to *Wiltshire*.'

'Don't you want to go to Wiltshire?'

'No, not at all.'

'Why go, then?'

'Mummy says I must.'

'Then I suppose you must.'

The girl's moody expression intensified. 'I don't know how I shall bear it.' Her gaze flicked round the bar. 'I thought Lewis would be here.'

'Lewis who?'

'Lewis Finch. He's the most divine man. I want to marry him.' She said this aggressively, thrusting her chin out.

'And your mother doesn't want you to?'

'No.' The girl — and she was just a girl, so very young — looked so utterly desolate that Sadie felt sorry for her.

'Cheer up. Oh dear, I used to hate it when I was hopelessly in love with a man and someone said that to me. You are in love with him, aren't you?'

'Yes, for ages and ages.'

'It is quite difficult, often, being in love with someone.'

The girl gave her an incurious look. 'We haven't met, have we? Were you at the Maxwells' thing?'

'No, I wasn't. My name's Sadie Lawless.'

'I'm Pansy Wade. That's a sweet frock.'

'Thank you.' She was wearing her coffee-coloured silk.

'I can't wear those colours, they make me look washed out. Do you think this coral pink is too girlish? Oh, gosh, there he is.'

The chair tipped forward and Sadie put out a hand to steady it. Two men had come into the bar and were striding towards Alma's group. The taller man was startlingly handsome, well made, with a roguish glint in his eye and curly chestnut hair cropped close to his head.

'Is that him?' whispered Sadie, looking at him.

'Ssh. Not him.' Pansy's mouth pursed up scornfully. 'That's only Kit Massingham. No, *him*.' Her gaze focused on the second man, a ratty little fellow whose brown hair was smoothed back from his forehead in the style favoured by Ramon Novarro. He kissed Alma's cheek and dragged up a stool to sit and talk to her.

Pansy dropped her bag on the floor. 'Oh, gosh. Oh, gosh.'

'Talk to me. Pretend you haven't seen him.'

'I can't.'

'Of course you can. Tell me something – tell me what you like to do.'

A shake of the head. 'Nothing, really. It's too shattering. Why doesn't he look at me?'

'Do you like to ride? Or to dance? To play tennis or read novels? You must do *something*.'

They managed a halting conversation for twenty minutes or so. More cocktails were ordered and Lewis Finch continued to talk to Alma, while Pansy chewed her nails. When everyone had arrived, they left the Savoy and piled into taxis.

Cataclysmic events had taken place in the weeks that had passed since Edith had visited the Egg – the resignation of Prime Minister Ramsay MacDonald and the formation of a National Government, in an attempt to resolve a financial crisis that threatened to tear apart the fabric of society. The hot, humid weather exaggerated the feeling of impending catastrophe. The sky had an ominous cast, and bruised, anvil-shaped clouds were piling up over the city to the south of the Thames. The tall buildings and traffic-strewn streets intensified the cloying heat and, in the taxi, Sadie picked at her skirt as it clung, clammily, to her legs. And yet she felt relieved to be away from the Egg. She was tired of the shadows and reflections that seemed to magnify and distort what was real, tired of feeling exposed to scrutiny.

In the Trocadero, half a dozen more of Alma's friends joined them. The waiter, a fragile-looking old man, hauled several tables together. A watercress salad was served and glasses of champagne poured. The man sitting next to Sadie talked of the house he was building in the countryside. She exclaimed and admired, but did not mention that she was an architect's daughter; all that seemed poisoned.

Forget about wretched Edith – if only she could, though! The things they had said to each other and the finality of their parting weighed on her. Had it been wrong of her to sell the Gull's Wing? It had been one of the most difficult decisions she had ever had to make. It was true that she, far more than Edith, had known what the house meant to their father, but she knew she would never forget Edith's accusation: *You ought to have kept the Gull's Wing in the family.* It was iniquitous of Edith to hold that against her. Her parents' Hampstead house had been mortgaged to the hilt to finance the building of the Gull's Wing. She had had to raise a substantial sum to pay estate duties. If she had sold the Egg instead, it would not have raised enough money.

Her father had been returning to England to oversee the final details of work on the house when his plane crashed. Was there a part of her that blamed the Gull's Wing for his death? Was that why she had sold it? These questions were unanswerable, and, in the two and a half years that had passed since the crash, she had evaded them. But she recalled her father's single-minded pursuit of his dream, and how it had become an obsession that had blinded him to the needs of others, and she felt herself distancing herself from him, though she had defended him to Edith.

The salad was cleared away and a fish course served. A shriek from the far end of the table; the handsome man who had arrived in the company of Pansy Wade's crush was setting up rows of champagne glasses, one on top of the other.

'Oh, Massingham's jolly good at that,' said the man with the country house. 'What fun.'

'I can't do it if I'm watched,' said the man, Massingham.

'Tommyrot, Kit,' a young woman called out. 'You only do it because you like to be watched.'

Sadie's neighbour said, 'Don't you care for sole, Miss Lawless?'

'Not awfully.' Edith had once served her the same dish, cold sole in a horseradish sauce, in her York Street home. Sadie had disliked it then and she disliked it now – the chill slither of the fish, the hot bitterness of the sauce. A melancholy descended over her and her head ached. She put her knife and fork on her plate and struck up a mildly flirtatious conversation with the man on her other side.

When the tower of glasses was complete, Kit Massingham poured champagne into the uppermost glass. Martin Rathbone, traces of theatrical paint clinging to his distinguished features, joined them as the liquid fizzed and spilled to the lower tiers. Everyone applauded. Martin took the seat next to Alma and ate, very quickly, the three courses that had been put aside for him, while telling an amusing story about a member of the audience who had fainted during the night's performance.

Speeches were made, a bouquet of orchids was presented to Alma and more wine bottles were uncorked. Ciro's was mentioned, and they walked in a sprawling, noisy band along Piccadilly, Pansy Wade clinging to Lewis Finch and laughing as she caught her sandal now and then in the trailing satin hem of her evening dress. A taxi sped by, the face of a girl pressed up against its window, and the air was thick with dust and ozone. A man in a ragged and stained shirt and trousers was folding himself into the doorway of a shop and unpacking his belongings: a newspaper, a tin of tobacco and some cigarette papers, and a brown glass bottle containing, Sadie supposed, beer.

Martin Rathbone fell in beside her. 'Good to see you, Sadie. How are you?'

'Very well. And you? Is it a good play?'

'It's a dreadful play. A farce that isn't funny enough. It's not my finest hour. I expect it will fold soon. What are you doing these days?'

'A friend of mine has offered me work, editioning a big print run. I'm moving to London for the next few months.' Lachlan had offered her work as his technical assistant, which she had gratefully accepted. She would be sharing a room with a friend who lived in Earl's Court.

Martin said, 'I don't think it's done Tom and Di any good, burying themselves out there. They were always self-obsessed, but it's made them worse.' He gave her an amused smile. 'What? I know what you're thinking. I'm supposed to be the self-absorbed actor.'

'I wasn't thinking that at all. But you're right — I'll be pleased to get away.'

'I wanted to play Hamlet,' he said, 'but I'm already too old. So, go for it, Sadie, and I'll come along and cheer when

295

your work's in a West End gallery. Oh, God, she's as drunk as a skunk.' Martin was looking at Pansy Wade.

'Do you know her well?'

'She's my cousin. She's an absolute pest. I'd leave her to her fate, but my aunt will kill me if she ends up getting blotto and going to bed with some scoundrel.'

They went into the nightclub. As Sadie and Martin foxtrotted, the reflections of the dancers blurred and mingled in the glass floor, the pinks and blues and silvers of the women's frocks whirling hypnotically against the dark chips and smudges of the men's evening dress.

The dance ended and Martin thanked her and returned to Alma.

'Would you like to dance?' a voice said, and Sadie turned to see Kit Massingham.

As they quickstepped, she felt her spirits rise like bubbles in champagne.

'That was clever,' she said to Kit, 'that thing you did with the champagne glasses.'

His dark blue eyes crinkled. 'It's my party trick. What's yours?'

'I'm not sure I have one.'

'I don't believe you. Everyone has a party trick. It fills in the time when you can't think of anything to say. Unless, perhaps, you remain forbiddingly silent.'

'Do I look forbidding?'

'Can't say. Maybe a little. Delightfully forbidding.'

'Delightful is better than forbidding.'

'Do you think so? The odd glower can come in handy, I find.'

They were flirting, she thought, and she was enjoying it enormously; it was just what she needed, to flirt with an

296

attractive man. Damn Edith and her rancorous, critical ways, and damn Tom Chiverton for forcing himself back into her life.

She gave their conversation only part of her attention as she admired the shape of Kit Massingham's mouth and the clever symmetry of his profile. He was older then her and he was fun and confident. He had the air of a man who knew his way around.

They left Ciro's. Rain was falling in heavy dark blots on the pavement and a wind had whipped up, stirring the leaves of the plane trees. She tucked her hand through Kit's arm and felt the brush of his shoulder against her own. They talked of unimportant things and she was thankful for that.

A drumroll of thunder, and Kit stripped off his jacket and flung it over their heads before they ran along the pavement. Beneath the jacket, his arm was around her shoulders and she felt him caress the curve of her neck with his thumb. They stopped in the shelter of a doorway to kiss.

Later, another nightclub, where the waiters were dressed as devils and the tables made from coffins. Lamps in the form of skeletons swayed and danced from the ceiling. Sadie went to the ladies' cloakroom to sort out her hair, which was dishevelled from the rain. Pansy Wade was leaning over a basin, white faced and weeping. Alma grimaced over her shoulder to Sadie, then went back to comforting the girl. The attendant was kneeling on the floor, pinning up the torn hem of Pansy's dress.

It was gone two in the morning and some members of their group were drifting away to their homes, or in search of different entertainment. Sadie stood on the fringes of the dance floor. Behind her, a group of men talked loudly over the three-piece band.

'The government needs to cut the dole and cut it hard, or Austria won't be the only country with its bloody banks collapsing.'

'Mosley's talking a lot of sense.'

'Can't stand the fellow. Preening fool, thinks too much of himself.'

Sadie recognised a face in the crowds. A young man with distinctive, high-cheekboned, mobile features was standing by himself. She swayed to the rhythm as she tried to place him. When he began to move his body in a magnetic, sinuous response to the tango, she recalled where she had met him.

She tapped his shoulder. 'It's Rufus, isn't it? We met at the Chivertons' house.'

He turned and smiled. 'Sadie.'

'You remember me.'

'Naturally, I remember you. I was terribly rude about the house your father built.'

She laughed. 'It doesn't matter; I'd forgotten. How are you?'

'Oh, jogging along. And you?'

She was fine, she said. 'Weren't you working on a ballet with Tom?'

'Not any more; it fell through. I say, may I get you a drink to make up for my past failings?'

She asked for a whisky and soda. The venue was crowded, but they found a space on the edge of a coffin.

She said, 'Do you see them any more? The Chivertons, I mean.'

'Not since the ballet fell by the wayside.' He made an ironic smile. 'I'd thought we were friends, but apparently not. What about you?'

She shook her head. But there was something she wanted

to know. 'When you used to go to the Gull's Wing, Rufus, did you ever think that Tom . . . ?'

'What?' he said.

'That he flirted with women. Women other than Diana, I mean.'

Rufus laughed. 'Oh, all the time. Tom's an inveterate flirt, everyone knows *that*.' He ran a hand along the edge of the coffin. 'There are always girls with Tom. So many of them go silly for him. I don't think any of them last long. Apart from anything else, Diana keeps him on a close rein. Why do you ask?'

'No particular reason. I just wondered.'

They finished their whiskies and Rufus went off to dance with someone.

After she had finished working for Lachlan, Sadie planned to go abroad. There were other printmakers, in France or Spain, for instance, in need of a good technical assistant. She would work and travel, and build up a portfolio full of work that she was proud of. Then she would contact Madge Danford, at the gallery, and ask her to take her on as a client.

I don't think any of them last long, Rufus had said, when talking about Tom Chiverton's women. And that was a huge relief. By the time she returned to the Egg, Tom would have forgotten her. He would have moved on to someone else. And Diana – if it had been Diana, and not Tom, who had vandalised the collage – would by then hate some other woman instead.

A hand touched her arm. 'We're moving on, I think.'

She looked up and saw Kit Massingham. She let him drape her stole round her shoulders. The rain had washed the dust off the parked cars and sent the litter and matchstick ends running along the gutters. Now, the air smelled fresh and clean and slipped over her skin, as cool as silk.

Two taxis drew up and they all piled in. Sadie sat on Kit's lap and he stroked the nape of her neck with the back of his fingers. She studied his features with seriousness, imagining how she might draw his strong chin and carved lips and the hooded eyes beneath arched brows.

'The others are going on to somewhere,' he murmured. 'But I wondered whether you'd rather call it a night and come back to my place for a drink.'

She would, she thought. She knew herself to be on the verge of an adventure, and an old excitement, one she had almost forgotten, jolted through her. His mouth brushed against hers and he drew her close and they kissed as the taxi sped through the rain-glazed streets.

Chapter Fifteen

London and Surrey – January 1971

Because the postal workers had been on strike for over a fortnight, making it difficult to send letters and documents around the country, Rose had agreed that she and Dan should come to their client's offices in the City for the final negotiations for a new contract. The client was a short, burly, red-faced man in his fifties called Peter Rickman, lacking in charm but mercifully direct, who wore a pinstriped suit and a shirt too tight in the collar, which he pulled at now and then. By half past three, the last details of the agreement had been hammered out; by four, the contract had been signed and Rose and Dan were putting on their coats.

Rickman looked outside at the misty streets. 'The place is falling apart. They should get the army in. Can't have the country held to ransom by a bunch of rabble.'

They shook hands and Rose and Dan left the office. Out in the street, Rose let out a breath.

'That was just about signed in blood.'

'Rickman's a hard nut.'

'I thought he'd never actually sign. He let the pen touch the paper *three times* before he wrote his name.'

301

They were walking to Liverpool Street Underground station. Dan grinned at her. 'You counted?'

'Of course I counted.' She gave him a gleeful glance. 'Five years' work for us, Dan. *Five years!*'

'I know. It's terrific.' Even Dan, a cool customer, was looking pleased with himself. 'You did well, Rose. You read him well.'

On the train, Rose sank gratefully into the last vacant seat, while Dan stood in the gangway. She felt exhilarated. Martineau Aviation, which had teetered on the brink of collapse just three months earlier, had, with a limp and a stagger, clambered back on to its feet. The order books were full, they were taking on more customers, and her father's generosity meant that they had not had to sell any of the planes. If the business continued to grow, they should be able, within the next couple of years, to repay both the bank loan and her father. And then the firm would be secure.

She was making a success of the business. She was *good* at it, she knew she was.

The carriages swerved through the tunnels. When the lights dipped on and off, Rose gripped her briefcase tightly. Normally, travelling in London, she took buses and taxis. She was going on the Underground because she was with Dan, because she didn't want him to think her the sort of silly woman who went into a flutter about riding on the Tube.

She heard Dan ask, 'How are the girls?'

The train had drawn into Chancery Lane Station. It was all right being at a station; it was the tunnels she disliked. 'Eve has a cold, poor thing,' she said. 'I was in two minds about whether to send her to school this morning, but she wanted to go.'

'And her sister? The aeroplane enthusiast?'

302

They rattled off again. She liked that Dan remembered Katherine, though he had only met her once or twice.

'She's well. She's getting used to her new school. She used to cry sometimes, last term, when she was getting ready in the mornings, but she hasn't this term, so I think she's settling in.'

The train came to a halt between stations. This was what she most hated: the creeping anxiety that came over her when a train stopped in the sooty, black, enclosing walls of a tunnel. It was hard to prevent herself from thinking about things she usually managed not to think about: fires, accidents, bombs.

Dan said, 'It'll be waiting for a green light. It'll be off in a minute.'

'Yes, of course.' She saw that her knuckles, gripping the briefcase, had gone white, and wondered whether Dan had noticed. If only the damn thing would move. Why wouldn't it move? And why were the other passengers in the carriage, the men and women reading their *Evening Standards* or thumbing through paperback novels, apparently untroubled? Why didn't they mind? Why must she be the one with the stupid, infantile fears she couldn't control?

Dan spoke again. 'That aunt of yours, the one you told me about, who lived in Sussex—'

'Great-aunt,' she said automatically.

'Great-aunt. Have you had any luck trying to trace her?'

She couldn't breathe. Her throat was closing over, trapping the stale air. She willed herself to focus on Dan's question, on Sadie.

'She quarrelled with Tom Chiverton,' she said. 'The woman at the shop, Winnie, Winnie Ferrers, told me.'

'Do you know what they quarrelled about?'

303

'Um . . . I don't know . . .'

'It's all right, Rose.' His voice was gentle. 'We'll be off in a few moments, honestly.'

Oh, God – he *had* noticed. 'I know, I know,' she muttered, looking at him, wild eyed, as if seeing him could anchor her to rationality. 'It's so stupid. I know it's so stupid.'

'Try and think of something else.'

'Is this blasted thing ever going to move?'

'You know how often we have a plane stuck on the runway. It'll be some little thing. They'll soon sort it out.'

It was never a hardship to look at Dan Falconer. Cornflower-blue eyes and fair hair dampened by the mist to curls. And cool as a cucumber, in spite of being marooned in this horrible tunnel, God knows how many feet underground.

She made an effort to distract herself. 'I wondered whether Tom Chiverton had tried it on with her.'

'With Sadie?'

'Yes. Or whether, even, he and Sadie had had an affair and it went wrong. Something like that. He played around, Winnie told me.'

'Do you think she's still alive?'

'To begin with, I thought she might be, but now . . .' Rose realised with a pang that she had stopped believing Sadie might still be alive some time ago. 'No,' she said. 'I don't think so. I think she's dead, Dan. I think she died a long time ago.'

The lights suddenly extinguished, plunging the train into darkness, and she had to stifle her gasp of terror.

She heard Dan say, 'Give me your hand.'

Her hand brushed against his. She felt better, holding his hand: not so alone. He began to talk about the contract they had just signed, all the little details they must keep an eye on, and she forced herself to concentrate on the sound of his voice, the pressure of his fingers, as she took shallow little breaths.

The lights flashed on and the train shuddered and began to move slowly along the track. Dan let go of her hand.

As they pulled into Holborn Station, he said, 'Do you want to get off? Get a taxi?'

'No, I'm okay.'

At Tottenham Court Road, they changed to the Northern Line. Embarrassment began to take over from fear. 'I should try hypnotism or something,' she said apologetically.

'You're afraid of flying, too, aren't you?'

The casual way he flung it into the conversation, as if he had known for months, jolted her. She stared at him. 'You know?'

'I guessed.'

'You didn't *say*, Dan.' She'd thought she had hidden her phobia rather well.

'I assumed you'd prefer me not to.'

'*How* did you know?'

'Oh . . . all those times Eric's asked you if you'd like to go up for a spin and you've found something else to do. That.'

Rose was irked to detect a glint of amusement in his eyes.

'And . . .' He was listing it on his fingers. 'And that time you refused to go into the cockpit and have a look round. Oh, and when Roy had the rough landing in the crosswind, you went green.'

She felt mortified. 'Does everyone know?'

'Eric and Roy are placing bets on who can persuade you to go up with them first.'

'You're kidding, Dan, aren't you?'

He smiled. 'Eric's pretty confident.'

'Don't you dare laugh.'

'Oh, come on, Rose. You must admit it has its funny side – the boss of an aviation company, afraid of flying.'

'Oh, *hilarious*,' she said as the train drew into Waterloo and they made for the escalators.

At the top of the stairs, as they reached the railway station, she looked at the noticeboard and saw that there was a Weybridge train due to leave in five minutes.

'Thank you for today, Dan.' The words burst out of her spontaneously. 'You were terrific; I could have done it without you. And thank you for stopping me making a blithering idiot of myself on the Tube. It's been a brilliant day, hasn't it?'

And then, taking herself by surprise, she hugged him. And somehow they were kissing, his lips cool and firm, his body crushed against hers, and she was breathing in the scent of his aftershave as commuters jostled by them, and she wanted to go on kissing him for ever, and catching her train be damned.

They parted. 'Have to run,' she said. The words were muffled and breathless, and she rushed off to the platform without looking back.

Later, reaching the flat with the girls trailing satchels and mackintoshes, Rose automatically checked her pigeonhole for post, though, with the strike, there was unlikely to be anything there. But there *was* a letter; she saw that it bore the stamp of a private postal service and tucked it into her handbag.

Make supper, eat supper, homework and bath. Don't think

about the extraordinary thing that happened; don't think about kissing Dan Falconer at Waterloo Station. She made herself put it aside and leave it for later, when she was on her own.

Eve's cold seemed better and Katherine was quiet, lying on her stomach on the floor, nose to book.

Rose said, 'Where are your glasses, love?'

'I don't want them.'

'You'll get a headache, reading like that.'

'I hate them. I can't find them.'

'Darling, you have to look after them,' said Rose crossly. 'They were expensive.' She searched through Katherine's coat pockets and satchel, and found the glasses under a crumpled PE shirt.

She heard Katherine say, 'Is Daddy coming today?'

'Not today. He'll pick you up from school on Friday.'

'I wanted to talk to him.'

'Why don't I see if I can get him on the phone?'

She dialled the number and handed Katherine the receiver. She picked up scattered toys and items of clothing off the floor while Katherine spoke to Robert, mostly in monosyllables. After a while, she gave the phone to Rose.

'Daddy wants to talk to you.'

'Is she all right?' Robert's voice, concerned, on the other end of the line.

'I think so, yes. She just wanted to hear your voice.'

'It was hard work getting a word out of her.'

'She's tired. She might be coming down with Eve's cold.'

It was only once the girls were in bed that Rose remembered the letter and took it out of her handbag. She saw, with a flutter of excitement, that it was from Sadie's friend, Jimmy Corrigan, whom she had written to after talking to Constance Meyrick, in Cambridge. Jimmy Corrigan – the red-headed

307

Scot with the flat in Victoria and the political journal, *Splinter*. Jimmy Corrigan – who, according to Constance, had been in love with Sadie.

In his letter, Jimmy had written:

Dear Mrs Martineau,

You wrote to me last year, enquiring about Sadie Lawless. I've been away for some months and I'm afraid I've only just received your letter. I tried phoning you, but was told you had moved house. The new residents gave me this forwarding address. I hope my letter reaches you, because I remember Sadie with great fondness.

Then a suggestion that Rose visit him at his house, along with a phone number. She dialled the number, but there was no answer.

Afterwards, she put the letter aside and thought about Dan instead. She probably shouldn't have kissed him, but she didn't regret it because it had been lovely, warm and unexpectedly passionate, and, God, she missed all that, and it made her feel happy just to think about it. She had kissed Dan Falconer and she had clinched a deal that would give the business an income for the next five years. Not a bad day's work, all in all. As she made herself a gin and tonic, a fizz of joy rose inside her.

A hard frost greyed the airfield the following morning and the fields that surrounded it were white and gripped by the cold. Rose was in her office, going over the flight schedule for the next month with Lennie, the loadmaster. She had not yet seen Dan.

Lucy put her head round the door. 'Telephone, Rose.'

'Could you tell them I'll call back?'

'It's your daughter's teacher.'

Rose went to Lucy's desk and picked up the phone.

'Rose Martineau.'

'Mrs Martineau, it's Miss Lomax.' Miss Lomax was Katherine's form teacher. 'I'd thought you must have kept Katherine off school today, and yet I've just spoken to Mrs Kent and she says she dropped Katherine off here this morning.'

Nadine Kent was the part-time nanny Rose had engaged to help with the girls.

'Katherine should be in your class, Miss Lomax,' said Rose, bewildered.

'I'm afraid she isn't. Jonathan was unwell in assembly, so Mrs Kent had to come in to collect him. I happened to run into her and I asked her whether Katherine had the same bug. Mrs Kent told me that she'd dropped Katherine off, as usual, but she wasn't in my class for register. I've spoken to Eve and she said Katherine was at school, but we've had a quick check round and there's no sign of her.'

Confusion rapidly mutated to alarm. 'Check again.' Rose spoke sharply. 'I'm coming over. I'll be there in ten minutes.' She put down the phone.

Lucy held out her coat and handbag. 'It'll be all right,' she said gently. 'There'll be some muddle.'

'Yes. Yes, I'm sure. Can you phone Clément?'

'Dan and I will deal with everything. Just go.'

Bundling on her coat, Rose left the building. The starter motor of the Mini coughed in the cold and her hands clutched the steering wheel. 'Start, damn you.' She took a deep breath and tried again, and the engine whirred into life.

As she drove, fast, to Weybridge, wisps of fog drifted across the road. Lucy would be right. Someone must have made a mistake. She had dropped Katherine and Eve off at Nadine's house a little earlier than usual this morning, at eight, because she had a lot of work to get through today. Nadine had taken the girls to school, so Katherine must be there, somewhere. Maybe she had been in the girls' toilet when Miss Lomax had taken the register, or maybe she was hiding in the library, reading a book. She'd get to the school and Miss Lomax would have found Katherine and everything would be all right, and the sick feeling inside her, which had sprung to life as soon as Miss Lomax had said *she wasn't in my class for register*, would vanish.

She parked on the school driveway. Miss Lomax was waiting for her in the secretary's room.

'Have you found her?' asked Rose.

Miss Lomax shook her head. 'She's not here. Miss Harper and I have checked everywhere.'

'But she must be! The playground—'

'Mrs Martineau, Katherine isn't here. Please, sit down.' The teacher frowned. 'How did she seem this morning?'

'Katherine? She was fine.'

'Not upset?'

Rose thought back. Because she had an early start, she had rushed the girls out of the house. She could hardly recall what they had said to each other. It occurred to her that Katherine hadn't said much.

'She was quiet,' she said reluctantly. 'She's never at her best in the mornings.'

'Katherine's behaviour has been difficult recently. I've been intending to write to you. She answers back and she's unco-operative, and I'm afraid her work has deteriorated. I've had to speak to her several times. I wondered whether there had been any problems at home.'

Rose tried to absorb the shock of the teacher's words. 'My

husband and I are separated,' she said. 'I explained that to you when the girls started here. Katherine's found it hard.'

'Children can take a while to get used to changes of circumstance.'

'Might one of her friends know where she is?'

'That's something else I was hoping to discuss with you, Mrs Martineau. Katherine seems to be finding it difficult to fit in. She doesn't really have any close friends.'

The thought of her daughter, alone in the school playground, cut her to the quick. But even that must be put aside now. 'I have to find her.' Rose stood up. 'I expect she's gone back to the flat.'

'Yes, I'm sure you're right. Would you let me know when she turns up? And we should make an appointment to discuss the other problems.'

Rose left the school and headed for the flat. The cold terror had settled under her ribs, a dread far more piercing than her panic in the Underground yesterday. Had that happened only yesterday? It had, but it seemed an age ago.

As she started up the car again, she thought, I don't know where Katherine is. My seven-year-old daughter, and I don't know where she is. All those other discoveries tumbled through her mind as well – that Katherine had been behaving badly and her work had deteriorated. Why hadn't she, Katherine's mother, known about that?

She recalled the glib confidence with which she had spoken to Dan the previous day: *She used to cry sometimes, last term, when she was getting ready in the mornings, but she hasn't this term, so I think she's settling in.* The fact that a person had stopped crying about something didn't mean they had stopped minding – Rose, as much as anyone, should know that. How long was it since she and Katherine had spent a whole day together, just the two of them? Not since she had started work at Martineau Aviation.

She took the road that led to the block of flats, keeping an eye on the pavements. Unease uncoiled nauseatingly in her stomach. Katherine wouldn't be able to get into the flat, because she didn't have a key, so she must be waiting outside. Rose turned off the road, into the parking area, and quickly scanned the building. There was no royal-blue coat standing out against the red brick.

Someone would have let her indoors. She would have rung the bell and a neighbour would have let her in.

Rose parked, let herself into the building and ran upstairs. The corridor and landing were empty. 'Katherine?' she called out, but her voice echoed back at her.

She unlocked the door to the flat. The hope that Katherine might have taken the spare key was a fragile one, and it dissolved as soon as the emptiness of the rooms folded around Rose. Where was she? The horror of what was happening washed over her and she pressed her knuckles against her mouth.

Stay calm; you need to think clearly. She dialled Nadine's number. Nadine confirmed what Miss Lomax had told her: that she had taken the girls to school, as usual, that morning.

'You saw her into the playground?'

'Yes. We said goodbye, just like we do every day, and she went in with Eve and Jonny.'

'Did you wait till she went inside the school?'

'No.' The fear in Nadine's voice carried down the telephone wire. 'Martha was crying.' Martha was Nadine's baby daughter. 'I'd just got her off in the pram and then she woke up as soon as we stopped at the school. We'd had a bad night and I wanted to get her off again. Rose, I'm so sorry.'

'It isn't your fault.' The fury she felt was, she knew, unreasonable. 'I need you to do something, Nadine. Could you have a good look round your house and garden, and make sure Katherine isn't there, somewhere? She knows you, she's fond of you. She might go to you. She doesn't know many other people in Weybridge.'

'I'll do that now. Give me five minutes, Rose, and I'll get back to you.'

Waiting for Nadine to phone back, she stood at the window, looking down to the car park and road. A part of her found it impossible to believe that this was happening. If she concentrated hard enough, she would see Katherine, her beloved, eternally scruffy daughter, her coat undone and her shoes unlaced, heading through the entrance to the flats, trailing her school bag on the tarmac. When she sat down for tea tonight, she'd look at both her daughters and remember the nightmarish terror she had felt, and feel eternally thankful that it was over.

But another part of her rushed along dark alleyways to a dreadful dead end, and she saw Katherine, lost and wandering alone through the streets of a town she hardly knew. Or she saw some man, with a promise of sweets or puppies, beckoning Katherine out of the school playground.

Please, no. Please, not that.

The phone rang.

Let Nadine have found her. Please, let Nadine have found her.

She picked up the receiver. 'Hello?'

'She's not here, Rose.'

She fisted her hand, pressing it against her chest. 'Thank you for looking, Nadine. If she turns up, you'll ring me straight away, won't you? I'm at the flat.'

'Yes, of course.'

'I have to go.' She cut off the call.

She stood for a moment, fear welling up inside her. Should she call the police? Her hand touched the phone, then fell away. She went into Katherine's room. Toys and clothes were strewn over the floor and the bed was unmade.

She saw it, then: Katherine's money box – a red, metal toy postbox – lying on its side, on top of the chest of drawers. The stopper at the bottom had been removed and the box was empty. Katherine was an assiduous saver of pocket money and birthday pounds. Rose could not see any coins or notes on the drawers or table. She began to sift through the contents of the wardrobe and shelves and the clutter on the floor. She was looking for her daughter's floral plastic purse.

If Katherine had decided to run away, where would she go? To her father? To her grandfather?

She must call Robert. He might know something – Katherine might have said something to him. She flipped through the pages of her address book and dialled the numbers of each of his businesses in turn, leaving messages for him to call her urgently. She was about to dial the engineering company where her father worked, when the phone rang.

She snatched it up. 'Robert?'

'Rose, what's wrong?'

'It's Katherine.' Her eyes welled up; she looked upwards, pressing her lips together, forcing the tears back. Quickly, she told him about the school, and Nadine.

'Her money box is empty and her purse doesn't seem to be there,' she said. 'So, I think . . .' I don't think someone's taken her; I think she's chosen to go. 'I think she's run away, Robert.'

314

'How much money did she have?' He was crisp and businesslike.

'Five or six pounds. Dad gave her some money for Christmas. You know what she's like; she never spends anything.'

'I'll get someone to go and check my flat. What about your father?'

'He's at work today. I was just about to phone him.'

'I'll call by his house. Damn it, Rose, where would she go?'

'I don't know. I thought you might.' Her voice rose, shrill and panicked.

'I wouldn't have thought she'd go to my place. It's a hell of a long way for a seven-year-old.'

'Oh, God, Robert, she's so *young!*' The words shook and cracked.

'Rose,' he said, 'you need to stay strong. We'll find her, I promise you.'

His calm voice steadied her. 'Yes.'

'What about the airfield? She likes the planes.'

A surge of hope. Why hadn't she thought of that? Robert was right: Katherine adored watching the planes. She said, 'I'll ask the staff to search the grounds and buildings.'

'She'll be okay,' he said. 'She's a sensible girl.'

'It wasn't sensible to go off on her own! It was a stupid, stupid thing to do! And on such a cold day! I keep thinking of her, out there . . .'

'I'm going to call the police.'

Ice settled around her heart. A missing child . . . You heard such things on the TV and radio, and could hardly bear to think of the agony the parents must be going through. The police calling on the public for information. Or dragging the rivers and canals. She dug her nails into her palms. 'Yes,' she whispered.

'I'm driving over now, Rose. I'll stop at your father's house and then at the school, because I want to talk to Eve. She may know more than she's letting on. And then I'll come to the flat. You call the airfield and wait where you are, in case she comes back. I'll be with you in about an hour, okay?'

'Okay,' she murmured.

'I'm sorry, Rose. I'm so sorry.'

'It's not your fault.'

'Oh, I think it is.' He put down the phone.

Rose called Lucy, who promised to organise a search of the airfield and buildings. Then she phoned her father at work. He told her that he would leave for home straight away.

Her gaze settled on the street outside: the postman, on his bike; a woman pushing a pram, a little girl holding on to the handle. Robert was right; she should have thought of talking to Eve. The girls might squabble a lot, but they were equally as often in cahoots over something. Eve might, out of misplaced loyalty to Katherine, have kept her sister's scheme a secret. Miss Lomax had said that Katherine was finding it difficult to make friends, which might mean that she was more likely to confide in Eve.

Making friends . . . She remembered Katherine saying furiously, *I hate that school*, Katherine talking of her best friend from her previous school, whom she missed – Abbie, that was the girl's name. There had been some plan to invite Abbie to tea, which Rose had forgotten about.

Might she have gone back to her old school? Might she have gone to look for her friend – taken her pocket money to pay for a train or bus, and travelled to Walton-on-Thames, the place she still thought of as home?

316

Rose looked at the clock. It was quarter past ten. Robert had told her to wait at the flat, but that was impossible and unendurable. She had to find Katherine. She grabbed her coat and keys, and dashed out to the car.

The fog was thickening and the light leaching into greyness by the time she reached Walton-on-Thames. The traffic, maddeningly busy and slow and clogged by roadworks, meant that she often drove at walking pace. She had left a key to the flat for Robert with a neighbour, as well as a note telling him where she was going. The neighbour had promised to look out for Katherine. As the Mini crawled along, Rose's gaze flicked frantically to the pavements as she searched for a child in a blue coat.

She parked in a side road, because of the yellow lines near the school, then got out of the car and hurried along the street. You thought something was important, but then you discovered it wasn't important at all. She had allowed herself to become distracted from the main purpose of her life: the bringing up of her daughters. She had failed to make sure they felt safe and loved. She had spent too much time on matters of secondary importance – the business, her own unhappiness and anger, even the search for Sadie. She had held Robert solely responsible for the break-up of her marriage and the destruction it had wrought on her children's lives, but she was not blameless. When she reflected on her behaviour, it seemed tinged with insanity: visits to the Egg . . . too many late nights and early-morning starts.

She recalled how she had felt as high as a kite yesterday, so pleased with herself because the contract had been signed, while Katherine, at school, must have been lonely and miserable. And then, she had kissed Dan Falconer. What had she

317

been thinking of, messing around with an employee, when the only things that had ever been of importance were her children's health and happiness? Since the scandal, she had lost her way, and just then she was afraid that the price she might pay would be terrible.

As she turned into the street that led to the school, the muffling charcoal mist added to her sense of unreality. The day was becoming darker, not lighter. The swirl and density of the fog made the trees and houses, which she had once passed morning and afternoon when taking her children to school, unrecognisable. Katherine was such a trusting child. To think of her alone and at the mercy of any malicious stranger was unbearable. The thought that had been at the back of her mind since she received the call from the school could no longer be put aside: she might never see her daughter again. The quick kiss she had given her that morning, her mind already on the working day ahead, might be the last kiss.

She was approaching the school. She looked up, searching through the clogged air. No one was there; there was just the empty pavement and the colourless mops of the lime trees. She should have phoned the police as soon as Miss Lomax had told her Katherine was missing. She should not have waited.

Out of the grey, a flicker of royal blue. A shadow, a shape, given substance by the tenuous glow of a street lamp. 'Katherine?' Rose called out. She began to run. 'Katherine, is that you?'

They went to a café after calling Robert, who was at the flat, from a phone box. Katherine had no gloves or hat, had left them on the train she had taken from Weybridge to Walton-on-Thames, and felt cold to touch. Rose was too shaken to drive, and, anyway, she sensed that they needed a conversation on neutral ground.

In the café, she ordered hot chocolate and teacakes. Katherine scoffed her teacake, then Rose's. *What were you doing? What were you thinking of? Don't you know how frightened I was?* All these things must be said, but not now, not yet.

Instead, she said, 'It was a very long way to go on your own, love.'

'I knew how to do it, Mummy.'

'Yes, but still, it was a long way. Taking a train, all by yourself . . .'

'I just asked for a ticket at the station. I couldn't remember the way, when I got off the train, but there was a man and he said I could walk with him. He had a dog called Raffles.'

Rose suppressed a shudder. That Katherine had asked a kind and caring person for help had been only a matter of chance. She could not yet feel safe. She didn't know whether she would ever feel safe again. With only a small twist of fate, events could have turned out so differently.

Katherine leaned her head against Rose's arm. 'I wanted to see Abbie.'

'She's your best friend, isn't she?'

'I miss her, Mum.'

'I know, darling. Do you miss Dad, too?'

Katherine nodded. 'All the time.'

'I'm so sorry, sweetheart. I'm going to try to make it better, I promise.'

'I want Daddy to come home.' Rose only just heard Katherine's mutter.

She held her daughter while she cried. She could have easily cried herself, but blinked a lot instead. The coffee machine made hissing noises and the door of the café opened now and then, letting in a customer and the cold and the fog.

Twisting round, Katherine looked up at her. 'Do you miss him, Mum?'

With a paper serviette, Rose wiped away Katherine's tears and her chocolate moustache. 'Yes, sometimes I do.'

'Then why can't he come home?'

Had she ever sat down with her daughter and tried to explain to her, in terms that a seven-year-old might understand, what had gone wrong with their marriage? She thought she had, but she had obviously made a lousy job of it.

'You know how you sometimes fall out with a friend, love – how there's sometimes things you don't agree about. That was what happened with Daddy and me. He did something that made me sad, so we agreed to live apart for a while.'

'Did Daddy do a bad thing?'

She met her daughter's gaze and tried again, choosing her words carefully. 'He did something that wasn't very kind, something that upset me. Remember that other friend of yours, that girl with the twin brothers . . . ?'

'Margot.'

'Yes, her. Do you remember how sometimes she used to do mean things and you'd feel upset?'

'*Daddy* did something mean?'

'We all do, now and then, sweetheart.'

'At school, Sarah Robinson is always saying mean things to me.' Katherine's gaze turned to the floor while she swung her foot to and fro, kicking the table leg. 'She calls me goggle-eyes.'

'Oh, Katherine.'

'I hate my glasses. I hate that school.'

'Oh, love.' She scooped her daughter on to her lap. 'I'm so sorry. I'm going to make it all better for you, I promise.'

'Has Daddy said sorry?'

'Yes, he has.' So many times.

Katherine twisted round to look at her. 'Then can't you make friends again? Can't you, Mum?'

Could she? Was it possible? Could she take the step that might repair her fractured family?

She whispered, 'I don't know, darling. I don't know.'

Rose's father was clearing up the last of the supper dishes when Robert came back into the room, after putting the girls to bed.

'I think they'll settle,' he said.

'I'll make coffee.'

'Rose, I'll do it,' said Giles. 'Sit down.'

Rose ached with tension but couldn't keep still. She tidied up the sitting room, putting toys in boxes and books on the shelf. The sense of having narrowly avoided disaster persisted.

The phone rang and she answered it. It was Mary Martineau, checking on Katherine. They spoke for a few minutes.

When she finished the call, Robert was standing at the window, his back to her. Her father put the tray of coffee things on the table. 'I'll head off now,' he said.

'Dad, there's no need. Stay and have coffee with us.'

'No, I should head home. Give them a kiss from me, in the morning.'

They embraced and Giles gave Robert an awkward pat on the shoulder, then left the flat.

Robert went into the girls' bedrooms to turn off their

321

lights. When he came back to the sitting room, he said, 'I could do with a drink, couldn't you?'

'Please. The coffee can wait.'

He made gin and tonics and sat down beside her. He shook his head slowly. 'I hope to God I never have to go through a day like that again. There was a moment today when I thought . . .'

'Me too.'

They were silent, absorbed by the enormity of what might have happened. Then Robert ran a hand over his face and said, 'Eve knew. I practically had to apply the thumbscrews to get it out of her. Loyalty, I suppose.' His smile didn't reach his eyes. 'She must have inherited it from you.'

'Robert,' she said gently.

'This was my fault.'

'No, I'm to blame as well. I didn't listen to her.'

'Rose, this was down to me – absolutely and completely – I know that. It wouldn't have happened if I hadn't been such a cretin. No, that's not right; it makes it sound as if I made a mistake, an error, when the truth is that I did what I did because I was selfish and greedy. I took what I wanted because I thought I'd get away with it. So I was stupid as well. And I've hurt the people I love most, and I'm so sorry, Rose – I can't tell you how sorry I am. I wish I could wipe it all away, but I can't – not ever.'

She put her arms round him and held him for a long time, resting her forehead against his shoulder. Though he had hurt her almost beyond endurance, he was, at least, familiar. It comforted her to be with him, because she knew he understood their odd, quirky little elder daughter.

When she could speak, she said, 'We both messed up. Look at me, so intent on proving to myself that I was still

322

worth something, I didn't even notice my daughter was unhappy. So pleased with being Rose Martineau, owner of Martineau Aviation, I neglected the most important job in the world.'

She had taken her daughters away from the home they knew and out of the school they loved. Eve had adjusted quickly enough, but Katherine had struggled. *You'll make new friends*: the facile remark she recalled making shamed her.

'Maybe I should give it up. Give up the job.' The thought had been in the back of her mind all day.

'Don't you dare.'

The vehemence of his response made her say sharply, 'I can't be in two places at once, Robert. I seem to end up doing one or the other badly. And I'm not cutting corners with the children again, not after this.'

'You don't need to cut corners. We'll manage. We'll find a way round it. What sort of message would it give the girls, if you gave up work now? You're doing the right thing. It's me who's got to change. You're doing a great job, Rose. You're a good person – it's in your nature, but it's not in mine. I'm not a good person; I act on impulse. And sometimes it's a damned destructive impulse and I ruin everything.'

'There's no point arguing about who did what. We just need to do *better*.'

'I don't want to "do better". I want it to be like it was before. I miss them. I don't feel involved in my daughters' lives any more. I've turned into one of those one-day-a-week fathers. I never thought I'd be like that. I've made an absolute bloody disaster of the only thing I was proud of.'

'Robert, that's not true. The girls love you. They need you.'

'But I've made them unhappy.' His hands clenched.

323

'Children need consistency. They need the two of us working together, not fighting. They need us, Rose.'

He stood up and went back to the window, as if he was looking for something he had lost. He was right; in her heart, Rose knew it. It was inarguable that Katherine and Eve needed both their father and mother.

'People can change,' he said. 'I've changed, and I promise you, Rose, I'm trying to make myself a better person. There's nothing more important to me than my family. Nothing more important to me than you, and I'll do anything to make you believe that again – anything at all. Because, the thing is, I love you.'

There were tears in her eyes and her head pounded. She knew what she must do, but could not quite take the step.

'I want us to try again.' He made a chopping gesture with his hand. 'I'm not suggesting moving in, anything like that; I know I haven't the right. But I'm asking you – I'm pleading with you, Rose – to let us try to be friends again. To do things as a family again. For the girls' sake. Take it slowly, and then, maybe in time . . . It was good, Rose, wasn't it? Before I destroyed everything, it was good.'

It was true, it had been good once. They had been a happy family once.

'Yes,' she murmured.

'Can we try again?' His dark eyes implored her. 'For Katherine and Eve? Can we be a family again, not because I want it, but because our daughters need it?'

A few days earlier, Dan had had a phone call from Kevin Goode at Westfield Air. Kevin had suggested they meet for a drink. It had been put casually – two old friends getting together for a few pints – but Dan knew Kevin well and had gone to the pub mentally prepared, and so had not been completely startled when his friend made him the offer of a job at Westfield Air. The salary Kevin suggested *had* taken him by surprise, though.

'I'm buying another plane,' Kevin explained, 'and I'm looking for a second airfield. Westfield's can't handle the volume of traffic we're building up. I need an operations manager who knows the business and can work independently, someone who's got his head screwed on and doesn't need to be nursed along. Yours was the first name that sprang to mind, Dan.'

Dan thanked Kevin, but told him that he wasn't looking for a new job. He liked working for Rose and was content where he was.

'Rot,' Kevin said, tipping the last of a packet of pork scratchings into his palm before slapping them into his mouth. 'You're not *content*. You're never *content*, Dan. You're an ambitious sod, like me – you know you are. If the money's not good enough, then say so, and I'll see what I can do.' Rising, he pulled on his coat. 'Think about it.'

Two days later, Dan and Rose had gone to London to sign the Rickman contract. And then, that extraordinary and shocking kiss at Waterloo Station. It had changed everything. Parting from Rose at the station, buoyed up by an optimism for the future, he had considered Kevin's offer in a different light. It was clear to him that if, miraculously, Rose felt something for him, if the kiss had been more than an expression of delight at a lucrative deal and relief at escaping the Underground, then he could not go on working for Martineau Aviation. If workplace relationships always created difficulties, a liaison between the boss and her junior would be ten times worse. There would be murmurings of favouritism. The staff would be uneasy and resentful. Clients and competitors would revel and gossip in club and pub: *She didn't wait long* or, *Do you think she's planning to go through the lot of them?* Prejudices would be reinforced and all that Rose had worked so hard to build up would be negated. If they were to be anything more than colleagues, he must resign from Martineau Aviation.

Then, the following morning, Lucy Holbrook came into his office and told him that Rose's daughter, Katherine, had gone missing. The staff had dropped everything and Dan had organised a search of the premises and airfield. He had been tramping along the boundary of the airfield, wondering whether he might find the poor kid freezing in a hedgerow, when a shout made him look up. Lucy was jumping up and down on the tarmac, waving her arms. 'They've found her, Dan!' she called out. 'They've found her!'

Of course, he longed to phone to check that Rose was all right, to comfort her; of course, he knew he must not. Rose must be left in peace with her family. This was when niggles of doubt began to chip away at him. He had no place in her life. She had a family and her loyalties must always be with them. Whatever the failings of her faithless bastard of a husband, Robert Martineau was the father of her children.

Get real, Dan, he thought, as they all got back to work. That he might have any sort of relationship with Rose was pure fantasy. Pretend the kiss never happened.

Rose came in late to work the next day. Dan went to her office and tapped on the door.

'How's Katherine?'

'She's all right now, thank you. She's at home with her father.'

'And you? It must have been very worrying.'

326

'I'm fine.' Her tone was clipped and unrevealing.

There were purple shadows under her eyes. 'You look tired, Rose,' he said. When he reached out a hand to her, she made a sharp movement away.

'Dan, no.'

His arms fell to his sides. 'I'm sorry.'

She made a brushing-aside motion of the hand. 'I have to get on.' She had moved behind her desk and was holding a sheaf of papers against her chest, like a shield. 'What happened the other day . . .' She looked at him, her eyes stony. 'It was a mistake.'

Her words struck him with a physical force. 'Is that how you see it . . . ? As a mistake?'

'Yes. And so do you, I assume, Dan.'

'No.' He frowned. 'I don't.'

As she put the papers into a folder, her brow creased into deep cuts and lines. Then she said, 'Robert and I are trying again.'

'I don't understand.'

'For the sake of the children. I have to put them first.'

'But you don't love him.'

Her head jerked up and this time he read fury in her expression. 'You don't know that. It's no business of yours. How dare you, Dan? How dare you think you can pass judgement on my marriage? I think you should leave.'

He went back to his office. Alone, he closed his eyes for a moment, letting out a breath. Rose was giving her marriage a second chance. He, the child of a destructive divorce, understood why she would choose to do that. But he loved her – this, he also knew – and so he could not stay where he would have to see her each day, because that would be intolerable.

327

He looked out at the frosty airfield. The low rays of the sun flashed silver on the wings of the Argosy standing on the tarmac. Dan picked up the phone and dialled Kevin Goode's number.

After Dan had given in his notice, Rose found herself thinking of Sadie: whether she had ever loved again after her broken engagement; whether, if your heart had been bruised too often, it might refuse to spring back to shape, and remain distorted, squeezed and mangled, a relic of what it once had been.

Forget Sadie. Sadie was dead and gone and not worth wasting any more time on. Sadie had hidden herself away and the years had covered her like a blanket of leaves.

Dan was her employee. She was a married woman with two daughters. To be attracted to a man – to fall in love with a man – would only complicate a life that was already relentlessly demanding. Whatever her feelings for Dan – whatever, in different circumstances, she might have wanted – to feel anything more than friendship for him would be a terrible miscalculation, and so she must forget him, too.

Chapter Sixteen

Madrid – July–August 1933

After a winter spent in London, working for Lachlan Brodie, Sadie had travelled to France in 1932, where she stayed with various artist friends, and sketched and painted. Her travels were punctuated by sojourns at the Egg, where she concentrated on building up a portfolio of work which she planned to show to Madge Danford at the Jermyn Street gallery.

She spent the summer of 1933 in Madrid, working for a printmaker called Gabriel Martinez, assisting him in producing an edition of two hundred prints. The studio was on the top floor of a tenement block. The floors were tiled and the walls whitewashed, and the high, tall windows, which were north facing, permitted only a fine, clear light to filter into the room. There were wooden tables and chairs, and the shelves were cluttered with all that was familiar to her: pots of printing ink, rollers and cutting tools, and the smell of turps and white spirit permeated everything. The walls and windows muffled the noises of the barrio, but Sadie could hear, while she was working, sounds from the other tenants in the block: crying babies and barking dogs and arguing couples.

Gabriel was a short, barrel-chested, bearded man in his fifties. Sometimes he spoke to Sadie in English – he had lived, when he was younger, in London – and sometimes in Spanish; he didn't seem to mind that her fumbling grasp of the language meant that she missed a lot of what he said. When he was working, he bent with intense concentration over the copper plate on which he was drawing a composition, brows lowered, responding to any interruption with a grunt.

She soon discovered that Gabriel was prone to moods. He was often jovial, greeting her cheerfully in the mornings and pronouncing her work good, and often the last to leave whichever café or bar in which they had spent the evening, but his temper could change like the sun going behind a cloud, making him touchy and prone to sudden explosions of anger. Sadie learned to recognise the signs, the scowls and silences, the impatient pacing of the floor.

When he was in a good mood, Gabriel let her use his studio space and etching press to do her own work. She was making a series of prints taken from the photographs and sketches she had made when travelling through Spain.

She had fallen in love with the country almost from the moment they had crossed the border from France. She and Jimmy Corrigan had travelled in his Austin 7. The car broke down with dismaying regularity, but Jimmy was adept at nursing it back into life. Together, they explored the high Castilian plain, taking rooms in towns and villages, the churches and houses of which were built of stone the colour of sand. In the smallest villages, skinny children ran barefoot in the dust, and the women peered at them from shadowed doorways, their seamed, hollowed faces half hidden.

They drove out on to the dirt roads that traversed the flat, sepia-coloured plain which extended for mile after mile, cut up by stone walls, dry creeks and rocky outcrops. In the distance rose ranges of mountains, purplish against the sapphire blue of the sky. Some days, they drove for hours and hardly saw a soul, coming across only a scattering of ruined cottages and a herdsman and his cattle, the same red-brown as the dusty earth. Lizards sheltered in cracks in the rock, and, at midday, Sadie and Jimmy took refuge from the heat in the shade of a copse of lollipop-shaped trees. The shadow of an eagle, soaring high, skated over the tawny land, and the click and whirr of Sadie's camera pierced the hot silence. Jimmy wandered around, then sat on a rock and wrote. In the evening, back in the village, they drank *vino tinto* and he read out to her some of what he had written that day.

They parted in Madrid, Jimmy to drive on to Italy, Sadie to work for Gabriel. She liked Madrid straight away – liked its bright, dry heat and the way the sunshine flared white on the cobbles; liked the cheerful evening gatherings in street and plaza, the ambling families with beribboned babies and black-garbed grandmothers, who stopped to peer in the shops and squeeze the fruit at the market stalls.

She took a room a short walk from the studio, saving money by sharing with a woman called Vera Butterworth. Vera was short and busty, with bristly, dark curls; she was from Manchester and engaged to a Madrileño, and spoke Spanish with a strong Lancashire accent. She believed, she informed Sadie, in speaking her mind. She was frank when the tea wasn't strong enough, and given to suggesting improvements Sadie might make to her appearance. But she was good-hearted and they worked different hours – Sadie in the studio all day, Vera teaching English at night school – so their paths did not cross too often.

The room was a decent enough size – though, because it was on the attic floor of a five-storey block, it captured and concentrated Madrid's summer heat. There was a lace-curtained window and two narrow, iron-framed beds. On the dressing table, Vera arranged embroidered mats for her Yardley talc and Coty scent and red Elizabeth Arden lipstick. In a corner of the room, a small cupboard held their crockery and packets of tea, sugar and biscuits. There was a circular table on which they ate their breakfast of oranges and pastries bought from the baker's at the corner of the road.

Gabriel introduced her to his friends, who frequented the cafés and bars of the Lavapiés neighbourhood of the city. They were artists, musicians, poets and journalists, a mixture of nationalities: Spanish, French, Irish, English, American, the odd Pole and Czech. The talk was of a concert someone had been to, a book some of them had read, or a scandal, political or sexual, or, even better, both. And of the rise of Hitler and Mussolini, men that they had written off as buffoons and demagogues when they had first appeared on the political scene, but then the buffoons and demagogues must have had an attraction, a charisma, and a knack of voicing people's anger and resentment, because, dismayingly, they gathered votes and built up power, and then they weren't funny any more, but frightening.

Spain had its own intractable problems, its own seething resentments: the Catalans and Basques, who murmured about home rule; the power of the Church and the nobility, with their vast holdings of land; and the evictions and use of migrant labour in the countryside, which led to lower wages for a dirt-poor peasantry, whose tastes inclined towards anar-chism. There had been uprisings against the Second Republic, and the right wing was gathering strength, brooding about cuts to the army and the introduction of liberal measures, such as divorce and votes for women. Madrid, in the uneasy early years of the thirties, was a fertile ground for new ideas, and for fear of and fury at new ideas. The talk in the streets, bars and cafés that summer was of politics, until someone cried out that they were sick of politics, that it was making them miserable, that there must be other things to talk about.

One evening, Sadie and Gabriel were invited to supper by a couple who lived in an apartment on the Calle del Mesón de Paredes. Padraig – Paddy – O'Connor was a journalist and writer; his wife, Mary, a brisk, no-nonsense, freckled blonde American, was a nurse. Two other couples shared the table, old friends of Paddy and Mary. The sixth guest was a man who arrived on his own – a Spaniard who had excellent English. He was slim and slender boned, and Sadie noticed, when he rose to help Mary with the coffee tray, that he moved with grace and economy. When he spoke, it was in a thoughtful, considered fashion. She thought him the sort of man who would be as much at ease in the gilt drawing-rooms of the wealthy as in Paddy and Mary's small apartment. He had one of those complicated Spanish surnames with a *de*, which she forgot instantly, only registering that Paddy and Mary called him Andrés.

So, she didn't particularly pick him out, just then. It wasn't – on her part, anyway – love at first sight, or anything like that.

She met him again a few days later, in the Café Barbieri. A place of pillars and mirrors and scrubbed wooden chairs and tables, it was a favourite with Gabriel's crowd. There was always a loud buzz of conversation and laughter, so you often had to shout to make yourself heard. There were shady sorts, pickpockets and sellers of hashish and ladies of the night in

333

frayed lace and patched bright silks, as well as a musician who sang and played a guitar. But even the pickpockets fell silent when a poet with a threadbare shirt collar, and worn-out shoes, recited his work, closing his eyes and speaking in a low, passionate voice.

Gabriel and his friends always sat to the rear of the café, pulling together five or six tables to make one big, long one. When they arrived that evening, Sadie caught sight of Andrés at the end of the table. She had only met him once before, but, sitting down next to him, she had the warm, happy feeling of coming across an old friend. As they talked, she registered that his features were strong and fine: an aquiline nose; a humorous, definite mouth, with little curved lines of kindness around it; and green eyes, framed by long lashes. There were threads of silver in his short black hair. Though his clothes were of good quality, they were well worn.

At the end of the evening, in the small hours, he offered to walk her back to her lodgings. They talked of this and that, comparing the merits of Spanish wine and English beer, and Andrés provided Sadie with a rough translation of one of the poems they had listened to. All too soon, they reached her lodgings. She could not offer him coffee, she explained, because she shared her room with a friend. No matter, he said; and then, hesitantly, he added that perhaps, if she liked, if she was enjoying their conversation, they might walk some more?

They wandered around the barrio, arm in arm. A moon of enormous clarity illuminated the courtyards and narrow alleyways, painting the cobbles in lush, silvery tones. He asked her about the political situation in Britain, and then they talked of how, in these strange, exciting times of the Second Republic, fissures were tearing apart the fabric of

Spanish society. Extremists from the right and left wings were taking the chance to escape through the cracks.

'I can't tell where it will end,' Andrés said soberly. 'Nowhere good, I fear.'

But, after they parted, finding to their mutual surprise that several hours had passed, what remained with Sadie was a sense of peace and serenity. Trying to drop off to sleep that night, she thought of the way he had tucked a few pesetas into the palm of a child sleeping in a doorway. And how he had put his arm round her protectively as they walked by a group of ragged men, whose eyes had followed them along the street. And the touch of his lips, pressing against the back of her hand before they parted.

Sadie phoned Mary, the American nurse, and asked her out for lunch. She asked her about Andrés, sliding it into the conversation cleverly, she thought, after they had finished their salad and cheese, and had spoken of other matters for a respectable amount of time.

'He's a swell guy,' said Mary, helping herself to a little pastry filled with cream. 'An absolute sweetie. He'd do anything for you.'

'He told me he was a writer.'

'He's a journalist mostly, now. Started off as an academic – a historian. Paddy's read a couple of his books about some Spanish king or other and he said they were very fine. His articles are published in a whole lot of papers and journals.' Mary looked up from her cake. 'Has he told you about the castle?'

'Castle?' Sadie said.

'Andrés has a castle in . . .' An open-palmed gesture, conveying to Sadie that it was somewhere in Madrid's vast, hot, empty hinterland.

335

Mary said, 'Are you keen on him?' and Sadie felt herself blush. 'I hardly know him.'

A snort. 'As if *that* ever made any difference. He's married.' She shot a glance that seemed, to Sadie, to contain sympathy. 'Andrés has a child — a son. I met his wife once. Talk about blocks of ice. He isn't *happily* married, I'll tell you that.' Mary rose, patting her blond curls into place and flicking a crumb of pastry from her blue dress. 'I have to get back to the clinic.'

It was very hot, that afternoon, and the sunlight seemed to find its glaring way into the studio. The heat drained the air of oxygen and Gabriel was in one of his moods. The first print Sadie took was a fraction out of registration. 'Can't you even get that right?' he snarled at her. 'Expensive paper, wasted because of a careless idiot.' He crumpled up the print into a ball and hurled it into a corner of the room. After that, she concentrated harder.

At seven o'clock, Gabriel declared that it was too hot to work, threw down his cutting tool and thumped out of the studio. Sadie cleaned up, and then worked for a while on one of her own prints. As she cut lino, she thought of Andrés, who was married and had a son. She thought of Pearl, and the unhappiness that her affair with a married man had brought her, and she thought of her own foolish and disastrous encounter with Tom Chiverton. There must be moments of joy in some of these affairs, but were they enough to compensate for knowing you would never be first in the eyes of the man you loved, and that you were running the risk of hurting someone else? Mary had said, *He isn't happily married.* Did that make any difference?

The following morning, a breeze had got up, stirring the hot air. Gabriel was pale and hungover, but his bad mood had gone. What little he said was mild and conciliatory, and they did a good day's work, successfully completing a run of twenty prints.

A week later, Sadie went to a party in rooms near the Puerta del Sol. Beneath the roar of conversation, the music of the piano was detectable only as a vibration. She laughed at her neighbour's jokes and a friend offered her a cigarette and Sadie cupped her hand round the match as he lit it. She became aware – she could not have said how – that someone was watching her, and, when she looked up, she saw Andrés. Their gazes met; he began to wind up his conversation with a smile, a gesture of the hand. As he made his way to her, her heart lifted.

Though she was attracted to him, they need not become lovers. They could be friends. He might not want any more.

At the end of the evening, he offered, once again, to walk her back to her lodgings. Sadie draped her silk stole round her shoulders. 'Won't your wife be expecting you?'

'My wife is with my son, in France. She has family there.'

They left the building. His hand touched her elbow, guiding her through a group of revellers in the doorway, their loud conversation echoing off the buildings in the plaza. It was past midnight and the city was still busy, trapping the heat.

Andrés said, 'I should have told you. If I said that I couldn't find the moment, it would sound like an evasion. But, to tell you that I was married, that I have a wife and child . . . You might have interpreted it as meaning that I was expecting . . . something.'

'I don't think,' she said carefully, 'that you're that sort of man.'

'I would not expect,' he said. 'But I might hope.'

A little bubble of excitement rose up inside her. Though

logic and hard experience might tell her to walk away from him now, she knew that she had already made her decision. She kept in step beside him.

As they walked, he told her that his wife, Isabella, was the daughter of his mother's closest friend. The two women had met at boarding school when they were girls; they had married on the same day and each had given birth to her first child – in Andrés' mother's case, her only child – a week apart. So, his marriage had been planned, you might say, in the cradle.

At the age of twenty-four, seeing Isabella again after a five-year separation, during which he had studied at the University of Salamanca, he had fallen deeply in love with her.

'She was a beautiful woman,' he said. 'She had this dark austereness that attracted me when I was younger.'

He had been twenty-five, Andrés went on, when he and Isabella had married. How long had it taken before they had realised the enormity of their mistake? Not so long.

'What happened between us – I am to blame. I wasn't the man she thought I was. She thought she was marrying the Señor Moreno with the manor house and the land and the unassailable position in society. But I'm afraid I disappointed her, and instead she found herself bound to someone who makes a pittance out of writing books that few people read and articles that neither she nor many of our friends and neighbours approve of. And who has steadily lost, I'm afraid, what possessions he owned. Worst of all, Isabella is a devout Roman Catholic. She believed she was marrying a man who shared her faith. But my religious beliefs have shrunk over the years to . . .' He held his thumb and forefinger a fraction apart. 'This, she can't forgive. After our son, Raoul, was born, she made it clear to me that she

338

felt she had done her duty towards me. We have not lived as man and wife since.'

'I'm sorry,' she said.

'I'm not seeking your sympathy, my dear Sadie, nor to justify myself. Nor, most certainly, to voice resentment. Only to explain to you.'

He was laying his cards on the table, she thought. He was telling her, *This is what I am.*

They passed a wall pasted with political posters and advertisements for concerts, poetry readings and bullfights.

'Isabella and I live in Madrid for nine months of the year,' he said. 'In the summer, she takes Raoul to stay with her family in Pyréneés-Atlantiques. They have a place by the sea. She prefers the climate there.'

They turned down a long, dark, narrow street that ran like a chasm between the high tenement blocks.

'I don't think,' he said, 'that she ever loved me. Isabella has a strong sense of duty. A long time ago, I came to the conclusion that she married me because her mother wanted her to. To the best of my knowledge, she hasn't loved any other man. Sometimes I think it would have been easier if she had.'

'Why?'

'Because it would have given me something to rail against, someone to feel angry with. Misery's always easier, don't you find, if you can blame it on someone else?' He smiled crookedly. 'I find consolation from time to time. I am not a monk.'

'One feels lonely.'

'Yes, exactly. I'm always discreet. I've no wish to humiliate Isabella more than she feels she has been humiliated already. And, besides, there is Raoul.'

339

They had reached the street where Sadie lived. She did not yet go inside; they remained in the hot, dark, moonlit air, talking. Andrés told her that, in the twenties, difficult economic times had meant that he had had to sell the family home and some of his land. He and his wife had moved into a house in Madrid.

'Isabella expected to live in a different style,' he said. 'I don't mean that she demanded luxury; she's not the sort of woman who cares about that. But she saw the sale as a loss of status . . . an indignity. I regret that, but, believe me, I had no choice. For me, it was a relief. I was able to think of something other than the cockroaches in the kitchens and the drains and ceilings that were on the point of collapse. I try to improve the lot of those who live on what land I have left. I've built a school so the children can be educated, and I make sure the sick have access to the services of a doctor. Isabella has a more rigid view of these things. She believes that a man's status, his future and opportunity, is set in stone at birth. The aristocrat's son will attend school, the peasant's will not.'

'Mary O'Connor told me that you have a castle.'

He gave her an amused glance. 'I think Mary imagines turrets, battlements and moats, that sort of thing. I've tried to explain to her that the roof's fallen in and the castle's only occupants are wild goats, but she doesn't want to listen. It's a beautiful place. There are lemon trees and the ground is carpeted with thyme. I haven't been there for years. I would like to take you there some day, Sadie.'

A horse and cart, loaded with sacks of onions and kindling, passed by. Sadie watched the flicker of expression across Andrés' face and the way the moonlight moved on his features.

She said, 'And your son, Andrés? How old is he now?'

'Raoul is fourteen years old. He's a fine boy. Isabella is a good mother to him, patient and affectionate. I miss him. The apartment feels very empty when he's not there.'

He asked her about herself. She told him that she had never married and that she had no children. She had been engaged once, she said, but it hadn't worked out. Then she talked a little about Kit Massingham and a man she had met in the south of France the previous summer – an artist called Jules.

'He was good fun,' she said. 'The least serious person you can imagine. Not as good a painter as he thought he was, I'm afraid, but fun.' But then, sensing what it had cost him to talk honestly about the failure of his marriage, she said, more frankly, 'Kit was a good friend – he still is – and Jules and I send each other postcards now and then, but I wasn't in love with either of them. I was in love with Felix, my fiancé, though, very much. After we broke up, I had a break-down. I can see now that he wasn't right for me and it wouldn't have worked, but it changed my life and I wasn't the same person afterwards. I'm sorry, Andrés, that things haven't worked out better for you.'

He gave a little shrug. 'Sometimes these things happen. But they cast a long shadow. Isabella believes divorce to be a sin, and, in the eyes of the Church, we have no grounds for divorce. Nor would I wish to inflict on her something so utterly against everything she believes in. I've visited on her quite enough disappointment and humiliation in the past, without adding to it. We live separate lives, Isabella and I. She has her friends and occupations, and I have mine. We try not to bring our quarrels into the open, to keep what conversation we have civilised, for the sake of our son. I'll

341

go to the house in the Pyreneés-Atlantiques for the last two weeks of the summer. I like to swim and ride with the boy.'

Sadie would return to England in the first week of September, to prepare for her exhibition at the Danford Gallery in November. There had been a moment, earlier in the evening, when she had warned herself not to get in too deep, that she, who had fallen in love so speedily and disastrously before, and who had been burned by desire, should be wary. But that moment had already passed.

They were standing beneath a street lamp that pooled a greenish light on to the cobbles. The impulse to touch him could not be resisted. Sadie stroked his face with the back of her fingers, then his cheek and the corners of his mouth, as if to make him smile.

'I'm afraid that Vera, my room-mate, will be fast asleep in bed by now,' she said. 'Did you say that your house is empty, Andrés?'

He took her hands in his, kissing her folded knuckles. 'I should so very much like you to come home with me.'

They kissed, and a fire flared inside her.

'Shall we go?' he murmured, and they walked away, arm in arm.

The bedroom hangings were of faded green-and-gold brocade: very *ancien régime*. Andrés removed her clothing with smooth efficiency; each layer slipping off and falling to the floor made her want him more. His body was compact, lean and well muscled, and she ran a hand over the wings of his shoulder blades and down the straight hollow of his spine, and then he laid her on the bed, a monstrous four-poster of carved black wood. Spiteful-looking cherubs glared at her disapprovingly from the corners of the tester, so she closed

342

her eyes and gave herself up to sensation. His fingers, running from breast to waist to belly. His mouth, against the curves and folds of hip and thigh. His palm, moving closer to the place she longed for him to touch, coaxing, prompting. Sweat pooled between her breasts and pleasure burned inside her, scorching her, and she opened herself for him.

In the morning, after they had made love again, Andrés went out to the baker's to fetch them something to eat. Sadie wrapped the green silk brocade bedspread round her and went off to the bathroom. All the rooms she peered into were cavernous and imposing, the furniture vast and uncomfortable, made for giants. They were old and ugly, those sideboards and bureaux, those hefty wooden chests with their iron and leather locks. On the walls were gloomy oil paintings of men and women with big noses and bulging eyes; near the fireplaces, bronze horses reared, snarling, and oversized majolica pots were decorated with shades of mustard, salmon pink and khaki. Ceilings soared above her, encrusted with leaves and flowers, and the landing floor was paved with marble tiles the colour of potted meat. The house was designed, Sadie decided, not to welcome, but to intimidate. Only in the books in the glass-fronted cupboards, the scattered heap of newspapers and magazines on a side table and the block of writing paper covered with notes in a strong, elegant hand did she see the man to whom she was coming to feel so close.

A shabby, seen-better-days air pervaded the rooms. The paintings and bronzes were not, she felt, of good quality. During their conversation the previous night, Andrés had intimated a shortage of money; she wondered whether more valuable pieces had been sold off. Dust had gathered on the architraves and polished tabletops: she could have written her name in it. It would take an army of maids to keep so large a house clean, and she had not yet encountered a single one.

The bathroom contained a huge bathtub resembling a modestly sized swimming pool: you'd want to be confident of your breaststroke. The throne-like lavatory necessitated a barefoot trek across a chilly black-and-white tiled floor, and she washed her hands in a cement-grey marble washbasin, the tap of which had gone green with age.

She studied her reflection in the mirror. Did she look different, now that she had fallen in love again? Because she had. Love and happiness made her as ringing and transparent as glass, and she existed with perfect contentment in each perfect moment. She couldn't remember feeling like this with Felix. She had never felt certain of him, and so had been dogged by jealousy and insecurity. It interested her that she did not feel the same with Andrés, even though their relationship would always be constrained by circumstances. She peered at her reflection more closely, trying to divine the truth from the shade and form of her features. Perhaps she had become older and wiser. It was pleasing to think that the last few years, which had often been lonely and full of turmoil, had made her stronger. Or perhaps she felt differently because she knew instinctively that Andrés was different.

As she walked back to the bedroom, a door opened downstairs. Peering over the balustrade to the floor below, Sadie caught sight of a black-clad woman carrying a mop and bucket. Silently, she scuttled back to the bedroom.

She said, 'I don't even know your name. I mean, your full, proper name. I only know Andrés.'

They were in the bath. The housekeeper had finished her work and left the house, and they had breakfasted in bed on the doughnuts Andrés had bought. Gleaming grains of sugar adhered to their skin, so they had decided to have a bath.

'My name?' He was washing her hair. He rubbed shampoo into her scalp. 'It's Luis Andrés Kindellan de Moreno. Easy, you see.'

'Easy?' she scoffed, through bubbles, then repeated it.

'Kindellan was my mother's name,' he explained. 'She was Irish.'

'It's awfully romantic. So much more romantic than Sadie Victoire Lawless.' She leaned forward and he tipped a cup of water over her head to rinse.

'Sadie Victoire Lawless is delightful. And very romantic. And very beautiful. Which is just as it should be, for such a beautiful woman.' He squeezed the excess water out of her long tail of hair and they shuffled up the bath to kiss, water swooshing in a soapy wave.

He said, 'Why Victoire?'

'After my mother, who was French.'

'Do you speak French?'

'Yes, not too badly. Better than my Spanish.'

'I adore your Spanish.'

'It's an impossible language. All those hrrr noises.' She rasped her throat. 'How many languages do you speak?'

'Just five.'

'Which five?'

'Spanish, English, French, Italian and German. Tell me about yourself, my darling Sadie. What sort of house do you live in? Is it grand or is it modest? Is it in the city or the countryside?'

'It's in the middle of a wood,' she said, 'in Sussex, in the south of England. It's a little house, a very little house, and it's called the Egg.'

'The Egg?' He laughed.

'It would seem, to you, tiny – a miniature. I expect you could fit it in your drawing room. My father built it. He was an architect, rather ahead of his time. He imagined lots of little Eggs, in fields and forests, where people could bring up their children away from the smoke and noise of the cities. When he died, I inherited it.'

'And why did you leave your little house in the forest?'

'To see the world. To meet you.'

'I'm so glad you did, querida.'

She kissed him, then climbed out of the bath. He wrapped a towel round her. He had some business that must be attended to, he told her, kissing her again. She should read some books, have a siesta. He would be back in an hour or two.

Andrés left the house. Sadie untangled her hair with the comb from her handbag and then lay down, naked, on the bed. It was hotter than ever and the heat settled round her like a blanket.

She drifted off into a shallow sleep and dreamed that she was at the Egg again. The rustle of the leaves, birdsong and all the little noises the house itself made; the tap of a branch against glass and the scratches of a squirrel running over the flat roof. Or perhaps the footsteps belonged to someone who was running through the trees, their breath quick and panicked as they slipped and stumbled in the mud.

She woke. Downstairs, a door closed. The footsteps she heard now belonged to Andrés; already, she recognised them. Delight washed over her and she went to meet him.

* * *

He was an only child; both his parents had died during his teens. In his twenties, he had published two books: one exploring Spain's Golden Age, the other a biography of Charles III. He was interested in all sorts of things: the art of making Persian rugs; the workings of the human mind; the origins of the various languages of Spain; English Romantic poetry; motor cars (he possessed a Lancia Lambda); and politics, of course – he was enormously knowledgeable about the politics not only of Europe but of America and the Far East as well. He played the piano rather well – classical mostly, but some jazz too, especially sentimental numbers such as 'Ain't Misbehavin' and 'After You've Gone', that sort of thing. He read novels and poetry and liked to go to the theatre. Sadie, who had considered herself reasonably well read, discovered that, when she compared the scope of her literary knowledge to his, it was sadly parochial.

He couldn't cook at all and was disproportionately appreciative when she prepared a simple breakfast or a late supper for them in his cold and unnecessarily large kitchen. Most of the time, they ate out. Another cavernous room in the house was lined with shelves containing bottles of wine. He took wine seriously, considering it important to match it to the food they were eating, even when what they were eating was only cheese on toast. They shared an interest in Russian music and dance, and in modernism, both in art and architecture, and in the works of Velásquez and Goya. He liked to see the paintings in the Prado through her eyes, because he thought that she could teach him something. They both loved sunlight and warmth and disliked the winter, though they didn't talk about that much, because, at the first intimations of a cooling in the air, they must part.

* * *

347

They fell into a routine. Five days a week, she worked at Gabriel's studio from early in the morning to late in the evening. Sometimes, when Andrés was not too busy, he met her for lunch, waiting for her in the square before they headed on to a café.

Blissful days were the ones when, after lunch, they went to his house and made quick, breathtaking love, while sunlight fell in blinding slices through the slats of the shutters.

Their love affair fuelled Sadie's creative energy. After Gabriel left for the Café Barbieri at seven or so in the evenings, she worked on for hours. When Andrés finished work, he came to the studio and sat on a windowsill to keep her company. Then they left the studio and walked back to his house, stopping for a drink or something to eat. Or not, when their need to be alone was urgent. Then, they would make their way along the street, arm in arm, hip to hip, her head resting against his shoulder. Inside the cool, marble vestibule of his house, she would peel off her blouse before he had finished bolting the door. In the mornings, he gathered up their clothes from where they lay, strewn like fallen leaves on the treads of the stairs, before the housekeeper arrived.

By halfway through August, Sadie had completed eight of her Castilian landscapes, with their bands of orange, russet and Titian red, and strong, shadowy dark greens and blue-greys, redolent of forests and mountains. She decided that she was pleased with them; they were bold and confident, and yet each hinted at a mystery. She wrote to Madge Danford, whose gallery in Jermyn Street had recently taken her on, and told her about them. She also wrapped up a print in layers of cardboard and brown paper and mailed it from the post office in Madrid to London.

Her work, dancing from her fingertips with an ease she had not experienced in years, and Andrés, her lover: she had never been happier.

One day, Sadie told Andrés about Edith. Her room-mate, Vera, had gone away for the weekend with her fiancé; Sadie and Andrés were wrapped around each other in her narrow bed.

'We quarrelled,' she said. 'And now we don't speak any more. I write to her, but she never answers.'

He ran his fingertips from her throat to her belly. 'What did you quarrel about, *querida*?'

'The house. Edith minded that my father had left it to me. She thought it meant he didn't love her.'

She remembered that day, two years ago now, when Edith had come to the Egg: the clumsy, hurtful atmosphere between them, her own resentment and anger, and the things Edith had said to her.

I've never loved you. What chance did we ever have, you and I, to love each other as sisters should? I'm not a fool; I could see how it was. From the day you were born, you were Father's favourite. None of this, after lengthy reflection, seemed to Sadie to be untrue.

He said, 'What's she like, your sister? Is she like you?'

'Not to look at, no. She's taller and a little darker. I used to wish I was tall, like Edith. She carries off her clothes so well. And she's a very organised person, the sort who always does everything just so. When I was going through my bohemian phase, I used to be rather scornful of that, but then I came to admire it.'

'Did you have a bohemian phase?' He sounded amused.

'Yes, I'm afraid so. Tasselled scarves and beads round my forehead and droopy skirts. I grew out of it, fortunately.' She let out a sigh. 'I expect that I chose to think of Edith as dull and conventional because I knew I'd never have the things she had: a husband, a child, a proper, ordinary household.'

'Don't be sad, *querida*. Now you have me.'

'Yes, now I have you, my darling.'

They kissed. After a while, Sadie put on her robe and made coffee. The scent of the ground beans, as she poured boiled water on to them, filled the small, hot room.

She said, as she brought the coffee pot and cups back to the bedside table, 'I can see, now, that my father was in the wrong. You shouldn't have a favourite child. My father gave me so much – too much, I think now. The house should have been Edith's. It's funny, but I don't love it as much as I used to.' She let the grounds settle, then poured coffee into two small cups and thought of a collage of ice and feathers, obliterated with red paint. 'It hasn't always been a happy place, Andrés.'

'So,' she said, 'your lovers. How many? Did you adore them? Were they as pretty as me?'

They were in the four-poster bed with the silk brocade hangings. They had made love and were lying side by side, satiated, their skin sticking sweatily at shoulder and hip. A triangle of sheet lay over them, all the covering they could bear in the heat. They had put off the lamp and their cigarettes were red pinpoints in all the blackness.

He said, 'There were one or two.'

'What were their names?'

'Juana . . . Bianca. Galina, a Russian, a ballet dancer, as strong as a man, with muscles like a coal miner's. Fine women, but I didn't love them. I love you, though, Sadie. I love you so very, very much.'

It was the first time they had spoken of such things. She

had known that she loved Andrés for what seemed like a long time – though, if you counted up, it was only three weeks. But she had not said so. It was not that she was afraid he was the sort of man who might turn tail and run at such a declaration – no, not at all – but saying the words could only spell out the impossibility of their position. *Here is this wonderful thing we have, but it can't last.* Words could be salt rubbed into wounds.

'I loved you even before we were lovers,' she said soberly. 'I think it was that first evening in the Café Barbieri. I remember all the streets we walked along that night. I remember everything we said.' She turned to kiss his shoulder, sensing with her touch the solidity of muscle and bone beneath the skin.

'The next day,' he said, 'I walked past Gabriel's studio. I couldn't stop myself. I knew you were there. You were outside, leaning against the wall, sunning yourself in the heat, smoking a cigarette. I watched you for a while. You were wearing overalls with paint stains on them and you had tied back your hair with a scarf, and I thought you were the most beautiful woman I'd ever seen.'

In the silence, she heard laughter from the street and, distantly, the bell of a police car.

'It's a disaster, isn't it?' he said softly, to the night. 'Forty-one years old and I've found the woman I'd like to spend the rest of my life with. Good God, my timing is abysmal. I wish I could give you more.'

'I don't want anything, Andrés. Well, only your heart.'

'Oh, you have *that*.' There was a gentle sadness in his voice. 'It's been in your keeping, Sadie, for quite some time now.'

One Saturday morning, the four of them, Sadie and Andrés

and Paddy and Mary, drove out of the city, searching for a respite from the blistering summer sun. Andrés drove them in his Lancia to a countryside of pools and granite outcrops.

As soon as they found a quiet spot, they changed into their bathing costumes and dived from the hot rocks into the cold water. They swam for hours, fooling about and splashing each other, racing from one side of the pool to another. After a while, Sadie clambered out and sat on a rock while the sun bleached her hair, which she had spread out on her shoulders. At midday, they picnicked in the blue shade of the scrubby trees. Mary had brought some loaves of bread, slices of dried ham and a jar of salty butter which they immersed in the water to keep cool. Sadie contributed bags of chocolate pastries and plump, warm peaches. The men uncorked bottles of wine.

Afterwards, they dozed, lying limp and motionless in the heat, like fish cast up on the rocks. Waking, they stretched and stirred, moaning that someone should have brought along a Thermos of coffee. Andrés and Mary went back into the pool for a last swim; Paddy and Sadie sat in the shade of the trees.

Mary's head emerged, dark and sleek, dripping with water, while Andrés lazed in the shallows. Sadie balanced the block of paper on her knees while she drew. She couldn't imagine ever forgetting this day, but you never knew, sometimes memory didn't cooperate, and if she made a decent drawing, the perfection of the moment could never completely vanish.

'Andrés is a good fellow,' said Paddy. 'He's one of the best. I'm glad you found each other, Sadie. He deserves some happiness. God knows, he's had to put up with enough. Of course, he loves the boy, that must be a consolation, but, Jesus, what a miserable situation. I'm not saying Mary and

I never have a cross word, she's a temper on her and she'd say I was an obstinate fellow, so we have our disagreements. But, on anything important, we think the same. It must kick you in the teeth to be shackled to a woman who believes the opposite to you about everything that matters. Another thing, Sadie: we've never had money, Mary or me. My da scraped a living from farming a bog in Donegal and Mary was brought up in a slum in Chicago. Her parents worked in a meat-packing factory. What you don't have, you don't miss. We've a house and food and clothes on our backs, so we think ourselves blessed. But Andrés' family were land-owners. I get the impression that what they owned dwindled over the decades. And then he gave half of it away and what was left vanished, one way or another. Old money can be a millstone round your neck. I daresay he'd get rid of that mausoleum he lives in, if it weren't for his wife.'

She couldn't resist asking, 'What's Isabella like?'

'Oh, you must know the sort. Rushing off to Mass every five minutes and bristling with sanctimonious self-righteousness.' Paddy lit a couple of cigarettes and passed one to her, then leaned back, propped on his elbows, tipping the brim of his straw hat down over his face. 'Ah, maybe I'm being unfair. I hardly know the woman. What will you do when you go home, Sadie?'

'I'm having an exhibition at a London gallery,' she said.

'That's great. Good for you. Hey, Mary!' he shouted in the direction of the pool. 'Sadie's going to be a famous artist!'

'I know; Andrés told me. Isn't it wonderful?'

Andrés, who was floating on his back, lifted a languid hand.

Two days ago, a telegram had arrived from Madge Danford. It said, the capitalised words redolent of Madge's vivacity

353

and enthusiasm, *ADORE IT! CAN'T WAIT TO SEE MORE.* Sadie knew that she should have been ecstatic, and yet a part of her was also afraid, because time was narrowing to a pinpoint, and in that black fragment of a moment, she and Andrés must part.

Paddy shot her a glance. 'When will you leave?'

'The end of the week. I have to get ready for the exhibition.' She picked up a handful of rust-coloured earth and let it trail through her fingers. 'And, anyway, Andrés is to go to France to join Isabella and Raoul.'

'The trouble with real life,' he said sympathetically, 'is that it sometimes gets in the way of what you care about most.'

But which of her lives was real? Sadie wondered. She had had a number of different lives: the indulged daughter, the carefree student, the tired teacher and jilted bride, and then the solitary inhabitant of the Egg. There were entire months of her sojourn in Sussex that she found hard to recall, and yet every day of her stay in Madrid seemed soaked in intense colour.

She put down her pencil. 'You'll look after him for me, won't you, Paddy?'

He puffed out smoke and gave his mouth a little twist. 'Mary and I have talked about going back to America. We love Spain, but we fear for it. We want to have children, we want them to have decent lives, a future, and we're starting to think that might not be possible here. A lot of people's noses have been put out of joint. You attack the interests of the wealthy and powerful, and sooner or later there's a backlash. There are places I'm not welcome any more and newspapers that won't publish my work. I've had the odd letter making threats, you know the sort of pleasant thing, telling me to leave Spain or I won't make it back home with the usual number of eyeballs. The same with Andrés. He doesn't pull his punches, either. He's made a name for himself as a liberal commentator – the worst sort of liberal, in many people's eyes; they see him as a traitor to his class. He'll criticise the far left too, and they don't care for that. Spain has its iconoclasts, just like every other European country right now – people who'd like to tear everything to bits and start again.'

He gave Sadie a smile. 'Look, I'll do what I can. But Andrés can be a stubborn devil when he digs his heels in and I'll probably be wasting my breath.'

Sadie walked down to the water's edge. She caught sight of her reflection in the pool, tendrils of damp hair escaping from the scarf with which she had tied it back, a frown incised between her brows. She dipped her toe in the water and the ripples broke the image to pieces.

That night, when they were finishing dinner, she told Andrés what Paddy had said. They were in a dark little café, being served by a very old, thin waiter in a high collar and white apron, who leaned against the panelled wall when not needed by the clientele, and dozed. Few of the tables were taken, many in the city having gone to the country or the coast to escape the worst of the summer heat. Their meal had been dismal; perhaps the chef, too, had gone away.

She said, 'You'll be careful, won't you, Andrés?'

He was holding her hand across the table. 'I'm always careful.'

'Paddy doesn't think so.'

'Damn Paddy.' He frowned. 'I won't be silenced, Sadie. You speak through the pictures you make, I speak through what I write. I love my country, and I can tell by the way you talk about it that you love yours. I have to go on writing what I believe to be true, or what's the point?'

'I see that, but I fear for you.'

'Don't.' He squeezed her hand. 'I'll be fine.'

Why did it have to be him? Why couldn't it be someone else who put themselves in danger by telling the truth? But she did not say it aloud.

He split the last of the carafe between their glasses. The thick, dark wine left purple flecks on the side of the glass. She must not feel heavy-hearted tonight. She must be happy, because that was how she wanted him to remember her.

He took her hand again. 'I've been lucky enough to have been given a voice,' he said quietly. 'I'm not the only one; there are plenty of others pushing for a decent future. Sadie, darling Sadie, I'm not a fool. I don't walk down dark alleyways at night and, if I'm meeting someone I distrust, then I'll make sure it's in the open. But if a man behaves like a bully then I have to say so, whoever he is, whatever he is. At least the left has the excuse of years of ignorance and deprivation. People can be quick to say that, no matter how things are managed in other countries – in Great Britain or France, for instance – the Spanish worker and peasant isn't educated enough or intelligent enough to be trusted to make the right decisions. I happen to think, if you treat people like animals, then they'll behave like animals. Spain has used men as beasts of burden for far too long and we're paying the price for it. You under-stand, don't you, Sadie?'

'In my head, yes. I love you for what you are. For your courage.'

'Oh, yes, the head and the heart.' She thought there was an edge of bitterness to his laugh. 'If only I could disregard the one or the other, how much simpler life would be.'

'Andrés, of course I understand. I've never been good at

sticking my own head over the parapet. I like to hide away in my woodland.'

'And I'm glad of that.' His eyes softened. 'This wasn't the life I imagined for myself when I was younger. I thought it would be book-lined rooms and students waiting keenly on my every word. Life takes its own direction.'

'Yes, darling, I know.'

The waiter came to clear away the plates and asked whether they wanted anything else. Andrés ordered coffees.

He said, 'My democratic sympathies have been one of the subjects on which Isabella and I have disagreed most profoundly.'

'Have you ever wished you could just stand back – or walk away?'

'Often. Since I've met you, all the time. For Raoul's sake, too. I haven't always made life easy for him, and I regret that. Since we're talking about honesty, then I'll admit something else.' He paused, frowning, then took her hands between his own. 'There have been times when I've found myself faltering, when I've begun to doubt my own principles. But I have to go on believing with all my heart that democracy is desirable and inevitable, no matter how flawed and imperfect it is. Whatever my reservations, I'll always come down on the side of democracy. I pray that, here in Europe, we go on trying to find our way to a more just and equal society – in my lifetime, I hope, but, if not, in my son's. But I'll be careful, Sadie, I promise. And you must be careful, too.'

'Darling, I lead a dull little life.' She stroked his cheek. 'Nothing will happen to me.'

On her last evening in Madrid, Sadie and Andrés did the usual things: a drink, a light supper and then back to his house, where they made love. Sadie was to take a train to Barcelona first thing in the morning, from there changing for a train to Paris. The day after, Andrés would drive to France, to the town where Isabella and Raoul were staying. They didn't talk about the future, because they both knew there might not be one. Next summer, Isabella might choose to stay in Madrid – this had happened before.

He offered to come to the station with her. No, Sadie said, she didn't want him to. She hated goodbyes. She didn't want them to say goodbye, not tomorrow, not ever.

'I'll write to you,' he promised. 'In your little house in the forest.'

She would write to his office. She could not write to the Madrid house because of Isabella. She imagined how different the house would seem with Isabella and Raoul there. She had come to think of it a little as her own, in some way, but it was not hers at all.

They slept on and off that night. There was a time when she woke and, moving quietly so as not to wake him, shifted to look at him. It was still dark, and the sadness that comes at the heart of the night washed over her as she picked from the gloom the angle of his shoulder and the blurred outline of his features. Would she ever see him again after tomorrow? She could not, at that moment, tell. It was easy enough to see how an affair like theirs might end – the letters that came further and further apart, the one unanswered. Apologies, perhaps, eventually, but then a slow change of tone, from passion and need to nostalgia and friendship.

All the difficulties of living so far apart, and of his obligations, seemed insurmountable. She would have given anything to make it otherwise. Tears sprang to her eyes at the thought of the life they might have had, the journeys they might have taken, the houses they might have lived in. The children — the green-eyed, dark-haired boy and the blonde, blue-eyed girl — that she would have loved and adored, and who would have filled the gap in her heart that she hardly ever dared acknowledge was there. The things they would have seen, the laughter they would have shared, the sorrows they would have wept over. They would have grown old together: he, sitting by the fire on a cold winter's evening, writing a history of some Spanish monarch or politician she had never heard of; she, her eyesight fading a little, drawing the proud angles of his face, the curves and folds of his clothing.

She must have made a sound — a sigh, a breath — because he shifted and took her in his arms again, stroking her hair and murmuring to her. Enclosed in his embrace, she shut her eyes, willing herself back to sleep. Be brave, Sadie, she said to herself. Might as well begin now, being brave.

Chapter Seventeen

London, Suffolk and Sussex – April 1971

Dan had been working for Kevin since mid-February. He had thrown himself into the setting up of the new airfield south of Croydon until late into the evenings and for much of the weekends. He was using the flat in Kew for little more than a quick shower and sleep, and the rooms had taken on a spartan air. The pots of herbs Celia had arranged on his kitchen windowsill had died because he had neglected to water them, and he had taken to drinking his coffee black because there was never any milk.

A part of him was aware that beneath his industriousness lay a deep discontent. It emerged in a lack of patience with those who worked for him, especially when he had to explain something to them a second time. He cancelled a visit to Southwold to see his father, using the excuse of too much work. He couldn't face it and found it hard to see why he should have to.

One Friday evening in April, the phone rang as he was going out to buy fish and chips. He answered it.

'Am I speaking to Daniel Falconer?' A woman's voice.

Dan said that she was. The caller introduced herself as a

nurse at West Suffolk General Hospital in Bury St Edmunds. She went on to break the news to him that his father had been admitted to the hospital, suffering from serious burns. He had given Dan's name, address and phone number as his next of kin.

Dan's heart seemed to pause before it restarted, a heavy, anxious thump. 'How bad is he?'

'We've treated the injuries and sedated him. He's doing as well as can be expected.'

'I'll be there as soon as I can.'

The nurse gave him the address of the hospital and Dan put the phone down. As he gathered his belongings and grabbed his car keys, he struggled to absorb the shock. He should have gone to Southwold weeks ago. More than three months had passed since he had last seen his father. Burns, he thought, feeling nauseous. Christ.

His journey to the North Circular was grindingly slow, the route clogged by traffic. When, at last, he reached the main road, he drove at speed until, overtaking a lorry, a near miss and a blaring of horns brought him to his senses. Shortly afterwards, he stopped at a garage for petrol and a Mars Bar, which he ate as he headed for the A11.

Driving north, he was haunted by a vision of his father in a hospital bed, limbs bandaged, in agony. His emotions jolted from fear to guilt to anger. His fear was for his father, that he might not survive, and his guilt was because of the miserly affection he himself had measured out so rationally and judgementally over the years. He was angry with his father too, for not looking after himself. What the hell had he done, to land himself in hospital with second- and third-degree burns?

He navigated through Bury St Edmunds with the AA map

open on the passenger seat beside him. By then, dread that he might reach the hospital too late swam uppermost in his mind. Another quick glance at the map and he made his way to Hospital Road, where he slipped the Cortina into a parking space before going inside the building.

A nurse showed him inside a curtained cubicle. Both of his father's arms were covered in white bandages and raised up in slings. Dan went to stand beside the bed.

'Dad?' he said softly, and Mick's eyes opened.

'Son. I told them to leave it till the morning. Didn't want to drag you all the way out here at this time of night.' His father spoke in a croaky, opiated whisper.

'Dad, it's fine.' He wanted to say more, but couldn't get the words out, eventually managing, 'How are you feeling?'

'A bit groggy.'

'What happened?'

Mick raised his eyes to look at him. 'I was trying to dry my trousers. I thought I'd go to the pub. There's this feller sometimes, we have a drink together. I'd spilled oil on my good pair. I'd washed them, my other trousers . . .' He screwed up his face.

'Dad, don't worry about it.'

But his father's halting tale continued. 'They were still damp, so I dried them over the oil stove. Pegged them to the wire that holds the curtains up. I've done it before and it works well. Thought I'd have a quick go at the crossword in the *Mail*, keep the old brain working, but I must have dropped off. There was this burning smell, I couldn't think what it was at first, thought I hadn't put out my fag.'

'Dad . . .'

'They must have slipped down on to the burner. It caught

the curtains. I tried to put it out. Bloody stupid . . .' A pause, before his father added, 'I'm sorry, Dan.'

'It doesn't matter.' Gently, Dan patted his father's shoulder. 'Try not to think about it.'

'How's the caravan?'

'I don't know. I came straight here. I'll go and have a look at it tomorrow morning, okay?'

'It was a nice little caravan.' Mick's eyes were closing again.

'You're going to be okay, Dad, and that's the only thing that matters.'

Mick did not respond. Dan drew up a chair and sat down by the bed. He thought of his father, setting the caravan alight and trying, by the look of it, to put it out with his bare hands. He could have been killed. It was horrible to see him brought so low, and all his anger vanished and what he felt instead was a deep misery, so that he could have wept, sitting there among the noises of the hospital, the quick clack of shoes on lino and the snores and groans of the patients, and beeps from machinery.

Love remains. The phrase popped into his head from God knows where. Mick Falconer had always been a man of optimism and easy charm and, until comparatively recently, not much conscience. Dan was never sure whether, at the time, Mick had felt guilty for his desertion of his wife and son. Dan suspected he regretted it now, though he had never said so. So, he had often been hurt by his father and had often felt contemptuous of him and had sometimes disliked him. The problem was that he loved him too. It would have been easier if he didn't, but there it was and he must accept it. His anger was fired by his father's desertion and neglect during his childhood, yes, but also by resentment of the ties that, in spite of everything, remained. He had fought against them, and had done so for a long time. It was exhausting, and, really, it was time to stop. It wasn't logical, it wasn't neat or tidy to love someone who had hurt you, and who had let you down over and over again, but nevertheless love was there, apparently indestructible.

Love remains. He loved Rose, too. He shouldn't love a woman who was married to someone else, a woman who had made it crystal clear to him that she was giving her marriage a second chance and that she regarded their only intimacy as a mistake, but he did, and that too he needed to accept. He recognised that this hopeless love, and the pain it inflicted on him, was at the root of the ill humour that had been his habitual mood since he had left Martineau Aviation. There wasn't much he could do about his feelings except wait for them to fade, though that might take years. Or maybe a lifetime.

But he had to stop taking it out on his subordinates. Go on like this and he'd end up the sort of operations manager that everyone loathed behind his back. Like his former imme- diate boss, Ted Wilkinson, who had made Dan's working life miserable during his early days at Martineau Aviation. What he found easy, others didn't, but that didn't mean they did not have qualities he lacked. He needed to learn to see the best in people, to value them for their good qualities. And that included his father. Mick had his good points. He was unmaterialistic, never made a fuss about living on a pittance, and always tried to put on a cheerful face, no matter how grim the reality. His admiration for his clever son was unqual- ified, as was his love.

Tears stung Dan's eyes again and he had to force them back with a blink and a cough when the nurse stuck her head round the curtain to tell him that his ten minutes were up. After checking on visiting times the following day, he headed out of the hospital.

Outside, it was a clear, crisp, cold night. As he unlocked the door of the Cortina, Dan discovered that he was shivering, wound up and wrung out from emotion and tiredness. He needed to find a chip shop and a bed and breakfast in which to stay the night.

Yet he remained where he was, sitting in the driver's seat, not moving, the keys in the ignition but the gears not yet engaged, arm crooked on the steering wheel, hand fisted, knuckles pressed against his cheek as he stared out at the dark, empty road.

At the end of April, Rose and Robert took the girls to the Egg. As Robert locked the Jaguar, which he had parked in the lay-by, Katherine and Eve, wild with pleasure at being let out of the car, ran through the trees, making hooting noises.

Rose had misgivings about this weekend in the country-side. *We should give it a try,* Robert had said, when the idea of staying at the Egg had come up. But what, exactly, were they trying out? Their ability to survive away from shops, cafés and cinemas — or their fragile reconciliation?

But the girls had not yet seen the Egg, and she herself hadn't been to the house for months, not since the roof had been mended, and she must check on it. Katherine and Eve had been enthusiastic about the visit and it would be good for them to escape the flat and be out in the fresh air. She had always intended to use the Egg as a weekend retreat, Rose reminded herself as she tramped over earth and dead leaves. Glimpsing the house, pale and austere amid spring greenery, it bewitched her, just as it had done the first time.

365

Since that terrible day when Katherine had run away, Rose and Robert had made changes. Robert now picked up the girls from school on Tuesdays, taking them to the Weybridge flat, where he stayed on until Rose arrived back from work. Then they all ate supper together. Sometimes Robert even cooked the supper. He continued to pick up the girls on Fridays, taking them to his Chelsea flat, where they stayed overnight. Rose finished work mid-afternoon on Wednesdays, so that she could collect Katherine and Eve from school. On Sunday afternoons, they often went out as a family. Their outings, to Bushy Park or the Thames towpath, went well enough. Superficially, at least, Rose found herself thinking they must look like a happy family.

Rose had moved Katherine back to her former school in Walton-on-Thames. She had an arrangement with the mother of Katherine's friend, Abbie, and dropped Katherine off at Abbie's house before taking Eve back to Weybridge. The picking-up arrangements were similarly complicated – in fact, having two children at two different schools was horribly difficult, but it must be made to go well. Rose compensated for the hours she missed at work by catching up in the evenings and early mornings, before the children were up. Though the knife-edge on which Rose balanced her family and work obligations seemed to have sharpened considerably, Katherine was happier. And, really, that was all that mattered.

She unlocked the door of the Egg and switched on the lights. The hall was dry, thank goodness, but the house was desperately cold, as if the winter's weather was still trapped inside the small building.

Robert caught up with her, arms full of bags and boxes. 'I nearly measured my length in all that mud,' he said. 'Couldn't your great-grandfather have run to making a path?'

He put down the bags, seized the girls' hands and they went off to explore the house, while Rose sorted out the sleeping arrangements and made up the beds. Katherine and Eve would sleep in the small back bedroom, on camping mattresses. Rose would have the double bed in the main bedroom and Robert the living-room sofa.

They had picked up bags of kindling and Coalite from a garage on the journey – there were no radiators in the Egg. While Robert was making the girls cocoa and toast, Rose knelt in front of the living-room stove, arranging firelighters and kindling. She struck a match and shut the stove door and the flames flared. The wind in the trees made branches tap against the huge glass windows, as if someone was trying to get in, so she drew the faded cream-coloured curtains and the room became cosier. The bright orange light of the fire, contained in the diamond pattern of the window of the stove, made the room seem warm, even if it wasn't yet.

'I'll put them to bed,' called Robert from the kitchen.

'Okay. Thanks.'

There were footsteps on the stairs, followed by shrieks and laughter as her daughters were settled in their makeshift bedroom.

Now and then, an image of Sadie in this room – reading a book, perhaps, or sketching the view – crept into her mind, but she pushed it away. The first time she had come to the Egg was on the day Robert had told her about Debra Peters. He had lied to her and he had betrayed her, and so she had embarked on her search for Sadie, hoping that it might fill the painful, gaping wound that had opened up inside her. But she was through with all that, had put it out of her mind, because Sadie Lawless had been a distraction, a waste of time, a puzzle without any prospect of solution.

The second time she had come here, she had been with Dan. She remembered the rainwater sloshing in the hall and him crouching beside her on the roof as they constructed their makeshift repair. And, later, in the pub, her attraction to him. Thinking of Dan hurt. And there was, in those thoughts, the danger that she would weigh her feelings for Dan on one hand and those for Robert on the other and not get the answer she wanted, the answer she needed to find for her daughters' sake.

She went into the kitchen and began to prepare the steak and mushrooms she had bought for their dinner. Robert came downstairs a while later and opened a bottle of red wine and poured out a couple of glasses.

'How's it going?'

'Just waiting for the potatoes, then I'll put on the steak. This stove's a bit cranky.'

'It smells delicious. You smell delicious.' His hand rested for a moment on her shoulder. 'Do you remember our first flat?' he said. 'The Islington one? It would have made this place look enormous.'

'The landlady, always poking her nose in.' Rose moved away and began to scrub mushrooms under the tap. 'God knows what she thought we were doing. Growing pot, perhaps.'

'And the fold-down couch. I had to kick it to make it fold down.'

'Do you remember the couple in the next room? They used to have arguments at three in the morning.'

'The making up was worse.'

She laughed. 'Yes.'

She served the dinner and they drank the wine. There was no television at the Egg and they hadn't thought to bring a radio, so they read their books. The silence was companionable, she thought, and she began to believe that they had done the right thing in going away together for a weekend.

At eleven, Rose went up to bed. Moths had got at the bedroom curtains, and ravaged shreds drifted like flakes of snow to the floor when she pulled them. Between the torn folds of fabric, she could see outside to the flat roof and the trees beyond. She remembered Winnie Ferrers telling her that Sadie had taken to sleeping in the back bedroom because she was afraid of being watched. Listening to the wind and the rustle of leaves, it seemed to Rose that it would be all too easy, if you were alone in the house, to translate the sounds into footsteps. Footsteps in the woods or, if you were feeling particularly fraught, tap-tap-tapping across the roof itself.

She, too, heard footsteps: Robert's, on the stairs, heading for the bathroom. Something tightened inside her and she glanced at her reflection in the mirror. After a few moments, the half-expected rap on the door.

She opened it. Robert said, 'That sofa's bloody uncomfortable.' She read the hope in his eyes. 'Can I come in?'

She let him take her in his arms. This was the logical conclusion of the path they had followed over the last few months. The wine and her year of celibacy would make her want him, wouldn't it? Desire flickered as his palm ran down her spine and over the curve of her hip; she willed it to flare and burn.

When he drew off her nightgown over her head, she felt naked and exposed, and slid quickly beneath the sheets. How out of practice she was – but if she repeated the movements they knew so well, the familiar steps of the dance of the years of their marriage, she must feel again and she must

369

want him again. She needed this to work, to prove to herself that she would be capable, one day, of loving him again.

And yet their bodies did not seem to fit together as they once had, and, like a clumsily made jigsaw, they shuffled and grated and muttered apologies to each other, and the chink of desire faltered and cooled and she could not retrieve it. The memory of that other kiss, on Waterloo Station, a kiss that had seemed to reach into the depths of her, crept into her mind, no matter how she tried to push the recollection away. Tonight, her body was made of stone: it was dry and cold and dense and without grace, and, in the end, she pretended pleasure and felt only relief as he shuddered and came. When she held him, it was not with passion, but with pity.

He fell asleep, but she lay awake. She was careful not to move, because she did not want to wake him. She couldn't lie to him any more; what they had just done had been deceit enough, but she couldn't yet face the conversation she knew they must have.

She did not want Robert. She wanted Dan. She had known this for a long time, but had been afraid to confront the implications of her knowledge. She had told Dan she was giving her marriage a second chance, but that had been an act of cowardice. Out of kindness to herself, she replaced the word: it had been an act of *desperation*, born out of fear the day she thought she had lost her child.

Sunlight streaming through the wall of glass woke her the next morning. Robert was already up. Rose heard, from outside, shrieks and ripples of her daughters' laughter, and Robert's voice, a low thread of bass.

He had planned a circular walk that morning, along the

ridgeway and the slope of the Downs, then into the valley. The browns and greys of the woodland were lightened by the bright pale green of unfolding leaves, and they discovered white flowers, pungent with scent, on the edge of the sunken lane. On the ridgeway and in the open fields, the air was warmer and the sun had burned the dew from the grass.

They reached Nutcombe at midday. There was a pub with a beer garden, and Robert suggested they have lunch there. There were things she needed to do at the house, Rose said, but he and the girls should lunch at the pub. She walked away before he could disagree with her, and felt his gaze following her until she turned along the road that wound uphill from the church. If they had sat down together to eat, he would have read the truth in her eyes. She didn't want that to happen while the girls were in earshot, and she didn't want to have that conversation in the pub where she and Dan had talked.

She headed up the hill, her jacket slung over one shoulder. Warmth seemed to rise up from the damp undergrowth: you could almost see the steam. The future that she saw for herself was hard and unforgiving, and punctuated by snares.

Her eye was caught by an animal – a fox, she thought – moving through the trees in a red-brown flicker. As she approached the Egg, she saw with a jolt that a woman was standing on the terrace. Tall and slim, she was dressed in a long, black coat and black hat, and was staring at the house. No, she was staring into the house.

'Hello; may I help you?' Rose called out.

The woman turned to her. She was old – in her seventies or eighties, Rose estimated. Her hair was white, her face gaunt and angular, and her mouth, outlined in scarlet lipstick, was a harsh streak against slack skin the colour of putty. And yet her eyes were remarkable dark, lustrous hollows.

'These woods are privately owned,' the woman said coldly.

Rose saw that what she had mistaken for a fox was, in fact, a dog. A second dog was rushing through the undergrowth, elongated head down, neck straight out, tail up, muscles moving beneath the glossy russet coat. Rose remembered her visit to the Gull's Wing, and the dogs that had leaped up against the gate. This woman was Diana Chiverton, she was sure of it.

She stepped on to the terrace. 'Forgive me, but are you Mrs Chiverton?'

A frown. 'I am, yes.'

'I've been trying to trace my great-aunt, Sadie Lawless. I believe you knew her. I wrote you a letter. Do you remember? My name's Rose Martineau.'

'I'm afraid you're mistaken. I've never heard of her.'

'It was a long time ago,' she persisted, 'but I'm sure you knew her. I was told that Sadie used to visit you and your husband at the Gull's Wing when she first lived here, in the early thirties. It's wonderful to meet you, because I've been hoping to talk to you about her for quite a while.'

The chill in those great, dark eyes remained, but there was something else there now. It shook Rose to realise that what she saw there was fury.

'No, you're wrong,' Diana Chiverton said.

As they spoke, Rose watched the emotions that crossed the older woman's face. 'Sadie was about my age, fair haired and pretty,' she said. 'She was an artist – a printmaker and painter. You must remember her.'

Diana bent, tenderly fondling the long, narrow head of one of the dogs. Then she straightened and took out a pair of black glasses from her coat pocket and put them on. 'Luna, Bran, come here.' She walked haltingly off the terrace, leaning on her walking stick.

Beneath the shadow of the trees, she turned and looked back. The dark lenses of the glasses turned her eye sockets to featureless pits.

'Tom and I entertained a great deal, back then. I can't possibly be expected to remember every guest who came to the house. You must not try to contact me again, Mrs Martineau. I shall instruct my solicitor, if you do.'

The dogs skittered around Diana Chiverton, now and then rushing across her path as she made her effortful way uphill. The arrogance of the woman, Rose thought. Diana Chiverton's assumption of superiority and power was presumably born of a status that she seemed to believe still existed. It was outrageous.

She called out, 'Do you know where Sadie went after she left the Egg, Mrs Chiverton?' and Diana stilled, then walked slowly on.

Robert and the girls arrived, having bought some groceries in the village shop. Unpacking them in the kitchen, Rose thought about what Diana Chiverton had said to her. Sadie's letters to Edith had been full of her visits to the Gull's Wing and her friendship with Tom and Diana Chiverton. Winnie Ferrers had confirmed that Sadie had socialised with the Chivertons when she had first come to live at the Egg. Had Sadie been so unmemorable that Diana had forgotten her?

No. Rose slotted a bottle of milk into the fridge. She had seen, when she had first said Sadie's name, a flicker of recognition in Diana Chiverton's eyes. Rose had taken her by surprise and Diana had been unable to suppress her automatic cognition. Diana had known Sadie, Diana remembered Sadie.

So why had she chosen to deny it? Why had she lied? What was she afraid of?

In the evening, when the girls were in bed, Robert went out to get a sack of Coalite from the wood store. When he came back into the sitting room, he said, 'Damn, it's cold out there.'

She watched him top up the fire. They needed to talk, but she didn't know where to start.

He rose, brushing his hands on his jeans. When he turned to her, his eyes were hard and his mouth set. He said, 'I'd hoped, coming here, we'd get to know each other again. But I get the impression you don't feel the same.'

'I've tried, Robert.'

'Is there any point in asking you to try harder?'

'No.'

He gave a humourless bark of laughter. 'Well, that was blunt.'

'We need to be honest with each other.' She raised her gaze to him. 'I think it's best, don't you?'

'Best for whom?' His voice had an edge. 'For you – or for Katherine and Eve?'

'In the end, best for all of us.'

'Not for me. Don't try to make out it's what I want, Rose, because it isn't. I still love you.'

'Do you?' She searched for the truth in his face. 'Do you really? I was enough for you for a while, Robert, and then I wasn't. You wanted something else. You wanted more.'

'I've tried to explain to you. That was stupidity – it was folly.'

'No, I don't think so. You've always been a restless person. Maybe you'll find what you're looking for some day. I hope you will.'

They had not yet drawn the curtains and he stood, framed by the night, his stance taut and angry. He said slowly, 'Everything we had, everything we've built up over the years . . . don't you care about that? What are you saying? That you're just going to walk away from it?'

'Robert, there's nothing there any more,' she said quietly. 'Nothing at all. Surely you can feel it. I've been trying to pretend to myself that there might be something left, but I can't any longer. I can't live a lie. Not even for Katherine and Eve.'

What lay between love and hatred was indifference; that was what she had discovered. At least with hatred, you felt alive.

He exhaled sharply. 'So you still haven't forgiven me.'

'It's not that. Actually, I think I have.'

'You've a funny way of showing it, then.'

'I think we need to talk about a divorce.'

He looked at her with dislike. 'No, Rose, let's not talk about divorce, because it's not what I want.'

A silence, then she said carefully, 'The one thing we've always agreed on is that we need to do what's best for the children.'

'And what's best for the children is having their parents living in the same house.'

'Is it? Is it, Robert? Won't it harm them if they see a bad marriage, day after day? Do you honestly believe that would help them to form relationships of their own, when they're old enough?' She was struggling to find the words that would reach him, that would make him understand. 'We've both come a long way these past few months. We've tried to do our best, we've tried so hard. And I can see that the girls are happier – Katherine, particularly.'

'Katherine's happiest when you and I are together.'

'When we're together in harmony, yes. But we wouldn't be in harmony if we lived with each other again. I can't make myself want you. I can't make myself love you again. I can't, Robert – I've tried, but I can't. And you would see that, and you'd resent it and we'd quarrel and dislike each other, and the children would see us quarrelling. They'd see that we resented each other – that we hated each other. And that would be awful – awful – and I won't do it.'

She saw him trying to control his anger. 'You've hardly given it a chance. These things take time.'

'No.' Her words cut through his. 'All the time in the world can't make me love you again.'

'Jesus, Rose.'

She knew how deeply she had hurt him and felt an equal pain in her forensic dismemberment of the limping remains of their marriage. Once, to see him, to hear his footsteps, had filled her with joy. Once, she had believed him to be her soulmate, the man who made her complete. She was putting a match to all that. She had ignited the pyre and was watching it turn to ashes.

He said, 'And if I don't agree to a divorce?'

'Robert, I don't want to fight with you.' Drained of emotion, she spoke softly. 'We've fought enough.'

He stooped and stabbed at the fire with the poker. The flames flared and roared. 'You seem to expect me just to keel over, to give you everything you want. And I'm finding it hard to see why I should.'

'It would be better if we tried at least to be civilised.'

'Oh, I'll be civilised. But don't imagine for a moment that I'll be *soft*, Rose. Because that would be a big mistake, a very big mistake.'

She felt no answering rage. She was through with all that, had spent her allowance of it a while ago.

She tried again. 'We have to be civilised because, if there's nothing left between us but bitterness and rancour, then that'll hurt the children. It will, Robert. It'll hurt me, too, yes, but maybe that's what you want.'

'Yeah, I'd like to stick the knife in. I'd like to twist it, shove it in deep.' But then shame shadowed his face, and he let out a breath and sat down in an armchair, and bowed his head.

'Who am I kidding?' he said quietly. 'If I hurt you, I hurt Katherine and Eve. And, anyway, I've hurt you enough already. There's a limit, isn't there?'

'I think so.'

He looked up, his eyes bleak. 'I wish it could be different. I wish I'd been a different person. You're going to make me start again, Rose, and I'm not sure I can. And, whatever I end up settling for, it'll be less than what we had.'

'It doesn't have to be.' She felt exhausted by the conflicting emotions that fought in her heart.

'But it will.'

Moonlight spilled on the terrace; in the darkness, a bird was singing. At last, Robert said, 'I'll speak to my solicitor.'

'Thank you.'

'We'll leave first thing tomorrow.' He stood, his gaze circling the room. 'I don't think I can stand being in this place any longer. It's driving me nuts.'

Had Sadie, like her, lain awake in this bedroom, wrenched in two by the breakdown of her relationship and her parting from the man she had once loved? Had the fear she had written about to Edith in her final letter − I don't want to live *here any more; it frightens me* – been born of the thoughts that come to you in the depths of the night, while mind and body long for sleep, but fail to find it? Perhaps Sadie, like her, had kicked off the blankets and turned over the pillow in an attempt to find a cool place. Perhaps, hearing the tap and thwack of branches, she had risen and gone to the window to look out, straining to see through the darkness.

In the early hours of the morning, Rose put on her socks and pulled a jersey over her nightgown, then padded downstairs. In the hallway, she slipped her feet into her wellingtons, fastened her jacket and opened the front door – quietly, because Robert was sleeping on the sitting-room sofa. Taking the torch, she left the house.

Outside, the air was sharply cold, heading for an April frost. She tramped up the sunken lane, making for the top of the ridge. Because there were no street lamps, no artificial light masked the thousands of stars that dusted the sky. Their glory should have lifted her spirits, but she felt only a dull, cloying sense of failure. Her marriage was dead and she was struggling to repair her children's lives. She wanted Dan and yet she had pushed him away, and, though she regretted that deeply, she could not see a way to repair it. She was unsure whether he had any feelings for her. When you looked at it closely, nothing much had happened. She had kissed Dan and he had responded, as any red-blooded male would have. After Katherine had run away, he had tried to comfort her – a friendly hug, a few kind words – that was all.

In the darkness, she heard the sounds of the woodland loudly and pressingly: the beating of wings and a fox's dog-like bark. The higher she climbed, the more densely branched and closely packed became the trees, their leaves a dead black, and it took an act of courage to push on through them when she could not see what lay beyond. She had failed her grandmother, too. Sadie Lawless had vanished like a drift of smoke blown away by a spring breeze, along with so many of the other unknown, unmourned young women of her generation. Rose's search for Sadie had ground to a halt and all that remained was a persisting sense of disquiet whenever she thought of her, a conviction that something wrong had happened.

She had reached the road. Ahead, she saw with a shock that all the windows in the Gull's Wing were illuminated, so that it blazed like a beacon in the night. The soles of her boots crunched on loose stones and dried mud as she walked towards the house.

She stood at the gate, looking up at it. She wondered whether Diana Chiverton turned on the lights every night, unable to bear her solitariness, shut up in that big house with her memories. Or whether she, too, was wakeful tonight; whether something had happened today that had disturbed the older woman.

As she walked back to the Egg, Rose could no longer hold back the tears. They coursed down her face and she crouched in the sunken lane, unable to stand for the ferocity of her sobs. When the storm subsided, she wiped her face on her sleeve and walked on, the torchlight a fragile disc in front of her as she stumbled along the path.

Chapter Eighteen

Segovia and Sussex – September–October 1934

Madge Danford was delighted with the success of Sadie's first exhibition at the gallery, in November 1933, and had offered to stage another exhibition in October 1934. Sadie's creativity had blossomed, and she felt confident of the originality and power of the prints and paintings she had made during the past year. She was hopeful that the second exhibition would strengthen her reputation.

She spent the summer of 1934 in Segovia, staying with Andrés in a flat he had borrowed from a colleague. The city was only sixty miles from Madrid, so Andrés was able to return there whenever necessary to collect his mail and keep in contact with the editors of the newspapers and journals he worked for. He often had to go away for a several days at a time, travelling to far-flung parts of the country to research an article he was writing. Sometimes Sadie went with him; on other occasions, when he deemed the situation too volatile or the man he was trying to interview too untrustworthy, she stayed at the flat, painting and teaching herself to cook a few Spanish dishes. It was the happiest summer of her life.

The flat was beyond a gateway on one of Segovia's cobbled

medieval streets, which gave into a courtyard planted with herbs and sunflowers. The courtyard was alive with white sunlight and dense, purplish shadows. The front door opened into a tiled entrance hall that was always cool, even on the hottest of days. Sadie had placed a pot of lavender on the deep stone sill of a latticed window. There were shutters on the inside of the window to keep out the heat, and when, in the early mornings, she opened them, she could see, outside, the fat green leaves of a grape vine.

Stairs took her up to a landing and into a series of small, sparsely furnished rooms. In the kitchen, there was a huge enamel-tiled stove and a ceramic sink. Black earthenware pots and copper pans, green with age, were arranged on the wooden shelves and suspended from an iron rail. A corridor led to a dining room furnished with a table and chairs of dark wood. The gazes of the subjects in the photographs arranged on the dresser, those men with their high, stiff collars and broad-brimmed hats, followed her. Her fingertips drifted across the frayed, lumpy spines of a row of books, and the cool air was redolent with the scent of chamomile and oregano from the bunches of dried herbs that hung from hooks on the walls. She helped herself to a peach from the green bowl on the circular table, tasting the sweetness of the juice and feeling the chill of the terracotta tiles beneath the soles of her bare feet.

In the bedroom, there was a dressing table, mirror and washstand, and a brass bed, made up with white linen sheets. Andrés came to stand beside her and she rested her head in the hollow of his shoulder. Their fingers threaded together and they kissed. 'You taste of peaches,' he said.

Sadie thought of the flat as their home. 'Let's go home,' they would say to each other after dinner, and they'd head off, away from the square with the Roman aqueduct, to the gateway that gave into the courtyard with the sunflowers and the herbs and the shadows.

'I'm going to give the Egg to Edith,' she said.

It was evening and they were sitting in the courtyard, drinking a glass of wine. Andrés had returned that afternoon from Barcelona and there were thumbprints of tiredness beneath his eyes. They were sitting side by side on a stone bench in the shade of the wall. The day's lingering heat was perfumed with the scent of rosemary and lavender.

'It should have been hers in the first place,' she said. 'My father left me both his houses, and that was wrong of him, Andrés. I expect he did it because he was trying to protect me. He knew that I'd have to support myself. I wonder whether, if he'd lived longer, and if he'd managed to recover his financial situation, he'd have changed his will. Those houses ruined him. He must have known, when he drew up his will, that he'd be able to leave Edith and me only the small amount of money that he had put aside in trust funds for us when we were born. Everything else had been spent.'

'It can cost a lot,' he said, 'to pursue a dream.'

'Yes.' Sadie watched a fat, white moth flutter around one of the candles they had lit in the garden. She wondered whether, in that dreadful moment when her father must have realised that the aeroplane could not right itself from its tailspin and that everything was lost, he had judged the cost of his dream too high.

She said, 'A father shouldn't give more of his love to one child than the other. It took me a long time to realise that. I didn't fully understand how much harm it had done. I'm trying to put things right, Andrés.'

He said, 'And if you give the Egg to Edith, where will you live?'

She looked at him, smiling. 'Here, of course, with you.'

They had had this conversation so many times. Now, with only a few days to go before she returned to England, she knew it must reach a conclusion.

'My darling . . .' He picked up the carafe of wine and topped up their glasses. 'There is nothing I want more. But, for you, my love, it would not be a good thing.'

'Rubbish,' she said crisply, snuggling up to him. 'For me, it would be the very best thing.'

In the silence, she heard, distantly, a woman singing, the melody strange and high and soaring.

'But you are so very English, Sadie,' he said.

'My mother was French. My father was English, but he studied in Germany and we travelled all over the continent. I'm English, yes, and I'm proud of it, but I'm also European.'

'I hear the way you speak of your home. I hear in your voice how much you love it.'

Yes, and sometimes I've hated it. 'I love it here too,' she said. 'I couldn't paint in Spain if I didn't love it.'

That summer, she had abandoned angles and straight lines for curves and loops and coils. When she looked back, she wondered whether, living at the Egg in the aftermath of her engagement to Felix, she had been afraid to allow vividness and luxuriance into her life. Her Spanish landscapes burst with deep, rich colours, with lush limes and leaf greens and the hot, baking maroon, sienna and ochre of the Castilian countryside. You would almost think that, if you put a hand to the canvas, you'd feel the heat coming off the rocks, or that you might breathe in the hot, oily scent of the tough, silvery leaves of the plants.

383

He took her hand. 'You mustn't give up the life you have for someone who can offer you so little in return. You mustn't leave England, which is safe, for Spain, which is not.'

'Nothing's safe. You know that.'

'*Safer*, then.'

'You're talking about the possibility of revolution.'

'More than a possibility. A likelihood. Revolutions often lead to civil war. There's no more terrible fate for a country.'

'I understand that. But there may be another war in Europe too. You believe that, don't you?'

'Yes.' A sigh. 'We live in an age of anger and irrationality. Leaders tell lies and people choose to believe their lies. So, yes, I believe that there will be.'

She took off the ring she wore on her right hand and showed him the inscription inside the band. He read it, frowning at the old-fashioned script. '*In thee my choys I do rejoys.*'

'I rejoice in *you*, my love,' she said gently. 'You are my choice. There are all those other ifs and buts, yet none of them will alter my choice.'

He drew her to him. 'I wish I could offer you more,' he said.

'I don't need more, I don't want more. I have so much, and if I had any more I'd burst from happiness.'

'I wish,' he said gently, 'I could give you a home, a child.'

Sometimes, thinking of what it would have meant to her to have Andrés' child, she could have screamed in pain. She had learned to gather in that part of herself, to hide it away, to cover over her yearnings by doting on her friends' babies and children, but it was always there, raw and beating, a wound to the heart, that she would never be a mother, never a grandmother.

She said, 'For a long time, I felt lost. I had to teach myself to do without the things most women expect, though I always found comfort in my work. And then I met you, Andrés. I can be happy here, I know it. I'll go back to England for the exhibition, but, once it's over, I'll return to Spain. I'll live quietly in Madrid, or, if it's better for you, I'll take rooms here in Segovia. I understand that you have responsibilities to your family and your work. I have my work, too, and I've no intention of being a little wife at home, nagging you because I'm feeling neglected.'

He smiled. 'You are so far from being the nagging wife at home . . .'

'While I'm in England, I'll instruct my solicitor to prepare the documents to make over the deeds of the Egg to Edith.'

'Will she accept it?'

Sadie had considered this. Since their quarrel, since Edith had gone to live in India, Sadie had written to her sister two or three times a year. But Edith had never written back.

'I don't know,' she said honestly.

'She may not love you for it.'

She understood what he meant. Edith might see her gift as condescending or aggravating. She might hate her for it. But she thought she had to try.

'Edith should have the house,' she said. 'I'll have no further use of it, after the exhibition. She's the only other person who understands what it means to our family.' She looked into his eyes, that deep, olive green. 'You understand, don't you?'

'I understand.' With a fingertip, he brushed back a lock of her hair that had fallen over her forehead. 'I'd like you to promise me something, Sadie.'

'Whatever you want, my love.'

'I'd like you to promise me not to make up your mind now. Go back to England, my darling, and make a great success of your exhibition. Make your final decision when it's over.

Maybe you'll have second thoughts. I'll understand, if you have second thoughts.'

'I won't.'

'Still, I'd prefer you not to burn your boats – that's the correct expression, isn't it? – until after the exhibition is over.'

Reluctantly, she promised him. Then she said, 'Are you happy when I'm not here, Andrés?'

He looked down at her. 'How could I be?' His eyes seemed to darken. 'Whatever difficulties I have, and however much I sometimes despair for my country, when I'm with you, all that fades away.'

'So. You see.' She kissed the palm of his hand.

'I've done my duty by my wife, I think.'

Frowning, she studied him. 'What do you mean?'

'When Raoul goes to university, I shall leave Isabella. So we'll only have to skulk in corners for another year or two.'

'Andrés . . .' She pressed her teeth into her lip. 'You don't have to do this.'

'I think I do. I can't ask her for a divorce, but I can put an end to this sham of a marriage.'

A fat moth, the colour of bone, bumbled among the lavender. 'I don't want to make you unhappy,' she murmured.

'You could never make me unhappy. I shall leave Madrid, too.'

'But your work, Andrés.'

'I'll retire to my land. I have a little farm there. I wish I'd taken you there, Sadie; I wish you'd seen it. I'll grow olives and make wine. Do you think I'll make a good olive farmer?'

'I'm sure you'll make a wonderful olive farmer.'

'I'll be a farmer and you shall paint. We'll still be living there when I'm a wrinkled, white-haired old man.'

386

'And I'm a fat old woman.'

He shook his head. 'No, you'll always be incomparably beautiful.'

They kissed. Closing her eyes, she made herself remember the taste and touch of him for the weeks of parting ahead, even though she knew him by heart already.

When she returned to England, it was autumn. Russet and gold leaves drifted from the trees in Paley High Wood and white fungi pierced the leaf mould on the forest floor. Rain slanted from a sky the colour of steel – and then the clouds parted, letting in a flurry of blue, and the Downs flooded with sunlight.

Her attachment to the Egg had faded and her residence there now felt temporary. It was a place to eat and sleep and put the finishing touches to the work she hoped would cement her reputation, but Spain was her real life and she yearned for it. Often, she thought of Andrés, rising in the morning and drinking a coffee in the Café Barbieri. Or in his study, among the books and the portraits, sitting at his desk, writing. Or dining at their favourite restaurant, served by the old man who leaned against the wall and dozed between courses.

She went to London to arrange for a couple of paintings to be framed, staying overnight in Jimmy's flat. The evening news, broadcast on the wireless, spoke of unrest in Spain in the aftermath of the general strike in Madrid. There were rumours of a revolutionary uprising among the miners of Asturias, in the north of the country.

After returning to the Egg, a letter arrived from Andrés, telling her that he was travelling to Asturias to report on the miners' strike. They had taken over several towns and seized the Civil Guard barracks. It was, he wrote, not so much a

387

strike as a revolution – or the beginnings of a terrible repression; it was hard to tell.

Sadie pictured a cobble, prised up from a street and hurled through the air, or a militia man's gun, wildly spraying bullets. Or Andrés, who loathed violence, caught up in some atrocity: the destruction of a church, the execution of a priest, the rape of a peasant woman. First thing every morning, she cycled down to the village to buy a copy of The Times, flicking through the pages as she walked out of the shop, scouring the columns for information.

Fog was rolling white down the hillside, turning the tree trunks into disembodied grey columns. The birches and hornbeams that marched up to the ridge were shifting and vaporous, as if they too were made of fog.

A shape solidified; she saw Tom Chiverton. She steeled herself. All that folly, all that misplaced passion, she thought.

'I had to see you, Sadie,' he said. 'I knew you were back and I had to see you.' There was resentment and a dry disappointment in his voice.

An old nightmare was revisiting her, one she'd thought she'd got out of her system, but which had returned with sickening inevitability.

She made to go into the house, but he grabbed her arm. 'Please, Sadie. Just hear me out.'

'Let me go, Tom.'

His grip slackened. 'Forgive me. A moment of your time, that's all I ask.'

There were streaks of grey in his black hair and a fan of lines at the corner of each eye. Some of the gloss had rubbed off Tom Chiverton.

'You shouldn't have come here.' She spoke softly, as if, in

388

the woods, in the fog, someone might be listening. 'You have to go.'

'I've tried to forget you.' He pushed back his mist-damp hair from his forehead. 'I'm not a stupid man; I know you don't want me, and I know that I degrade myself, coming here to plead with you. But I can't forget you, I can't pretend to have no feelings for you. I can't pretend that night wasn't extraordinary and magnificent.'

But that was lust, she thought with distaste, lust and desire. And they don't last. But she had said all that before and he had not listened then. Something occurred to her as she stood there in the fog. She had always dismissed his feelings for her as a sham, a sort of conceit, short-lived and shallow. But perhaps she was mistaken. She herself had pursued Felix after he had broken off their engagement, had followed him to a party and, in front of a roomful of people and Dahlia Knight, the woman he had left her for, had begged him to love her again. She must have wearied Felix as Tom wearied her.

'I don't love you, Tom.' She spoke quietly; she needed him to listen. 'I can never love you. The truth is, I'm in love with someone else.'

A short expelling of air; he kicked his foot at the dead leaves. 'Then he's a fortunate man.'

'Yes.'

'I'm glad for you, Sadie – truly, I am. I want you to be happy.'

She longed for him to leave, but he remained there, his gaze on the wooded fall of the valley. They were alone, and yet the skin on the back of her neck prickled and she seemed to feel eyes, hostile and watchful, on her.

'I've just finished the final edits for *Ellipse*,' he said. '*Lumu* was like pouring water from a jug. With *Ellipse*, blood out of a stone comes to mind. See, I've exhausted myself – I've reduced myself to cliché. And yet they're some of the best poems I've ever written.'

'I'm sure it'll be a success.' Go home, Tom.

'Oh, yes, it'll be a success.' His upper lip curled in a sneer. 'Fine reviews in *The Times* and an interview in the *Telegraph*. They'll ask me to do a recitation on the wireless, and someone, some bore, will write a critique to stir up controversy. And I'll have given away a few more pieces of myself to preserve the myth. That's what it's all for, that's what the source of my joy has become: a fuel to manufacture that thing, that *creature* that is Tom Chiverton. And I myself have created it . . . with the help of my wife, damn her . . . I've created a monstrosity. Monsters have to be fed, Sadie. Do you know what this one dines on? Snippets and titbits and photographs. Articles in the newspapers and dinners with the rich and famous. People touch his hand, as if he possesses a magic power. Women squeal when they encounter him in the street. They read the captions of the photos: *The poet, signing books in a New York store. The poet, attending a reception given by the Prince of Wales.* The poet, selling his soul.'

'Then walk away from it, Tom,' she said quietly. 'Just walk away.'

He touched her arm. 'Do you know why I find it so hard to do that? Success is addictive. You come to depend on it. You know what it's doing to you and you hate it for that, but you can't seem to stop. You're afraid you won't be able to live without it, that there'll be nothing left of you. And all the time, all the time you're watching it devour your soul.' A smile twitched across his features and then was gone. 'And then there's Diana,' he muttered. 'She's like a millstone round my neck. She'll never let me go. She'd follow me to hell and back. Have you any idea how tiresome devotion can become?'

Whatever betrayals and bargains made up the dance of the Chivertons' marriage, and whatever small role Sadie had once played, she was no longer a part of it. All she wanted was never to see him again.

'I'm sorry, Tom,' she said.

Shapes moved in the mist. Was that a deer, that charcoal shadow that she seemed to glimpse beside a tree, or a fox, perhaps?

He spoke again. 'I'll always love you. It won't go away. You've lit a fire inside me, and sometimes it warms me and at other times I detest and loathe it. Well, it looks as if that's my punishment for all my failings, to have to live with that. I won't trouble you again, Sadie, I promise.'

He frowned, turning aside. 'Perhaps you're right, perhaps I should just walk away. Sometimes I picture it. I imagine leaving the Gull's Wing. How wonderful it would be to shut the door behind me and stride off over the Downs! How relieved I'd feel to live simply again, sleeping in shepherds' huts or under hedgerows, as I used to when I was younger. I've never felt happier than I did then.'

He headed away, up the hillside, and within moments the fog had swallowed him up.

Sadie went back inside the house. Her hand trembled as she put on the kettle. It was over, she told herself. She spooned tea into the pot. It was over for good, now. Tom had told her that he would not trouble her again and, this time, she believed him. She leaned against the sink, closing her eyes, and her thoughts of Andrés were accompanied by a yearning so intense it frightened her.

Chapter Nineteen

London and Surrey – May 1971

The taxi dropped Rose outside Ursula Palmer's flat in Holborn. A soft evening light washed over the white tassels of a lilac tree that drooped beside the railings.

'Honky Tonk Women' blared out of a second-floor window and a heady whiff of pot mingled with the scent of lilac as Rose picked her way over the white cat sprawling across the stone steps. She rang the doorbell.

The door swung open. 'Rose!' Ursula shrieked.

'Urse. Happy birthday.'

They embraced. Ursula was wearing a sleeveless purple crêpe midi-dress, rather creased, and her limp, fine brown hair hung loose to her shoulders. They had met at school at the age of twelve. In the sixth form, when Rose had studied science subjects, Ursula had chosen the arts. She had become Dr Palmer after writing her Ph.D. dissertation on the Elizabethan sonnet, and was now a junior lecturer in the department of English Literature at University College London.

As Rose followed Ursula up flights of stairs, they exchanged news. The music became louder and they had to step round couples perched on the stairs, drinking and smoking.

Ursula led the way into her flat. 'It's a bit of a hole,' she said cheerfully. 'When my book sells in the millions, I'll buy somewhere bigger.'

'Might it sell millions?'

Ursula snorted. 'Fifty, a hundred copies, if I'm lucky.'

A plasterboard wall suggested that the original room had been split in two. The division ruined its proportions, pushing the fireplace against the new wall and leaving space for only modestly sized pieces of furniture. An alcove to the side of the fireplace was crammed with books, magazines and papers, which spilled out of envelopes and folders. A mushroom-coloured rug, splotched with the ghosts of red-wine spills, lay in front of the fireplace and, in a small brass Buddha, patchouli-scented joss sticks burned.

'Come and get a drink,' Ursula bawled over the music. 'There's someone I want to introduce you to.'

Most of the guests seemed to have crammed into the small, square kitchen, which led off from a narrow corridor. Ursula fired off introductions and poured Rose a glass of a plum-coloured wine. There were crisps in earthenware bowls and hunks of cheese and the sort of French loaves that split into shards when you tried to slice them, as well as bottles of wine and Party Seven beer cans, one of which a man with a blond moustache was struggling to open with a screwdriver. A girl in a flowery kaftan perched cross-legged on a work surface, sticking together Rizla papers to roll a joint, and a spirited conversation was going on around her.

'Scientific experiments are a sort of exploration,' a boy with John Lennon glasses was saying earnestly. 'It's impossible to know where you're going.'

A girl in a frayed lace blouse said, 'But if the experiments

393

end up with another bomb, or something worse than the bomb . . .'

Ursula chinked her glass against Rose's. She said, 'Are you still interested in Tom Chiverton?'

Rose helped herself to some crisps. 'I've pretty much given up. I've reached a dead end.'

'I met this bloke, Ivan Merchant. He's at Keele, and a bit of an expert on your Tom. There he is.' Ursula waved a hand towards a man who was wearing a yellow shirt and denim jacket. He was standing in the corridor, talking to a short girl in a knitted tank-top. 'Isn't he gorgeous?'

Rose shot a glance at the tall, slim man in the corridor. 'Not bad.'

Ursula called out, 'Ivan!' and he looked round.

He came to join them. 'I don't think I've said happy birthday to you, Ursula.' He did so and kissed her cheek.

'This is my friend, Rose Martineau. Remember, I told you about her.'

'The friend with the relative who knew Tom Chiverton? Pleased to meet you, Rose.'

They shook hands. Ivan had light brown hair, blue-grey eyes and a mouth bracketed on either side by deep, half-moon indentations, so that he seemed permanently on the verge of smiling.

'I teach Chiverton on my course,' he explained.

'"Speaking Through Nature: English Poetry of the Nineteenth and Twentieth Centuries",' quoted Ursula. 'You should think of a snappier title, Ivan.'

He flashed her a smile. 'It's a quick zip through the canon.'

Rose said, 'My great-aunt, Sadie Lawless, was a neighbour of the Chivertons, back in the thirties.'

'Is she still alive?'

'I don't think so.'

'Did she know Tom well?'

'Quite well, I believe, to start with, but then I think they quarrelled.'

Ursula moved away, leaving Rose and Ivan standing in the doorway to the kitchen. Ivan gave a wry smile. 'Both Tom and Diana had a way of falling out with people.'

'Did they?'

'Oh, yes. Diana was a snob and Tom had a temper. He once broke the jaw of a bloke who dared to trespass on his land, and there was an incident — hushed up, of course — where he beat to a pulp some idiot who broke into his house. He wasn't your pale-faced, tubercular poet, Tom — quite the opposite, in fact. He used to regularly have boxing matches with one of the gardeners who worked at the Gull's Wing, a gypsy, and it was bare-knuckle fighting, so not for the faint-hearted. He was a fine shot, too. He used to go to country fairs and win every prize going. His father was a gamekeeper, his grandfather a blacksmith, so all that was in his blood. And he wasn't a squeamish man, either; he'd wring a hen's neck, and Tom was the one who used to slaughter the pigs they reared at the Gull's Wing.'

'The biography I read didn't talk about any of that.'

'Was it the Geoffrey Cranham one?' Ivan shrugged. 'Everyone knows that's a complete whitewash.'

More partygoers squeezed into the kitchen, edging Rose and Ivan into the corridor. 'Why?' she said. 'In what way?'

'It leaves rather a lot out.'

'Is there a better biography? Could you recommend one?'

He shook his head. 'The Cranham biography's pretty much the only one. It was published eight or nine years ago, with

395

Diana Chiverton's blessing. Other writers have tried, but she always puts a stop to it.'

'How?'

'She sues them – or threatens to sue them. So publishers run scared and biographers envisage their meagre advances going down the drain, and eventually they give up. Diana also denies them access to Tom's papers. You can't make a decent job of a literary biography if you haven't read your subject's letters or seen the early workings of their poems. Everyone knows that the Cranham biography, apart from being pretty much unreadable, leaves an awful lot out, but the fact is that there isn't a decent one, because Diana's made it impossible for anyone to write one.' Ivan glanced at Rose's glass. 'Let me get you another drink.'

'Thanks.'

He disappeared into the kitchen, reappearing minutes later with a couple of glasses of wine, and half a French loaf tucked into the pocket of his jacket. They agreed to find somewhere quieter to talk, and ended up perched at the foot of a flight of stairs.

Ivan offered the French loaf to Rose, who tore off a chunk. 'I've tried to contact Diana Chiverton a few times,' he said. 'She wrote me a rather threatening letter. I'm yet to meet anyone who's got anywhere near her.'

'I have.' An image of Diana Chiverton flickered into Rose's mind: hollow black eyes against a white face, standing beneath the trees, near the Egg.

'Really?' He looked at her with interest. 'You're one of the few, then, Rose. She has a reputation for being a hermit.'

'It was by chance.' Though she had since wondered whether that was true. Diana had given the impression that she thought of the woods that surrounded the Egg as her own. In appearing at the house, she had been warning off trespassers.

'She was formidable,' Rose said. 'She refused to speak to me about Sadie. She denied ever having known her, though I know for a fact that she did.'

'She's over eighty. Maybe her memory's shot.'

'Maybe.' Though Diana *had* remembered Sadie, Rose was convinced of that. 'She was a beauty, wasn't she, when she was younger?' she said. 'There was a photo in the biography.'

'She was tall and dark, and very striking.' Ivan gave her a flirtatious smile. 'Just my type.' Leaning towards her to allow a man carrying a couple of glasses of beer to clamber over them, he added, 'Diana's life work has been to preserve the Chiverton myth. She's the ferocious guardian of Tom's legend. Woe betide you if you should even hint that he wasn't a saint or that their marriage wasn't the most perfect since . . . I'm struggling to think of a perfect marriage.'

'Are there any?'

'I wouldn't know. No direct experience.'

She saw him flick a glance to her left hand. Since Robert had agreed to her request for a divorce, she had stopped wearing her wedding ring.

She said bluntly, 'Do you think Diana's trying to hide something?'

'Of course she is. Tom took lovers. Everyone knows it, but, while Diana's alive, no one dares to say it out loud.'

'Do you think she knew?'

'How could she not have?'

Rose hadn't known that her husband was visiting a prostitute. The newspapers had worked it out before she had.

'If you love someone,' she said slowly, 'you trust them, and you want to go on trusting them. You have a belief

397

in them, and it can be very hard to accept that you're mistaken.'

Ivan ripped off a piece of bread. 'Tom Chiverton didn't take one or two lovers, Rose. There were dozens of them. He saw some of his women for years, on and off, but others were one-night stands. No, Diana *knew*. If she didn't, she must have been walking around blindfolded, with her fingers in her ears.'

But, if that was true, then why had Diana tolerated it? And why should she continue to try to conceal Tom's true nature? Pride, thought Rose. Fear of humiliation. Tom's infidelity had diminished her.

'There's a certain amount of respect for Diana,' Ivan went on. 'Tom wouldn't have become what he was without her help. She did everything for him — acted as the initial sounding board for his writing, told him which invitations to accept and which to reject, ran the house, made sure he was fed and clothed, kept journalists at bay. You could say that she protected him from the world.'

'I don't suppose Tom Chiverton ever had to worry about what to have for dinner,' said Rose dryly.

'I don't suppose so, no.' His smile was amused and impish, his mouth tilting up at the corners. 'Diana was of a different social class to Tom. Her family came over to England with the Norman Conquest, or so she claims. I think there's still a hangover from the days of deference, when you kept quiet about the failings of your betters. That's why she gets away with it.'

'I would have thought there's quite an appetite for broadcasting the failings of the great and the good.' Rose brushed breadcrumbs from her brown velvet loons. She wondered whether Ursula had told Ivan about the scandal.

'But not for being hauled through the courts,' he pointed out.

'I suppose not.'

'Maybe people are more prepared to forgive poets than, I don't know . . .'

'Politicians. Businessmen.'

'Yes.'

She could tell from the sideways flicker of his eyes that he *did* know.

'Poets are allowed a certain leeway,' he said. 'People see them as romantic heroes, as trailblazers. It's okay – in fact, it's almost obligatory – for a poet to be carried away by passion. If you were to make a list of the dozen or so most important English poets of the first half of the twentieth century, Tom Chiverton's name would have to be among them. He isn't just admired academically, Rose; his collections go on selling. Plenty of people still read him for pleasure. Maybe there isn't much of an appetite for tarnishing a hero. Still, if I was a biographer, I'd be sharpening my pen right now.'

Rose frowned. 'Why now?'

'Diana's unlikely to last much longer. She had a stroke a year ago and her health is frail. How long will she have the strength to go on fighting? Someone's going to spill the beans about Tom's love life soon. And it'll be explosive.'

Rose thought of the woman she had met in Paley High Wood. The fragility of her physical appearance had seemed at odds with the fierceness of her demeanour. Perhaps Diana Chiverton was clinging on to life in order to preserve the myth she had helped to create.

'Are you familiar with Tom Chiverton's work, Rose?'

'A little. Not very, to be honest. Ursula and I rather went our separate ways at university. I studied physics.'

'What do you do now?'

'I run a freight-aviation company.'

'Wow.' He sat up, smiling. 'I don't think I've ever met anyone who runs a freight-aviation company. Does that leave much time for reading poetry?'

'Not really. I've read Lunar, though.'

'What did you think of it?'

'I loved it.' And she had. Tom Chiverton had soaked the southern English countryside in magic and myth. Now, when she visited the Egg, phrases from the poems flickered through her mind, making her see the fields and woodland differently. The landscape had shaped Tom Chiverton, but he had shaped the landscape of his readers' minds.

'The poems Chiverton wrote in the late twenties and early thirties were his greatest,' said Ivan. 'Both Lunar and Ellipse are masterworks. Nothing he did afterwards comes anywhere near them. He always claimed himself to be the product of the landscape that nurtured him, that he was only able to write when he was living in the country. And it had to be the right sort of countryside: the southern English down-lands – Sussex, or Hampshire. Ursula's very scathing about that. She says that a poet writes from the heart, and physical location shouldn't matter. Her chap, Sir Thomas Wyatt, wrote poetry while he was imprisoned in the Tower of London. Keats wrote while he was coughing himself to death with TB. But, for Chiverton, place was integral.'

He offered her the stub of the French loaf. 'Would you like any more of this stale bread?'

'It's okay; no, thanks.'

He said casually, 'Why don't we see if we can find a decent restaurant, and go on with our conversation there? You could tell me all about your aviation company.'

And why shouldn't she? It would be fun to go out with a good-looking, interesting man, eat a dinner that someone else had cooked, drink some decent wine instead of Ursula's rotgut, flirt a little and maybe afterwards go back to wherever he was staying, for coffee. And then, who knows? For a moment, she was tempted.

But she said, 'Thank you, Ivan, it's kind of you, but I should get home to my daughters.'

'Ah.' A disappointed downward turn of the mouth, then he smiled. 'It's been good talking to you, Rose.'

Outside, heading for a bus to take her to Waterloo Station, she wondered why she had turned down Ivan Merchant's offer. Her father was looking after Katherine and Eve and had told her not to hurry back.

She knew that it was because of Dan. She met other men and felt a flicker of attraction towards them, and then she thought of Dan and it always died. One lousy – but beautiful – kiss, and she couldn't seem to shake him off.

She had accepted that she might never see him again. She had wondered whether she might run into him when she was visiting Kevin Goode at Westfield Air, but he had always been away, working at Kevin's new site. It was just as well, she told herself. Though they had not exactly quarrelled, they had not parted on good terms, she and Dan. She could not have picked up a phone and said, *Sorry, Dan, I made a mistake.* In retrospect, she saw that she had put him into a situation where he had little alternative but to resign from Martineau Aviation. He had no reason to think of her fondly. He was probably blissfully happy, was enjoying his new job, had found a new girlfriend and had forgotten her months ago.

The thought depressed her. She missed him. His replacement at work, the new operations manager, Alan Stubbs, was pleasant and competent enough, but he was no replacement for Dan. Alan had a habit of noisily clearing his throat, which she was finding increasingly grating, and his reports, penned with a blotchy biro, were a nightmare of crabby figures crammed into narrow columns, so different from Dan's organised clarity. Journeys with Dan had been a pleasure; even that awful time on the Underground, when she had suffered from claustrophobia, she now thought of with a sort of affection. Car or train journeys with Alan were a trial, what with the throat clearing and his lack of conversation about anything other than contracts and schedules.

She was blaming Alan for not being Dan, she thought, which wasn't fair. Thinking about Dan made her miserable, so she should stop. Think of Tom Chiverton, think of Sadie.

A bus pulled in and she climbed on board, paid her fare and found a seat beside the aisle. She remembered Diana's dogs, barking through the gate of the Gull's Wing, and the flicker of movement she had glimpsed behind the windows. During the days when reporters had camped out on the pavement outside her own home, she too had drawn the curtains and hidden indoors. She could see why you might shut yourself away when the vultures were hovering, preparing to rip at your frailties. Public exposure brought with it humiliation and distress, it rewrote the story of your life in a way that devastated and disorientated, it threw you into a void. In her eighties, long after her husband's betrayals had taken place, Diana's only hope might be to reach the end of her life with his reputation intact.

If Tom Chiverton had been a serial philanderer, why hadn't Diana left him? That woman outside Katherine's school, the woman who, in the immediate aftermath of the scandal, had accused Rose of being a doormat, had judged her the sort who would settle for betrayal in exchange for the stylish house, the nice life and the respectability of marriage. No doubt there were other women who would judge her for the opposite sin: for failing to stand by Robert, for divorcing him.

Perhaps Diana had persuaded herself that Tom's affairs were unimportant. Some women weren't all that interested in sex. Perhaps all she had cared about was knowing she was first in Tom's heart. Perhaps she had been content with her role as Wife of the Famous Poet.

But it seemed to Rose far more likely that Diana had known about Tom's infidelities and had hated them. Forty years ago, divorce had been far harder to obtain and had brought with it social disgrace, particularly for women, however blameless. Diana would have had to prove in court that Tom had been unfaithful. Perhaps she had been unable to face the lawyers and the ignominy, the unutterably sordid process of sharing your worst secrets with strangers.

Or Diana might not have been able to afford to get divorced. She might have been tied to Tom financially, with no income of her own. A woman of a different time and class, it was likely that she had never worked outside the home. Poor old Diana should have got herself a job, then she could have kicked the lying rat out of the house. Diana Chiverton's social value had been dependent on her youth and beauty. Plenty of women still traded in those commodities. Debra Peters sprang to mind. Diana must have come to recognise and fear the signs: Tom's unexplained absences, the letters quickly hidden, the phone calls that went dead as soon as she picked up the receiver. And his demeanour, cock of the walk, whenever he made a new conquest.

Perhaps Diana Chiverton had been made so powerless through financial dependency that she felt she had no alter-

403

native but to turn a blind eye to her husband's love affairs. Her position in society had been dependent on Tom's reputation. The newspapers that had blazed headlines about Johnny Pakenham, Debra Peters and Robert had done so with apparent disapproval, but beneath the thin pretence of moral outrage had lain a prurient glee. What would public opinion of sexual scandal have been in the thirties? A king had been forced to give up his throne because he had fallen in love with a divorced woman. Would Tom Chiverton's career have survived the truth being revealed about him? Would Diana's reputation? Would the Chivertons have continued to lunch with the great and the good, with royalty and bishops? Would they have been invited to smart parties in great houses if someone had spilled the beans about Tom's love affairs and his canoodling with the maidservants?

Was that enough, though? Were old love betrayals, however painful, sufficient to imprison Diana Chiverton in the Gull's Wing for the rest of her days, cut off from the world, her sole reason for living apparently the protection of her husband's good name? Or had something else taken place in that remote little patch of Sussex woodland, something unspeakable?

It was past eleven by the time Rose arrived home. Both the girls were asleep. She gave her father a hug and promised to cook him Sunday lunch the following day to say thank you.

After Giles had gone, she began to search the sitting room. She couldn't remember where she had put the letter from Sadie's friend, Jimmy Corrigan – the letter she had received the day before Katherine had run away. She did not think she had thrown it away.

404

She found it eventually, sensibly filed away in the small desk in a corner of her bedroom. *I hope my letter reaches you,* Jimmy Corrigan had written, *because I remember Sadie with great fondness.*

Taking off her make-up in the bathroom, another possibility occurred to her: that Diana had loved Tom so much, she wanted him on any terms. Whatever sins she had been complicit in concealing, she had gone on loving him.

A week later, she went to lunch at Jimmy Corrigan's house in Alwyne Place, in Islington.

Jimmy answered her ring of the doorbell, shaking her hand and beckoning her indoors. He was tall and thin, like the house, verging on gaunt. He wore faded jeans and a navy-blue sweater over a white shirt, and now and then the tails of the white shirt untucked themselves and he shoved them untidily back into his jeans. His pink complexion was blotched with freckles, and the hair that had once been red had turned white, a thistledown corona framing features which, if they had perhaps never been handsome, were made remarkable by the sharp blueness of his eyes.

She gave him the bottle of wine she had brought and he thanked her. 'Come through to the kitchen, Rose,' he said.

Photographs, prints and political posters crowded the walls of the narrow hallway. Persian rugs were scattered on the polished floorboards.

'I hope you don't mind,' he said as she followed him through the house, 'but I've invited a friend to join us.'

The kitchen was at the back of the house, a sunlit room big enough for cupboards, oven and fridge, but also a pine table, dresser and a brown denim sofa, on which was sitting a small, dark, elegant woman wearing a midi-length rust-brown skirt and a loose black cashmere sweater.

'Rose,' said Jimmy, 'this is Pearl Massingham. Pearl, this is Rose Martineau, Sadie's great-niece.'

'Pearl?' said Rose. 'Sadie's friend, Pearl?' Sadie's friend, Pearl, who she hadn't ever had a hope of tracing, because Sadie had never mentioned her surname in her letters to Edith.

'Yes.' Pearl held out her hand to Rose and smiled. 'I was Pearl Foster, back then.'

'I'm so pleased to meet you.'

Rose's anticipation whirred into a higher pitch, like the engine of an aeroplane gathering up speed as it makes to leave the runway. Forty years had passed, and yet here she was, with Sadie's closest friends, Jimmy and Pearl. If anyone knew what had happened to Sadie, it had to be them.

Drinks were offered and seats assigned at the dining table, which was laid for three. There were plates of quiche and cold meat, and bowls of salad.

'I have a house in Majorca,' Jimmy began, once everyone had helped themselves to food.

'It's so glorious, Rose,' interrupted Pearl. 'On a promontory, overlooking the most utterly divine beach.'

'I've been finishing a novel. Can't do it here – too many interruptions. Do have some bread.'

'Jimmy writes thrillers.' Pearl passed Rose a ceramic butter dish. 'They're awfully good.'

'They're not, but they pay the rent and I enjoy writing them. I write books about politics too, but they don't sell half as well. Help yourself to the ham, Rose. It's good; I brought it back from Majorca.'

'It's divine, Jimmy,' said Pearl.

'I had a deadline, so I shut myself away in my place in Majorca for six months. That's why I didn't get your letter,

Rose. When you didn't reply to mine, I wondered whether you'd forgotten Sadie.'

'Or given up on her,' said Pearl. 'You mustn't give up on her, darling. We've always longed to know. When Jimmy told me you were coming, I simply had to see you.'

'Pearl lives in the Highlands. Hell of a long way away. Came down on the sleeper train.'

'Just a splash, darling.' Jimmy was poised with a jug of water over Pearl's tumbler of whisky.

'You've always longed to know what?' said Rose.

They both looked at her. 'What happened to Sadie,' said Pearl, gently. 'She was our dearest friend and she just disappeared. I thought – I hoped – you would tell us at last.'

Some of Rose's pleasure in the encounter diminished. 'I'm afraid I was hoping you could tell me.'

'You don't know where she went, then?' Pearl, too, looked disappointed.

'Of course she doesn't,' said Jimmy. 'I told you she wouldn't.' He squeezed Pearl's hand.

Rose explained about her inheritance of the Egg from her grandmother and her discovery that Edith had had a sister. 'I've been trying to speak to people who knew Sadie,' she said. 'I spoke to her psychiatrist.'

'Philip? Such a sweetie.' Pearl beamed.

'And her friend, Constance. And the woman who owns the gallery that used to represent her. She told me about Sadie not turning up for her private view.'

'Bloody awful evening,' said Jimmy. 'Crowds of people, everyone expecting Sadie to turn up at any minute, and she never did.'

'Madge was spitting mad,' said Pearl.

'And Sadie didn't phone or write to explain?'

Jimmy shook his head, then lit a cigarette after offering the pack round. 'We spoke the day before the private view, in the afternoon. Neither of us had a phone, but she called me from the booth in the village – what's its name . . . ?'

'Nutcombe.'

'Yes, Nutcombe. I was working for an advertising agency, so she rang my office. We arranged to meet up in a café near the gallery the following day, a couple of hours before the private view opened.'

'But she didn't show up?'

'No. I assumed she must have missed her train and would be coming on a later one. But, no. So I sat there, like an idiot, waiting, and then I thought she must have forgotten about our arrangement, so eventually I went off to the gallery on my own.'

'But she didn't turn up,' said Pearl.

'Neither of us ever saw or heard from her again.'

'Might she have felt nervous about the private view?' Rose remembered Winnie telling her that Sadie was the nervy type. 'Might she have decided she couldn't face it?'

'I don't think so.' Pearl pushed back the sleeves of her black cashmere jumper. 'She was looking forward to it. She'd had another exhibition a year or so before, and that had gone well. Sadie had confidence in her work. She knew she was good.'

Rose took the ring out of her handbag and showed it to Pearl. 'I found this. I wondered whether it might have belonged to Sadie.'

Pearl stared at the ring and put a hand to her mouth. 'Oh,' she whispered. Looking shaken, she put on her reading glasses.

'Is it hers?' Jimmy frowned.

'Yes, of course it is. You remember, Jimmy – Felix gave it to her. See, there's the inscription. *In thee my choys I do rejoys.*' Pearl held out the ring to him. 'Oh, my goodness.' There were tears in her eyes. 'Where did you find it, Rose?'

'At the Egg. It was lying in the undergrowth, a short distance from the house.'

'She should have got rid of the bloody thing,' said Jimmy sourly. 'I told her often enough.'

'She never told me she'd lost it.' Pearl gave the ring back to Rose.

'She was still holding a torch for that wee bampot.'

'No, no, she wasn't, not at all,' said Pearl. 'Sadie was over Felix, you know that.'

Jimmy lit another cigarette from the stub of his first.

Pearl murmured, 'Darling, remember what the doctor said. You don't want that awful cough again.'

Jimmy made a hissing noise, but balanced the cigarette on the edge of the ashtray before addressing Rose. 'I went to the Egg a few days after the private view. I wanted to find out what the hell Sadie was playing at. She wasn't there. I'd a key with me, because I'd stayed in the house in the summer, so I had a look inside, in case she'd been taken ill or something. All her stuff was gone. Her clothes, her handbag, her sketchbook and paints. Even the etching press. So I assumed she'd gone away somewhere.'

'She wouldn't have gone away without telling us.' Pearl's soft remark had the patient echo of an argument returned to many times.

'She might have. Sadie had her secretive side. She could be a very private person, when she chose.'

Rose said, 'If she'd gone away, where would she have gone to?'

'To Europe,' said Jimmy. 'She liked to travel.'

'She went to France, one year.' Pearl stabbed an olive.

'The two of us drove to Spain in thirty-three,' Jimmy said. 'We travelled round Castile, she painted and I wrote a piece for *Splinter* about the conditions in the countryside. Sadie stayed on in Madrid to work, while I went on to Italy. Spain was fascinating then, before Franco. Immense poverty and upheaval, brewing like a saucepan about to boil over, but beautiful, even so. I've never forgotten it. It took my mind off what was going on in the rest of Europe. I fell in love with it.'

'When she came back, Sadie was so happy,' said Pearl. 'It was so marvellous to see her happy again.'

'*He* might have been a complete idiot as well,' growled Jimmy. 'She always had lousy taste in men.'

'Jimmy, darling, how can you say that? What about Kit? Kit's my husband,' Pearl explained to Rose. 'He and Sadie had a little fling, long before he and I got together. Anyway, he wasn't like Felix at all, Jimmy; I'm certain of it. Sadie told me all about him.'

'Who?' said Rose. 'Who wasn't like Felix?'

'Andrés.' Pearl put her knife and fork on her plate. 'He was her lover. He lived in Madrid.'

'Oh.' None of Sadie's letters to Edith had mentioned a lover in Madrid. So she can't have wanted Edith to know about him.

'What was he like? What did he do?'

'He was a writer.'

'A journalist,' said Jimmy. 'Left wing. So, if he stayed in Spain, I doubt he'd have survived the Franco regime.'

'He was a duke or a count or something,' said Pearl with a vague wave of her hand.

'Rot,' said Jimmy. 'Andrés was descended from the impoverished Spanish aristocracy – had land and money once, but didn't any more. He was a bit of a mixture, like Sadie herself. His mother was Irish, his father Spanish.'

Pearl patted his hand. 'Sadie was always afraid that she might lose him. It was difficult for them, you see, Rose. Andrés was married. He had a son. The marriage wasn't happy, but Andrés and his wife were Roman Catholics, so there was no possibility of divorce. She went back to Spain the next summer, in nineteen thirty-four, because she wanted to be with him.' A soft sigh. 'It was hard for Sadie to fall in love again, after Felix, and it must have been hard for them to believe they had any sort of future. But Andrés was the love of her life.' Pearl looked sad. 'I truly believe that.'

'Mightn't she have gone back to Spain?' asked Rose. 'Might she have missed Andrés so much that she couldn't bear to wait until the private view was over?'

Pearl knotted her hands together in her lap. 'You see, Sadie always wrote to me,' she said quietly. 'Always. Wherever she was, whoever she was with. Even when she was in that awful hospital, after her breakdown. She'd write letters and send postcards, dozens of them. She used to do little sketches – some divine scenery or a cartoon.'

Rose remembered the cartoon on the postcard she had found in Edith's effects – the fashionable woman teetering down the street in high heels and cloche hat. *Don't I look just le dernier cri, darling?*

'But, this time, she didn't write?' she prompted.

'No. Not to me, not to anyone. Jimmy and I asked around. Sadie had a lot of friends. None of them had heard from her.'

'I went to the police,' said Jimmy. 'They weren't interested.

411

Sadie was an adult and there was no evidence of foul play. When I told them about the private view, they assumed . . .'

'She was an artist,' Pearl pointed out. 'What Jimmy is saying is that they assumed she had bohemian habits.'

'They told me she'd probably gone off with a man. I told them they didn't know what they were talking about.'

'You didn't put it like that, darling.'

'No, I didn't. So they threw me out.'

'She'd have written,' repeated Pearl. 'She would have, Rose.'

Rose believed her. She said, 'Did Sadie ever mention Tom Chiverton to either of you?'

Pearl gave her a long, steady look, then said, 'She had an affair with him.'

'She didn't.' Jimmy scowled at Pearl.

'Jimmy, she did, I'm afraid. She told me. She made me promise not to tell anyone, but I can't see that it matters now. Rose should know. It wasn't much of an affair, just one night, and she felt very ashamed of herself afterwards.'

Jimmy downed his whisky in one. 'Bloody hell,' he said. He began to clear away the plates.

Pearl gave him an affectionate look. 'Sadie was lonely, living there on her own. Tom Chiverton came to the Egg one evening, and, well, you can guess. He was a very attractive man then. He went to seed later, of course.' Pearl made a resigned face. 'We all do, I'm afraid.'

'Not you,' said Jimmy, loyally.

'Sweetie, thank you.' She smiled at him. 'Sadie regretted the fling with Tom Chiverton awfully. But, you have to under-stand what it was like for women of our generation, Rose. An awful lot of us never married, never had children, because of all those poor boys who died in the war. One was desperate for love and companionship – and sex, of course. I was

412

thirty-five when I married Kit, older than that when I had my boys. I'd given up all hope of a family and I know that Sadie often felt the same.'

'So she wasn't in love with Tom Chiverton?'

'No, not at all.' Pearl narrowed her eyes. 'It was more to do with desire. Such a traitorous emotion, don't you agree?'

Rose thought of Waterloo Station, and kissing Dan Falconer. Yearning, and finding what you hoped was an answer to yearning. If she hadn't kissed Dan, then he wouldn't have left Martineau Aviation. He would still be working there and she would see him every day. Would that have been better or worse?

'So, it was a short-lived affair. And did he – did Tom – accept that?'

'No, I'm afraid not. She told me he used to watch her when she was in the house. You know it, don't you? Those great big windows.'

Rose thought of Sadie, in the little Egg, and Tom Chiverton, less than a mile away. It must have been awkward, to put it mildly. The idea of Tom watching Sadie through the windows of the Egg made her feel cold inside. A theory was putting itself together in her mind, a dark suspicion, an answer to the mystery of Sadie Lawless's disappearance.

'Tom Chiverton was part of the reason Sadie decided to go abroad,' said Pearl, 'but he wasn't the most important reason. Sadie wanted to make something of herself. She had so much talent. She knew she needed more experience, so she used to go and work for other printmakers as a technical assistant. Some printmakers are brilliant draughtsmen or colourists but have no skill at the technical part. Sadie was good at it all. She had the lot.'

'Show you something,' said Jimmy. Standing, he indicated

413

to Rose a series of framed images on one of the walls. 'Sadie did these.'

Rose saw that they were covers from the journal, *Splinter*. The prints were abstract in style, the motifs jagged and angular, the colours sludgy and sombre, enlivened with dashes of red. She felt the same flicker of excitement she had experienced when she saw Sadie's paintings in the Danford Gallery – of being transported back to forgotten days and hidden lives.

'I couldn't pay her,' Jimmy said. 'The blasted paper never made me a penny, so I'd take her out for a meal instead. Fish and chips, when I was very poor.'

'They're marvellous.' And they were: bold, striking and powerful.

'I was trying to link up themes in politics and the arts.' Jimmy snorted. 'Hell of a lot of politics going on in the nineteen thirties. Hell of a lot going on now, if it comes to it. It's a fallacy to think you can stand aside from the events of the world.' His gaze was focused on the images as he said, 'I think something happened to her, that day.'

'Jimmy,' murmured Pearl.

'It needs to be said, hen. As you said, Rose should know. I think she met someone. Some stranger stopped to offer her a lift when she was walking down the hill, or she got talking to the wrong man on the train to London. She'd talk to anyone, Sadie. She was young and pretty, and she was friendly. She'd take a liking to someone she'd just met. Maybe she was unlucky. She was the sort of woman . . . Well, a man would look at her and want her.'

In Jimmy's voice, Rose heard echoes of an old sorrow. And Pearl must have heard it too, because she took his hand.

'Maybe Rose would like a coffee, darling. Shall I make it?'

'I'll do it. Give me a moment.' Jimmy left the room. His footsteps faded, a door opened and shut.

Pearl said in a low voice, 'He adored her. He never married, you know. He went to America, a few months after poor Sadie disappeared. He was in the first war and he saw it was all going to happen again and he couldn't bear it, he just couldn't bear going through it all over again.'

She pulled the collar of her sweater up to her chin. 'Jimmy's always believed that something bad happened to Sadie. Maybe he's right. All I know is that she wouldn't have been able to live without Andrés. She loved him so much, you see, Rose. And there's a limit to the amount of heartbreak you can endure, isn't there?'

After she left Jimmy Corrigan's house, Rose took a bus to Chelsea, to Robert's flat, to collect the girls. Robert and Katherine were playing Monopoly when she arrived, and Eve was drawing a picture.

Eve threw herself into Rose's arms. Katherine said, 'I've bought Park Lane, Mummy.'

'Wow.' Clasping Eve, she went to stand by the Monopoly board.

'We've only just started,' Robert said. 'Poor Katherine never gets to finish a game.'

'I don't mind waiting.'

'I'd have liked to have taken them out for some fresh air.'

It was on the tip of Rose's tongue to remind him that he had had plenty of opportunity to take his daughters out that morning, but she bit the remark back. She sat down on the sofa with Eve, pressing her cheek against her daughter's dark curls while the game continued. She could see Robert resenting her presence and working himself up to another sour comment. Since he had agreed to a divorce, their conversations had been punctuated by cold remarks and sarcasm.

Robert would never respond to rejection with physical violence, but a different sort of man, a man with a hot temper, might. You read about that sort of thing in the papers. A relationship ended and a woman was stalked in the streets, then strangled or beaten to death by the spurned boyfriend. The cheaper papers called it a crime of passion. Rose didn't see it like that; the outrage was to their ego, she thought, and not to their hearts. They killed not for love, but for jealousy, possession and pride.

Chapter Twenty

London and Surrey – June 1971

A couple of weeks later, Rose took a taxi to Brook Street. She had been invited to a reception at Claridge's Hotel, in celebration of Kevin Goode's fortieth birthday. In the black-and-white tiled vestibule, she was directed to a function room on the ground floor. Pausing in the doorway, she saw that the women's bright frocks were dotted among the men's dark suits like jewels in the dust. A five-piece band was playing in one corner of the room and a few couples were dancing.

Making her way through the crowds, she steeled herself, knowing that at any moment she might come face to face with Dan. Knowing Dan as well as she did, she had no doubt that he would be polite and civilised. They would talk about aviation and then one or the other of them would find an excuse to leave. This thought gave her no joy, and she found herself longing for the evening to be over.

Finding Kevin, she kissed his cheek and offered him her congratulations. 'Costing me a fortune, this shindig,' he grumbled. 'Kelly insisted.' Kelly was Kevin's new young wife.

They talked for a few minutes and then another guest

arrived and Kevin excused himself. Rose took a glass of wine from a tray and wandered round the room. Here were groups of men who knew each other from school and university, from golf club and Rotary club and the Freemasons. She was not part of any of these associations. In her line of business, this was not a new feeling.

She caught sight of Dan, standing on the far side of the room. Her gaze lingered on him and she felt a mixture of pleasure and pain, and was torn between a desire to run away — no one would notice, she felt — and a longing to speak to him. She would try to make everything all right again. She would explain to him how she had been ripped into pieces by her anxiety about Katherine. She took a step in his direction; she must speak to him.

Then a blonde woman in a short cobalt-blue dress came up to him and kissed his cheek. Dan leaned towards her and the blonde woman placed a hand on his shoulder and murmured something in his ear. Dan smiled. He might have laughed. Turning away, Rose weaved through the crowds to the other side of the room.

A voice said, 'You look like you could do with some company.'

The speaker was a man of around her own age. Curly reddish hair, a heavy jawline, his face flushed, blue eyes that were focusing on the V of the neckline of her cream-and-gold halter-neck dress.

'Nice to see a girl here,' he said. 'All these bloody men. And such a beautiful girl. My name's Russell Litchfield.'

'Rose Martineau.'

'Why aren't you drinking champagne, Rose? You look like a girl who likes a glass of champagne.'

He wandered away. She hoped he had gone, but he returned a few minutes later, a glass in each hand.

'Here you are, Rose.' Drops of champagne splashed on her fingers. Staring at her, he gave a burst of laughter. 'I've read about you, haven't I? *Rose Martineau* . . . You're married to that chap, aren't you?'

Instantly, she became wary. People assumed things, because of Robert. Men assumed things.

'How do you know Kevin, Russell?'

But he was not to be deflected. 'That chap in the papers,' he said, looking pleased with himself. 'The one with the hooker. Yes, I'm very pleased to meet *you*, Rose. He likes his fun, doesn't he, your old man?' A suggestive raise of sandy eyebrows. 'I expect you like a bit of fun, too.'

'I don't know what you're talking about,' she said coldly.

He shrugged. 'What's sauce for the goose, and all that.'

'Would you excuse me, please?'

'Oh, come on. Relax. Drink up. We're just getting to know each other.'

Rose was standing by the wall. Russell was on her other side, uncomfortably close. She tried to move away, but found herself trapped.

'Excuse me,' she said firmly. 'I've just seen someone I need to talk to.'

He looked annoyed. 'Don't take offence. I was only joking. Where's your sense of humour?'

'I think she wants you to go.' Dan's voice, as hard and cold as ice.

Russell swung round, his face creased into a scowl. 'Shove off, why don't you? Can't you see we're talking?'

'Mrs Martineau would like you to leave her alone.'

'Dan, it's fine,' Rose said quickly.

'See? Mind your own business, Falconer.' This from Russell, belligerently.

'You're drunk, Mr Litchfield. Perhaps you should go home.'

'Oh, bugger off.'

There was a scuffle. Dan gripped Russell Litchfield's shoulder, or Litchfield tried to hit Dan, Rose wasn't sure which happened first, or maybe both happened at the same time. But then Russell hit Dan hard on the mouth and he staggered back. Rose heard herself gasp and start to go to him, but he was already regaining his balance. Dan's fist then glanced off the other man's jaw and Russell tripped over a table leg, taking down with him the table and a number of empty wine glasses. A woman screamed as Russell Litchfield hit the floor with a thunk and a brittle tinkling of broken glass.

Everyone in the room turned to look at them. Rose clasped her hands over her mouth. Dan flexed his fist and offered Russell his hand to help him off the floor. Russell told him to fuck off.

'Watch out for the glass,' someone said.

Two men hauled Russell Litchfield to his feet. He gave his head a shake. 'You bloody *arse*,' he spat angrily at Dan.

'Are you all right?' Rose murmured to Dan.

'Yes. Fine. Ouch.' With a dazed expression, he was examining his knuckles. 'I don't usually do that sort of thing.'

'I know, Dan. Let's get some fresh air.'

She took his elbow and steered him out of the room. In a corridor, they stood beside an open window as she searched in her bag for a handkerchief.

'Here, let me.' She dabbed at the blood on his split lip. His hair was dishevelled, his suit rumpled. 'You look a mess.'

A waitress was passing with a tray of empty glasses; Rose asked her to fetch some ice.

Turning back to Dan, she said, 'You didn't need to do that.'

Dan was pressing her handkerchief against his mouth to staunch the bleeding. 'He was pestering you, the idiot,' he mumbled.

'Yes, he was, but I can look after myself. Are you sure you're all right? Nothing broken?'

He shook his head, then put a hand to his bruised face. 'You okay, Rose?'

'I'm fine.' She felt shaken and upset – and yet, at the same time, just being with him made her heart lift.

'How's Martineau Aviation managing without me?'

'We're struggling on.' She smiled. 'I'm trying to train your successor, but it's an uphill task. How's Westfield?'

'Fine, up till now.'

'What do you mean?'

'Litchfield is one of our most important customers. We fly his products all over Europe.'

Appalled, she stared at him. 'Oh, Dan.'

He brushed at his jacket, which was splashed with champagne, and straightened his tie. 'I'd been thinking of leaving, anyway. I've never settled there. It's not the same as Martineau Aviation.' He gave a smile, then winced.

The waitress came back with the ice. Rose wrapped up some cubes in her handkerchief and instructed Dan to put it on his cut lip. He asked, in a muffled way, after Katherine and Eve, and she told him they were well.

'Katherine's back at her old school,' she said. 'She's happier now.'

'Good,' he mumbled.

Then there was a silence, during which neither of them seemed to know what to say. They were standing next to each other, she thought miserably, but there was still a barrier between them.

421

She began to speak, but, with a clack of high heels, the blonde woman in the cobalt-blue dress turned up. 'Ah, there you are, Dan,' she said briskly. 'I've been looking for you everywhere. You need to come back inside. Kevin's insisting you apologise.'

'I'll be a minute,' said Dan curtly. 'Tell Kevin I'm on my way, please, Jenny.'

Jenny went off. Dan said to Rose, 'Are you still doing a lot of work with Pearson's?'

'Yes, a fair bit.'

'Don't take on any more.' His lip was puffing up, making him lisp. 'I've heard they might go bust. Not a certainty, but it doesn't look good. Make sure you're not overexposed.'

'Thanks, Dan. I'll do that.'

'Have to go,' he said.

'Dan . . .'

He looked back at her.

'I'm sorry,' she said.

'No need.'

Then he was gone before she could explain to him that she hadn't been apologising for Russell Litchfield, but for everything that had taken place between them. Conflicting thoughts rushed through her head. She tried to make sense of what had happened, to slot it into a pattern, but could not. Dan had intervened with Litchfield and had warned her about Pearson's, which must mean that he cared about her – or did it? Perhaps he had acted through gentlemanliness, or a sense of duty. He clearly didn't *hate* her, which was something.

But they had failed to slip back into the easy friendship of his last months at Martineau Aviation. Nothing was resolved; only harm had been done. She hadn't even told him she and Robert were getting a divorce.

She couldn't face going back into the venue. She must have attended more disastrous parties, she reflected, as she went downstairs to the porter to collect her jacket and brief-case, but she couldn't, at that moment, think of one.

At eleven the following morning, Rose phoned Westfield Air and asked to speak to Dan Falconer. The voice on the other end of the line informed her that he wasn't available.

'Could you find out for me when he will be?'

'Mr Falconer's left the company, Mrs Martineau.'

Rose murmured a thank you and ended the call. She thought for a moment, and then, leaving her desk, stuck her head round the door of her office to speak to Lucy.

'Lucy, do we still have Dan's home phone number?'

'I'll have a look.'

A few minutes later, Lucy came into the office with the number. Rose dialled it.

The phone rang out. Rose was about to put the receiver down when a man's voice – not Dan's – said, 'The Falconer residence.'

She said hello. 'My name's Rose Martineau. I wonder if I could speak to Dan.'

'He's not here, love. He's at work.'

Or on his way home from work, Rose thought grimly, having just been fired. She said, 'Who am I speaking to?'

'Dan's dad.'

'Oh, I see. Good morning, Mr Falconer. Please forgive me for disturbing you.'

'Mick – call me Mick. I'm staying with Dan until I get better.'

'I'm sorry to hear you've been unwell, Mick.'

'My caravan set on fire. I was almost burned to a crisp.'

'How awful,' she said, shocked.

A tap on the door; she looked up. Alan, Dan's successor, was in the doorway. Rose mouthed, *Just a minute.*

'I hope you make a speedy recovery, Mick,' she said, into the phone. 'Would you mind giving Dan a message from me?'

It was hard to know what to say, and, in the end, she settled for, 'Please tell him that Rose Martineau phoned.' She spelled out her surname.

She put down the phone and pressed her knuckles against her teeth. There were so many things she wanted to say to Dan, but she hadn't said any of them. She wasn't even sure whether she should have said them.

She was wearing Sadie's ring today. She slipped it off her little finger, glancing at the inscription on the band. *In thee my choys I do rejoys.* She had an inkling that joy might one day again be possible, and it seemed a long time since she had felt that. But she couldn't see her path to it; the forest was in the way.

Chapter Twenty-One

Sussex – October 1934

Sadie's bicycle had a puncture, so she took it to the garage, where Mr Boxell promised to repair it. Walking back to the Egg, she had almost reached the turn-off through the woods when she heard a motor car coming down the hill towards her. Looking up, she recognised, with a flicker of disquiet, the Chivertons' Wolseley. She stood on the verge, hoping that Tom would drive past. But the motor car slowed, then came to a halt, and she saw that Diana, not Tom, was driving, and that she was alone.

Diana climbed out of the car and marched across the road to Sadie. 'You shouldn't have come back here,' she hissed. 'How dare you come back here?'

'What do you mean?'

'Why couldn't you have stayed away? Why have you come back here to torment me?'

Sadie made herself speak calmly, trying to soothe. 'It's my home, Diana. I came back because it's my home.'

Fury continued to contort Diana's features. She said, in the same enraged tone, 'I dare to hope you've gone for good, and then here you are, back again, on our doorstep, throwing yourself at him, trying to entice him away from me. Well, I won't let you have him!'

'Tom?' Sadie could almost have laughed. 'Are you talking about Tom? But I don't want him!'

'Liar!' Diana's scream echoed against the trees.

Sadie found herself backing away, afraid that Diana might strike her. 'It's the truth,' she said. 'You have to believe me.'

'How could I ever believe you? You were lovers, weren't you!'

The phrase was a howl of pain. A chasm seemed to open up beneath Sadie; she could not deny it. Her horror that Diana knew, and had perhaps always known, mingled with her lasting shame.

'I'm sorry,' she murmured. 'It wasn't—'

'I saw you yesterday.' Diana's low, tormented mutter broke through an apology Sadie knew to be utterly inadequate. 'I saw you with Tom.'

She recalled sensing, while she had been talking to Tom, that they were being watched. How much of their conversation had Diana overheard? A cold sweat washed over her. Had Diana heard Tom tell her, Sadie, that he would always love her? Had she heard him say that his wife's devotion had become tiresome to him?

'I sent him away.' She heard her own voice rise, defending herself. 'I didn't ask him to visit me, and I certainly didn't want him to.'

'And that's how you do it, isn't it?' Diana's mouth stretched into a contemptuous sneer. 'You blow hot and cold, because you know that's how to keep him wanting you. You manipulate my poor Tom like a piece of clay. You're a clever woman, aren't you, Sadie?'

'That's not true. It's ridiculous.' That Diana should put all

426

the blame on her, labelling her as a scheming temptress, and exonerate Tom was both ludicrous and unfair. 'I have no feelings for Tom,' she repeated. 'You have to believe that.'

'But I don't, because I'm not a fool.' Diana drew closer, leaning towards her so that Sadie, standing on the verge, was level with her gaze. 'Listen to me. I won't let you destroy my marriage. Tom is everything to me. I can't live without him. Oh, I know his faults, I know he gives in to these silly women who pester him at book signings, but he always comes back to me. *Always*. But you – you're different. You've always been different. I look at him and I can tell he's thinking about you. I read the poem he's working on and I know it's about you. And it hurts me so much; it hurts me *here*.' Diana clenched her fist and thumped it against her chest. 'It *torments* me. I can't live with this any more.'

'Diana,' Sadie tried again. 'I'm sorry; it was very wrong of me.'

'Go away,' Diana said. Her eyes had narrowed to black pebbles. 'I won't let you do this to me any longer; I won't let you have him. You should have stayed away. Get out now, before it's too late. Go away, Sadie, and leave us alone, and don't ever come back.'

Sadie's shock changed to anger. Her anger was at the disruption and anxiety the Chivertons had brought into her life, and the arrogance of the pair of them. They were as bad as each other, she thought, using people for their own ends, as pawns in their complex emotional games.

'You have no right to demand that of me,' she said coldly.

'I have every right!'

A fleck of spittle struck Sadie's cheek just before, weary of trying to reason with Diana, she turned away.

Diana's voice, screaming at her – 'Go away and never come

427

back!' – followed her as she headed along the path. Crows rose screeching from the trees and her breath was shallow, as if her lungs refused to take in air.

She went inside the house and bolted the door behind her. She found herself going to the window and looking out, nervous that Diana, in her rage, might have followed her. But there was no one, the woods were empty.

Go away and never come back. And that was exactly what she intended to do, though she had chosen not to give Diana Chiverton the satisfaction of hearing her admit it. She would leave the Egg as soon as she could, after the exhibition was over, not because Diana demanded it of her, but because she loved Andrés and longed to be with him.

She put the kettle on the stove to make tea and cut herself a piece of bread. But she could not seem to swallow it and found herself going back to the sitting-room window over and over again and peering out into the trees. She drew the curtains, shutting out the woodland that surrounded the Egg, but that was worse, because it made her wonder what lay beyond. With them drawn, it would be easy for someone to creep up to the house unseen, and, in the end, she pulled them back again.

Though she tried to dismiss her fears, telling herself that she was becoming as irrational as Diana Chiverton, she could not. The expression in Diana's eyes, one of wild anger, had frightened her. What would Diana do if she believed herself to be threatened? How far would she go to keep Tom, whom she adored? Sadie had tried to convince Diana that she did not want Tom, but she knew she had failed. She would never be able to convince her.

She did not feel safe in the Egg any more. Acknowledging that sent a wave of fear through her, but it spurred her to action. Her private view at the Danford Gallery was at seven o'clock the following evening. She had planned to take the train to London tomorrow, in the early afternoon. She was to attend the private view and stay in the capital overnight, before returning to the Egg the day after, to pack up and clean the house before leaving for Spain.

She did not want to come back to the Egg. She hated the thought of returning to it. She made her decision as she went upstairs to pack. If she sorted out her affairs today, she would never have to come back to the house after leaving for London tomorrow. She would never have to risk seeing either of the Chivertons again.

First, she went through the studio, stacking her sketches and drawings in her portfolio and tying it up. Camera, paints, pencils, charcoal and brushes she put in a holdall. The etching press — what should she do with the heavy, cumbersome etching press, which took two or three men to lift? When in London, she would find someone to buy it, she decided. One of her artist friends would be glad of it. She'd give them a spare key and they could make arrangements to collect it themselves.

A clattering downstairs made her heart jolt. Opening the bathroom window a crack, she saw with relief that the postman was heading back up the path. She hurried down-stairs to pick up the post from the mat, quickly flicking through the letters and bills. There was nothing from Andrés and a terrible disappointment washed over her. More than a week had passed since he had last written, and the fighting in Asturias, where he was reporting on events, had inten-sified. What had begun as a revolt had turned into an armed rebellion and the Madrid government had sent in the mili-tary. In *The Times* that morning a report had stated that General

Francisco Franco had been sent to suppress the insurrection.

Sadie stuffed the letters and bills into her handbag. She should be with Andrés. She should have stayed with him; she should have gone where he had gone. Tears sprang to her eyes and longing gnawed at her.

She took a steadying breath and went upstairs to the bedroom. Hauling her suitcase out from beneath the bed, she began to pack her clothes. Her gaze drifted back to the window and the trees. Concentrate, Sadie. She tied up Andrés' letters with a ribbon and put them safely in her writing case, and then put that in the holdall. She would have to manage her suitcase, portfolio, handbag and the holdall on the train. She couldn't take anything more, she simply hadn't enough hands.

But the suitcase wasn't large and, though she sat on the lid, trying to force it shut, it refused to close. Sadie flung out everything and started again, packing the clothes she would need in London for the private view, and those for Spain. Her evening dresses she would have little use for, so she decided to package them up and post the parcel to Pearl, at the school in Hertfordshire, where she was teaching. She had run out of brown paper and must buy some at the shop.

The kitchen. Things to take, things to leave behind. She was categorising her old life ruthlessly, putting most of it aside. The pots and pans, crockery and cutlery could be left for whoever next lived in the Egg. Edith might use it as a base when she returned to England for holidays, or she might let it out to a tenant.

The sick feeling that had come over her when she learned that Diana Chiverton knew she had slept with Tom was intensified by her fear for Andrés. Though she told herself not to worry – that one could hardly expect an efficient postal service from a region in the grip of chaos – anxiety pecked away at her. What if something had happened to him? She would not be able to bear it. Diana had said that she could not live without Tom. So they had something in common, after all, because Sadie had not the resilience to live without Andrés. She had survived heartbreak once; she could not do so again.

She sat down at the kitchen table and wrote a letter to Edith:

The Egg is now yours, Edith. I have posted the papers to Mr Copeland. I don't want to live here any more; it frightens me, and besides, it was wrong of Father to give it to me – I see that now. Whatever the differences between us, Edith, you are my sister. I wish you every future happiness.

She addressed the envelope, then put on her jacket and left the house. Taking the path through the trees, she speeded her pace, glancing over her shoulder. Reaching the road, she felt better, though the sound of a motor-car engine made her look round, her heart hammering. But it was only a brown van, the name of a plumbing firm inscribed on the outside, and the cloth-capped driver nodded his head in acknowledgement as he passed.

She posted her letter, then bought brown paper and string in the shop. Opening her purse to pay, her fingers fumbled and coins spilled over the floor. Winnie came out from behind the counter to help her gather them up. They talked about the private view and about Winnie's wedding to Colin Ferrers, in December. She should have told Winnie she wouldn't be able to attend, she thought as she left the shop, but she couldn't face the explanations. Not today. She would try again

431

tomorrow morning, when she felt calmer, before she caught the train.

From the telephone box, she called Jimmy's office and arranged to meet him in a café a couple of hours before the private view. Then she walked back up the hill. As she made her way along the path to the Egg, she heard the dull thud of gunshots. Diana must be shooting crows at the Gull's Wing again.

Back in the house, a quote from one of Tom Chiverton's poems repeated over and over again in her head as she went through books and papers in the sitting room:

> The owls have come back,
> I hear them calling to each other
> Remnants in the dead leaves,
> a feather, a bone, a claw . . .

She stuffed papers to be burned in the stove. Tom's poem was about her wood, Paley High Wood. She had found bones and feathers under the trees and had made a collage of them, but Tom had made a poem. A poem, a collage: you peeled back the skin and exposed the heart and sinews.

Kneeling in front of the stove, she ran the pad of her thumb over the quincunx of emeralds on her ring as her gaze returned to the window. A mist swirled round the forest floor, blurring the roots of the trees. She should have gone today, before the fog came down. The thought of spending another night in the house appalled her. *Get out now, before it's too late,* Diana's voice echoed, a chorus to her sudden sense of urgency. It came to her then that she should not have been afraid of Tom, only Diana.

She glanced at her watch. If she hurried and gathered her

belongings now, she still had time to catch the next train to East Grinstead. Yes, she would go today, she thought, and relief flooded through her.

She hauled the suitcase, holdall and portfolio down the stairs to the hall. Then she went through the rooms one last time, opening drawers and cupboards, making sure she hadn't left anything valuable behind. In the studio, catching sight of an etching tool stranded on the window sill, the flailing hem of her jacket brushed against a bottle of turpentine she had left on the press. It crashed to the floor and the glass shattered. She hurried downstairs for a bucket and dustpan. By the time she returned, the room stank of turps. A friend of hers had once set his studio alight by spilling a bottle of turps. She picked up the shards of glass, cutting her thumb, and had to run downstairs and open the suitcase to find a handkerchief to bind it up. Hauling buckets of water from the bathroom, she scrubbed the floor.

When she had finished, she looked at her watch and saw that the train was due to leave Nutcombe station in less than fifteen minutes. With dull horror, she knew she hadn't a hope of getting out of the house and down the hill with her belongings in time to catch the train. She wished she had a kind neighbour with a motor car; she wished she had a telephone to call a taxi. The next train wasn't due for another two hours and she couldn't remember whether it met an onward connection to London.

She sat on the studio floor, exhausted and tearful. She could grab her handbag and cycle down the hill and be damned to her luggage; Jimmy would, she knew, agree to come to the house after the private view and collect her belongings for her. She rose — and then, with renewed despair,

433

remembered that her bicycle was at the garage to be repaired. However fast she ran, she wouldn't catch the train.

She went downstairs. In the kitchen, she swallowed the last half-inch of cooking sherry in the bottle and leaned against the stove, her eyes closed. She made herself imagine the court-yard in Segovia, sitting with Andrés on the bench, watching the shadows lengthen. She could feel the heat and hear his voice, warm and reassuring, and she smiled to herself. Not long now, she thought. Not long till we're together for always.

Dusk had fallen and she went into the sitting room to draw the curtains. Standing at the window, she thought she saw a movement in the trees. There it was again: the sudden shiver of a branch; a bird rising from the silver birches, as if disturbed.

Sadie opened the glass door and walked to the end of the terrace. She looked out into the woodland. There was nothing, only the night's multiplying pools of blackness. She was about to turn away, to go back into the house, when a red-brown dog snaked out of the undergrowth. Then Diana emerged from the trees and walked towards her; she was holding a shotgun.

Sadie stared at her, frozen with fear.

As Diana propped the gun against her shoulder, she said, 'You should have gone. I told you to go.'

Sadie began to run away from the house, through the trees. Stumbling in her panic, she slipped in the mud, then scrambled back to her feet, making for the sunken lane.

The report of the gun echoed against the tree trunks. She felt a searing pain and, when she put a hand to her leg, it came away soaked in blood. She limped on, driven by terror, but her pace was slowing and her strength was leaching away from her. Diana, behind her, had time to take aim.

434

Sadie fell to her knees in the undergrowth. She knew then that she would die here, far from Andrés and everyone she loved. She would die and Diana would bury her body beneath the trees and no one would ever know what had happened to her. Andrés would never know.

She wrenched the ring from her finger and dropped it on to the dead leaves: a message, her last.

She lay on the forest floor, feeling the cool caress of the earth. The woodland that surrounded her was blurring, as if it was dissolving into the fog. The tree tops spun in a great circle and then were obliterated by Diana's figure. The scent of the leaves faded and darkness fell.

Chapter Twenty-Two

London, Surrey and Sussex – June 1971

These days, there were always splashes of tea on the work surfaces in the kitchen of Dan's flat. His father, who had been living with him since he had been discharged from hospital, drank a mug of tea every half-hour or so. Dan had to avoid watching Mick's tea-making routine, because it put him in a state of tension. *Don't carry the tea bag across the kitchen to the sink*, he longed to say, *because you'll drip tea on the floor en route. In fact, don't dump your tea bags in the sink at all, where they leave brown stains; put them straight in the bin.*

But he didn't say any of that, because at least Mick was able to use his hands again, which had been badly burned. And Dan was trying hard to refashion their relationship, even though it reduced him to teeth clenching; he was trying to forgive his father for causing the neglect he had suffered during childhood and to respond to the changed circumstances in which they found themselves. He wondered whether his father would ever work again. Mick was almost sixty, his hands lacked dexterity, he had a cough from smoking too much and unemployment was soaring.

One Thursday afternoon, while his father was out for his

436

walk, Dan tidied the flat. He sorted out the heaps of *Daily Mirrors*, puzzle magazines and gardening leaflets, and the clothing — anorak, jumper, shoes, socks and handkerchiefs — that Mick had discarded at random in the rooms. Once he had returned the items to their appropriate places, he emptied ashtrays and gathered up a dozen mugs with puddles of cold tea at the bottom and put them beside the kitchen sink. He couldn't put them in the sink because a great many used tea bags lurked in it, like leeches in the depths of a pond. Then he collected all the pieces of paper — receipts, shopping lists, reminders — that his father generated. *Take painkillers. Library book. Dogs' Home* — Mick fancied keeping a dog.

He discovered a scrap of paper down the side of the sofa, extracted it and smoothed it out. Reading what was written there, he stilled. *Rose Martineau*, pencilled in his father's handwriting. Frowning, Dan put it on the kitchen table.

Fifteen minutes later, Mick came back into the house, talking of the weather and brandishing a string bag of purchases he had made for Dan at the Spar. 'They didn't have brown bread, so I got white,' he said. He patted his stomach. 'It's better for the tummy. Brown bread makes me burp.'

'What's this, Dad?' Dan showed his father the piece of paper with Rose's name on it.

Mick fiddled for his glasses in his jacket pocket, put them on and peered at it. 'Oh, yes. She phoned.'

Dan fought to contain his frustration. 'When?'

'A while ago,' Mick said vaguely. 'Shall I make us a cup of tea?'

'It's all right — I'll do it.' Dan filled the kettle. 'Do you remember why Rose phoned? What she wanted?'

His father was unpacking the shopping and putting everything in the wrong place. For once, Dan didn't care.

'She said to tell you she'd called,' Mick said, as he carefully placed a packet of sugar among the soup tins.

Rose had phoned the flat. Dan wondered whether she had called after Kevin's party, a fortnight ago – it seemed likely. He had thought of phoning her then to check that she was all right, but hadn't. There seemed little point in churning up emotions that could only cause him pain, and he had made a fool of himself with her too often.

When his father was settled with the crossword and a cup of tea, Dan went into the hall and dialled Martineau Aviation. Lucy Holbrook answered. He asked to speak to Rose.

'She's not here,' said Lucy. 'She's just called to say that she's going straight home after the hospital, because of the girls.'

'Hospital?' he repeated. 'Is she ill?' He felt a pang of fear.

'Not Rose, Dan – it's Eric.' At the end of the line, he heard Lucy let out a breath. 'It's been an awful day, simply awful. One of the DC-3's tyres blew on landing and it went off the runway.'

'Good God. Was Eric badly hurt?'

'Just a few bruises, but he had chest pains, so they took him to hospital. Rose was afraid he was having a heart attack, but she phoned an hour or so ago to tell us that the doctor thought it was angina.'

'And you think she's gone home?'

'Yes; she said she had to pick up the girls from the nanny. Sylvia's staying with Eric, at the hospital.' Sylvia was Eric's wife.

'Is Rose with her husband, in London?'

'No, not that I know of.' Lucy sounded surprised. 'She should be at her flat, in Weybridge. Have you got her home address, Dan? Shall I give it you?'

* * *

438

Nadine had kept the girls until half past six and given them their tea. When they got home to the flat, Rose ran a bath and let them splash about for twenty minutes. As she helped Eve dry herself and put on her pyjamas, she kept thinking of the plane skirling off the tarmac. And Alan and Max, helping Eric out of the cockpit, and Eric, his face screwed up with pain, clutching a hand to his ribs.

The intercom sounded; she answered it.

'Rose, it's Dan.'

'Dan?' She couldn't, at that moment, work out why Dan had come to the flat. It was lovely to hear his voice, but it didn't make sense. She let him into the block.

A rap at the door; she opened it. Seeing him, her heart gave a joyful little flip.

'Is this a bad time, Rose?'

'No, not at all. I was just getting the girls ready for bed.' It had been a bad day, but Dan coming to the flat had transformed it. 'Come in.'

'Lucy told me about the accident. How's Eric?'

'Resting. He'll be in hospital for a couple of days, so they can keep an eye on him. I saw it happen,' she said quietly. 'I thought it was going to turn over.'

'Are you okay, Rose?'

'I'm fine. Just . . .' She let out a breath. 'So relieved it wasn't worse.'

'Have you eaten?'

She thought about that. 'Not since breakfast.' There was nothing to eat in the flat; she had meant to call in at the shops on the way home.

'Shall I get us some fish and chips?'

'Yes. Yes, that would be nice.'

He went away again. In his absence, Rose made a vague

439

attempt to tidy the flat. Eve got out her plastic tub of crayons and felt-tips and upended them on the dining-room table. Rose thought of telling her it was too near bedtime to start drawing, but decided not to. Life seemed too fragile to fuss about routine.

She had looked out of the window as the DC-3 had come in to land. The incident must have taken place within a few seconds, and yet, in her memory, the events – the tyre bursting in a cloud of white, and small flames stabbing at the tarmac; the plane swerving off the runway and on to the grass, while Eric and the co-pilot fought for control – were like a slow-motion film.

When Dan came back, she cleared a space on the table. 'Mum,' said Eve reprovingly. 'All my crayons are in *order*.'

They spread out the portions of fish and chips Dan had bought in the middle of the table and ate from the paper wrappings. Rose was ravenous, hadn't realised how hungry sheer terror could make you feel. Eve took a chip and carefully blobbed tomato sauce along it and Katherine dashed round the table, taking chips now and then, for which Rose would have normally gently reprimanded her, but today did not.

Dan asked her about the plane.

'The wheel rim's damaged, but Max said he can repair it. It'll take a day or so. But I don't think Eric will be able to fly again.'

'Is he going to die, Mum?' asked Katherine.

'No, love.'

'But you said he was in hospital.'

'Yes, but they'll make him better. It'll break his heart, Dan. Flying's been his whole life.'

'He fought in the Battle of Britain. A Hurricane.'

440

'I know. Eve, mind your sleeve with that ketchup.' Rose sighed. 'I've been trying to think whether we can offer him something else in the company, something on the ground – if he'll accept it. And meanwhile . . .'

'Meanwhile, you're a pilot down.'

'Yes.' What a relief it was to be able to discuss the events of the day with Dan, who understood the business and knew the people involved. She had been stiff with tension and now some of it had slipped away.

'Have a word with Kevin,' Dan suggested. 'He might be able to recommend a pilot. There are a lot of good people around, Rose – experienced men, ex-RAF. It shouldn't be too difficult to find someone.'

'Are you and Kevin still talking?'

'Oh, yes.' Dan rescued a chip that Eve had dropped on the floor. 'He thinks Litchfield's an ass, too. He's just done a better job of keeping his thoughts to himself.'

'I'm so sorry, Dan, about what happened. I feel responsible.'

'You weren't. It was time for me to go. I knew it; Kevin knew it, too.'

'Dan, I got you fired.'

'Actually, no; I managed to get my resignation in before Kevin could fire me.'

'Dan,' she said, a little exasperated, 'that's splitting hairs. There's no need to be so literal.'

'Sorry. Bad habit of mine.' His blue gaze settled on her. 'Rose, I needed a change. Believe me, I've no regrets.'

'Who are you working for now?'

'For myself. I'm going to start up my own freight-aviation business.'

She considered him. Of course he would do that, and of course he would do it well.

'Good for you,' she said. 'Actually, it's about time, Dan. You'll be brilliant. And thanks for the warning about Pearson's. I've heard they've filed for bankruptcy.'

Eve went back to her drawing – an undersea scene. Katherine drew a jellyfish on the paper, fat and pink, bobbing between the fish.

While the girls were occupied, Rose said quietly, 'I was so sorry to hear about your father. A fire – how awful. How is he?'

'Recovering. Getting better all the time.'

'He's staying with you?'

He gave a muted groan. 'Yep.'

'How's it going?'

He spread out his hands. 'It's driving me nuts, Rose. He tries to help. He washed my shirts, but he put a duster in with them, so now they're all yellow. He's set the grill pan alight a couple of times. The whole place will go up like a furnace one day, like his caravan. And he answers the phone when I'm out and then forgets to tell me who's called. I wouldn't have found out you'd rung if I hadn't come across a piece of paper with your name on it.'

So Dan hadn't failed to call her back because he hated her, or because he had forgotten to or couldn't be bothered – all thoughts that had frequently tormented her during the last fortnight. The discovery planted a seed of happiness inside her.

While Dan drew a lobster for Eve, Rose put the chip papers in the kitchen bin and made coffee. When she took the tray back into the dining room, he was standing by the window, examining a proof copy of a book that had arrived in the post, earlier in the week.

She paused in the doorway to look at him. She was feasting

442

her eyes on an attractive man, yes, but it also struck her, an arrow to the heart, how at ease she felt with him, how natural and delightful it was to talk to him, to be with him. Desire and contentment mingled: it was as if she had been on a long journey and her destination was becoming clear at last.

Dan looked up. 'Is this good?'

The book was called *Dark Fire* and it was a new biography of Tom Chiverton, written by a *Daily Mail* journalist called Ricky Walker. Ursula's friend, the academic, Ivan Merchant, had sent the proof copy to her. In it, Walker had listed, with forensic detail, Tom Chiverton's many love affairs. The list of mistresses had become tedious as Rose read through them – the mopey ones and the tiresome ones; the famous ones and the nobodies; some greedy, others importunate – and all, ultimately, were spurned by Tom. Diana had been spared nothing and the Chiverton marriage had been exposed as an unhappy sham. The biography would make headlines in the newspapers when it was published in a few weeks.

'It's very revealing,' she said. 'I'm going to go and see Diana Chiverton on Saturday.'

'She's agreed to talk to you?'

She gave a dry laugh. 'No, but I'm going to sit outside her house and hammer on the gate until she gets so tired of me she tells me the truth. Diana knows what happened to Sadie – I'm sure of it, Dan. That's why she lied to me. I think he hurt her. I think Tom Chiverton hurt her.'

He frowned. 'Seriously?'

'Yes. It's the only thing that makes sense. I think Diana's always known, and she's trying to protect him.'

'Rose, be careful. Maybe you should wait.'

'I can't. Diana isn't well; she may not survive much longer.

And, anyway, I've made up my mind.' She gestured to the book. 'You can borrow it, if you like.'

'You've finished it?'

'I couldn't put it down.' She smiled at him. 'It's trashy, but it's very readable trash.'

Eve, who had been trying to balance the box of crayons on her head while standing on a chair, lost her balance, fell off the chair, and the crayons went everywhere. She howled.

Rose picked her daughter up and comforted her. 'Bed, you two. Now. It's gone eight.'

The phone rang as she carried Eve out of the room. She picked up the receiver. It was Robert, complaining that she had missed a solicitor's appointment that afternoon.

'Robert, I'm just in the middle of getting the girls to bed; can I call you back? Yes, I know, and I'm sorry, but we had a problem at the airfield. Yes, I realise it's important; I didn't mean that . . .'

'I'll head off, leave you in peace,' murmured Dan.

She called thanks after him – for the chips, for the company, for being there when she needed someone. With Eve balanced on her hip and Edith Fuller's flat scattered with crayons and the odd chip, she tried to placate Robert. Then she settled Katherine and Eve in bed.

It occurred to her as she left the bedroom, propping the door a few inches ajar, as her daughters liked it, that, when Dan had spoken to her of his father, Rose had recognised the same emotion in his eyes that she herself had experienced earlier that day as she ran out to the airstrip, terrified that the plane would burst into flames. And she knew that Dan, too, was familiar with that knife-edge, where horrors lie to one side and a precarious safety to the other.

* * *

444

Dan spent Friday visiting an airfield to the east of Woking. In the evening, he and his father went out for a curry and a beer. When they returned to the flat, his father sat down on the sofa, opened the *Daily Mirror* and fell instantly asleep.

Dan made himself a coffee and began to read the proof copy of *Dark Fire*, the Tom Chiverton biography that Rose had lent him. She had been right in her assessment of the book. It was an easy and compelling read that avoided any analysis of Chiverton's poetry, concentrating instead on his messy private life. Dan had thought his parents feckless, but they were nothing compared to Tom Chiverton, who had had dozens of liaisons. Chiverton had had the opportunities, Dan reflected, as he gently roused his father, made him a cup of tea and helped him to bed, that fame and good looks created. A fan at a book signing, a continuity girl at the BBC, a publicity assistant in New York: all these women and many more had shared Tom Chiverton's bed, sometimes for a single night, at other times in an affair that had lasted, on and off, for months or even years.

Had he been driven by passion, Dan wondered, as, at around midnight, he cleared up the kitchen, or had Chiverton's faithlessness been provoked by some other emotion? The love affairs had increased in number from the mid-thirties. Dan did not believe you could say it was for love, that level of promiscuity. Love was deeper, love took time, it persisted, it ran through your life like a bright thread, remaining there even when you tried to unpick it. Seeing Rose again, spending an hour with her in pleasant domestic surroundings, had brought home to him the depths of his feelings for her.

And now, mixed in with love, he felt hope, too. Rose had seemed to welcome his company. Perhaps, still, just as a friend, but he did not think so. She and her husband were not living together. Her voice, as she had spoken to Robert Martineau on the phone, had been laced with a studied patience, rather than affection. Dan remembered her using that tone to soothe a difficult customer at Martineau Aviation. Presumably, the attempt at a reconciliation hadn't worked out.

He rinsed out a milk bottle. He wondered whether Tom Chiverton had disliked the women he slept with. There was a type of man who despised women, even as he wanted to have sex with them. Maybe Chiverton had been that sort of man. That would fit in with Rose's theory. *I think Tom Chiverton hurt her . . . I think Diana's always known, and she's trying to protect him.* Was it possible? You couldn't, after reading the biography, with its lurid descriptions of Tom Chiverton's hot temper and appetite for women, rule it out.

The author of *Dark Fire* also emphasised how deeply Diana had loved Tom. Diana's love for Tom had been without limit. She had had no children; all her love had been focused on one man. There was no suggestion that Diana had ever been anything other than faithful and loving to Tom, so his affairs must have tormented her. As Dan checked that the front door was locked and made sure his father hadn't woken to have a smoke and left a burning cigarette in an ashtray, something niggled. He felt uneasy when he remembered Rose telling him that she was going to see Diana Chiverton. He almost picked up the phone and dialled her number, but it was past one o'clock, and calling at this hour might wake the children up. And, anyway, he couldn't put his finger on exactly what was troubling him, and he was probably imagining things.

* * *

Saturday dawned fine and bright. The sky was a wash of forget-me-not blue and the hedgerows were starred with wild roses as Rose drove to Nutcombe. The woods and copses on the slopes of the hills were countless different shades of green.

Ivan Merchant had told her that Diana Chiverton was dying; Ricky Walker, the author of *Dark Fire*, had implied the same thing, so her journey had acquired an urgency. Walker's publishers, too, must have believed that Diana was by now too infirm to sue them.

Dark Fire had made use of the same photograph that had been printed in *Poet of the Downs*: Tom Chiverton, with his soulful dark eyes and windswept black hair. But Rose had come to believe that the attractive exterior concealed a dark secret.

Sadie goes to live at the Egg. She's young, beautiful and raw from her broken engagement. She and Tom are neighbours; they get to know each other. Emotionally vulnerable, she falls for him on the rebound. He's a womaniser, confident of his charisma and good looks. She breaks off the affair, but Tom won't accept that and watches her through the windows of the Egg. Sadie begins to be afraid of him. She goes abroad – in part, to get away from him. She thinks he'll forget her, but he doesn't. She's frightened of being in the Egg, where the great glass wall exposes her to him, so she decides to give the house to Edith, the sister with whom she has quarrelled. On 15 October 1934, she writes to her: *The Egg is now yours, Edith. I have posted the papers to Mr Copeland. I don't want to live here any more; it frightens me.* But she leaves it too late and Tom comes to the house one day, angry and vengeful.

And then . . . what? As Rose steered the Mini round a tight corner, her imagination tried to fill it in. Tom loses his temper and strikes Sadie, and she falls and hits her head? Maybe. Yes, maybe.

Dark Fire had portrayed the Chivertons' marriage as a mesh of resentments and dependencies. Diana had needed Tom's love, his magnetism and genius, but Tom had also been dependent on Diana's protection, which had allowed him to write.

Mick Falconer, an early riser, brought Dan a cup of tea in bed that Saturday morning. The brown liquid slopped into the saucer and on to the bedroom carpet as he padded into the room. Dan skimmed through the final chapters of *Dark Fire* as he drank the tea. Diana Chiverton had nursed Tom during his last, dreadful years, until his death from lung cancer in 1957. The biographer claimed that, by then, Tom had come to hate Diana, and their marriage had been a sham. If that was true, his dependence on her during his long illness must have been terrible to him. Tom and Diana had remained bound together in a simulacrum of intimacy until death had parted them, and yet, after her husband's death, Diana had continued to fight to protect the name of the man who had deceived her and despised her.

Dan's sense of unease remained as he went about the morning's business. *I think Tom Chiverton hurt her . . . I've made up my mind.* He thought of Rose, driving to Sussex to confront Diana Chiverton. He phoned her flat, but there was no answer.

He had intended to go to the airfield that morning, before accompanying his father to a football match in the afternoon, and he was cooking Mick eggs and bacon when it struck him. What if Rose had got it all wrong? Because there was another solution to the mystery of Sadie Lawless's disappearance. What if Tom hadn't killed Sadie? What if it was Diana,

448

the loving wife who had been wounded over and over again, and who would have done anything for love? Grabbing his car keys, he gave his father a quick hug, telling him that he was going out.

Rose swung the Mini round by the church and up the narrow, winding road through the woods, past the bend in the road and the path to the Egg, up and up. The branches of the trees cast dappled shadows on the tarmac. Sometimes a shaft of sunlight pierced the canopy and, when she looked into the woods, she saw that they had taken on an opaque blackness.

The car window was open, so she heard the dogs barking as soon as she reached the ridge road. As the Mini came to a halt, she noticed that the metal gate to the Gull's Wing was swinging open. Parking on the opposite side of the road, she walked through the gate. She knocked on the door, but there was no answer, so she traced the sound of the dogs' wild yelps and yips to the courtyard at the side of the house.

Diana Chiverton was sprawled on the cobbles, a shotgun at her side. Her dogs were whirling round her, panicked.

'Are you hurt?' Rose called out. 'Let me help you.'

'Those damned birds. They foul the courtyard . . .' Diana's voice was a weak gasp.

'Here, take my hand.'

With obvious reluctance, Diana took Rose's hand. Once she was sitting upright, she shuffled back a couple of feet to lean against the wall. Her white hair was matted by mud and a trickle of blood ran down one side of her face from a graze on her temple.

'I slipped,' she muttered.

'Let me get you a glass of water,' Rose said.

'Luna, heel. Bran.' Diana clicked her fingers and the dogs stopped their barking and came obediently to her. 'You can go now,' she said to Rose.

'You're hurt. You need a doctor.'

'What good would *that* do?' Diana jabbed at her clothing with odd, repetitive little movements of the hand, as if trying to tidy herself.

'At least let me help you indoors.'

'Go away, I said. Get off my land!'

What had made this woman so solitary? What had changed Diana Chiverton, giver of parties and pivot of a glamorous social circle, into a recluse who shuts herself off from the rest of the world?

Rose stood her ground. 'I came here to talk to you about Sadie,' she said. 'I spoke to you about her when we met at the Egg. Do you remember? She was my great-aunt and I've been trying to trace her. She lived here, on and off, for four years, and then she suddenly disappeared. I've spoken to plenty of people who knew her and loved her, but none of them has any idea where she went.'

A snarl. One of the dogs joined in – a low, menacing rumble.

'It's odd, isn't it?' Rose spoke gently, aware of the older woman's frailty. 'On the fifteenth of October nineteen thirty-four, Sadie made an arrangement to meet a friend in London, but she never turned up. So, I think – and I've spoken to quite a number of people and have no reason to believe that I'm wrong – that Sadie was last seen alive here, at the Egg.'

The repetitive hand movements stilled. The Vizsla pricked up her ears before resting her long, coppery head on her mistress's thigh.

Rose said, 'I think I know what happened to her.'

'Really?' Diana gave a secretive smile. 'I doubt that.'

'You remember her, don't you?'

Diana's dark eyes, which still possessed a certain fire, settled on Rose. She murmured, 'How could I ever forget her?'

Rose felt a ripple of excitement. 'Tell me.'

'What is there to say? She was a bitch – a greedy, evil little bitch.'

The venom in Diana Chiverton's voice shook Rose, but she persisted. 'Sadie and Tom had an affair, didn't they?'

'She seduced him.' Now, Diana Chiverton's features were contorted by rage. 'She wouldn't leave him alone. She kept coming back here to tempt him, trying to entice him away from me. But I wouldn't let her have him.' Diana's tone softened; momentarily, a tender smile rubbed away the lines on her face and made her appear youthful.

She spoke quietly, as if telling herself a story. 'No one ever loved as deeply and as truly as Tom and I. He was my life and I was his. How dare she think she could have him? I had to put an end to all that. I had to make sure she couldn't torment me any more.'

Rose felt, then, an impulse to walk away. Old jealousies and old betrayals – for the first time, it crossed her mind that it might have been better to have left them in the past.

But she said, 'I think Tom killed Sadie. And I think you knew, and you've been protecting him all these years.'

Diana gave a cackle of laughter. 'Is that what you think?'

Then she raised the shotgun. The black circle of the barrel pointed at Rose, who took a step back.

'What a fool you are,' Diana said. 'Tom didn't shoot Sadie – I did. And then we buried her in the woods.'

* * *

451

The roads narrowed, becoming more winding as Dan approached Nutcombe. Rose had told him that the Gull's Wing was on the ridgeway; *Dark Fire* had described in atmospheric detail the way up the wooded hillside from the village.

At the ridge, the trees fell away and the sudden intensity of the sun almost blinded him. He saw a house, tall and magnificent, ahead, at the side of the road. Light flashed on its many windows. As he braked, the sound of a gunshot ripped through the air and Dan hurled himself out of the car and began to run.

Rose, who was kneeling on the cobbles beside Diana Chiverton, heard footsteps and looked up. Dan Falconer appeared round the corner of the house.

'Are you all right?' He yelled it at her.

'Yes. Yes, I'm fine.' Though her voice trembled.

'My God, Rose . . . Are you sure you're okay, you're not hurt? I heard a shot.'

Shock was running through her like water down a hillside and her muscles were weak. Diana Chiverton had collapsed before she had been able to pull the trigger.

'I think she's had a stroke.' She pressed her fingertips into the flesh of her arms, in an attempt to stop herself shaking. 'She dropped the gun on top of her and I tried to move it away so that I could help her, but it went off.' She dug her teeth into her lower lip. 'I don't know anything about guns, Dan.'

'Hey,' he said gently, touching the crown of her head. He picked up the shotgun, which had fired harmlessly at a hen coop, broke it, and placed it on top of the woodpile. Then he helped Rose to her feet.

She sat down on a rusty chair while Dan crouched beside Diana Chiverton. 'I'll call an ambulance,' he said.

452

He went inside the house. Rose stared at the woman who lay motionless on the cobbles. *Tom didn't shoot Sadie — I did. And then we buried her in the woods.* Diana Chiverton's words still seemed to reverberate in the courtyard of the Gull's Wing. Diana would have shot Rose, if her strength hadn't failed her at last. People said, didn't they, that they would do anything for someone they loved. For Diana Chiverton, that easy phrase had contained a literal truth.

Dan came out of the building. He gave Rose a glass of water. 'The ambulance should be on its way.'

Carefully, he spread over Diana a grubby orange blanket that he had found in the house. Upset by the gunfire, the dogs had retreated to a far corner of the courtyard. Now and then, they made little forays towards their mistress, whining.

Rose sipped the water. 'She's dead, isn't she?'

'Yes, I think so.'

'She killed Sadie, Dan. She told me. Hold me. I need you to hold me.' Closing her eyes, she rested her head against his shoulder and he put his arms round her, and they stood in the courtyard, wrapped together, not moving.

They remained in the courtyard of the Gull's Wing as Diana Chiverton's body was loaded on to the ambulance. When it was gone, they went inside the house to find leads for the dogs. Rose suggested that they take them to Winnie Ferrers, at the shop. Winnie would know someone — a farmer, a dog lover — who could look after them until a suitable home could be found.

As Dan attended to Luna and Bran, Rose wandered through the rooms of the Gull's Wing, weaving between heaps of clutter — stacks of yellowing newspapers, rags and old clothing, mounds of letters and bills, many unopened. In the kitchen, flies buzzed round an open tin of dog food. A stench of sour milk and rancid meat made her stomach heave.

She went upstairs. On the landing, double doors led into a drawing room that ran almost the length of the house. Here, too, time and neglect had laid waste to a room that must once have been breathtaking, and yet, if she part closed her eyes, she could picture it as it must have been forty years ago, when Sadie had first been invited to a supper party at the Gull's Wing. There are brightly coloured rugs and vases of roses and pictures on the walls. Someone is playing the piano, some seductive old melody, and the Chivertons' beautiful and celebrated guests are talking and laughing. And Sadie looks up and sees Tom Chiverton, and from that moment her fate is entwined for ever with his.

Closing the doors quietly behind her, Rose went downstairs. Dan was waiting, the dogs on leads, in the courtyard. Hand in hand, they walked down the hill.

In the early afternoon, they drove to the police station at Crowborough. Dan went to find a phone box to call his father to explain that he wouldn't be able to make the football match, while Rose spoke to a Detective Sergeant Nesbit. Nesbit had fairish hair, washed-out blue eyes, and wasn't bad-looking, though he had the beginnings of a paunch.

She told him what Diana Chiverton had said to her: *Tom didn't shoot Sadie — I did. And then we buried her in the woods.*

When she had finished her story, DS Nesbit looked up from his notepad. 'Diana Chiverton was in her early eighties, you said?'

'Yes.'

'You think she had a stroke?'

As Diana had pointed the gun at her, one half of her face had seemed to collapse, to lose shape, like ice turning to water. The shotgun had fallen from her hands.

'Yes, the ambulance men thought so.'

'So she'd have been confused.'

'When it happened, yes.' Diana had tried to speak again, but had made only incoherent sounds. 'But not before.'

'I shouldn't worry about this nonsense, Mrs Martineau. She was a sick woman, by the sound of it. In her dotage, muddled up – you know how they get. Or you may have thought she said something about, um, Sally, and been mistaken.'

'Sadie. And, no, I'm not mistaken. Diana Chiverton told me she'd killed Sadie and buried her body in the woods.'

'Let it go, love – that's my advice.' As he ushered her out of his office, Rose saw on his face that he thought her a silly, hysterical woman.

Dan drove her back to Nutcombe to pick up her Mini. As the Gull's Wing came into view, Rose said quietly, 'She was insane, Dan. She was quite, quite insane.'

'Yes.'

And then, 'I've missed you.'

He parked the car and turned to face her. 'Are you talking about work?'

'Oh, yes.' A sigh. 'Alan hasn't your flair. But, no, not just work.'

'Oh? That's good.' Smiling, he stroked back her hair from her forehead. 'I've missed you too, Rose. I've missed you so very much.'

Then his mouth brushed against her forehead, a light whisper on the skin. She moved to meet him, her own kisses raining over his face, her lips pressing into the hollows and angles of it, as if she was learning it by touch.

Waking in the middle of that night, Rose thought of buying a shovel and looking for Sadie herself. Peeling back the evidence of Diana Chiverton's rage; picking at the earth and leaf mould until she uncovered the white bones. But Paley High Wood stretched on for more than a hundred acres. It must be littered with animal bones. Tom and Diana could have hidden Sadie's body anywhere. Sadie's story would never quite have an ending, and that saddened her.

Chapter Twenty-Three

Lake District, Surrey and Paris
– Autumn 1971–Spring 1972

Rose often thought that she and Dan had messy lives. Arrangements were made and then broken. Tickets were booked for the theatre, but then Katherine and Eve contracted chicken pox. She had put complicated plans in place so that they could have a weekend in the Cotswolds, when, suddenly and devastatingly, Dan's mother died. Mary Martineau came to stay at the flat to look after the girls so that Rose could travel to the Lake District to attend the funeral with Dan. A neighbour had promised to keep an eye on Mick Falconer. The two businesses must be kept running smoothly in their owners' absence.

The Buddhist funeral at the commune where Angela Falconer had lived and died was simple and moving. That evening, Rose tried to comfort Dan.

'I blamed her,' he said. 'I was always so angry with her.'

They were walking beside Lake Windermere. The leaves on the trees were beginning to turn to gold.

'You kept trying, Dan.' She rubbed his shoulder comfortingly. 'You never gave up on her. You always loved her and you cared about her and you tried. And that was brave and good of you.'

'I never told her I loved her. I've never found it easy to say. I love you, Rose; I love you so much.' And he took her in his arms, crushing her to him.

She was careful, knowing she must not hurry him into her daughters' lives. They had had too many upheavals during the last year and a half, and should not be required to endure any more. She let Katherine and Eve and Dan get to know each other gradually. He joined them for supper now and then, but did not stay overnight. After a few months, he began to come along to some family outings – a pantomime in Richmond, sledging on Box Hill.

Just before Christmas, Jimmy Corrigan phoned her. 'I've been making some enquiries,' he said. 'There was a journalist I knew when I was living in Chicago, so I contacted him to ask him if he'd ever heard of Andrés. He has a friend called Paddy O'Connor, who lived in Madrid in the thirties, before the civil war. Well, anyway, he spoke to him about Sadie. And this Paddy remembers a man back then – Spanish, a journalist, who had an English lover. And get this, Rose: the girlfriend was an artist.'

'What was the Spanish journalist's name?'

'Luis Andrés Kindellan de Moreno. *Kindellan*, Rose. It's an Irish name. Sadie's Andrés had an Irish mother.'

'Do you think it was him?' she said. 'Do you think he was Sadie's Andrés?'

'There's a good chance of it.'

'What happened to him? Might he still be alive?' As she spoke, she recalled Jimmy saying to her that, as a left-wing journalist, Andrés would have been unlikely to have survived the Franco dictatorship.

From the other end of the phone line, a sigh. 'I'm sorry, Rose; it's not a happy ending. This guy died in nineteen thirty-four. He was in Oviedo, in northern Spain, at that time, reporting on the miners' uprising. Spain was in turmoil, back then, and what started off as a strike turned into a revolution that threatened the government. It was all suppressed very brutally by the army. Andrés was arrested and imprisoned for trying to tell the truth about the torture and executions. A couple of days later, he was shot by some officers of the Foreign Legion.'

When she had a moment, Rose did a little research in Weybridge library on the miners' revolt in Asturias. It had begun in early October and had been crushed by the military before the end of that month. So Sadie's lover, Andrés, had died at much the same time as Sadie herself. Presumably, Sadie had never known her lover's fate. Perhaps that was just as well. The heart could only be repaired so many times.

Rose was trying to trace Sadie's works of art. She hated that Sadie had been forgotten, her reputation as an artist buried by the passing years. Nerissa Taylor, at the Danford Gallery, was helping her and had promised to curate an exhibition, if enough material could be found. Nerissa owned two paintings and Jimmy had offered to show the prints that Sadie had made for *Splinter*. Pearl Massingham also possessed some early works.

Rose's brother-in-law, George Martineau, had offered to help her in her quest. It was the sort of task he enjoyed. He and his boyfriend, an interior designer called Hal Tillyard, spent happy weekends driving round the countryside in Hal's Morgan, following up leads. George had come out, and had introduced Hal to his family. He was a delightful man and Rose adored him, and so, in time, did the

Martineaus. George and Hal discovered an oil painting in a gallery in the Cotswolds, and a set of a dozen prints in the sale of the furnishings of a stately home in Oxfordshire. Using the money she had inherited from her grandmother, Rose bought them. One of the prints was of the Egg, seen from the viewpoint of the forest. In this image, the house appeared to be being consumed by the trees.

In the spring, Rose planned to sell the Egg. The Gull's Wing was in the process of being bought by a group of enthusiasts who had set up a trust to preserve the work of Edward Lawless. They already owned a house in Hampstead, a villa in Berlin and a folly in the gardens of a grand mansion in Buckinghamshire. They had expressed an interest in the Egg, and, really, the house had too many dark associations for Rose to wish to keep it.

The DC-3 was waiting on the tarmac, its engines turning. The pilot, Chris, who would take the plane to Paris, was Eric's replacement. Eric now worked part-time at Martineau Aviation, helping to bring in new business. Chris and the co-pilot, Tony, were already on board.

Lennie, the loadmaster, stowed Rose's overnight bag as Chris welcomed her. There was some chit-chat about the weather as, with nervous fingers, she secured her seatbelt. If only she couldn't see into the cockpit, to where all the fingers on the dials were jittering as they made ready to taxi down the runway. If only she could stop thinking about tyres bursting, undercarriages collapsing, landing strips missed in a fog, and a snowstorm causing a plane to crash near the Sussex coast.

The DC-3 began to move, the engines roaring and gathering up speed as it headed down the runway. Sixty miles an hour . . . a hundred . . . Rose held her breath. The nose rose up and every rivet and joint creaked as the plane achieved the seemingly implausible and pulled away from the ground. The shuddering and bouncing of the fuselage made her mouth go dry. Breathe, Rose, breathe. Though she knew, both as a physicist and a rational human being, that it was ridiculous to feel that the DC-3 required her faith and concentration to stay in the air, nevertheless, at some level, that was what she felt, and it was a while before her mind was able to move back to her usual preoccupations: the children, the business, Dan.

'You've chosen a good day, Rose,' Chris said. 'Look at it. Isn't it beautiful?'

The tilt of the earth was revealed through the cockpit window. The patchwork of golden fields and green woodland was intersected by a criss-cross of darker-coloured roads and hedgerows. The plane was still rising up into the sky and Rose found her gaze fixing on that great wash of blue. Yes, it was beautiful. It was. Her heart soared.

Philippe, Martineau Aviation's import–export agent in the French capital, met her at the airport and drove her to her hotel, where she left her case. He had arranged meetings for her that morning with some of the firm's regular customers. In the afternoon, she was to visit a manufacturer in Le Bourget. A new and very promising opportunity had come up for Martineau Aviation to provide transport for machine parts to factories in the UK. If she was able to pull it off, it might transform the future of the company. As Philippe already had a commitment to another client, she would be carrying out the negotiations on her own, which was why it had been imperative that she, a fluent French speaker, go to Paris. She had thought of taking the Channel ferry, but that would have meant being away from the girls for longer. And, anyway, you had, in the end, to face up to your fears.

After her meeting at Le Bourget, she took the metro to Châtelet Les Halles and then walked through the Marais to the Place des Vosges. It was early spring in Paris, and people were sitting at the pavement tables beneath the colourful awnings of the cafés and restaurants.

Walking beneath the grand colonnades of the Place de Vosges, Rose's attention was caught by a man sitting at a table at a café in the far corner of the square. She stood for a moment, enjoying the lines of his profile and the shape of his shoulders beneath his navy shirt. Even when sitting, he had always, she thought, a suggestion of barely contained movement and energy.

'Dan?' she called out, and he stood up. He took her in his arms and kissed her.

'How was the flight?'

She made a gesture towards herself: *See – I survived.* 'I almost enjoyed it,' she said.

She wanted to kiss the little hollows at the corners of his mouth and to run her fingertips along his spine. She wanted to shut her eyes and breathe in the scent of him and feel the warmth of his skin. She wanted to be alone with him.

He said, 'I thought, either dinner, then back to the hotel, or, back to the hotel and then dinner. It's up to you, Rose.'

'Are you hungry?'

He shook his head.

'Me, neither,' she said, and they walked, arm in arm, to their hotel.

* * *

She flew back to Britain the following morning on a Trident from Orly airport, while Dan stayed on in Paris to look at a plane. Arriving at Heathrow, she caught a taxi to Weybridge. She planned to leave her case and collect her car, and then drive to the airfield.

Her father had looked after the girls overnight. He had left the flat looking immaculate; it was always so. She knew how lucky she was, how her complicated life could not have worked without the help of friends and relatives.

She changed out of the dress and jacket she had worn in Paris, into a white blouse and navy-blue suit. She was touching up her make-up when the phone rang. She went to answer it.

'Mrs Martineau?' A man's voice.

'Yes; who is it?'

'It's DS Nesbit, from Crowborough police station.'

A moment's thought, and then she remembered the detective sergeant who had been so dismissive of her when she had gone to see him on the day Diana Chiverton had died.

'Yes? How can I help you?'

'If I might just go over something you mentioned to me, Mrs Martineau. When we spoke, let me see, on the eighteenth of June nineteen seventy-one, you said that your relative had gone missing.'

'My great-aunt, Sadie Lawless, yes.'

'When was that?'

'It was in October nineteen thirty-four.'

'Am I right in recalling that you said she was an artist?'

'Yes, she was.'

'What sort of an artist? Painting? Anything else?'

'Sadie painted, but she was a printmaker, too.'

'Ah.'

The way he said it made her senses sharpen. She said, 'Detective Sergeant, do you know something?'

'We appear to have found a printing press. Rusty old thing, but that's what it is. An etching press – that's the correct name for it.'

Her throat had tightened. 'Where? Where did you find it?'

'It was buried in Paley High Wood. That was why I thought of you, Mrs Martineau. Huge great bloody thing, weighs a ton, but someone had taken the trouble to bury it in the ground next to your house.'

Chapter Twenty-Four

Sussex – April 1973

The Edward Lawless Society had bought the Egg and had spent the past year on its restoration. The Society's chairman, an academic and architect called Richard Spencer, a slight, genial man, met Rose outside the house on a Sunday morning in spring.

'Rose!' He offered her his hand. 'I'm so *pleased* you were able to come. Such a *privilege* to be able to show Edward Lawless's great-granddaughter our work. A *treat*, one might say.' He had a habit of peppering his speech with italics.

'It was good of you to invite me, Richard.'

They went inside the house. Mr Spencer offered her coffee, which Rose politely declined. As they toured the rooms, he spoke to her of the work the Society had carried out: the fragments of old paint and paper discovered in hidden corners and matched and restored; the paring of the house back to its original state; the sixties appliances – Edith Fuller's tenant's fridge and washing machine – removed and replaced by the type of kitchen equipment in use between the wars; the plumbing of bathrooms and kitchen, cleaned and restored.

'Of course, there is inevitably a certain amount of *guesswork*,'

Spencer added. 'Though we have many of the original draw-ings, some of Edward Lawless's notes on the final details of the building are believed to have been lost in the plane crash.'

They went upstairs. Richard Spencer opened the door to the smaller room and Rose looked inside.

'You decided to furnish it as a bedroom, then?' she said.

Inside the room that had once contained Sadie's etching press was a narrow bed made up with a white coverlet, and a small chest of drawers, art deco in style.

'We've tried to recreate the house as it was when Edward Lawless was alive, to make it what it would have been, if you like, had he not died in such an untimely fashion. We've tried to be true to his original intent. We discussed this at length, I assure you, Rose, and it was one of our more difficult deci-sions.' He said, as he closed the door of the bedroom behind him, 'I hope you don't mind. I know that your grandmother owned the Egg for a considerable time.'

'Yes, though she never lived in it. Her sister, Sadie, lived here for four years, though.'

'Sadie, yes – Lawless's younger daughter.' He fell silent, perhaps realising that he had strayed into an unhappy area.

'Sadie gave the Egg to her sister, Edith – my grandmother – just before her death.'

'A terrible thing.' He shook his head. 'A terrible, terrible thing.'

Sadie's remains had been discovered, buried with her etching press, beside the house. She had been identified by a Bakelite bead necklace, still strung round her neck, that Pearl Massingham had recognised. Lead pellets from a shotgun had been found embedded in her leg bones. The coroner's court, to which Rose had given evidence, had concluded with a verdict of unlawful killing.

466

DS Nesbit had agreed with Rose that Diana Chiverton had had the means and the motive, and had, in all likelihood, murdered Sadie, and that Tom had helped her conceal her crime. Even a woman as tall and strong as Diana could not have moved the heavy etching press alone. The motive for burying it would have been to persuade anyone enquiring after Sadie's disappearance that she had left the house voluntarily. Her smaller possessions – clothes, books, papers and paints – could have been incinerated, but not the press. But, from such a long distance of time, and with all of the principal players dead, nothing could be proved.

As Richard Spencer opened the door to the main bedroom, light flooded in through the windows.

'Were Lawless's daughters close?' he asked Rose.

'No, not at all, I'm afraid. There was a big age difference. And Edith, my grandmother, went to live in India in the early thirties.'

Whatever her grandmother had felt about the sister with whom she had lost touch – guilt, relief or anger – she must have, in the end, known regret, too, because she had left Sadie's letters in the padouk cabinet for Rose to find.

She looked out of the window. 'I expect they were close sometimes. I'm sure there must have been occasions when they got on well. I wouldn't know; I'm an only child.'

He began to talk about the roofs. They had been in most urgent need of repair. Some of Edward Lawless's contemporaries had criticised him for using flat roofs in rain-soaked England.

'It's true that they lend themselves more readily to a Mediterranean climate,' he said. 'However, the expense and difficulty of restoring the roofs in this building are nothing compared to restoring those in the Gull's Wing. It's a huge

467

project and I expect we'll be working on it for at least the next five years. I'd be delighted to show you round the house today, Rose, if you have time.'

'No, thank you, Richard. It's kind of you, but I must get back to my fiancé and children.'

'Another day, then.'

Rose murmured her appreciation. She knew that she would never go back to the Gull's Wing. Nor would she visit the Egg again, after this day. Perhaps she would come to Nutcombe from time to time, to put flowers on Sadie's grave in the churchyard, but that was all.

They went back downstairs to the sitting room. 'We'll be opening the house to the public shortly,' Spencer said. 'Odd days, to begin with, but if there's interest, and I believe there will be, we'll open for a more substantial period in the future. Long-term, we plan to use it for an archive of Edward Lawless's papers. I envisage this room being used as a library.'

'And the Gull's Wing?' she said.

'We may well arrange restricted openings before the restoration is complete, to pay for the work.' He gave her a resigned smile. 'I'm afraid that the house's, um, notoriety will be of help to us. The workmen tell me they often have to chase away sightseers and journalists.'

'People will always have an appetite for scandal.'

'Yes, that's true.' Then he said, with genuine passion, 'We're all so grateful that you agreed to sell the house to us, Rose. Edward Lawless was ahead of his time. He was attracted to the new and the groundbreaking; he was an experimentalist, a pioneer. They're both such remarkable houses, which is why it's so important to preserve them for future generations. You should be proud of him.'

She was, she said, and she thanked him.

'Are you interested in architecture yourself, Rose?'

'I'm afraid not.'

Three months ago, she, Dan and the girls had moved into a house on the outskirts of Weybridge. It was a resolutely ordinary house, large and comfortable, built of red brick in the 1950s. She had sometimes mused on whether living in an extraordinary house, as the Chivertons had done, had encouraged them to feel that they, too, were extraordinary, and that the normal rules of society did not apply to them. Her family – the new family she was making with Dan – would make its mark on the house, rather than the other way around. Dan, Katherine and Eve, and the undistinguished home that she loved: these were her future.

They said their farewells outside the Egg and shook hands, and then she walked away through the trees, towards the sunlit fields beyond the sunken lane, where they planned to have a picnic. There was a moment when she turned her head, as if she half expected to catch sight of Sadie in paint-splashed overalls, coming out of the house. But then, hearing Dan's voice and her daughters' laughter, she walked on, and did not look back again.